The
NIGHT in
VENICE

Also by the author

First published in Great Britain in 2024 by Weidenfeld & Nicolson,
an imprint of The Orion Publishing Group Ltd
Carmelite House, 50 Victoria Embankment
London EC4Y 0DZ

An Hachette UK Company

1 3 5 7 9 10 8 6 4 2

A CIP catalogue record for this book is
available from the British Library.

ISBN (Hardback) 978 1 3996 0802 2
ISBN (eBook) 978 1 3996 0804 6
ISBN (Audio) 978 1 3996 0805 3

Typeset by Input Data Services Ltd, Bridgwater, Somerset

Printed in Great Britain by Clays Ltd, Elcograf, S.p.A.

MIX
Paper | Supporting
responsible forestry
FSC
www.fsc.org   FSC® C104740

www.weidenfeldandnicolson.co.uk
www.orionbooks.co.uk

The

NIGHT *in* VENICE

A.J. Martin

WEIDENFELD & NICOLSON

The Morning in Venice

'Each day passed in the water-city will add to its charm, but from the first all is novel and enchanting: the very cries of the gondoliers have something most wild and picturesque.'
From *Venice*, by Augustus J.C. Hare & St Clair Baddeley

Monica woke and put her hands behind her head. She lay on a narrow, iron bed, which was not as grand as the room. That could also be said of the bamboo table, the wicker chair and the mysterious little green cabinet. These articles looked temporary – and over there was her trunk, still packed and corded, as though Monica were about to leave, whereas she had arrived only last night. She felt as though she didn't quite belong in this house but might belong eventually; it was giving her a wary welcome.

The walls of the room were not papered but painted dark blue, and the plaster was rough in a beautiful way. Of course, it was not so much a house as a palazzo, so it could afford to look a bit worn out. The heavy wooden shutters were open. When she'd gone to bed, there had only been darkness beyond the windows, but something nice had seemed likely to appear opposite, and now it had done: a sunny sky above a row of palazzos ('palazzi', she supposed), with a showy little church wedged in between them, like somebody trying to squeeze into a photograph.

Monica began staring at the ceiling, where a curious shimmer was flowing over the roof beams: something between a reflection and a shadow. Quite possibly, there was no word for it. Charles Dickens had written about the silence of Venice, and her uncle Leo's good friend, Arthur somebody-or-other, had also written a poem on the theme. Leo had shown it to Monica soon after it was written, which was about two years ago, and Monica had looked at it again when she knew she would be coming to Venice. It began:

> *Water and marble and the silentness*
> *Which is not broken by a wheel or hoof*

You had to admire the man's nerve, using that word 'silentness'. Of course, it was only there to rhyme with another word that would be coming up later on. Leo had called his good friend's poem 'fey', which Monica thought an excellent word: small but lethal. She said it out loud, for Monica often spoke to herself.

Oddly enough, thinking about silence always made her think about noise, and she began counting all the noises that were not occurring but *would* have been occurring on the Holloway Road: men whipping up their poor horses; the clip-clop of hooves; the grinding of electric trams; the roaring of motor buses; quite often the great bash and tinkle of an accident, and the uncouth shouts of policemen chasing criminals. And there was sometimes an extra noise in the background of the Holloway Road, like the loud squeaking of a pencil on slate, the true cause forever out of sight.

Just now she heard nothing but the sound that went with

the shimmering light, which must be the sound of water. Of course, she'd known in advance that the streets of Venice were full of water, but she'd never really believed it, and she didn't quite believe it now, even though it was perfectly clear that, last night, she and Driscoll had been rowed rather than driven to what was called the 'water door' of this palazzo. Venice was like a dream that continued even after you knew it was real.

Monica sat up.

She had dreamt in the night that she had killed Driscoll. Yes, she had gone into Driscoll's room to find her standing near the open window, whereupon she had run over to her and shoved her. She shook her head to dislodge the image, but the image remained.

'You really killed her,' she said, and her voice sounded very loud in the silence. She looked to the right. The bamboo table and the green cabinet looked back at her innocently enough, but the blue gingham travelling dress, draped over the back of the chair, seemed to say, 'You'd better put me on quick and get out of here.' Her white shoes on the floorboards and her sailor hat on the back of the door said the same.

'Or was it a dream?' Monica asked the room aloud.

The ivory hand mirror, which had been on the table, now lay on the floorboards. It was performing a peaceful enough function – reflecting the reflection of the water on the ceiling – but it ought not to have been doing it from down on the floor. There had definitely been agitation in the night. She seemed to recall getting out of bed quickly, before she'd gone to sleep, and walking fast into Driscoll's room.

Monica was now sitting on the edge of the bed, her hands on her lap. If she sat in a contained way, she might *feel* contained. 'If I killed her in the night,' Monica said, 'then I must have gone back to bed and to sleep immediately after. Was that a very likely thing to have happened?' Yes, because any great shock or time of anxiety would make Monica more, rather than less, likely to drop asleep. It was a means of escape, and Monica had been very tired to begin with, as Driscoll had pointed out about fifty times on the train from Calais.

Monica stood. Of course, the shock would have been greater still for Driscoll. To be standing on the stone balcony of one's holiday bedroom, only to be rudely shoved from behind by one's ungrateful ward, so that one toppled over the little ornate wall. Monica had begun removing her nightdress and, with it halfway over her head, she froze, thinking of the right word. 'Balustrade,' she said, as she completed the removal of the nightdress.

She walked over to the trunk that contained her clothes. Then she stood still, in order to think. Had she merely dreamt it all? But it had not been a very dreamlike dream, which, of course, suggested it had been real. She had simply walked into the room and pushed Driscoll out of the window, not waiting to see where she landed. Then she had turned around and walked out again, just as though she had done a simple domestic chore. She might as well have gone into the room to turn out the light. But then not all Monica's dreams *were* dreamlike. They were of all kinds; she had such a very great variety of them. Most mornings, she would sort through her dreams, as other people did with the post, but sometimes there was one big one, and it might take her a while to realise it hadn't been real; and it followed that, on other occasions, what she thought she had dreamt might turn out to have actually happened.

Monica reached into the trunk and picked up the topmost dress, the one earmarked for First Day, meaning first day of the holiday. In her stultifyingly methodical way, Driscoll had arranged them in order. The First Day dress was referred to by Driscoll as 'the white cotton with spot', for it had a spot pattern woven in; it also had a sailor collar. Well, they *were* at the seaside, in a fancy sort of way. The blouse for First Day was underneath, with a high but soft collar for protection against the sun.

Driscoll had been preparing the holiday clothes for weeks, and almost every evening the sewing machine had been trundling away in the living room of the flat, and before every meal the cottons and linens and flouncy little snowdrifts of lace had to be removed from the dining table (which was in the living room, there being no dining room). Driscoll was addicted to lace, and other unnecessary embellishments, such as velvet ribbons. She dressed like her mother . . . not that Monica had ever met Driscoll's mother, who was, of course, dead – one of the many ghostly presences in orbit around Monica. Or, at any rate, Monica *assumed* that Driscoll's mother was dead, on the strength of the following evidence.

A tall chest of drawers – called a tallboy – stood opposite the end of Driscoll's bed in her Holloway bedroom. Monica was forbidden to enter Driscoll's bedroom, which was the very reason she frequented it when Driscoll was out. The tallboy culminated in a locked top drawer, the key to which Monica had discovered in a rolled-up pair of white leather gloves in the next drawer down. The top drawer held a great froth of silk, lace and crepe de Chine, mostly scraps awaiting Driscoll's needle. There were also two wicker crucifixes and one small silver one, a box of sugared almonds, a Japanese silk fan, a corkscrew (no such shameful item was in the kitchen), an unsuitable – but, as it turned out, boring – novel called *Three Weeks*, by a person called Elinor Glyn, and a locked cedarwood box that didn't rattle, about eight inches by four. There was also a flouncy Valentine's card, with a mound of stuck-down confetti-like stuff forming a blurred heart on the front. The inscription was infuriatingly obtuse: 'I hope you will . . .' followed by three illegible words, the first two separated by an 'a', then 'to', followed by 'this particular' with a large 'A' on the line below, and three kisses underneath that. This card was not contained in an envelope, but in a custom-made pasteboard folder with a yellow-ribbon bow skewered to the front. There *was* an envelope in the drawer, however; it was marked 'Mother' and contained a single photograph in a florid frame. It showed a thin, Driscoll-like woman, perhaps slightly prettier, and evidently with the same dress sense, for she was swathed in velvet with a lace mantle over the shoulders, and her high blouse collar seemed a lacy attempt at self-strangulation. It was the fact of the photograph being in the envelope that made Monica think Driscoll's mother dead – because the envelope was like a coffin.

Monica began dressing, thinking of Driscoll's mother as she did so. Had she, like her daughter, been clever with a needle? Driscoll always put too much lace on the dresses, whether the woollen winter ones or the cottons and ginghams for summer. She was quite good about removing the lace when Monica protested, but she would save herself quite a few rows with Monica if she left it off to begin with.

But now Driscoll was dead. Or, at least, she was according to what might, or might not, have been a dream. Monica ought to have been able to say that it *must* have been a dream because she would not, in actuality, be capable of killing her guardian. But Monica couldn't honestly say that – what with various things that had gone on this year.

She appealed to the bamboo table, the green cabinet and the blue gingham travelling dress. 'Surely I wouldn't have?' But the continuing silence of these objects seemed telling.

Half dressed, Monica sat back down on the bed to listen for any sound that might be coming from the next room. She wished she knew the time. If it was after quarter to seven and Driscoll were not dead, she would be awake. 'That goes without saying,' Monica said, for Driscoll had never *not* been awake after that time. But there came no sound from next door, so either Driscoll was dead, or it was before quarter to seven.

Monica feared it might easily be past quarter to seven, going by the amount of light in the sky. She looked towards the windows. They *were* only windows, albeit tall ones, whereas Driscoll's room had proper French windows, and the small balcony to step onto. If Monica were to walk over now to her own ordinary windows and look to the right, she would be able to see whether Driscoll's French windows were open. If they were, that would be bad, because they were open in Monica's recollection – whether dream or reality – of pushing Driscoll into the canal.

Monica would also be able to look *down* from her own windows. She would be able to see whether Driscoll was floating in the water. Did bodies float? It was a question that had come up in one or more unsuitable books she'd read, but she couldn't remember the answer. The corpse might or might not float. It depended on a number of terrible things.

Monica did not have an image of Driscoll's entry into the canal, but Driscoll couldn't have avoided it. The canal was all that lay below the window, apart from the little landing stage in front of the water door. She might have bashed her head on that on her way into the water, but it would have been a miracle if she'd come to rest on it, since it was only about two feet wide.

And Driscoll couldn't swim.

You'd have thought she could, since – while not in the least graceful – she was quite athletic, and she frequented a gymnasium near King's Cross with her one friend, Mary Kelly, who worked in an accounting office, and was surely also destined for spinsterhood. Mary Kelly was a thin, careful person who always gave the impression of thinking a great deal about Monica that she wasn't willing to say. She would nod warily at Monica as she entered the flat, removing the wide, round hat she always wore, which made her look like a foreign priest, and saying, 'Hello, Monica. Are you well?' and Monica would say, 'Tolerably, Miss Kelly. I hope you are, too,' before quitting whatever room the encounter had occurred in – usually the kitchen. Once, Mary Kelly had brought a rattling tin of mathematical instruments, for use by Driscoll in the training of Monica, so she was what was known in the *Notable Trials* books as 'an aider and abettor'.

In the first weeks after the move to Holloway, Monica had been required to accompany them to the gymnasium. They would change into blue serge tunics with snake-buckle belts, then swing Indian clubs while facing one another and doing identical movements, like a person in front of a mirror. That was to warm them up, which it certainly did. They then played each other (or sometimes other people) at a game that involved batting something resembling a large insect over a high net. Monica had watched them from a high viewing gallery, marvelling at the way their exertions, often accompanied by involuntary gasps, would make the gas lanterns above them sway.

Monica, who had been rolling on her white cotton stockings, paused to recollect the name of the game. Badminton, that was it. You could also call it shuttlecock or battledore, so there were three horrible words for the price of one. But Driscoll loved the game, even though she had to wear her glasses to see the flying shuttle, or whatever it was called, retaining them by a rubber band in an unbearably poignant way.

But there was never any swimming. While Driscoll made regular use of the public transport, public conveniences, public libraries and occasionally (Monica suspected) the public houses in the vicinity of Holloway Road, she would never go into public baths. She had once half explained this prejudice to Monica. They had been passing the baths on Hornsey Road, which lurked behind the Holloway Road, so to speak, and, seeing some young men coming out with flat, wet hair, she said, 'I don't know how they nerve themselves to go in.'

'Off the diving boards, you mean?' Monica had said.

Driscoll shook her head. 'The water. It's not clean. How can it be with all those people in it?'

'So you've never been in a swimming baths?'

'As a girl, yes, but not to swim.'

She had then changed the subject, as she usually did when Monica (out of sheer morbid interest) attempted to quiz her about her past, leaving Monica to conclude that she must either have resorted to public baths to wash clothes or to wash herself, presumably in company with her mother. In Manchester, where this depressing scenario had unfolded, the public baths must be very factory-like: big and echoing, towered over by great chimneys.

Monica herself could *nearly* swim. She could probably do it *in extremis*, as Driscoll would say, if a boat she was in happened to capsize, for example. Leo had begun teaching her in his casual way when she was in the sea at Brighton. 'Keep your chin up,' he had said.

Monica looked at the windows again. She still dared not approach them. She now had her petticoat, blouse, stockings and dress on, and they were all white. Her shoes, gloves, sailor

9

hat and parasol would also be white when she got around to those. She would look like a ghost, were it not for her very black hair and very dark eyes.

Monica noticed the ivory-handled hairbrush at the end of the bed. She vaguely recalled throwing it there after brushing her hair last night. Monica tended to fling hairbrushes about a lot, finding them very frustrating objects. She reached out for it, and, while sitting on the bed, she applied it to her hair, which was not quite the same thing as brushing her hair. Monica's hair could *not* be brushed, although Driscoll had spent hours trying.

'It's so woolly,' she would say.

'It is *not* woolly,' Monica would furiously reply. Later, Driscoll decided that the word for Monica's hair was 'frizzy', which Monica denied even more hotly. But, in truth, it was. Officially, Monica wore her hair down, being still only fourteen, but in practice her curly hair was always naturally up, and if she put pigtails into it nobody could tell, especially if she used black ribbons. Monica chucked the hairbrush aside and rose to her feet.

There was nothing for it: she would have to cross the room and look.

When she arrived at the window, her heart was pounding as if she had run there. She looked across at the palazzos opposite. She still dared not look to the right to see about the French windows, but she believed she had the courage to look down.

She did it.

The water was the colour the ink from her Swan pen became when she washed it under the tap: turquoise; and there was no corpse floating in it, but then there wouldn't be. The velvet cape Driscoll had been wearing (incredibly, given the heat of the night) would have taken her straight down like a diving bell. Yes, she would have made a splash and a ripple or two, but seconds after her entry into the water, there would have been no sign of the event having occurred. It would have been like when you gave a biscuit to Billy Jackson's dog.

The air was warm, and a dirty-water smell came up from the canal, but it was not unpleasant. It was quite *pleasant*, in fact . . . intoxicating . . . there was something excitingly foreign about it. Monica began to hear voices echoing on the canal, but they came from that part of it that lay around the corner, because in Venice canals could – and did – turn through ninety degrees. The voices gradually became English, and they were accompanied by echoing drips, splashes and all the fumbling clatter of bad rowing. The boat came bumping around the corner, and it was being very badly rowed indeed by one of the two people in it. The rower was a man; his companion was a woman. Monica stepped back a little, not wanting to be seen by them, in case she had killed Driscoll.

The man was saying, 'When in Rome, we are advised to do as the Romans do, and I hold the corresponding view, darling, that when in Venice—'

'Get to the point, Henry.'

'The point,' said the man, 'is that the Venetians don't really go in for breakfast.'

The way this idiot was rowing . . . he was stirring up the water, in a manner likely to bring a corpse to the surface.

'But I'm absolutely starving,' said the woman.

'All right, we'll have coffee and a bun when we get back to the hotel.'

'*If* we get back to it.'

'But this is such fun, darling. I really can't see why people go to all the expense of a gondola.'

'I think you're going to find out.'

'How do you mean?'

'When you come to a canal too narrow to row on.'

Their faces were obscured by their hats. The man wore a wide straw hat, the woman a white sun bonnet with flowers on it. Evidently, her hat was a pleasanter thing than she was – prettier, too, probably, judging by the tone of her voice, which echoed against the stone walls. They had come to the junction, where the little canal met a bigger one.

'Turn us left here, darling,' said the man, as they crashed into the stone bank. '*Left*, Ada.'

She was supposed to be in charge of the rudder. She said, 'The correct instruction, if you want me to go left, is: "Pull on the right-hand rope."'

'Sorry, darling. Pull on the right-hand rope.'

'What's that horrible thing they eat here that's savoury but looks like custard?'

The man made no reply; instead, he very unexpectedly looked up and saw Monica. She leapt back, but he had certainly seen her. He said, 'Shall I tell you a peculiar fact about Venice, darling? They never have Venetian blinds at the windows. It's always those lovely old wooden shutters.'

The man had been reasonably handsome but with one of those purple birthmarks – port wine stains, they were called – on his left cheek. And now, from the centre of the room, Monica heard him say exactly what she hoped he would *not* say: 'Did you see that girl at the window?' Monica retreated right to the bed and put her hands over her ears. She didn't want to overhear any more. When she removed her hands from her ears, the Venetian silence had resumed.

She replayed their voices in her mind. They had sounded horribly English – as though they owned the place. About half the people on the train had been English. But then it was 'the season', being late summer, when it was still warm but not too hot. That was the theory, but Monica thought it might well be very hot today. She returned to the window and looked down again, although she still dared not look right. She watched the ruffled water of the canal gradually settle back down. Was Driscoll beneath it? If so, she had been spared a day of heat. Driscoll minded the heat terribly, but it would be nice and cool at the bottom of the canal.

Monica walked back towards the bed, over the wooden floor that rose and fell like the sea. She stood, listening. Driscoll usually snored in her sleep – a thin snore, because of the thinness of her nose – but no sound at all came from next door. Did Monica have the courage to walk out of her own bedroom, turn left down the corridor and knock on Driscoll's door? She did not. The silence from next door was too unsettling, and the dream – if that's what it had been – was not fading away as it was supposed to. 'Try to think,' she said. 'Try to think about last night,' and, of course, last night began yesterday *morning* – on the train.

The Train de Luxe

'It is perhaps best, and no mere romantic idea, to enter Venice for the first time by moonlight.'

From *Venice*, by Augustus J.C. Hare & St Clair Baddeley

It was a 'train de luxe', and when you looked up its timings in the Continental *Bradshaw*, which Monica and Driscoll had done many times in the days prior to departure, you saw at the foot of the column a capital 'D'. If you then looked to see what D denoted, you saw that it was 'The Simplon Express'. (Well, that was the confusing world of *Bradshaw* for you.) The train, therefore, definitely went to Simplon, but what – and indeed where – was that? It was a place in Switzerland where a new tunnel through the Alps began, and Driscoll had difficulty believing that this tunnel could be en route to Venice, even though it certainly was, albeit via Milan, where the Simplon Express 'terminated', hence a thick black line in the *Bradshaw*. From Milan, it was necessary to take another, more ordinary, train for the short final journey to Venice.

Not trusting the *Bradshaw*, Driscoll had brought it with her, even though it was about four inches thick, and even though all the train timings and associated documents, such as tickets and coupons for meals, had been supplied to her in a big, silky envelope by the booking clerk of the International Sleeping Car Company. When she had first heard of the Venice expedition, Monica had assumed the arrangements would all be made in Boulton's Archway Excursion Office, which was about the one bright spot in Upper Holloway, its interior resembling an art gallery, being lined with posters, fantastically coloured, and with slogans that seemed made up of words thrown randomly together, but they were always interesting words. 'Orient Line to Australia', for instance, 'Canadian Pacific', 'Continental Boat Trains', but some of Boulton's posters were a bluff, Driscoll explained (albeit not in so many words). He mainly supplied English holidays, and for a trip like their own, it would be necessary to go into town – to Cockspur Street, just off Trafalgar Square, where the offices of the International Sleeping Car Company were located in a giant building, suggesting a great deal of sleepiness in the world. Cockspur Street was crammed with international booking offices: tall, white ship-like buildings all staying open late at night, and with the flags of all nations flying from their roofs. Driscoll – dragging Monica with her – had made two return visits to make sure the Simplon Express really was still intending to do what the timetable said.

It was, of course, several trains really, starting with the one from London to Dover that preceded the Channel steamer, and which departed from Victoria Station at eleven o'clock in the morning. Before they had boarded, Driscoll began rummaging through her gigantic satchel because she thought she'd forgotten something or other. Driscoll had sent away for the satchel from a company that supplied 'Serviceable Garments to Take with You on Your Holidays'. All Driscoll's things were either depressingly serviceable or fussily over-elaborated, nothing in-between. Her other bag was in the second category, being a portmanteau or carpet bag of florid green-and-red check with a ribbon trim around the opening. Monica had only her chatelaine bag, which, being very small and dainty, could not be called serviceable, which was why she liked it. Their main luggage consisted of two trunks, and those were already in Venice – at least in theory. A railway carter had collected them from the flat a week ago, and Driscoll had watched him with great anxiety as he had disappeared with them into the traffic of Holloway Road. He had not looked very reputable.

As Driscoll hunted through the satchel, Monica looked along the train, trying – and failing – to spot any individual she'd less rather travel with than Driscoll. It was such a misalliance between the two of them. If Driscoll had been a little older or younger, prettier or uglier, then possibilities might have opened up. She might have been an amusing aunt, like Charley's aunt in the play (except that was a man), or some unfortunately blighted person in need of protection because of having one leg shorter than the other, for example . . . Or a big sister – wiser, yes, but still learning things herself, like Elinor in relation to Marianne in *Pride and Prejudice* – or was it *Sense and Sensibility*? Yes, it was.

Monica was fourteen, approaching what was supposed to be the most exciting time of life; Driscoll was thirty, exiting that period, and providing living proof that the excitement was not guaranteed to occur. She was from a different generation; you couldn't say 'damn' in front of her. And there was no intellectual companionship – not that Driscoll was stupid; she held a degree from the University of Manchester. It's just that she was clever in all those things – mathematics, science, geography – for which Monica had no aptitude. Even so, the year in which their relationship had been purely that of teacher–pupil had been tolerable, if not enjoyable. But now Driscoll stood in *loco parentis* – the second person, after Leo, to occupy that role in an apparent game of pass the parcel, except that in pass the parcel, people *wanted* the parcel. Leo hadn't seemed to mind having it (you wouldn't put it too much higher than that), whereas Monica believed that Driscoll had taken it out of a sense of duty, or possibly for the money.

When Driscoll realised she *hadn't* forgotten anything, there was a further pause before boarding as they both watched a railway official walk up to a blackboard on the platform. He self-importantly chalked the words 'Sea slight' before departing. 'That means it's going to be rough,' said Driscoll, and she used this as an excuse for them not to go to the dining car for the 'light luncheon' available before Dover. Monica believed that Driscoll had a coupon for this meal, but that she would somehow get the money back if they didn't claim it. Monica thought of picking a fight over this, but she wasn't very hungry, having eaten – at Driscoll's insistence – a 'solid' breakfast of bacon, bread, porridge and cocoa. In the event, she and Driscoll both fell asleep somewhere early in Kent and had to be woken up by the guard tapping on the compartment glass at Dover.

On the Channel steamer, there was not so much a restaurant as a cafeteria. Driscoll ate an omelette, while turning the pages of *An Italian Grammar*, by a certain N. Aldini. Every so often she would frown, as though questioning the Italian language, which was very irritating of her. Monica had a bread roll and a little butter, which was supposed to be the start of her meal, but it was also the end because the sea was a little more than slight, and she began to recall every detail of her breakfast bacon.

So far, the excitement Monica felt at the prospect of going abroad had been outweighed by the heaviness of Driscoll's presence, but the scales began to balance about halfway across the

Channel when they'd walked up on deck. They were watching the black smoke roll up from the funnel into a grey sky when, quite suddenly, the sun swung out from behind a cloud and the sky became bright blue, shaming the smoke. Driscoll smiled at Monica, who smiled back.

'You've found your sea legs, dear,' she said.

'They're the same legs I've always had,' said Monica.

Driscoll laughed, and they walked together to the rail. Before long, the Calais docks appeared, looking just like a propped-up postcard, with a grand sort of chateau in the middle, presiding over all the cranes.

The train from Calais was the Simplon Express proper, and very palatial it was. After boarding, Monica walked the length of it several times, passing through the two dining cars (which had pretty, flower-like lamps on the tables and handsome waiters), through the lounge car, where tea and coffee were taken, and along the corridors of the sleeping cars, which were not yet made up for sleeping. Driscoll remained in their own compartment, and Monica knocked on the glass and waved at her every time she passed, until, after the third time, Driscoll ordered Monica back into the compartment. For a while, Monica sat quietly, wondering how the compartment would change when it became a bedroom for the two of them. This being a train de luxe, there was inlaid wood, a good deal of tasselling (if that was a word) and an effectual chandelier in the centre of the ceiling; but it all shook rather suspiciously as the train thundered along, everything being held in place quite loosely, everything being *conditional*. Monica could see where Driscoll's bed would fold out from the wall above her seat. A violent shake of the train might see it come away prematurely, smashing Driscoll on her head, killing her immediately and flattening her 'sugarloaf' hairstyle in the process.

Driscoll had practically turned her side of the compartment into an office. She had her travel bureau full of papers, on some of which she had written itineraries for their five days in Venice. She called these 'First Day', 'Second Day', etc., and was continually amending them for some reason – probably so as to eliminate moments of freedom for Monica – and she was amending these even now, with reference to Messrs Hare and Baddeley's guidebook. The train had come to a stop; wide fields – bigger than English ones – rolled away on both sides.

'This will throw us late,' said Driscoll, after about thirty seconds of immobility.

'Trains do stop at signals, you know,' said Monica. 'It's one of their chief characteristics.'

When the train started moving again, Monica put her feet up on the seat next to Driscoll.

'Take your feet down, dear,' Driscoll said, hardly looking up from her notes.

They were now somewhere near Boulogne, and the sea was sparkling away on the right. A man and a woman in bathing costumes stood in the water, talking; the man had his hands on the woman's shoulders. It was obviously quite a serious tête-a-tête, even though they were in the sea.

Monica lifted up her legs to look at her holiday shoes.

'Put your feet *down*, dear,' said Driscoll.

'It seems I can't put them anywhere,' said Monica.

'You can put them on the floor.'

Monica did like the shoes. They were white canvas, as soft as pumps, but with low wooden heels that made a business-like sound when she walked. They were delicate-looking but tough. For example, the laces were ribbon-like but had steel tips so they wouldn't unravel. She and Driscoll had spotted them in the window of Ed's Original Boot & Shoe, which was one of the few jolly places on the Holloway Road and known to all as 'Ed's Original'. It was not normal to see shoes like this in Ed's, since he was chiefly a *repairer* of shoes – a cobbler, in fact – and displayed mainly practical things in the window like shoe polish, shoe trees and so on.

'They'd be just the thing for Venice,' Monica had said, when they saw them in the window.

'They probably won't fit you, dear. You have very small feet.'

But they did fit.

'They were just waiting for you to come along,' Ed said.

'It's like Cinderella,' said Monica, and both these remarks had irritated Driscoll, since she obviously found both Ed and his shop rather rough, and now she was going to have to fork out for the shoes.

Monica still hadn't put her feet back down on the carriage floor.

'They're quite "swaif", aren't they?'

'The word is "*suave*",' said Driscoll.

'I know, but Leo always pronounced it "swaif". It's how they used to say it in the fifteen-hundreds.'

Driscoll made no reply to that. They'd been over this ground before.

Monica said, 'They're wedding shoes really, aren't they?'

'Not necessarily,' said Driscoll, 'and put your feet *down*.'

As Monica did so, she began to hear – from the corridor that ran along the side of the carriage – the jangle of glass bottles on the move. By craning to the left, she could see a white-jacketed waiter – an emissary from the dining car – coming along the carriage corridor. His trolley held bottles of mineral water, all of the same type: the stuff that came in delightfully fat and pompous little green bottles – very fashionable in London, but probably quite everyday objects in France.

'This is promising,' said Monica. 'I'm going to buy one.' She slid back the compartment door and stepped into the corridor.

'Bonjour, monsieur,' she said.

'Bonjour, mademoiselle.'

How she liked that word. She indicated the bottles: '*Elles sont très jolie.*'

'*Et rafraîchissantes,*' said the man.

She leant into the compartment, asking Driscoll, 'Do you want one, dear?' Monica always liked to give third parties the impression that she and Driscoll were perfectly friendly. But Driscoll only shook her head while writing – an insult to both Monica and the bottle man. Monica slid the door half shut, so that Driscoll might half hear what she was about to say to the bottle man: '*Mon amie préfère les bouteilles d'une autre type.*'

The man was not shocked, as he would have been if he were English. He simply nodded and smiled in a worldly way. In the compartment, Driscoll was still writing, but she had coloured up. She had heard, all right. Her ears must have 'buzzed', as they say. Well, she ought not to eavesdrop whenever Monica spoke to a member of the opposite sex, and what Monica had said was perfectly true. Driscoll was what's called a secret drinker. Unsuitable novels were full of them; you very often read of such people in Sherlock Holmes stories – in 'The Adventure of the Blue Carbuncle', for example, or the 'Copper Beeches'.

Driscoll would sometimes leave Monica in the reference room of the Holloway Library, saying, 'I'm just popping out for a second, but you'll still have "me" for company.' This was one of her rare jokes and it was the prospect of a drink that brought it on, Monica believed. By 'me' Driscoll meant 'Mee', namely Arthur Mee, author of the tedious *Children's Encyclopaedia*, which the library took in instalments. Of course,

Monica would just immediately walk over to the fiction shelves and start reading something by Conan Doyle (her particular favourite), H.G. Wells or somebody fun like that, because if you read the right thing, the library faded away. Driscoll would have to seek her out on her return from wherever she went for her glass of afternoon wine, but she would never give Monica a ticking-off for abandoning Arthur Mee because of the guilt. So, in a way, Monica didn't mind about Driscoll's drinking. It was only because of it that she had her few minutes of freedom.

The water man had glasses on the lower shelf of his trolley. He slipped one over the top of a bottle, so she had her own private jangle. Both bottle and glass, Monica assumed, would be collected later. Back in the compartment, Monica sipped the water. She waited for Driscoll to say, 'Is that nice?' She didn't, so Monica said, 'This is very nice.'

It was the right way to drink water; there was one very *wrong* way of drinking it, which was to do so in public using a . . . Monica closed her eyes, so as to make a bad scene pass from her mind.

Driscoll was still sulking over Monica's remark to the bottle man, and she would continue to be silent until the issue came to a head – usually after about half an hour – when she would say, 'You know perfectly well why I'm cross, and I think you should apologise for your rudeness.' Sometimes Monica forestalled this painful process with an early – if grudging – apology, but that wasn't an option on this occasion, since she wasn't supposed to have said anything Driscoll had heard.

Monica sipped her water. She'd rather it was lemonade, of course, but lemonade was a childish drink, and the French were very grown-up people. She had bought the water because of the jangling noise the man had made on his approach, which had caused her to recollect the sound made by the Idris lemonade man, who played such an important role in her dearest memory of her parents, the one that seemed to summarise the sunlit perfection of her first nine years.

★

Like a butterfly, the Idris lemonade man appeared only on the very hottest days. He was called Mr Allsopp, and his horse was a very large Shire with an amusingly small name: Ron. Mr Allsopp and Ron went slowly around the wide, tree-shaded roads of Hampstead, and the jangling of the bottles was enough to announce their presence. People would wave to them from their front gardens, and they would pull up.

Monica's memory involved a summer's afternoon, when she was sitting on the bench in the front garden of the house in which she had spent her first nine years, namely the Oaks, otherwise known as 47 Sycamore Gardens (rather a clash of trees, but it just showed you how pleasantly leafy Hampstead was). The actual oaks were all to the rear, in a small wood – a copse – number 47 being a new house built on an old garden. Her mother was sitting on the bench, writing her diary. Monica, sitting next to her, had recently had a bout of German measles, but was now 'completely better', as she had been triumphantly asserting for days, and when her mother had mentioned that Father had no patients that day and would be joining them on the bench shortly, Monica had said, '*Nobody* is ill today' – a very fate-tempting remark.

When Mr Allsopp and Ron turned up, Monica's father came out of his 'consulting room', which was not a room but the coach house next door to the Oaks. To have, instead of a consulting room, a consulting *house*, with a telephone and a dispensary that smelt of the methylated spirit lamp, proved what a good and successful doctor he must be. Mother had also been a good and successful doctor but had given it up to raise Monica – or to help raise her, with the assistance of a veritable beauty parade of nannies.

Mr Allsopp had put the bottle of lemonade on the table in front of the bench with a joke about how he was being a waiter today as well as a carter, but he didn't mind. Anne, the maid, brought out some glasses and a plate of tiny, brown-bread lemon curd sandwiches, which were Monica's favourite, and so the three of them – Father, Mother and Monica – were all sitting in a line on the bench as they had their lovely lemony 'tea'. Well, they might as well have been the Three Wise Monkeys sitting there, for all they knew of the future.

For a view, they had first the green garden pond, which became even greener and more mysterious on a summer's day; then came the unexpected purple blossom of the jacaranda tree; then the low front-garden wall of pink brick; then the dusty street. Mr Allsopp and Ron were still present, albeit a bit further up the road and on the opposite side. The Oaks was at the top of the hill, and so they would have a rest at that particular spot. Ron was eating from his nosebag, and so the smell of hay added to the sensation of being in the deep countryside rather than Hampstead (which was countryside in a way, but hardly 'deep'). Mr Allsopp was sitting on his driving seat and reading a paper. Monica asked her father what it was. '*Sporting Life*,' he replied, and he'd hardly looked; he seemed to just know, confirming his cleverness. Also in the street was Harriet Beck, who lived opposite. Harriet was ten, a year older than Monica and a lot larger; she could skip forwards and backwards, and she was doing that just then: a little way forward, a little way back, kicking up dust. You might say she resembled a pendulum, except that a pendulum makes a clock go, and time in that street seemed to have come to a stop, as if too pleasantly fatigued by the sun to continue even to the next minute, let alone the next day.

If only Monica did not have the memory of saying, 'Nobody's ill today.' There was no question that she had done, however, because her mother had said, 'I will write that in my diary.' The diary still existed; it was in the hands of Mr Farmery, the lawyer, who had told Monica she would be given it when she reached the age of legal majority: twenty-one. But Monica's parents did not still exist. Both had died within a year of that day. First Mother (some unmentionable cancer), then Father (cancer of the liver), which was, on the face of it, terribly bad luck, but also perfectly understandable: they were, by profession, the enemies of disease, and disease had taken its revenge.

★

The train was going along by a river. Two teams of men rowed fast along it, competing with each other, or perhaps with the train. Monica was close enough to risk a wave, targeting one particular man, and she scored a hit, because he left off rowing to wave back, rather to the annoyance, it seemed, of his friends. Monica believed that men were going to be her allies in the world. Driscoll, on the other hand, was frowning at her. The train had overtaken the boats, but the river persisted. Monica finished off the mineral water, then she asked, 'What river's that, dear?'

'The Somme,' said Driscoll.

She did know geography, you had to admit.

'And don't you dare throw that bottle out of the window.'

It must have been the little notice above the window – 'Ne jetez pas d'objets par la fenêtre' – that had given her the idea of saying that. To throw something out of the window was to defenestrate it. Monica wished she could defenestrate Driscoll, but as she looked across at her now, she felt ashamed of her thought.

Whenever – as now – she wrote or read, Driscoll wore her slightly twisted wire glasses, and, of course, she was writing or reading most of the time. It was so unfair on her that she was short-sighted, especially given her many other disadvantages. Monica wished she could at least afford to buy her a more elegant pair of spectacles, with tortoiseshell frames, perhaps. And then there were her clothes.

Driscoll, as usual, wore a suit – one of her 'tailor-mades', as she called them, even though she made them herself. They were intended as plain, serviceable garments, which Driscoll then embellished by going to the opposite extreme. This one was new, and perhaps a little lighter than her usual two or three, but it was wool nonetheless, therefore much too heavy for Italy in the first week of September. It was in the usual colour of dark green, which Driscoll called 'the useful green', since it didn't show the dirt, but then why add braid of a lighter green to the cuffs? That could only be a hostage to fortune. The effect wasn't too bad, though. Driscoll had a reasonably good figure and could have looked quite 'chic' with some alterations of the *right* kind to her tailor-mades, as Monica often pointed out: a higher waist on the jacket, a higher hem on the skirt. Driscoll was quite a sporty person – why not try to look sporty? Of course, she also needed to throw out all her hats. They were all far too mountainous, squashing her reddish hair, which she always wore teased up in the 'sugarloaf' style, but even with a pad inside, this never had a chance against the hats. Her present hat – lolling about on the luggage rack above her head – had been bought specially for Venice. It was white, and vaguely nautical, with a rolling brim that rolled somehow too much, so you felt a bit seasick looking at it.

A great cathedral was coming up on the left.

'Where's this?' Monica asked Driscoll, just to see if she would reply again.

'Amiens,' she said, so perhaps Monica was off the hook as regards the apology.

'It's very viewsome,' said Monica, and she had used this word – which she knew Driscoll found provoking – in hopes of eliciting further speech from her companion.

'*Viewsome*,' Driscoll muttered with disdain.

It seemed her sulk was over. She probably reasoned that, drink being her true Achilles heel, it was too embarrassing to perpetuate the grievance.

Amiens seemed to consist mainly of the cathedral and a great expanse of railway sidings – a wonderfully spacious scene. There were few people about, but some of the engines were fuming like abandoned bonfires. Then came the approach to Paris, which was very exciting and unexpected, for they hurtled through a long, dark forest, the gleams of sunlight flashing in time with the rhythm of the train. But Monica remembered that they would not be penetrating to the heart of Paris; the Simplon Express would swirl around the edge of it – following the course of the prettily named Petite Ceinture railway.

This proved to be a strange process, with the train indulging in many long, thoughtful pauses, often while half buried in cuttings. Then it would slowly emerge, passing giant, church-like factories and tall, powdery white houses, parts of which seemed to have been sliced away. When the train was in another cutting, pondering its next move, an official knocked on the window glass and entered. Driscoll greeted him in French, but he was having none of that. In excellent English, he explained that they would soon be at Gare de Lyon, the station facing towards Italy. There would be a fifty-minute wait there.

'Is that in the timetable?' Driscoll asked.

'Naturally,' he said.

'So we are not late?'

'If anything, a little ahead of time.'

Monica had to get in on the conversation.

'Where are we now?' she asked.

'Paris, mademoiselle.'

Monica laughed. 'Of course, I know that, but where exactly?'

'Just now, we are near the district of Belleville.'

'Belleville . . . it sounds nice.'

A coal train was rumbling past the window.

'It *sounds* nice, yes,' said the man, and Monica laughed again.

'*Vous êtes très amusant, monsieur.*'

'*Et vous êtes charmante, mademoiselle,*' he said, nodding and departing.

Monica turned defiantly towards Driscoll. 'What a nice man.'

'It does not do, Monica, to be overfamiliar with people like that.'

'I was just being friendly.'

'It's the same thing.'

'Do you think so, dear? Do you suppose that if we looked up "friendly" in the *Oxford English Dictionary*, it would say, "the condition of being overfamiliar with someone"?'

Driscoll made no reply; she was checking the time by her watch, which resembled a wristwatch but was not. It was a timepiece prised from a brooch and now jammed into the socket of a leather wristband, and every time Driscoll raised it to one or other of her myopic eyes, you thought she was about to clatter herself with a backhander. She seemed even more agitated than usual.

After another twenty minutes of mysterious manoeuvring,

the Simplon Express was in the great, echoing hall of the Gare de Lyon station, and Monica was watching from the corridor as doors opened all along the train. 'People are getting out!' she called over her shoulder to Driscoll.

'Well, that's quite all right,' said Driscoll. 'We do have fifty minutes.' Driscoll was now collecting up the satchel. She obviously meant to leave the train as well, so this was quite a turn-up.

'I'm just going to stretch my legs, dear,' she said – and, of course, it's always a lie when people say that. 'I won't be more than ten minutes. You'll wait here, won't you?'

'I will, yes,' said Monica, because one lie jolly well deserved another.

Monica watched from the open carriage door as Driscoll walked quickly along the platform. Monica stepped down and began following Driscoll; this was all quite sensational, and the Gare de Lyon was a good place for an adventure. It was full of sunlight, albeit of the evening sort, and there was something of the conservatory about it, with palm trees in large pots along the platforms. Monica could dodge behind one if Driscoll should glance back. But she did not glance back, and when she reached the gate, she was not checked by the ticket collector; she waved vaguely at the Simplon Express, to show she belonged to it and was therefore important. Monica arrived at the gate just in time to see Driscoll quit the station through some grand stone arch that made her look very small – small but determined.

Indicating the direction in which Driscoll had gone, Monica said to the ticket man, *'Je suis avec elle,'* and continued her pursuit.

When Monica exited the station, she was on a busy junction, and there was Driscoll on the other side of the road. She was approaching a glass canopy in a kind of seashell shape. A sign said 'Metro', which was the Tube of Paris. It occurred to Monica that Driscoll was running away from her. Well, the nerve of the woman! But then Monica had a spasm of sympathy for Driscoll, who was standing next to the Metro entrance and looking bewildered. Had Monica really driven her to this extremity – to abandoning her young charge in a foreign capital, and doing so in a panic, for she had left her portmanteau on the train and wore no top-coat? Now, with her usual, straining, goggling gaze, Driscoll was consulting her watch. A woman was approaching her – a thin woman, whose fast, precise walk looked familiar. Could this be Mary Kelly, Driscoll's one friend? No, the hat was too good, rather 'swaif'. This was certainly a Parisian lady. Nevertheless, Driscoll was conversing with her, presumably asking directions, which were being duly given – too slowly for Driscoll's liking, evidently, and now, having heard the woman out to the limit of her patience, she was practically charging away towards another junction, which meant crossing a busy road. Monica tried to keep sight of her amid all the wagons, horse-drawn and motorised, carriages and buses – but it was like when a magician waves his handkerchief to confuse you momentarily (for which there was a word that Monica couldn't recall), because now the traffic was continuing, but Driscoll had completely disappeared. For a moment, Monica didn't know what to feel. Great happiness was preparing to contend with great loneliness in her. She spoke to herself, as she often did, fairly gasping, 'But this is the most . . . !'

She found herself walking into the road, tall French horses haughtily passing on either side, then she noticed a shop that appeared at first diseased, but this was only because it was decorated with huge purple plaster grapes: '*Cave à Vin*', Monica read, and here was sprinting Driscoll once again, making directly for it.

Well, the main thing Monica felt now was silliness for not having guessed what Driscoll was about.

Driscoll had gone into the shop. A man had joined Monica on the traffic refuge in the road. He smiled at her and touched his hat; he had what were called 'flashing eyes'. They were at a premium in London, but probably quite common in Paris. The man was now departing, crossing the next part of the road. A tram clanged by, making a quite unnecessary din. Were the London roads ever this busy? It would be the station, rearing up behind her – its great fancy clock tower pointing to the pink sky – that attracted all this traffic. Everything hereabouts was to do with the station: Rue de la Gare, Café de la Gare and so on.

At one street corner, a man was relieving himself into a sort of iron stall; the only protection from the gaze of passers-by a skimpy screen on legs, which encompassed him like a narrow belt. It was the most public of public conveniences! Well, that was the French for you. Very ungenteel at times. Even on so grand a train as the Simplon Express, the lavatories emptied directly onto the tracks, which might be *fairly* hygienic, Monica supposed, if the train were going fast enough . . . Or was it just a case of out of sight, out of mind? The man who had been so brazenly urinating was walking away now, perfectly unashamed. Monica was surprised that Leo hadn't mentioned this outrageous French practice to her. Of course, being a poet, Leo had very often been in Paris. In fact, the first time he had left her alone with Ethel, the maid, it had been to come here.

Monica looked over to the wine shop. Instead of Driscoll, a fat, sleek Frenchman emerged. He held no bottles – must have placed an order. Perhaps there was a queue in there. Monica revolved a little to the right. There, on another street corner, was a green iron turret plastered with colourful posters; alongside it, in the same dark green, statues of four Greek-looking maidens held up an iron dome. A trickle of water fell constantly from the dome. Monica turned away immediately from this worrying sight, looking back towards the wine shop, from which Driscoll was finally emerging, satchel bulging suspiciously. So Monica would not be free of her guardian after all, but at least she was still going to Venice. She intercepted Driscoll at the station entrance, with a humorous, '*Bon soir, madame!*'

Driscoll was gratifyingly shocked. 'I thought you were going to wait on the train?'

'Oh, I'm off back there now,' said Monica, holding out her arm, which Driscoll took gratefully, evidently certain she had not been seen buying wine.

Driscoll's tone was cheerful as she said, 'Don't say you're "off" anywhere, dear. It's milk that goes off, not young ladies.' Monica knew very well the satisfaction of having misbehaved and thinking you'd got away with it. A person could become quite addicted to the sensation.

★

An hour later, with the Simplon Express racing through dark fields towards the town of Dijon, Monica and Driscoll sat facing each other with a good deal of reading matter strewn about on the cushions to either side of them; Driscoll was making notes, possibly also writing a letter. The *chef de train*, or whatever he was called, had recently walked along the corridor tinkling a little bell to announce the first service of dinner, but Monica and Driscoll were down for the second one – an exciting prospect for Monica. Driscoll, too, seemed rather skittish, and had been smiling fondly while perusing Hare and Baddeley and saying things like, 'Now here's a church that really is a must.'

She had, so to speak, admitted to a half-bottle of wine, and this stood open on the little table projecting from beneath the window, together with the corkscrew Driscoll had presumably brought in her satchel from London. Monica believed that she had at least another half-bottle in reserve and remaining in the satchel . . . or it was possible she'd already seen that off, since she'd visited the lavatory twice since their departure from Paris, taking the satchel with her both times. Monica wondered whether Driscoll would be taking more wine with dinner. A menu had been placed in their compartment during the Paris pause; Monica was looking it over.

'I'm going to have *bas-bonds d'agneau de Pauillac pannés et persillés sauce diable*, mainly because it'll be such fun to say. I don't think much of the legumes, though: "*petits pois à l'anglaise*". I didn't come all this way to eat English peas. They'll be dishing up spotted dick next!'

'No, they won't, dear,' said Driscoll. She was drinking the wine from the water glass Monica had been given that afternoon, which Driscoll had stolen (only word for it) from the previous train.

'How's your Italian coming along, dear?' Driscoll indicated the little volume by N. Aldini.

'I can make certain emergency remarks.'

'What *do* you mean?'

'"*La casa è in fiamme.*" The house is on fire.'

'Mmm . . . not very likely in Venice.'

There was an Italian vocabulary at the back of Aldini's book that Monica had glanced at a few times, but the poor man's cause had been fatally undermined by the clerk in Cockspur Street, who had assured Monica and Driscoll that any reasonably educated Italian could speak at least some English, and, if not, French could always be resorted to. Everyone who'd ever had anything to do with Monica had been able to speak French, so she had a good grasp of the language, which she spoke, she believed (because Leo's friend Mr Harper had told her), with 'a very pretty accent'.

Driscoll had bought Aldini's book and the Hare and Baddeley at Hatchards in Piccadilly, after browsing and fretting in the travel department for about an hour while Monica sat on a hard chair attempting to divert herself by reading some rubbish about King Arthur and his knights, which was full of words like 'forsooth' and 'harken', and things had kept 'befalling' the characters. When she came to chapter three and saw that it was called 'Chapter Third', it was simply too much, and she had chucked it aside. Apparently, something had happened to the book when she did that: the cover had got an invisible crease in it somewhere, and Driscoll had had to pay for it, so they had both been in a bate when they got back to Holloway Road.

Monica reached over and picked up the Hare and Baddeley, which Driscoll had set aside, having returned to her writing. Certain passages had been underlined by Driscoll – for example, 'The votive pictures are to be seen on most altars of the Virgin . . . one of the most graceful Gothic churches of the city.' A number '1' was pencilled next to that, meaning it was for 'First Day'. It was quite surprising that Driscoll had not written '*The* First Day' and so on, for she was prone to cramming in the definite article where it was not required, as, for example, in '*The* blue gingham', which Monica was currently wearing, it having been selected long in advance for the honour of being Monica's travelling dress.

Monica said, 'I do wish you wouldn't bother with all this highfalutin stuff, dear,' and Driscoll looked up. 'Architecture and sculpture's not at all in my line, and as for paintings, I'd just as soon take them as they come.'

'How do you mean?'

'I don't want to actually seek them out, because they invariably disappoint when you've spent the best part of a morning tracking them down. And I'm not half as interested in art as you might think. Just because I'm useless at geometry and trigonometry doesn't mean I'm desperate to see paintings by . . . what's that Venetian painter who sounds like a sneeze?'

Driscoll removed her glasses. 'Titian?' she said.

'Bless you!' said Monica, and Driscoll smiled.

'Now, of course, granted, Leo asked you to take me to Venice—'

'He didn't just ask, dear. It was a term of his will.'

'But he didn't specify a cultural tour, dear. I'm sure he didn't; it wouldn't be like him. Do you know how Venice came up between Leo and I?'

'Leo and *me*, dear. Since the two of you are the object.'

'I did that deliberately. I like to keep you on your mettle, dear, as you know. Well, I was reading a lovely unsuitable novel by Wilkie Collins. It was called *The Haunted Hotel*, and it was full of disembodied heads floating about and so on. I happened to mention to Leo, "I wouldn't mind seeing Venice; it sounds so romantic and ghostly," and he said, "Then you shall do, dear."'

'And when was that, dear?' asked Driscoll.

'In January, just after New Year.'

Leo had died on 12 March, and Monica and Driscoll now both thought their separate – but possibly rather similar – thoughts about the strange manner of his death.

'So, you see,' said Monica, 'it was all quite whimsical.'

Driscoll said, 'It was written down in a legal document.'

'Yes, but you can have legal documents to require whimsical things. A man who believes in fairies might require his trustees to tell his beneficiaries to go out looking for them on certain days of the year.'

'Looking for what?'

'Fairies.'

'Why would he do that?'

'To prove they exist.'

'But you just said he believes they *do* exist.'

'Well, obviously, he wants to prove it to other people.'

'A trust like that wouldn't pass the legal tests,' said Driscoll. 'It would be void.'

'What a horrible word that is. Void on what grounds?'

'On the grounds of complete silliness, dear.'

'But Leo *was* quite silly,' said Monica.

'Your guardian was an Oxford don, dear.'

Driscoll wouldn't refer to Leo by name these days, the parcel he'd passed her having turned out to be something of a poisoned chalice. And it wasn't quite true that he was an Oxford don. Yes, he had been a 'Balliol man', and he'd taught in some place in Oxford, but it was only a crammer, as he would cheerfully admit to anyone who knew the Oxford scene. His profession, insofar as he had one, was that of poet, and the only reason he could afford to pursue it was the money he had inherited from Monica's father, who had been a doctor: the very opposite of a poet, in other words.

Monica thought about that Venice stipulation of Leo's. He had written it in a sort of appendix to his will called a Letter of Wishes. You'd have thought wishes belonged in fairy tales, but Letters of Wishes quite often accompanied wills, apparently. The will-maker simply put a clause in their will saying, 'I hereby leave the sum of . . .' (in Leo's case not very much) '. . . for the carrying out of the wishes in my letter,' and the letter could be quite a restless thing, constantly modified right up until the will-maker died. In the event, the wish about Monica seeing Venice had been the only one in the letter, so Monica ought to have been flattered by that, and certainly kindness was never entirely out of the picture where Leo was concerned, but Monica didn't believe that she seeing Venice was uppermost among Leo's true wishes. Unfortunately, he had given up on those shortly before he made his will . . . And *what* was a will-maker called?

Monica frowned, crouching forward – sometimes that would bring a word on, but this time it only caused Driscoll to say, 'I hope you're not travel sick, dear.'

The people who arranged for the wishes to be carried out were the executors of the will, and Leo's executors were Mr Walker and Mr Farmery, who were also *trustees*, by virtue of the trust created by an earlier will – the one made by Monica's father that would control her life until she came 'of age'. When looking for a suitable person to take Monica to Venice, these two – being quite unimaginative men – had looked no further than the person they had just appointed her next guardian, namely the elongated creature sitting opposite, who was just then taking a rather large gulp of wine.

She now began smiling in quite a worrying way and removing her watch, saying, 'How would you like to calculate our speed, dear?'

Monica said, 'Sherlock Holmes does that – in "The Adventure of Silver Blaze". He and Watson are travelling down to the scene of the crime. Holmes is bored – he does find Watson quite boring – so he computes the speed of the train.'

'And how does he go about it?'

'I've no notion.'

'But you've read the story.'

It seemed a maths lesson was in prospect. Monica wished she'd never mentioned 'Silver Blaze'.

'If you're going to read such stuff,' said Driscoll, 'you might as well learn what you can from it.'

If Driscoll wasn't careful, Monica would bring up the book she had discovered in the secret drawer: *Three Weeks*, by Elinor Glyn. Over the course of her delvings into the drawer, she had read perhaps about one-fifth of it in snatches. A few sentences had taken hold in her brain. 'Paul dressed for dinner; his temper was vile, and his valet trembled.' There was a lot of trembling in the book, taken all together. It was also, Monica had discovered, a famous – or infamous – book, so it would be quite natural to mention it.

Driscoll was saying, 'How do you think he might have done it?'

'Who?'

'Sherlock Holmes, for heaven's sake!'

'I believe he . . . times the distance between the telegraph poles.'

'It would be more logical to use the quarter-mile posts.'

'I don't think you can be more logical than Sherlock Holmes.'

Driscoll then said something like, 'If you have the distance in quarter miles, then multiply by 900 and divide by the number of seconds, you have the speed.' That was rather like when she said, 'The volume of a pyramid is the area of the base multiplied by the height divided by three,' or whatever it was, and it wouldn't do to ask her to repeat it, because she'd get cross, being so quick at things Monica was slow at.

'You should be able to see the quarter-mile posts,' said Driscoll.

'Where?' Monica said.

'Dateless girl – outside the window!'

'Dateless' was one of Driscoll's words. She'd brought it with her from Manchester.

Monica *couldn't* see the quarter-mile posts from where she sat, only dim fields flying by. 'Maybe they're on the other side.'

'That is possible,' Driscoll rather surprisingly admitted.

'Shall I tell you what I'd like to do?' said Monica. 'I'd like to have a hot chocolate in that famous café.' She indicated the guidebook. 'Apparently, it's "of worldwide reputation". I'd also like to have a ride in a gondola and see Lord Byron's house. Leo told me about Byron in Venice – swimming along the Grand Canal and having all those affairs, so that's naturally quite interesting.'

'Hare and Baddeley don't care for that house,' said Driscoll. She leant over, caught up the book and began flicking through the pages. 'Here's Byron's place,' she said, as if she'd just located it on the Holloway Road, and she began reading, at first aloud – '"Many are the quaint stories of his life here . . ."' – and then in frowning silence. Putting the book down, she said, 'I'm not sure I approve of Lord Byron.'

Well, of course, Lord Byron wouldn't have approved of *her*.

'When he swam along a canal,' said Monica, 'he'd do it on his back, so he could see the stars. It was also to keep his cigar alight, of course.'

'It *would* be.'

'And when he was in Venice, he learnt Armenian in a monastery.'

'All I can say,' said Driscoll, 'is that he must have had a great deal of time on his hands.'

'Is that any reason to disapprove of someone, though?'

'I disapprove of him because he was a rotten poet,' said Driscoll, and that word 'rotten' was because of the wine. It was also possibly apt. While not at all poetic, Driscoll read a good deal of poetry, and would regularly quote the works of Tennyson, whom Monica found rather a stiff read. Also, his name was peculiar – so close to being Alfred Lawn Tennis – but she was inclined to agree with Driscoll about Byron's writing. Leo hadn't cared for him either: 'A versifier, not a poet.'

Silence for a space between them; only the businesslike thrumming of the train. Driscoll was smiling rather vacantly – this, too, the wine's doing, of course.

'It's good that *we* have a palazzo,' Monica said at length, 'instead of being in a *pensione*. That always makes me think of the old-age pension.'

'Reasonable enough, dear,' said Driscoll. 'The root is "pension": payment or rent.'

They had been destined for a *pensione*, but Mr George Farmery, solicitor, had unearthed the palazzo at the last minute. It belonged to some people of his acquaintance with the un-Venetian name of Morris.

'What do you think it will be like?' Monica asked.

'I do know it's plumbed up to the third floor.'

'And you can't say that for many palaces, I'm sure. What floor are we on? Our bedrooms, I mean.'

'The fourth,' Driscoll said, pouring her third glass of wine.

'Remind me about the servant situation,' Monica said, grandly. 'They turn up on the evening of First Day?'

'The housekeeper,' said Driscoll, 'should be waiting for us this evening. She'll heat the water and get us a cold supper. Her mother, the cook, will be coming tomorrow evening to make the dinner. At least, that's the arrangement.'

'How wonderful. What's the housekeeper's name?'

Driscoll had to consult her notes for this. 'Zita.'

'I love that,' said Monica. 'That's *highly* promising.'

Driscoll, wine glass in hand, was smiling fondly at Monica. 'I do believe that's your favourite word, dear. Promising. It

41

does you great credit, given what you've been through in your young life.'

She meant all the passing of the parcel, and it was really very nice of her to say this, so Monica jumped into the seat next to Driscoll and kissed her on the cheek before resuming her seat opposite.

'As for the café,' said Driscoll, 'I assume you mean Florian in St Mark's Square. We'll be in the piazza tomorrow anyway – for the basilica and so on – so why don't we have luncheon there? It might be rather jolly.'

Monica was so amazed and delighted that she said, 'When?'

'At lunchtime, dear. Our lunches are kind of *terra incognita*. The arrangement with the servants is for evening meals only. I think we could fit in a lunch at, say, half past twelve without too much disruption of the itinerary.'

'But won't it be expensive?'

'Quite expensive, yes.'

'And will luncheon involve a *chocolat*? I would make very short work of a *chocolat*. I'm looking a gift horse in the mouth, aren't I?'

'You are rather, dear,' said Driscoll, removing her glasses and smiling so charmingly that Monica couldn't think why she didn't drink wine all the time.

★

About seven hours later, the train was thundering through Switzerland, passing who knew what mountains and gorges. Monica could only imagine, since Driscoll had insisted on the closing of the curtains as soon as the scenery became interesting.

The two lay in their respective beds, the compartment having been converted while they ate dinner. Four berths had been available in the compartment (two either side), but only two were required. Driscoll had chosen to have the lower of the two on her side made up; Monica, of course, had chosen the higher of the two on hers, and she had been awake ever since climbing up to her 'bunk', so much so that she was beginning to think the name of the International Sleeping Car Company a fraud.

By glancing down diagonally, she could see Driscoll clearly, for, while the light of the chandelier had been switched off (it was now swinging about wildly as though in protest), a small blue night light burnt alongside it. This was just about enough to read by, and Driscoll had at first been reading Hare and Baddeley for a while. Then she had stopped reading in order to lie silently, staring upwards like somebody who's died with their eyes open. Then she had begun snoring, with her glasses distressingly askew on her long, thin nose. Monica had climbed down and gently removed them, placing them on the little table by the window, so that Driscoll should not stand on them when she got out of bed. At the same time, Monica had claimed Hare and Baddeley and taken it up to her bunk. (She enjoyed going up and down the ladder because its rungs were carpeted.)

She had intended to read the guidebook, but it was just too dull, so she looked at the map at the beginning. The Grand Canal was in the shape of a letter 'S', albeit an 'S' the wrong way round. Monica revolved the book to see if she could make the 'S' come out the right way, but it was permanently backwards, which was quite all right. An 'S', whether backwards or forwards, is beautifully sinuous, quite unlike the Holloway Road, which had no sinuosity (and if there was no such word, there jolly well ought to be) whatsoever.

She started recalling their dinner, even though she didn't want to. It had not been a success. Driscoll, having drunk too much, or too little, wine in the compartment, had seemed to take against the whole event, perhaps because she resented the spending of the token. It hadn't helped matters that, as the hors d'oeuvres arrived, the idiotic waiter had told her that some signal soon after Paris had thrown the train late after all, which had caused Driscoll to start a bout of sighing. 'Poor Zita will have to wait up half the night for us,' she had said. 'And who knows when the gondoliers stop working for the evening?'

'I should think they wait for the trains,' said Monica, and Driscoll had touched her hand in gratitude.

'Sorry to be so grouchy, dear,' she had said. 'I'm awfully tired. I rather want to go to bed.'

'Why don't you have some more wine, dear? Look,' Monica had said, indicating the next table, 'they serve it in tumblers – so you'd get much more than in an ordinary glass.'

There had been silence between them, more or less, after that fatal remark, and Monica had detected pity in the occasional glances that came her way from the other diners, as they chattered away merrily, their talk seeming to chime with the tinkling of the cutlery. Among them had been the man with the flashing eyes. He had smiled several times at Monica, requiring him to lean over, so as to peer around his companion, whose back was towards Monica and who, like Driscoll, wore a large, unjustified hat. And then Monica had twice peered around Driscoll to smile at the *man*, so it was as if they were playing peek-a-boo, and this had caused Driscoll to turn around to see what, or whom, Monica might have been looking at. Of course, her gaze had immediately quelled the flashing of the man's eyes.

Lying on her shaking bunk, Monica was becoming intensely annoyed that the curtains were closed on the orders of a person currently unconscious. From her elevated position, Monica could control the top of the curtains, so she pulled them apart slightly, revealing an entire mountain with a white peak and an amazingly self-satisfied full moon presiding above. Monica whispered to herself, 'Everyone is a moon, and has a dark side which he never shows to anybody.' She was not the first person to say that, but she could not remember who *had* been the first.

A cracked voice came from below: 'Close the curtain, you *horrid* girl!'

'I am *not* a horrid girl,' said Monica, as she complied with the order.

It wasn't the first time Driscoll had called her that; it was about the fifth, and the first had only been a few weeks before, so evidence was accumulating that it was her true opinion, which would strengthen Monica's case – which she intended to put to Mr Farmery – for being taken away from her. She must escape Driscoll and the horrid reality that she represented, and Monica believed she was entitled to this escape, by way of compensation for the death of her parents.

'I am *not* a horrid girl,' Monica repeated, as the snoring from below resumed. Meanwhile, the train was making a different roar, a louder one than before. Monica tweaked the curtains, to see a cold-looking iron wall reeling away. They were in the great tunnel amid a mechanical cacophony, and yet Driscoll's snores were not drowned out. Why hadn't the Metro outside Gare de Lyon sucked her down, and carried her away for good and all?

Monica began to feel an agitation that had become familiar over the past year or so, a sort of feverish rage, manifesting in a total inability to keep still. She sat up, then climbed down the padded ladder to stand over Driscoll – this person who kept her from the world to which she truly belonged, her effectual gaoler, who really ought to be more careful about leaving

45

herself defenceless before her prisoner. The train, apparently free of the tunnel, was wildly speeding, bucking about more like a boat than a train, and Monica was shaking; but she would have been shaking anyway. It seemed to her that anything could happen at any moment: a disaster, a breakthrough or breakout – the necessary jolt.

But now the train was slowing; a signal, no doubt, for they had such workaday contraptions even amid the snowy mountains, and that signal was Driscoll's friend, for the dangerous moment had gone. Monica turned and regained her bunk.

The Gondola

'The impression produced when we have passed the great railway bridge, which has dissolved the marriage of Venice with the sea, and the train glides into the *Railway Station* is one never to be forgotten.'

From *Venice*, by Augustus J.C. Hare & St Clair Baddeley

As the train approached Venice station on a long bridge over the sea, Driscoll slept. She had slept intermittently ever since they had boarded this new train at Milan, even though it had no beds (and certainly no name). It was not the train they were supposed to have taken; that had departed long before their arrival in Milan, having grown impatient waiting for the Simplon Express, which had been running very late. They'd then had a long, exhausting wait for the Milan train's successor, not getting away until early evening; it was just gone ten now.

Boats, illuminated by lanterns, swooned about on either side of the causeway, as though providing a lazy overture to Venice. Their sails were either red or even deeper red, and the fat moon of the Alps was officiating here, too. As Monica watched the boats, Driscoll suddenly awoke and began digging about in her portmanteau. Monica had suspected she had something very heavy and superfluous in there, and now she produced the offending article: her velvet evening cape, and she was putting it on – actually on top of her woollen jacket.

'Why are you wearing that?' said Monica.

'It's suitable for the evening.'

'But not for the tremendous heat, dear. You know how you wilt in the heat.'

'I do not *wilt*, dear,' said Driscoll.

The train had stopped. Monica and Driscoll exchanged wide-eyed looks. There was nothing for it but to disembark. As they were walking along the corridor of the carriage, Monica had the opportunity to study the cape from behind. It was green with red lace trimmings and made Driscoll look like the top half of a Christmas tree. Or, then again, in combination with the satchel, it made her look rather Mexican. Monica had seen the cape once before, when she and Driscoll, and Mary Kelly, had gone to hear a piano concert at Islington Town Hall. Driscoll had worn it at the concert, Monica believed, for the benefit of a man who was a surveyor (or something like that) for Islington Council, but who nonetheless was artistic. He wore a rather fraying woollen jerkin instead of a waistcoat and he had a pointed beard. There was a meekness about his light blue eyes that he was apparently always trying to overcome. He knew a lot about music, or at any rate talked a lot about it as they all drank tea after the concert. He had made Driscoll laugh in the same way she laughed when she was playing badminton. He hadn't made Monica laugh. When Driscoll had introduced her to him, he had said, 'Ah, the famous Miss Burnett,' before going back to pontificating about the music. His name was Aubrey . . . something-or-other, and Monica believed he must have sent Driscoll the Valentine's card in the locked drawer. There were positively *no* other candidates, and his name did begin with 'A'.

They climbed down from the train into a station full of elegant, flowing people, dark colours, tremendous heat and swirling steam. 'But this is wonderful!' Monica said.

They were walking fast along the platform, and Driscoll was very evidently starting to perspire.

'My dear,' said Monica, 'you will faint in that cape.'

'It'll be chilly on the canals,' Driscoll said. 'We will, in effect, be on the sea.'

'How do you make that out?'

'Don't use that expression, dear. The Venetian lagoon is an enclosed bay of the Adriatic. And it is a palazzo we're renting, you know, not rooms in a boarding house. The servants will expect us to be presentable.' She suddenly stopped on the platform, so that Monica almost crashed into her. Driscoll was looking Monica up and down, smiling a worried smile. '*Might* you slip on your shawl, dear?'

Monica shook her head slowly, to indicate a very emphatic 'no'. The shawl was in the portmanteau, and that was where it was going to stay. It was a horribly complicated thing – made you look like you'd got caught in a net.

'Or the dust coat?'

Monica shook her head again. She rather liked her blue gingham travelling dress; she wanted the gondolier to see it.

The station – packed with travellers – was completely fascinating. The brick walls were discoloured, made both black by soot and green by salt water, and the place was filled with the smell of dirty water, which became stronger as Monica and Driscoll approached the *uscita*, which obviously meant 'exit'. But now Driscoll stopped again. She was looking towards a ladies' lavatory. '*Gabinetto*', it was called. 'Would you like to use the facilities, dear?'

'No.'

'I think we should.'

'Why do you say "we"? We're two independent people, you know.'

'I know that, dear. You always go out of your way to make it very clear. Please come in with me; I'm not leaving you alone out here.'

It occurred to Monica that the station had frightened Driscoll. There were so many people; the engines kept making loud barking noises, and it was amazing to think it could be so hot so late. Monica trailed into the Ladies after Driscoll, or she began to do so, but she never crossed the threshold, because Driscoll about-turned.

'We're not going in there,' she said.

'Oh, God,' said Monica.

The place was 'unhygienic', presumably.

Driscoll, standing amid the flowing crowd, was putting on her glasses as she tried to make out some document in her hand. She jerked the paper closer to her eyes, then removed the glasses to polish them with the little rag she kept in the case. How Monica wished she wouldn't do that – it was too like wiping away tears.

Monica touched her guardian's arm. 'What's the matter, dear?'

Driscoll directed a sigh up towards the station roof, then turned to Monica: 'I can't read my own writing.'

She passed over the paper. Monica expected it to show the address of the palazzo – for palazzos did have addresses, complete with very long house numbers like 1349. But the paper was a list of 'THINGS TO DO ON ARRIVAL', and, of course, the things were numbered. Number two was, 'Find gondola pier left of station,' but number one was hard to make out.

'I think it's something to do with travellers' cheques,'

Monica suggested. 'Yes, it says, "Cash first travellers' cheque."' Monica wondered whether the apostrophe was in the right place, and Driscoll had probably wondered about it, too, for there was something half-hearted about it. 'And look,' said Monica, pointing across the station, 'there's the Change.' She felt very grown-up, calling the brightly lit Bureau de Change 'the Change'. There was a queue coming out of the door, however.

'Not to worry,' Monica said. 'We can cash it on First Day. Tomorrow, in fact.'

'It's a question of whether I have enough for the gondolier.'

Driscoll was peering into her purse, which she had made herself and embroidered with a picture of some unknown English garden. It looked too innocent for a late night on the Continent.

'But you've got masses of banknotes, dear,' said Monica.

Driscoll looked helplessly at her.

'In your *wallet*,' said Monica, for Driscoll also had one of those among her many encumbrances. 'You could probably buy a gondola *and* a gondolier for what you've got in there.'

'I know, but I've just read something about how the gondoliers prefer coins. They don't trust the notes.'

Yes, Italian banknotes were untrustworthy. They were a murky purple-green colour and depicted a man of no more physical distinction than your average bank clerk, except for an enormous moustache. But he was the king of Italy, apparently. The Italians called their money 'lire', but other people, including Hare and Baddeley, called them 'francs', which must be very humiliating for the Italians.

'It ought to be the *right* amount,' said Driscoll, 'and I can't do it all in a minute. It'll be so awkward if he feels obliged to give change.'

51

'I don't think he will feel obliged. They're generally such rogues, you know.'

I shouldn't be trying to make Driscoll even more anxious, thought Monica, but she was so very irritating.

Driscoll said, 'According to the guidebook, it's usually about one franc.'

'Which means one lira,' said Monica. 'Look, do come on, dear. We'll be last in the queue.'

They began moving, but slowly, as Driscoll intoned, 'There are twenty-five and fifty cents to the pound so that makes a lira worth five and sixpence ha'penny, more or less.'

'That'll be all right,' said Monica. 'A cab ride's usually about five bob, isn't it?'

They would occasionally take cabs at home, but even London cabs put Driscoll into a dither of nerves. She didn't like dealing with working people. In a café, she'd always call out, 'Waitress!' whereas 'Miss' was so much friendlier.

'Don't worry, dear,' said Monica. 'I'll deal with the gondolier.'

She meant she would flirt with him, which she certainly would be doing. She'd been imagining her ideal gondolier for about three years (long before her own Venice trip was on the cards), ever since Leo had taken her to see the Gilbert and Sullivan opera.

They stepped out of the station, and it was immediately obvious that the trains could not have proceeded any further even if they'd wanted to, because here was a canal, presumably the Grand one, since it was almost as wide as the Thames, and with quite heavy traffic upon it. Many boats, all illuminated, criss-crossed before them. They included gondolas, steam launches, barges and everything in between. Red-and-white poles, like barber's shop poles, projected from the black water at all angles. The station shared the Grand Canal with churches and palazzos, some of which looked tumbledown, with balconies and arches half rotten, like coral, as if they had spent some time *under* the water and were resigned to doing so again.

The cab rank of the gondoliers did indeed lie to the left of the station, and Monica picked out her man right away. He was standing up in his boat and smoking a cigar while talking to an associate on the bank. But when he saw Driscoll and Monica approaching – that is to say, when he saw *Monica* approaching – he pitched the cigar into the water, even though it was nothing like burnt down. All the gondolas were hung with paper lanterns, mostly Christmassy greens and reds, but this fellow's were blue and yellow, like somebody *else's* Christmas, or the one you couldn't quite remember but that had certainly been a good one. The man smiled at Monica, so he was definitely going to be her choice.

'This one's lanterns are an original colour,' she said to Driscoll. 'I rather like them.'

Driscoll probably saw the true meaning behind that remark, but she nodded in a weary way.

'*Buona sera, signor,*' Driscoll said to the gondolier. With her piece of paper in her hand, she looked like someone about to give a speech.

'Evening,' said the man. Why, he might have been a cockney!

'*Conta costa*—' Driscoll began.

'I think he speaks English,' Monica interjected. 'I mean, he just *has* done.'

'How much,' said Driscoll, 'to go to . . .' and she read out the address, which was Calle something, with the number coming at the end, not the beginning. The man merely smiled when she'd finished. There was something mischievous about him, which might be said of all attractive men. Driscoll said, 'Do you know the place?'

'Everybody know it,' he said. Monica loved the way he rolled the 'r'. She couldn't have done that if you'd paid her a hundred pounds. She had quite often tried.

'Very good,' said Driscoll, 'but how *much?*'

He named a figure that Monica didn't quite catch (because, of course, the man's English was not *really* up to the cockney standard) and she wasn't sure Driscoll had done either, but she said, 'I don't think that will suit.'

'Oh, God,' Monica said.

Driscoll had turned her back on the gondolier in order to squint into the purse. The gondolier folded his arms. Perhaps he was regretting throwing away his cigar prematurely? But he looked neither pleased nor displeased. Another big steamboat came up, making waves that rocked the gondola quite violently, and the gondolier unfolded his arms to make a pretence of being about to fall over. It was really funny, and showed off his skill, because obviously his balance was excellent in reality . . . and it was very good of him to make a joke when Driscoll was behaving so ridiculously.

'She's just checking she's got the right money,' said Monica. 'She doesn't care for travelling, you see. It puts her in a great state of nerve tension.'

'Right-a money? For a-what-a?'

'The fare.'

'The fare?' said the man, as though that were the last answer he had expected. 'Fare ees fair.' He seemed intrigued by the word. Another gondola was pulling out into the canal with three passengers on board. There was a good deal of luggage on that boat, and its gondolier was extremely fat, so the whole thing was low in the water, but the fat gondolier didn't seem to mind; he started singing as he rowed away, at which Monica's gondolier put his fingers in his ears and pulled a face for her benefit.

Driscoll had stopped counting the money. She had turned back around to face the canal, but she didn't seem to have reached any decision, and she did look a state – very overheated and red.

The gondolier said, 'Your friend – she can pay what she like. I will take you and her for nothing.' Monica adored the way he spoke. He had left the 'h' off 'her' and thrown in about a dozen extra syllables.

'Of *course* we will pay,' said Monica, and she stepped onto the gondola, making it a *fait accompli*. She sat down on the halfway seat and indicated the one at the end to Driscoll. The gondolier held Driscoll's hand very tenderly as he helped her in, whereas he only just touched Monica's arm as he helped *her*, which was rather disappointing. Could it be that he preferred Driscoll? More likely, he was feeling sorry for her.

The decorated prow of the gondola looked like a seahorse, or the end of a violin. There were blue cushions, somewhat grubby. When the gondolier began rowing, he immediately became a figure from art, and Monica realised that the English way of doing it – sitting down with two oars – was very undignified in comparison, like rowing on the lavatory. Driscoll was smiling bravely while clutching her purse; there was a small breeze on the Grand Canal that might help her.

The canal was really a high street, like the Holloway Road, but whereas the dead-straight (and *generally* dead) Holloway Road was a travesty of the notion, the Venetians had got it right. Imagine wanting to spend a night riding up and down the Holloway Road? You'd have to be off your head, whereas Monica was finding herself hypnotised by the Grand Canal.

You might have been floating on air rather than black shining water. Of course, the gondolier himself played a part in the hypnosis. She liked his clothes: white-and-blue sailor shirt offset by crimson neckerchief, narrow black trousers; black velvet shoes with rope soles – a dancer's shoes, really.

They were turning right and leaving the Grand Canal. They entered an echoing, watery labyrinth. It was so unusual, like something between heaven and a sewer, and it was up to you what you made of it. The blue and yellow lamps were obviously not only for decoration; they showed the way along this back canal now, with little dead-end canals off to the side bounded by blank walls – water seemingly held in reserve for mysterious purposes. The stripy barber's poles had given way to burnt-looking black spars. They were passing houses, of course, but most seemed dark. Perhaps the lights were all burning on the other side. A corner lamp came into view, like a siren tempting you on, and making you feel sleepy at the same time.

But as they swept around the corner, the gondolier let out a cry, something like 'Oyeee popay!' Driscoll, who'd been half asleep, grasped Monica's knee.

It had certainly been a loud cry; even now, its echo had barely died away.

'Why do you shout?' Driscoll asked.

'It is-a for-a look-out,' he said, and he pronounced 'out' as 'hout'.

He resumed his graceful rowing, with the water just trailing away quietly off the oar. There was no splashing, merely what might be called 'plashing'. Occasionally he smiled at Monica, and he tried once or twice smiling at Driscoll, but he got no response from that quarter.

Then he stopped rowing, and the gondola was simply gliding along past windows that were mainly dark. Monica did see a dinner in progress, all in a golden yellow light made by many candles, but the diners had their backs to the window, which was strange, because you'd think some of them would be facing out. The law of averages would surely dictate that. The gondolier was looking directly at Monica. He took the single oar and laid it down along the length of the boat. He then made a praying gesture, and Monica thought: *He's asking for my . . . favours. He wants a kiss at the very least! Well, he's Italian; he just can't help himself.* But now the man rested his head on his hands, so it was not the praying gesture he was making, but the sleeping one, and he was pointing at Driscoll, who was asleep on her cushion with her head sagging. Well, here was his opportunity. Monica realised she didn't want to be kissed, and she regretted not having paid more attention to N. Aldini, who might, for all she knew, have given a whole page to 'When refusing a kiss'. But the gondolier had picked up his oar and resumed his rowing, so the whole charade had been about nothing more than making a little fun at Driscoll's expense, and Monica wondered why he'd bothered. Perhaps he was a bit simple-minded.

As a distant clock chimed eleven, they came into a short watery road with an illuminated doorway that gave onto a small dock – hardly more than a doorstep. Monica now saw that a figure was standing in the doorway, but this person was made dark by the light coming from behind. As they neared the light, the figure gradually ceased to be a forbidding giant and became a small, round Italian woman. They had arrived at their palazzo, and this was its housekeeper, the famous Zita. Monica muttered to herself, 'She's not as young as her name.' It was hard to believe she could have a mother (the cook) who was still alive. She looked very jolly, however, and she seemed to know the gondolier, because she called him Stefano. To be precise, she said what sounded like, '*Sera, Stefano.*'

He held on to Monica for slightly longer this time as he helped her from the boat, so she could smell his smell, which was that of cigars. 'Thanks ever so much, Stefano,' she said, and she wondered how she might, after all, capitalise on his obvious affection for her, but couldn't think of a way, which was just as well, for she was very tired. Perhaps she would be seeing Stefano again? He might become their regular 'cabbie' since there seemed no other method of getting to and from the house. But how would he be summoned? These were tired thoughts and another church bell, presumably also tired, had now got around to striking eleven.

'*Buona sera, signorina,*' said Zita to Monica, who thought the words sounded wrong somehow, coming from that lady – rather too stiff-sounding. Of course, they were Italian words, and Zita *was* Italian, but Monica recollected a footnote in the Aldini book: 'In Venice, servants, and people of that type, have a tendency to revert to their own dialect. It is recommend-ed that formal Italian be insisted upon.' Monica reciprocated enthusiastically, and now she and Zita stood on the little dock, gazing back at Driscoll, who had remained in the boat. The earlier travesty was being repeated: she had turned her back on the company to ferret through her wretched purse. Stefano had his arms folded again, and he was looking at Zita as if to say, 'Really, aren't these *inglesi* just the limit?'

Monica was tired of making excuses on Driscoll's behalf. Besides, she was immediately entranced by the room she now stepped into. It was like something between a scullery and a dockside warehouse, and this last element made it more, rather than less, beautiful. It was rather shadowy. A small fire burnt in a grate surrounded by porcelain tiles decorated with images of children doing things like feeding hens or sitting on gates. There was a long table with a supper prepared: ham, cheese, mineral water, olives (which Monica had only read about), grapes, sweet biscuits and a bottle of red wine, all laid on the planks of the table in rather a rough sort of medieval way, but good white linen was present in the form of rolled napkins, obviously of impeccable cleanliness and corresponding to the pristine white of three fat candles burning on the table.

Beyond the table, things slowly appeared out of the shadows: a chandelier lay on the floorboards, like a great, collapsed spider. Monica detected a shrimping net and a boathook. She knew about boathooks from her days of rowing with Leo on the 'other' river in Oxford – the one that was not the Thames. There was also a rocking horse, the largest one Monica had ever seen, but it didn't seem so large compared to the size of this room, which was obviously like the sort of goods station of the house. Things would arrive here and await their true beautification upstairs. But now one of the candles on the table had, for no apparent reason, started to smoke, and this Monica took to be a warning of something bad going on outside. She turned to see that Zita was remaining at her post on the small dock. She blocked the sight of what lay beyond, but her stance suggested anxiety.

Monica walked back to the doorway. Clearly, no progress had been made on the gondola. Stefano was now sitting down in it, which – Monica assumed – he only did when things came to a pretty disastrous sort of pass. It was like seeing a horse sitting down. He muttered something that sounded like 'Cazzo', and from his tone, she gathered that this was something a young English girl was not meant to hear. It was a comment on Driscoll, who was standing at the far end of the boat, and still counting her money like a female Scrooge. Obviously, the woman had suffered a total nerve-collapse. She was not capable of functioning beyond the bounds of her own mental Holloway. It was not her fault, but Monica must take charge. She marched onto the gondola, stomped right along to the end, rocking it in such a way that Stefano had to utter some word of caution, but Monica didn't care.

Driscoll turned around; she wore her glasses, and they were askew. She said, 'I must have got my purses mixed up. There's English and French in here as well as Italian.'

Monica grabbed at the purse: 'Give it here now, you idiot!' and while Driscoll, in her shock and alarm, had relinquished the purse, Monica had not quite grabbed it, and now it lay on its back in the black water, slowly drifting away, with the embroidered garden scene uppermost.

Monica's first instinct, when she saw what she had done, was to glance at Stefano. He shook his head and shrugged. Driscoll was crying and folding her glasses, as though having given up on the whole day. And now she simply began standing still, glasses in hand, eyes closed. Monica herself was on the verge of tears; she didn't know how to proceed. Soothing Italian words came from Zita, who was paying Stefano, seemingly from her own money, having collected the satchel and portmanteau from the boat. Monica called out to Zita, 'It was only small change in the purse, you know, just a few notes for minor expenses on the journey. She's amazingly organised, you know. Her wallet's in the satchel; there's plenty of money in that.' Monica realised she was talking about Driscoll as if Driscoll were a halfwit, or elsewhere – and certainly she did seem to be inhabiting her own world. She was now at least moving, however, proceeding in quite a stately and dignified walk along the gondola. Stepping onto the little dock, she nodded and said a formal 'Thank you', to Zita. 'I will now pay you back.'

Monica never saw Stefano's departure. She was once again in the large, hot room, staring at the fire. Driscoll, not so much weeping now as just loudly sniffing, was riffling through her satchel. She got hold of her wallet and, with many apologies in broken Italian, handed Zita a note.

Monica turned towards the two of them. 'Sorry,' she said, and even as she spoke, she didn't know whether she was apologising to Zita or Driscoll, but neither seemed to hear her. Driscoll was reaching for the wine bottle, while beginning to speak, half in her bad Italian, half in English, to Zita about the arrangements in the house. She didn't look towards Monica. Gradually, Zita became busy, which was obviously her natural condition. She bustled about the room chopping bread, stirring the fire; she attended to Monica, who ate and drank various things at the end of the table. All the while, Monica looked at Driscoll, who did not look back. She was again sorting through the contents of her portmanteau while sipping wine quite shamelessly. Then she asked Zita, 'Will you show the girl up to her room, please?' She had now ignored Monica for a good quarter of an hour. This was not unknown, when Monica had 'created' particularly badly. But after about this length of time, the ice would usually start to crack – a series of sharp remarks culminating in a moral lecture.

Monica was shown upstairs, to the third floor, where there was hot water in a small, charmingly misshapen room, cosy like a cabin in an old ship. It contained numerous candles, an antique lavatory, a copper on the boil next to a tin bath – also a small yellow couch, just in case one was exhausted after one's ablutions. A red dressing gown (it presumably belonged to the house) was draped over the couch. Monica asked Zita to put the hot water into the bath, which she did using a beautiful chipped red enamel jug – a very soothing process to observe, at once fast and slow. She got into the bath, and Zita departed.

Monica had nearly fallen asleep in the water when there came a knock on the door. This would be Driscoll . . . but it was Zita again. She had brought her a delicate cup of Italian cocoa to drink in the bath. Monica had never drunk anything in the bath before, except, accidentally, the bathwater. She asked Zita to enquire as to whether 'the mistress' (she thought she'd better call Driscoll that for form's sake) would want the water after her. Monica believed she had made herself understood. On the Holloway Road, Monica would always have 'the hot' when it came to baths. Early in their acquaintanceship, she had sometimes offered 'the hot' to Driscoll, who always refused so peremptorily – almost rudely – that Monica had stopped doing that.

Sipping her *chocolat chaud* (she thought the French term applied, given that the drink was so very rich), Monica predicted that Driscoll would come calling soon. 'We will not sleep on a quarrel, dear,' she would say, as night settled uncomfortably over the Holloway Road, somewhat reducing the perpetual din, and bringing to a merciful end one of those many evenings when the two had been fuming and recriminating (Monica usually out loud) in their respective bedrooms. Yes, there would either be a knock on this bathroom door, or later upstairs when they were both ready to turn in. After Monica's apology, Driscoll would say, 'Let's put today behind us, dear. Fresh start in the morning,' to which she might add, 'We'll win through in the end, you know!'

When Monica had finished the *chocolat*, she climbed out of the bath and put on the dressing gown, which was far too big, but very soft and welcoming. She ascended the ancient and dark stairs to the bedroom floor, where Driscoll's room came first. The door was open, and Monica peered in to see rather grand quarters, but faded and lit by only a single candle, with Driscoll standing by the opened windows, still draped in the terrible cape. Driscoll's back was to her, and she did not turn around even though Monica lingered in the doorway. So Monica proceeded to her own room, the next one, where her trunk lay waiting, and where she was joined a few moments later by Zita, who assisted with her preparations for bed.

Zita gave no definite answer beyond a polite nod to the question about the bathwater. Monica was being encouraged to think something had been lost in the translation. Zita departed, saying something like 'Sogni doro', a pretty and affectionate phrase, anyhow, presumably meaning 'Goodnight', and because Zita had spoken it so musically, Monica believed it was Venetian rather than Italian. Zita had turned the lamp right down, not quite extinguishing it, so perpetuating the wonderful mystery of Venice. Monica climbed out of bed to look down on what she already considered, in a possessive way, their very own side-canal, but all she could really make out was a single lamp over the way, reflected and lengthened in the black water.

She returned to bed; she was very tired, and she kept nearly dropping asleep – literally seeming to drop, even though she was already lying down. She would keep awake for the visit of Driscoll and one of her damp goodnight kisses, but there came no knock on the door. It seemed Monica had 'created' her way into uncharted waters, which disturbed her – but then again, her thoughts might be wrong-headed, and she was so very tired.

Departure from the Palazzo

'The *Calle*, as the narrow streets are called – the only streets in Europe free from mud and dust – are, in their way, as full of interest as the canals.'

From *Venice*, by Augustus J.C. Hare & St Clair Baddeley

Sitting on her bed in the strong morning light, Monica realised she had come to the end of her definite recollection. The images that followed were both real and unreal, and they were the crux: the key to the question of whether she had killed her guardian.

She had apparently woken up soon after going to sleep, or possibly not having slept; she had turned left out of her room and walked along the corridor to Driscoll's bedroom, where nothing had changed: Driscoll remained standing at the opened window in her velvets. Monica said, 'I'm sorry.'

There was no reply from Driscoll, but only this histrionic staring out to the dark and dripping city of Venice. Driscoll had always had her moods, but there was a new note of melodrama here.

'Well?' Monica said. She was looking for a response to the apology, renewing it in effect.

Then Driscoll had seemed to answer a question that had not

been asked. Half turning around at the window, she said, 'I was just thinking how sincerely I wished I had never seen your face.'

It was then, seemingly, that Monica had been overcome with the need to perform some rapid physical action. This person before her was literally in her way, blocking the light and blocking out Venice, keeping it from Monica. Therefore, Monica had walked quickly across the room and pushed her *out* of the way, which happened to involve tipping her into the canal — at least, presumably, for she had not checked. Monica had then returned directly to bed, being so very tired.

★

In her silent, sunlit room, Monica experienced a certain satisfaction at the notion that Driscoll might be gone forever. But a moment's thought told her how foolish that was. Driscoll might not have woken up this morning, but all the policemen, lawyers, gaolers and hangmen in the world certainly had, and their paths would soon be crossing Monica's, if the dream had not been a dream.

There was still no noise from next door.

If Monica wanted to hear a sound, she was obviously going to have to make it herself. She walked across the wooden floor towards her white shoes, which were next to the trunk. Even in her stockinged feet, her walking seemed loud. She sat on the floor to put on the shoes, and when she walked back to the bed with them on, the noise was, of course, louder still, because of the wooden heels. Her chatelaine bag lay at the foot of the bed. She had wanted it near her because it was new and she loved it. She picked it up.

The chatelaine bag was a kind of purse, really — certainly not much bigger than a purse — and her money was inside it. Driscoll had given her fifteen lire, with the usual injunction:

'Don't spend it all at once.' She counted the money. Still fifteen lire, in rather dirty notes of three, two and one. She and Driscoll had got the money from Cockspur Street, during the visit whose main business had been the obtaining of the travellers' cheques. These came with instructions, which Driscoll had read while frowning all the way home on the Tube. You'd think she would have comprehended them immediately, being a great hand at maths, but it had already become apparent that the prospect of foreign travel seemed to fairly terrify her.

Monica looked at the money again. She didn't know what she was going to do today, but you needed money in a strange town even if you weren't going to do *anything*. And, in the circumstances, she felt at liberty to spend – and to misspend – the lot.

She was putting the purse in the bag when she heard a church bell, laboriously counting the time. She began to count with it: '. . . Two, three, four, five, six, seven. Please stop now.' But the bell ignored her, and marched on towards eight, then nine. It was surely inconceivable that Driscoll would have slept until nine o'clock; it had certainly never happened before. Monica stood and seemed to wobble on her feet. She felt rather faint. She *had* fainted once, in the marquee of the flower show at Manor Farm, Highgate. It was the acrid scent of some funeral flowers – chrysanthemums, carnations and probably lilies – that had finished her off. The marquee had been very stifling, and a man had been whistling infuriatingly, but it wasn't really his fault. Those same flowers had been in 47 Sycamore Gardens after her mother's funeral.

Monica picked up the hand mirror again and, as she had suspected, her face was totally white. She seemed to have been painted with emulsion. She walked over to the trunk for another look. The dresses for Second Day onwards were all cotton, all white or dark blue, and all made by Driscoll. Driscoll had declared that dark blue was Monica's colour. None was entirely free of lace. The effect was somewhat old-fashioned, but undoubtedly pretty – and it was quite touching, the way that Driscoll had made attractive, lightweight dresses for Monica to wear in Venice while apparently intending to persist with her own heavy woollens and velvets.

Beneath the dresses lay Charlotte, Monica's bisque doll. In the flat, Driscoll had asked Monica, 'Do you want to take Small Charlotte?' and Monica had merely shrugged, since they had recently been arguing, and Monica didn't want to appear too soppy about what was, after all, a toy. But Charlotte had often proved herself a reliable ally of Monica's – she was a good listener, you could say, and Monica was glad to see her now. Charlotte was two and a half inches tall and probably a refugee from a doll's house that Monica couldn't remember. She dated from Sycamore Gardens days, anyhow. From a distance, she looked like a pincushion, on account of her fragile pink dress that could not be taken off; or, if it *were* taken off, Charlotte would immediately fall apart, so Driscoll had reinforced the dress with a red-ribbon belt. She had done this one rainy day in the Pond Square house when she was only a governess and not yet a guardian. She had not made a big fuss about doing it but had just let Monica discover the repair when she next saw Charlotte, which was on the night of the same rainy day, since Charlotte lived on Monica's bed. It was sweet of her, of course, and Monica had been grateful, but later on she began to suspect Driscoll's motive. Was the repair not part of her strategy to ingratiate herself? Thereafter, Driscoll's occasional references to 'Small Charlotte' would irritate Monica. Only Monica was allowed to call her that.

'Hello, dear,' Monica said to Small Charlotte, and she put

her gently into the chatelaine bag. If she was going to prison, she would take Charlotte with her. Next in the trunk came a red book: *Forty Patience Games*. That was for the evenings, and there would be a couple of packs of cards somewhere lower down. The book lay on a clean bundle of towels and other white flannelly things, bound by large safety pins like a suffocated baby. This had been transferred by Driscoll from the chest of drawers in Monica's Holloway bedroom to the trunk – because who was to say that Monica might not experience her very first 'monthly' in Venice? 'Monthlies' sounded so dreary, like grocery bills, and they were evidently very disobliging things indeed, so it would be just like them to start happening in an inconvenient location. Harriet Beck's had started when she was thirteen, but she was, as she admitted, 'a rather large girl'. The smaller the girl, the later in life she started having monthlies, according to Harriet, '. . . and you,' she had said, pointing rudely at Monica, 'are a rather small girl'.

Monica stepped out of the room into the corridor. Directly before her – this being a rather *thin* palazzo – was a window. Last night, there had been blackness beyond it. Now she saw that it looked down on a bit of garden behind the house. The garden had a red-brick wall around it and contained some dark trees in pots geometrically placed on flagstones. They resembled the serious trees you saw in graveyards, and they were elegant in the sunshine. She looked slowly to her left, towards the door of Driscoll's room. It was closed. If Monica had done nothing to Driscoll in the night, the door would have been that way because Driscoll, like most people above nursery age, wanted her bedroom door closed as she slept. But it was also possible that Monica had closed it having murdered Driscoll, because you would naturally want to close the door on a bad scene. The trouble was that the dream or the memory had been all about the pushing out of the window. That episode was brightly lit, but what had happened immediately before or after was in shadow.

Monica hurried past the door and gained the stairs. She clattered fast down the three floors and came to the big ground-floor room: the 'goods station', where the rocking horse seemed to have assumed a disapproving expression. Should she try to eat some breakfast? 'I am a great believer in breakfast,' Driscoll used to say – a dull remark, since most people were great believers in breakfast. In the Holloway house, Monica usually had bacon, bread and tea, with porridge added on red-letter days; and it was Driscoll who made the bacon and porridge, even on those days when Ethel was working. Just now, she felt full of love for Driscoll – to have been so boring in life, and then to be not only dead but murdered . . .

Monica turned her attention to the two doors. The front door, of course, gave onto the water; the way out was by the back door, which was very sturdy and red with brass studs in it – a baronial sort of thing. A small table stood beside it, and here Driscoll had laid out some items that would be needed for First Day: a large key, for opening the door, her gloves, the guidebook and their two parasols. Monica picked up her own parasol. No sign of Driscoll's wavy hat. Perhaps Driscoll had brought along another one, and had not been able to decide, in all the upset of the night before, which one to set out for First Day. There was a table by the door in the flat as well, and Driscoll always placed upon it the things that must not be forgotten. Monica picked up the guidebook. There was a sealed letter inside, unstamped and held between the last page and the back cover, on which Driscoll had written the address of the palazzo. It must be the letter Driscoll had been writing on the train. Obviously, it was for posting, and it was addressed to 'Miss S. Kelly, 37A, Preston Terrace, Manchester, Lancs, Inghiliterra'.

Now, it wasn't quite true that Mary Kelly was Driscoll's only friend. Driscoll was also acquainted with Mary Kelly's sister, Sarah (another potential spinster), but she was only by way of being a pen-friend, having remained in Manchester, where they had all been at the same brainy school together. Monica had never seen Sarah Kelly, but she would wander into her dreams occasionally, looking like a combination of Mary Kelly and Driscoll, which is to say too tall and thin, and always seeming to be accompanied by the dreary word 'Mancunian', which meant a person from Manchester.

Monica tried the big red door. It was locked, as she had expected. Therefore, Driscoll had not got up early in the morning and unlocked it. Monica herself unlocked it and, leaving the key in the door, stepped out. She closed the door behind her quite loudly. Surely that would have woken Driscoll if she were alive, but Monica, lingering by the closed door, could hear no stirring from within the palazzo. She walked fast through the small garden, which held the medicinal smell of its trees, to the door in the wall. She had forgotten about this third door, but it must have let Zita out, therefore it would presumably let Monica out as well. Or maybe Zita had had a key. If the door was locked, Monica would be trapped.

★

The door did open, releasing Monica into the Venetian world.

She was in a rectangular square with a church frowning down from beyond the far end, as though jealous at not being allowed in. The square was quite empty, except for a sort of carved stone well in the middle of it. In one corner of the square was a rather whimsical painted arrow with the words '*Per Ferrovia*' above it, which meant, 'This way for the railway station'. In the opposite corner was another arrow, reading 'Per Rialto', which meant the famous Rialto Bridge over the Grand Canal. She had learnt about these signs from a less pompous guide to Venice than the Hare and Baddeley effort. She had discovered it in the Holloway Library. It was written by a man (possibly an American) with the perfectly straightforward name of Louis Archer, and he wrote accordingly. But today Monica was stuck with Hare and Baddeley. At least it had a map. The station lay roughly west of where she believed herself to be, the Rialto roughly east. She would head for the Rialto because east was also the direction for the main place in Venice, St Mark's Square, and it would be absurd to come to Venice without going there, no matter whether you'd killed someone or not. Florian, the luxury café, which Driscoll had fixed on for the taking of luncheon at half past twelve, was in St Mark's Square, and perhaps Driscoll would be there after all, with her usual, 'Now you have some explaining to do, Monica,' and the prospect of policemen, courtrooms and prison cells would dissolve.

The first thing the Rialto arrow did was to direct her into a very obscure alley, where the houses on either side seemed to be the *backs* of houses. She was walking under a succession of washing lines hung with clothes, sometimes quite indecent ones. Well, it was a good drying day, although she supposed Italians seldom spoke of 'good drying days', since almost every day qualified.

She turned a few corners at the request of the Rialto arrows, but a couple of times they failed to materialise, and she had to guess the direction according to the position of the sun, which was still quite low, but climbing fast and clearly with big plans for the day. Many church bells were ringing, as though in celebration of the sun.

Monica had been starting to lose faith in the arrows, and now she was in a little square where two of them said '*Per Rialto*' while pointing in opposite directions, so here was what Driscoll would have called the '*reductio ad absurdum*'. The square was full of sunshine yet also deeply sleepy. On the one hand, it seemed to say, 'This is a good example of a beautiful place; it should inspire you to go out and see how many others you can find.' Or it might be saying, 'Don't trouble yourself about anywhere else: stay here,' and there was a man doing precisely that – reading a book on a balcony. Monica took note of him as she began to run. She was running for the simple reason that she wanted to make faster progress. She had liked the man's misshapen straw hat, which also made her hate him, because he was obviously not worried about anything. There weren't many people about, but some of those who *were* about seemed to be eyeing her with great suspicion. Almost all the streets in Venice were narrow alleyways, so fast running on the part of someone going the opposite way tended to be noticed. If Monica thought about why she was managing not to trip over her parasol, she probably *would* trip over it.

She stopped running when she came to a third square. There was a carved stone well in the middle of this one, too – so you could see the workings of the Venice dreamworld: it was all more or less the same, however much time you spent walking or even running. There was a stone balcony here, too. Nobody was peacefully reading a book on this one, but you had the sense that somebody might start doing so at any moment. This stone well had two steps running around its base. Monica walked over and sat down on the top step. 'I am completely lost,' she said.

Glancing to the right, she saw another new thing about this square. It had a drinking fountain: a sort of iron stump with a horrible face half buried in it, as though an ugly dwarf had been encased in the stump, and the water came from the mouth in a continuous, rattling spew. Monica hated drinking fountains, and with good reason. Turning away from it, she thought she might be about to cry, but she had only got as far as looking miserable when a well-dressed man – judging by his white trousers and highly polished boots – entered the square and walked up to her. He carried a cigarette, which smoked for a while in his hand, close to Monica's head, before he spoke.

'Who were you talking to just now?'

It came to Monica only slowly that he had spoken English.

'Myself,' she said.

'Are you looking for your parents?'

Monica considered. She knew she was going to give a clever reply; it was just a question of what.

'I know where to find my parents, thank you,' she said.

Because they were in Highgate Cemetery in London.

'Are you quite all right?'

'*Quite*, thanks,' and she still hadn't looked at this man who was standing over her in such an arrogant way, but she could tell he was taking a draw on his cigarette.

'Very well,' he said, and walked away, which was a shame really, because it might have been useful to have someone to talk to.

Monica stood up, since no tears had come. They would only have been tears for herself and not for Driscoll, who deserved them more, especially if she were dead. (For Driscoll's sake, Monica was making an effort to think grammatically.) There were no arrows at all in this square, so she walked down any old alleyway, and suddenly she was on the bank of a moderately wide canal and looking at a closed water door with a small dock before it. She had come back to square one, so to speak, and she realised that, as she had emerged from the alleyway, she had accidentally glimpsed the balcony of Driscoll's room. The shutters had been open, just as they would have been if she had pushed Driscoll into the water.

But they would also have been open if Driscoll had woken up after Monica's departure. Should Monica try calling up to her now? No; she still dared not discover the truth. All she dared do was look down at the water, which had a very knowing look; it had been there too long. It was decidedly not fresh or natural and it moved slightly against the stone banks, licking its lips. Monica, feeling sick, turned and walked away. 'I have killed her,' she said. 'I believe I'm too young to be hanged, but I will be detained at His Majesty's Pleasure.'

She pictured the king, sitting in a grand sitting room, relishing his freedom, with tall French windows open to a beautiful garden. A flunky entered. 'May I remind you, sir, that young Monica – who indeed is not so young these days – remains in prison. Is it your pleasure that she should be released?' The king shook his head.

But perhaps there might be clemency? It was something you appealed for – the kind of speech that a lawyer would make for you, which was possibly also called a plea of mitigation, and which might be written up in the *Notable British Trials* series, of which the Holloway Library had a complete set, and of which Leo himself had possessed a few volumes, since he had some of the same morbid interests as Monica. The funny thing about those books was that they were 'unsuitable', even though they were full of King's Counsels and Lord Chief Justices and so on. The most unsuitable – and therefore the best of the lot – was *Trials of Burke and Hare*, the 'body merchants' (the second of whom, Monica suddenly realised, had the same name as the co-writer of the Venice guidebook, which must be a curse to that presumably more respectable gent). The trial of Burke and Hare turned into the trial of Burke only, because the even more despicable Hare 'turned king's evidence', which is to say he 'split' on Burke. When Driscoll had found Monica reading it in Holloway Library, she had said, '*Honestly*, Monica,' and Monica had tried to explain that it was hardly her fault. Naturally, one gravitated to that sort of horror on a rainy winter's afternoon in that library, which was both too light and too dark (electric lights but not enough of them), and full of suspicious-looking characters, especially in the reference section, which was where Driscoll would dump Monica before going off in search of wine, and where the *Notable Trials* were shelved.

Monica believed that sometimes the defendant himself made the plea for clemency, perhaps as a result of being so evil that even his own 'brief' had deserted him. Monica thought she might as well rehearse her speech.

The Plea for Clemency

'Many pretty ornaments sold in Venice are made of the pearl shells of Lido, "flowers," *fior di mare*, the Venetians call them; they have no others.'

From *Venice*, by Augustus J.C. Hare & St Clair Baddeley

Monica began making her plea to the judge as she passed a *'Per Rialto'* sign on the wall of a pinkish church. (Her gigantic shadow was passing it at the same time, she noticed.) She spoke in a low voice, but not quite a whisper. 'To begin at the beginning of this sorry tale, your honour. I am Monica Alice Phyllis Burnett.' She paused, as she always did when she said her surname out loud, wondering about the effect it might have; it did seem rather prolonged. But it was only a name, so she pressed on. 'I was born on 29 May 1897, so I am fourteen years and three months old.' It was probably not necessary to say that; the judge's maths would be up to working it out. 'Both my parents were doctors, and both died within three months of each other in 1907, both of a cancer. I was just turned ten years old at the time.'

That did sound scarcely believable, and Monica recollected the time, about a year ago, when she'd been with Leo in the theatre at Oxford, watching *The Importance of Being Earnest* by

Oscar Wilde. Leo himself would soon be dead, but he probably didn't know that, and his main concern at the time was the play. Leo was an expert on Wilde, and he'd been muttering criticisms of what he called the 'line readings', before charitably – but also quite rudely – adding that this was only an undergraduate production so what could you expect? It had been an enjoyable evening to begin with. She and Leo had a bag of mint humbugs to share in the theatre (Leo ate as many sweets as the typical child), and the young man in the role of Lady Bracknell was very amusing, Monica thought. When he'd said, 'To lose one parent, Mr Worthing, may be regarded as a misfortune; to lose both looks like carelessness,' Monica had laughed, before remembering that this was exactly her situation. The question, then, was whether to take back the laugh, so to speak. She had noticed that Leo was looking at her sidelong; it seemed he had prepared a smile but was holding it in reserve. Monica herself smiled, which was his cue to do likewise, and so they exchanged their rather sad smiles, which was a bit soppy, but quite nice, really.

The next moment, Leo was laughing fit to bust at Lady Bracknell, and that was him all over: he was kind, but never mawkish or sentimental, and the quest to have fun always came first. In the theatre, Monica had thought about this for a while, then she said, 'I like you, Leo, but I no longer love you,' and a woman on the row in front had turned around to scowl at her for speaking, but Leo had obviously not heard, because he was still laughing. For the remainder of the play, Monica could think of nothing but her parents – in particular, her mother, and she began to panic, becoming very hot and restless, being unable to recall the colour of her mother's eyes. If Monica couldn't remember their colour, who could? Certainly not her uncle, Leo Burnett.

Another 'Per Rialto' was coming up. Approaching it, she passed an alleyway to the left, at the end of which was the Grand Canal. Monica walked a little way along the alley, where she stood watching the boats, especially the gondolas. Their pilots seemed to *stir* them along, rather than rowing. There were longer gondolas, as well, propelled by two men, and there were ferries, going at right angles to the other boats, so there was a busy warp and weft occurring. As for the palaces, they were beautiful, of course, but when you looked with a dispassionate eye, half of them needed a coat of paint, the other half a total rebuild.

'My mother died first, your honour,' she said. 'She died in the Royal Northern Hospital, which is on the Holloway Road, on which I would later be taken to live – which partly explains my dislike of that road.' She had visited the hospital only once, in a cab with her father. Her mother had a room of her own; it overlooked the Road and was stuffed with plants as an antidote to it, but the smoke and drone of the Road couldn't be entirely dispelled.

She didn't go to the funeral. It was a very hot day; Leo took her off walking on the Heath. Monica's father sat up with her for two nights afterwards, calling her his 'little gypsy', which was not characteristic of him. The name came from some children's book he'd heard of, and he no doubt applied it to Monica because she was becoming more and more gypsy-like herself, a result of gradually being taken into Leo's little house in Highgate, which was on the other side of Hampstead Heath. Highgate was not *quite* as pretty as Hampstead, but it was another London village on a hill, and, like Hampstead, it was touched by the golden halo of the Heath.

The Grand Canal was sending small waves along the paving stones of the alley, daring her not to move back. Perhaps one of the famous Venetian floods was in prospect. In the seventeenth century, according to the guidebook, an earthquake had caused the Grand Canal to run dry for two hours. So that was the *opposite* of a flood.

She said to the waters, 'After my mother's death, my father went into partnership with another doctor.' So there were two of them in the coach house. The other doctor was a large, gloomy man, name of Howell, and he didn't seem very good at his job. On two occasions, she'd thought it was the ambulance drawing up outside (quite a common event), but it was the hearse both times. 'I think Father took Howell on when he found out that he – my father, that is – also had a cancer, your honour. I believe he hoped he might recover if he had some assistance at work.' And what a silly idea that was. She turned and walked away from the Grand Canal; she'd be seeing it again soon, no doubt.

'I gradually moved in with my uncle Leo, your honour. I believe he tried to be kind to me, but even so, it was something of a shock.'

Whereas her father's house was like her father, being tall and solid, Leo's house was like Leo: small, endearing, ramshackle and (here, of course, the simile ended) overwhelmed with wisteria. It was on Pond Square, in the middle of Highgate. The pond had been filled in about twenty years before, but it was still a countrified spot. Widows lived there, or the better class of tradesmen. As Leo would cheerfully admit, there were 'no top-notchers in Pond Square'. He himself was probably the nearest thing to it, being a university professor, of sorts. The house was scruffy, and it made Monica scruffy, as did the Heath, which she had to cross to get to Highgate from Hampstead. Her woollen stockings acquired many small twigs and leaves; the washing of her blouses went by the board. The smell of the smoking fire in Leo's house permeated her hair and clothes. It didn't do to inspect the house too closely. There was gas only downstairs, where the burners made dark smudges against the green leaves of the Morris wallpaper. If you looked around the burner of any of the upstairs oil lamps, it would be full of dead insects. The graded enamel jugs in the scullery were all hung in the wrong order. There were many books in the house, but most were damp. Several competing families of foxes lived in Pond Square, and fights would break out between them in the middle of the night. It was quite a romantic situation for Monica. Leo was so impractical and disorganised that she saw herself as his young protector, like Amy Dorrit, supporting her father by seamstressing in the debtors' prison. Certainly, Pond Square postponed the terrible comedown she was destined to experience on the Holloway Road.

Monica had returned to an alley running parallel to the Grand Canal. Somebody was playing a piano somewhere: artistic, modern music, of the kind Leo had liked; fragments of something barely there.

'Father and Leo rubbed along all right, your honour, if you'll forgive the expression, but they had little in common, and didn't speak all that much. But I was aware that they had one very important conversation in the drawing room at Sycamore Gardens.' It had been on a dark day of relentless rain; her father had been terribly thin, about half his normal weight. 'The solicitor, Mr George Farmery, was present, and I believe that's when my future was decided.'

She was passing another alley to the left, and there was a further instalment of the Grand Canal at the end of it. This time, one of the motor launches was departing from a landing stage. The boat was going backwards at that moment, which perhaps caused it more effort than going forwards, hence the great quantity of black smoke rolling out of its funnel. You didn't expect to see a big boat like that going backwards. It was like Harriet Beck's skipping. Of course, not everything *could* go backwards. For instance, time: even in Venice, time was moving forwards, and by the end of the day, Monica assumed, she would discover, by some means or other, whether she had killed Driscoll.

'My father,' Monica resumed, 'made a will before his death.'

The words 'before his death' were, of course, unnecessary.

'I was to be left a capital sum of money . . .'

That was also wrong.

'I was left a sum of money in capital . . .'

That was wrong as well, but the judge would get the point.

'I believe it amounts to about a thousand pounds, your honour, which I will come into when I am "of age", which is to say at my "majority".' (Monica congratulated herself on not saying 'when I am twenty-one', although that's what it amounted to.) She was now on a footway by a small canal, on which a rather whiffy dustcart-boat was moored, looking thoroughly ashamed of itself. Then again, it was supposed to be lucky to walk past a dustcart. There were two giant seagulls strutting about on this one, picking at some rotting vegetables that had spilled from a dustbin.

'The will,' she said, addressing the seagulls, 'also appointed my uncle Leo – whose real name, incidentally, is Leonard – as my guardian. Naturally, he must have been consulted about this beforehand.' And it must be admitted that Leo never showed any resentment at being in that role, even though he had been a carefree bachelor before Monica came along.

Monica walked on, accompanied by her shimmering reflection in the water. She was not at all sure Leo had ever ceased living the life of a carefree bachelor. He continued to do most things 'for the fun of it'. He would often take Monica along with him, and when that was not possible – or when he simply didn't *want* to take her along – he left her in the care of Ethel, the servant he had acquired to help look after Monica.

The '*Per Rialto*'s had brought Monica to a bridge that went diagonally across a small canal rather than being at right angles to the water. It made an elegant variation. A gondola was gliding towards the bridge, and Monica's heart gave a leap, because she thought the gondolier was Stefano, but, of course, all gondoliers looked more or less alike, just as all gondolas did, and it was not Stefano. The man had to duck down low as he went beneath the bridge. There were no passengers on his boat, just empty red cushions faded to pink by the sunshine.

Descending from the bridge, Monica said, 'Father did not bequeath the house in Sycamore Gardens to Leo, you honour.' He did not bequeath it to anyone, for it turned out he had never got around to buying either it or the coach house, which was a bit annoying of him. 'But he did leave Leo an income to be paid from the interest on the above-mentioned capital. The will stated that this income was for the upkeep . . .' Or whatever might be the right sort of rickety Dickensian word. '. . . for the upkeep of himself and myself, and also for my education, about which the will had this to say . . .'

Monica was now in a very narrow alleyway indeed, which kept kinking left and right so you couldn't see ahead. It was a sort of ancient yellow colour, and the window shutters had faded to colours beyond the reach of names. The poet Browning had described an alleyway in Venice so narrow that he couldn't open his umbrella; it might have been this very one.

Monica had tried her best to understand the will; she'd once taken a long walk with Mr Farmery as he tried to put her in the picture. (Rather to the surprise of both, they'd ended up in

Finchley.) Of course, Mr Farmery had told her only what he thought she ought to know, and she was vague about exactly *what* the will had to say regarding her education; she believed it was something along the lines of, 'My daughter is to be educated in a manner suitable to her intelligence.' Farmery had used some such phrase . . . Her *high* intelligence, it must have been, otherwise her father wouldn't have brought it up. It was generally understood that a girl like Monica would be educated at home until aged fourteen, and that is what had happened so far, but Monica had now been fourteen for three months with no school on the horizon.

A bootblack had his pitch at the end of the alley. He seemed to have chosen the wrong spot, since there were no people about other than himself and now Monica – at whom he was rudely staring, probably because she had been talking to herself. He wouldn't have understood what she said, but you weren't supposed to speak to yourself in *any* language. When she passed him, Monica came to a junction of alleyways. As she turned right on the '*Per Rialto*' trail, she remembered to mention the trust to the imaginary judge. 'My father's will had established a trust, your honour.' No need to explain to a judge what a trust was, of course – which was just as well, because Monica wasn't entirely sure herself, but she understood that the purpose of this particular one was really to enforce her father's will: to make sure her guardian did indeed guard her, and to make sure she got her good education. 'There were three trustees,' she continued. 'The first was Leo himself; then there was Mr George Farmery, whom I have already mentioned.' She pictured Mr Farmery's premises – the only office among the shops where Highgate High Street became Highgate Hill. The office overlooked the tracks where the little tram crawled up and down the hill between Highgate and Holloway, always dependent on its wire, of course, just as a mountain climber requires his rope. She thought of Mr Farmery: a kind man with large, friendly ears; the 'farmer' part of his name was reassuring, seeming to connect him to the London villages of Highgate and Hampstead. Then again, he was also very friendly to Driscoll, who lived in Holloway, where no farms had existed for a very long time.

'The third trustee, your honour, is called Mr Walker.' She had never met Mr Walker and knew nothing whatsoever about him, except that he'd been a friend of her father's at the University. Whenever she pictured Mr Walker, she saw him walking *away*.

Monica was coming to a district of shops and people, so she spoke more quietly and quickly. 'The main one of the three as far as I was concerned, your honour, was Leo, because he became my first guardian. As I have already mentioned, he was very different from my father, even though he was his brother.' Was it worth saying that Leo, for all his faults, could find entertainment in anything? 'He knew the sort of things likely to interest a young girl,' said Monica, 'and they are not necessarily the things you would expect.'

When the council was metalling some new roads in Highgate, he took her to see the steamroller and the surprisingly handsome man who commanded it, driving while standing up, like the helmsman of a boat, and he did have what Leo called 'sea captain's hair', meaning too long, but Monica thought him fine-looking, and she believed Leo did, too. He would also take her to see the water cart that laid the dust on North Road, or to observe the performance of the man who posted the giant bills on the billboard on Muswell Hill Road. This began as comedy, because there would be about ten minutes of apparent confusion with a bucket of paste, a mop and some rolls of paper. Then, suddenly, there'd be a beautiful picture of a woman playing golf and 'Bovril – for health, strength and beauty'. You'd think the man would take a bow, but all he'd do was shoulder his ladder, pick up his bucket and trudge off.

She thought of Leo: a small, disorganised man in a brown moleskin suit and yellow waistcoat. His hair always stood up, so he looked like a cockatoo, and he wore a moustache, which he sometimes attempted to curl, when he was going out for one of his late nights in the West End. But when he succeeded in curling it, the moustache looked so different from the rest of him that it seemed to be stuck on. Monica had once said, 'A beard might suit you, Leo.' (Because the moustache certainly didn't.) He'd replied, 'I don't believe I could grow a beard however hard I tried.' He had been a very boyish man, quite unlike his brother.

'He would take me into town very regularly on the "tuppenny rides", your honour, known to most people as the London Underground, and we would often go to the theatre.' Usually to the Lyceum, especially for pantomimes, or to the Players' Theatre under the railway arches at Charing Cross, and with supper to follow, even if it was nearly midnight. 'We went often to Oxford, where he had a connection with a college – one of the smaller ones, not very famous.'

Insofar as Leo did any work, it was at Oxford: coaching students up for their exams, or giving readings of his poetry, after which he might sell a few copies of his books. There would be a small charge for admission, and it was Monica's job to sit by the door and collect it. She'd done that half a dozen times and at least twice nobody had turned up, but he never seemed to mind, and nor did Monica, since she was being Little Dorrit in her mind, or perhaps even Little Nell. Leo didn't let reality overtake him – not until just before the end of his days. He would just throw up his hands in a humorous way and say 'Banjanxed!' which was his catchphrase, you might say. It meant something like 'Ruined!' but he never was quite ruined and always seemed to have something 'up his sleeve'. Monica never understood why Leo didn't live in Oxford. It was something to do with the Pond Square house, which he didn't own, but had the use of very cheaply.

'You wouldn't say that Leo ran a "household",' Monica said, 'but he did employ a servant – namely Ethel – who was retained as a cook-general "assisting", in other words doing everything. Ethel was about seventeen when she first came. Her father had been quite literally lost at sea, your honour, and she came to us from the Sailors' Orphan Girls' Home, which is at 116 Fitzjohn's Avenue, Hampstead.' (She had supplied the address just in case the judge should think a place like that could never exist outside a children's story.)

For a while as she walked, she was thinking of Ethel, and wondering whether she would ever see her again. On the face of it, Ethel was like Driscoll personality-wise, in that she was tremendously dull, but unlike Driscoll, she was not in the least intelligent . . . although Monica did wonder about that sometimes. Ethel spoke so little, there wasn't much to go on; it might just be that she couldn't be bothered to make the effort. If you asked her what was for dinner, she might say, 'Stew.'

'Any particular kind of stew?'

'No.'

It was always pretty nice, though.

A few weeks after Ethel had come to Pond Square, they'd gone walking on the Heath, Ethel supposedly chaperoning Monica. They'd walked to the overgrown viaduct, which went over a green and dreaming pond. As usual, there'd been nobody about, except for a few squirrels crashing through the trees.

'I love this place,' Monica had said. 'It's so superbly pointless. Do you know what I mean?'

'No.'

'I mean, this pond has no reason to exist except to have a viaduct over it, and vice versa. The Heath is so very beautiful, don't you think?'

'It's very *muddy*. It's quite nice at bluebell time.'

'And at sunset, don't you think?'

'Everywhere's beautiful at sunset, if you like sunsets.'

'Ethel, dear,' said Monica, '*where* was your father lost at sea?'

'In the Atlantic Ocean.'

'That doesn't narrow it down very much. The Atlantic covers about three-quarters of the world, I think. Of course, geography's not my strong point.'

'It certainly isn't. He was lost in the Azores.'

'What are they? They sound beautiful, I must say.'

Ethel said, 'Islands,' and started crying in the process. Monica was completely mortified, because obviously she was the cause, but she knew what to do, and it was a twofold plan: first, *shut up*; second, march Ethel – still crying – over the viaduct and down into that little cluster of houses in a hollow called the Vale of Health. Monica was banking on there being a man there selling ices from a little van while his small white pony grazed nearby. He was there, all right. Monica bought two ices, and gave them both to Ethel, who was still snuffling a bit.

'But what are you doing?' she said. 'I can't eat two.'

'I bet you can.'

She could, as well.

Ethel was actually very pretty. 'And that,' Leo had told Monica, 'is a clue to the fate of her mother.' It must have been a terrible fate indeed if even Leo wouldn't talk about it, and after the performance on the viaduct, Monica realised she must never enquire about it herself. Ethel's prettiness – which might have been provoking had she not been so dull – had secured her a 'young man', in whom she was, as they say, completely 'wrapped up'. He was a plasterer called John, and he lived with his father, who was also a plasterer, a little way north of the Heath, at Golders Green. The two of them had met on the Heath, at the Model Boat Pond, which Ethel seemed to frequent, even though you'd have thought the boats would have reminded her of her poor father's fate, especially when they capsized, which they often did, causing the owner to have to wade in after them. Evidently, John had simply walked up to Ethel, raised his cap and said, 'Good afternoon. Would you like to take a walk over the Heath with me?'

'And what did you say to that?' Monica had asked Ethel.

'Yes.'

At that point, John had sounded quite an interesting man, which turned out not to be the case when Monica finally met him, but none of this would be of any interest to the judge.

'From time to time, your honour,' Monica resumed, 'we had a lodger at Pond Square, usually a literary gentleman, the last one being a Mr Robert Harper, whom Leo called Bobby, and who stayed two years, until only a couple of months before Leo's death.' At about the time of his departure, Monica believed she had dreamt that Bobby Harper was shouting at Leo in the night. Perhaps this had really happened. 'He was actually a barrister, your honour, but of an unsuccessful sort, so I doubt your honour would have come across him.'

As a rule, Bobby Harper wouldn't get up until about ten, but every so often he'd be out of the house at dawn, in order to bicycle to some railway station, from where he took a train to an obscure town with an obscure court. Winchester had been mentioned once. There he would do a 'plea' on behalf of some miscreant who, presumably, couldn't afford any barrister more famous than Bobby Harper.

He was a small man, like Leo, only neater. The word for him was dapper, which was the next best thing to handsome. He always had a flower, stolen from the Heath, in his button-hole, and he obviously loved stationery, of which a barrister, even an unsuccessful one, needs a lot. When he did get a brief, he enjoyed wrapping it up in pink ribbon. Being a lawyer, Bobby Harper could speak some Latin – *some*, not much. 'He gave me a little coaching in Latin, your honour, and a little in history. He was an expert on the British constitution, even though Britain doesn't have one. Leo would also teach me, in his casual way, and *his* great specialism, of course, being a poet, was literature. But I can't say I had much education from either of them . . . which brings us, your honour, to the late Miss Rose Driscoll.' (Because Monica would only be addressing the judge if Driscoll *were* late.)

She had finally arrived at the matter of Driscoll, and it seemed she was also about to come to the Rialto Bridge, since the crowd of pedestrians was thickening. (Why, incidentally, had Monica heard of the Rialto Bridge even before she came to Venice? It was because somebody in a play had said, 'What news on the Rialto?')

She thought about how, when she'd first heard the name Driscoll, it had reminded her of a rainy day. 'She became my governess in January of last year, your honour,' she said, 'which was a kind of promotion for her, since she'd merely been my tutor for the few months previously.'

Driscoll had placed an advertisement in the window of the Highgate Post Office, claiming various accomplishments, prob-ably truthfully, since she didn't have the imagination to lie. She never moved into the house in Pond Square but would come up on the tram from Holloway four days a week. 'Of course, I had no say in her becoming my governess, your honour, any more than I would have a say in her becoming my guardian. This is because I am a legal minor, and therefore a person of no consequence.' Monica took back that sentence; it was probably unwise to condemn the law when addressing a judge. When she had complained to Leo about being given into the clutches of Driscoll, he'd said she needed to be 'taken in hand', which was a shocking reversal of his previous policy. 'I believe, your honour, that he felt guilty about having neglected my education, and was trying to atone for that – and, of course, a governess is cheaper than a school, at least in most cases.'

Monica found herself standing alongside a chemist's shop, and highly decorative it was. She might go inside and buy a powder paper, for she feared the sun could be making her rather red, despite the sailor hat and parasol.

'I did not care for Driscoll, your honour,' she said, still looking at herself in the window. 'I wouldn't say I hated her, but we had nothing in common.'

Monica walked on.

'For example, she had no sense of humour. Anything funny was "no laughing matter". It appeared, your honour, that she was afflicted for much of the time by a morbid depression of the spirits, which could be relieved – although I only found this out later – by several glasses of wine.'

Mathematics also cheered her up, but she would explain things like equations with such great speed that Monica could never keep up, and finally she would become cross at her enthusiasm finding no response. 'It's as clear as day, for heaven's sake!' she would cry.

But there would also be her long 'silent goes', which happened about every three weeks, when she would set Monica the task of reading, say, a chapter on electricity and magnetism from Dr Brewer's *Guide to Science* while she stared out of the window, invariably at falling rain, and when Monica told her she had finished the chapter and not understood a word of it, Driscoll would say, 'Oh, well,' and that would be it. Or, while similarly staring, she would ask Monica to parse pages from Arthur Mee's *Encyclopaedia*, or a terrible book providing 'specimens' of literature for parsing, just as Burke and Hare provided the medical students with dead bodies to practise on. 'She considered almost every modern novel unsuitable, your honour, but she herself was unsuitable. Unsuitable for *me*, at any rate.

'As to my uncle, your honour, well, of course, you know what became of him.' She did wonder how the matter would be phrased in a proper legal way. Perhaps it would just be baldly stated: 'Run over by a tram.' 'It was six months ago, on 12 March, your honour, and it was the very tram I have possibly already mentioned, the one running down, or up, from Highgate to Holloway. It was coming down when it hit Leo. An inquest was held. The verdict was death by misadventure, and we must make of that what we will.'

In retrospect, Monica believed she had probably heard the moment of impact. It was early afternoon on a sunny day – sunny enough for the living-room window of the Pond Square house to be open. Driscoll was talking to Monica about the charm of mathematics when they had both heard shouts indicating a kerfuffle on the High Street. Monica had hoped this would amount to some drama that might impinge on them personally, forcing Driscoll to abandon her incomprehensible number-talk. It did so about an hour later when a policeman came to the door. Driscoll had answered, and Monica had blocked her ears because she had known it must be terrible news. Of course, Driscoll had attempted to break the news gently: 'My dear, you must prepare yourself for a shock.' But it was no such thing, really. It had to be that Leo had died, since Ethel was in the house with them, and everybody else connected to Monica was dead already. She had been thinking for some time that Leo's luck was running out. His shouts of 'Banjanxed!' had become rather hollow; he had started to go a bit bald on the top of his head. He kept going to the bank, and not because he wanted to. Bobby Harper had left, and there had been some trouble between them. Leo had stopped going to Oxford because he was economising, yet Oxford was where he earned his money, so that must be what's called a vicious circle. And when, over recent weeks, he came to say goodnight to Monica before heading off to The Flask or The Red Lion & Sun, he seemed not to have his notebook in his top-coat pocket – the notebook that had always nestled so cosily there. The world was out to get Leo, and the tram was just the agent sent to finish him off. The tram was the assassin.

On the evening of the day of his death, Driscoll and Ethel had concocted a plan to distract her. Ethel had said, 'Let's bake a cake.'

'What kind of cake?'

'Just a cake.'

'It has to be a special one,' Monica said. 'I want to make an upside-down cake.'

But when the cake was made, Monica hadn't been able to see anything particularly upside-down about it, so had started crying as though she were a much younger girl – and this was taken to be a show of grief on her part, but it was not as simple as that. Monica had still liked Leo, even though she had stopped *loving* him that night in the theatre. What saddened her was not so much his death as what the death represented: another victory for the real world.

There had certainly been something wrong about his death – even more than ordinarily when someone is run over by a tram. Whether he had deliberately jumped in front of it, Monica could not say. It seemed a strange way to kill yourself. It was quite a small tram, after all, and might not do the job. Also, the new bridge over the Archway Road (which ran parallel to Highgate Hill) was available for suicides, being a rare case of a high bridge over a hard surface rather than a river, and many people had already taken advantage.

She had been taken down to Holloway within two days of Leo's death. It seemed his tenancy (or whatever was the word) of the Pond Square house had expired some time before, and the house had to be given up to somebody who'd long been waiting to pounce on it.

Monica slowly realised she was looking in the window of a tobacconist's shop. She was surrounded by people, mainly Italians. They made low 'z' sounds as they spoke. Some of them were staring at her – because why would a young girl be looking in a tobacconist's window? She hoped the starers assumed she was part of a family walking in detachments. She often tried to give that impression in London, by looking forwards or backwards, perhaps waving or calling out, as though keeping tabs on other family members.

'By coincidence, your honour,' she said, 'if indeed that's what it was, my uncle had made a will shortly before he died, and he used his power as my guardian to appoint Driscoll as my *next* guardian.' He had done that in consultation with the two other trustees, Mr Farmery and Mr Walker, she supposed. If Driscoll were still alive, and wanted to pass the parcel of Monica again, she also would have to consult those gentlemen.

(It was possible Driscoll had become a trustee herself; Monica wasn't clear about that.)

She was on a shopping street about ten feet wide. The shops were fairly ordinary, selling things like buckets, brushes, buttons. Up ahead, she could see the Rialto Bridge. 'Why did Driscoll want to take me on, your honour?' Monica enquired. Out of Christian charity, perhaps? Or perhaps money had something to do with it, for she now came in for the income arising from the capital, and, of course, she was entitled to use a certain amount of it for her own expenses. 'The greatest horror, your honour, was being taken into her flat, in that infernal valley, where the tight rein she had already fashioned for me became tighter than ever.'

Monica pictured the flat, at once bleak and jumbled with china and brasses, bullrushes and aspidistras. It was on the second floor of a 'divided house' set a little way back from the actual Road, in what purported to be a separate thoroughfare, but wasn't really: it seemed as though Holloway Road Crescent had quickly lost its nerve about diverging from the Road and had re-joined at the first opportunity. When she had first seen the house, Monica had felt a rising panic. It was in the wrong place, hence the need for bars on the downstairs windows, to protect it from the Road. She was jealous of the house in the dead *centre* of the crescent, for that was a few feet further back from the Road. It still had barred windows, though. And it was all wrong inside, of course. Monica had immediately asked Driscoll if she might rearrange things, so she had moved the armchairs near the fire – which were long and low, with dark wood and studded red leather that made Monica think of coffins – a little further apart, to separate the fates of the two people who would be sitting in them. She had attempted to shift the heavy sewing machine, on its heavy table, a little further into the corner, so as to try to banish the drudgery it represented, but she had hardly effected any change. The pieces still on the board still represented checkmate.

'It's not quite what you're used to, dear,' said Driscoll. 'But we must both make the best of it for the present – and your own room is the largest.'

A wide, ghostly bedroom did await Monica, and a monumental-looking bed, somewhat higher than it was wide, therefore tomblike, and the room overlooked the Road directly.

It always took a long time to get in or out of the flat, for Driscoll must lock or unlock the three locks on the front door, like a prison warder. As she did this, Monica would gaze along the Road towards Archway, where Highgate Hill began. On certain days, you could see the Heath, looking like a great green cloud swelling gloriously above Highgate. At other times, you could only see Highgate Village (mainly the pretty churches), and that was heartbreaking in itself.

Monica dreaded those evenings when Driscoll would take her place in her coffin (always on the left as you faced the fire) and Monica was more or less obliged to sit in the other one. They would then read as the clock on the mantel loudly ticked, like a bomb waiting to go off, and on the hour it *did* go off, first with the Westminster chimes, that sinister little tune, like a kind of grown-up nursery rhyme evoking the Houses of Parliament in the rain; then came the pedantic chiming of the actual hour before the ticking resumed – or so it seemed, although in fact the ticking never stopped but was just drowned out for a while by the chime. Sometimes Driscoll would not read but would stare at the fire and hardly move. Monica longed for those evenings when Driscoll would sit at the table instead, in order to play patience or do her sewing, with the machine trundling away like a motor car with a flat tyre. It was some consolation that Ethel was also taken into the flat in her familiar role as cook-general 'assisting', but Ethel went out in the evenings – riding on the upper decks of buses and trams and looking out of the window – or retreated to her bedroom, where she must simply lie on the bed and stare at the grubby plaster rose on the ceiling, for she certainly never read anything.

Ethel had told Monica that she actually quite liked Holloway Road.

'Why?' Monica had demanded.

'It's convenient,' she said.

One stormy evening, soon after Monica had moved in, Driscoll had stopped her sewing to unpick a mistake, but the sewing-machine noise continued. It came from the flat above. 'A young lady and her mother live there,' Driscoll explained. 'They're very similarly situated to ourselves.'

'I hope to God, for their sake, that they're not,' Monica said, and so she'd been ordered to bed. That had been one of their first big rows.

Monica remembered about the judge she was addressing.

'I was still not put into a school, your honour, which I would like to have been, because then I would have been in a school *story*, if you see what I mean, and I generally like those.' Instead, there were lessons in the flat, then excursions to lectures and classes in draughty public buildings on, or just off, the baleful Road. She must make the judge see the difference between her old life and her new.

'In Leo's time, your honour, I used to go to oil-painting classes given by a lovely little lady in a cottage in Keats Grove, Hampstead, which is just as pretty as it sounds. I would paint flowers sitting in her garden, and it was all brushwork. Under Driscoll, I was taken to a Unitarian church hall – which is just as *horrible* as it sounds – for drawing lessons with a man who took a mathematical approach – all perspective and proportion, your honour.'

She was standing by a man who had taken a live eel out of a bucket. He laid it on a marble slab and cut it clean in two; then he swept both halves dismissively into the bucket on the other side, so she wondered why he'd bothered. Maybe he was in a bad mood, or possibly evil. Was she herself evil? She stood on the bridge; there were shops on one side of it. Perhaps she had become unhinged by all she had been through? She had to admit there was something new in her character since her parents had died: she had developed a terrible temper, sometimes with those jittery fits whereby she felt impelled to perform some drastic *action*. But there was no need to bring that up with the judge, and Monica was tired of addressing him anyhow.

It occurred to her, as she stood beside the entrance to a little café, that she was very hungry. She walked in. The place was like a golden grotto, and so warm that it was as if all the playfully shaped loaves and multicoloured cakes had just been taken out of the oven. She ordered a cream cake that resembled an ice cream in a cone, a glass of fresh orange juice (she had never had that before, except in the course of eating an orange) and a *caffè con latte*, which was so creamy it might have been another cake. She consumed them all standing up at a glass shelf under a golden chandelier. The shelf was next to a mirror, in which she looked very greedy, but she didn't mind. This was the best breakfast she had ever eaten, and it lifted her spirits, whereas the plea for clemency had depressed them. If she really had defenestrated Driscoll, then obviously she did not deserve clemency, and it would be wrong to ask for it. Monica knew that she often behaved very badly in Driscoll's presence, but she prided herself on not recriminating or moaning too much about the loss of her parents; that would be undignified, and, besides, they inhabited a sacred past realm of strictly private memories. The brave thing would be to make the most of the opportunities provided by Driscoll's absence, this breakfast being one. It occurred to Monica, as she stepped out of the café, that she had just had a bun and a coffee – exactly what the people rowing along the side canal had been going off to have. But they were not free, because the man, who was a 'drip', was trapped with the woman, who was horrible. It further occurred to Monica that, while she might be going to gaol, she was for the present freer than she had ever been.

She was walking past little curiosity shops now. They sold glassware, trinkets, souvenirs, lace. In the window of a toy shop, small clockwork figures were poised charmingly in the act of doing ordinary things. They had such modest aspirations. A barber was about to shave a customer; a soldier was about to march; another would probably (going by the position of his arm) salute . . . Monica was smiling to herself for the first time that day. She fancied one of the little soldiers, and she would certainly be able to afford him. But no; Charlotte would be jealous.

She came to a shop selling puppies. There were as many out-side as inside, playing or sleeping on straw in wooden crates. The ones outside were under shade, but they must have been too hot, nonetheless. One of them, quaking away sweetly, was black and white. As the tourists brushed past her on this street that was also a corridor, Monica thought of Billy Jackson's dog, which was also black and white.

★

Billy Jackson was about two years older than Monica. He got paid for looking after the sheep on Hampstead Heath, but it was his dog, Fred, that did the work, creeping about in the vicinity of the sheep, fixing them with intimidating stares, defying them to try anything. At first, Monica had liked both Billy and Fred. She considered Fred to be the more intelligent of the pair, but both were good-looking, and there was something decorative about the whole Heath-sheep set-up, what with Billy's headquarters being a quaint shack set in among the trees of that supposedly ancient hill on the Highgate side of the Heath called the Tumulus. From there, Billy could look down on his flock, and he sometimes gained extra height by sitting in a tree. Billy was perhaps a bit simple, or maybe just uncommonly sweet-natured. He looked as though he had spent too long in the sun – not that he was red-faced, but sort of hazy-looking, with faraway blue eyes that you'd have called 'cornflower' if he'd been a girl.

Monica had first noticed Billy when she had just turned twelve. In the summer of that year, she was often on the Heath, usually with Leo. They would lie on the grass, sharing a bag of sweets and slurping from small bottles (beer in Leo's case, cherryade in Monica's). Leo would often be trying to write a poem. 'What rhymes with pillow?' he might ask.

'Willow,' Monica might say.

'No good at all,' Leo might say. 'Give me another one.'

'Billow.'

'Now that's more like it,' he would say, and the poem would proceed in his little notebook. On a couple of occasions, Leo's friend A.E. Housman had come up to them. Like Leo, Housman (whose first name was Alfred) was a poet, but, unlike Leo, he made a good living at it, and he had a big house on North Road, Highgate. He would talk to Leo while Leo sat on the grass, but A.E. Housman would never sit on the grass himself. When Monica pointed that out, Leo said:

'That's largely why he's a success, you see. Takes himself very seriously.'

On the second occasion, Monica and Leo had been sitting near the Tumulus, and when A.E. Housman was walking away after their chat, Leo said, 'I believe he comes up here to look at the shepherd boy,' and he indicated Billy Jackson.

In the first week of that August, Monica had been freer than usual to wander about. Leo was busy writing and Ethel had gone on an excursion to the New Forest with some of her fellow sailors' orphans. (They never went to the seaside, for obvious reasons.) So Monica went to the Heath on her own, always reassuring Leo – not that he was really bothered – that she would stick to the 'tourist spots', of which the Tumulus was one.

Monica, having noticed Billy, required that he notice *her*, so, when she took her afternoon book onto the Heath, she would read it near the Tumulus, sitting among Billy's sheep, but Billy himself paid her no attention. He just lay about smoking and talking to some old man (who might, come to think of it, have been his father) about things like bicycles and motor cars. As Monica listened to the dream-making sound of a slight breeze wandering through the trees, she developed a plan.

That night, she asked Leo to recommend a poem about shepherds, or at least sheep, and he fished out a tattered volume of Wordsworth. Well, she should have guessed. The poem was called 'Michael', and it was a story of a shepherd, interesting and well told enough – perhaps – to appeal to Billy.

She took the volume to the Tumulus and tried to attract Billy's attention by signifying her great enjoyment of what she was reading, but that wasn't easy. The poem did not (to say the least) call for loud laughter, and tears would have been overegging it. Eventually, towards evening, when Billy was wandering up the Tumulus, with the late-afternoon sun blazing low behind him, so that she had to shield her eyes as she addressed him, she said, 'I'm reading something you might rather like.'

He stopped and smiled, as far as she could tell, what with the unhelpful light.

'My name's Monica,' she said. 'Your name's Billy, I believe?'

He nodded slowly.

'It's a poem,' she said. 'Can I read you a bit?' It occurred to her that she was implying he himself *couldn't* read. But he was still smiling.

'If you like,' he said, and he sat down about three feet away from her. She began to read, almost losing her nerve at the first line:

'Upon the forest-side in Grasmere Vale . . .'

But she carried on:

'There dwelt a Shepherd, Michael was his name;
An old man, stout of heart, and strong of limb . . .'

Billy said, 'It's not me, then.'

'I didn't say it was *about* you. I said it might interest you.'

'Yes. It does, Monica.'

'His bodily frame had been from youth to age
Of an unusual strength: his mind was keen,
Intense, and frugal, apt for all affairs,
And in his shepherd's calling he was prompt
And watchful more than ordinary men.'

'It's good,' Billy said, by which he obviously meant, 'Please shut up now.'

'It's in iambic pentameter,' Monica said, closing the book.

Billy was making a cigarette, at which he was expert. Before he lit it, he said, 'Do you mind?'

'Not in the least,' she said graciously. She'd thought the cigarette would make him philosophical along the lines of, 'Lovely afternoon, isn't it?' Or that he would at least say *something*, but he just commenced looking about the Heath, as if he'd never seen it before.

'What are you doing?' she asked.

'Counting sheep.'

'And does it send you to sleep?'

He laughed at that, and so began a friendship of sorts, although whenever she talked to Billy Jackson, Monica regretted that her own name could not be abbreviated, like Billy's or Fred's. 'Monica' seemed such a mouthful every time Billy said it.

One hot afternoon, Billy let her take Fred for a walk on the leader around the streets of Highgate. Billy seemed delighted to hand Fred over, and Monica was delighted to have him. The only one not delighted was Fred. He did not care for being on the leader (he kept trying to eat it) – at least, not when it was held by such a comparative stranger as Monica. Halfway up Fitzroy Park, he tried to bite Monica, and she kicked out at him. Eventually, Monica just had to trail behind Fred back to the Tumulus.

'He acted up all the way,' Monica said, while Fred was rudely demonstrating how pleased he was to see Billy, and how glad to see the back of Monica. Billy smiled his lazy smile and said, 'He doesn't like being on the leader, even with me.'

'Well then,' said Monica, 'why did you let me take him?'

'Because you wanted to,' said Billy, still smiling.

He had her there; that was perfectly true.

She had fallen out with both Billy and Fred that day, and when, about a week later, she saw one of the Heath sheep where it was not supposed to be – standing about gormlessly outside the Old Crown on West Hill, where it was liable to get knocked down by a tram or a motor car – she did not go and tell Billy. That sheep might have died, or indeed it 'may' have died. But she did not believe so, for the next day, she saw what was probably the same animal again (it was a ewe with horns, carrying the blue mark of the Heath flock). It was now on North Road, where there were no trams but regular sheep drives by farmers coming in from Finchley, who probably wouldn't feel any scruples about picking up an extra sheep on their way down to the slaughterers of Holloway.

This time, however, Monica had a new thought about the stray. The only reason it *was* a stray was down to the incompetence of Fred the dog. She could also have put it down to the incompetence of Billy, but she would rather blame Fred, since she was more 'out' with him just then. She decided she would take the sheep back to Billy on the Tumulus, and that this would be a way of paying Fred out for his stand-offish behaviour. She had learnt how to lead a sheep from Billy; or at least, she had watched him do it. You took hold of the creature by its jaw, oddly enough, and you must walk to the side, rather than ahead of it.

It did come along pretty well, but when she went past Lockwood's shop on North Road, which sold, essentially, everything, she went in and bought a bit of rope for a ha'penny from Mrs Lockwood. Monica then took the sheep around the corner to Clement Dodd, the blacksmith on Highgate High Street, because, just as Lockwood's sold anything, Clem Dodd could *do* anything (and he was also kind, as signified by the way he had let a tree grow up through the middle of his forge). He made a halter out of the rope and put it on the sheep. It was then just a question of walking back onto the Heath without pulling the sheep's head off.

When she reached the Tumulus, Billy was naturally pleased to see the sheep. Well, quite pleased at least. 'Thanks,' he said.

At this, Monica, who had expected more than a single word by way of gratitude, said, 'Did you not know she was missing?'

'I did,' said Billy, smiling.

'Did you not look for her?'

'I did, but not for too long.'

'Why ever not?'

'She's one of the clever ones. It was odds-on she'd come back.'

'She couldn't come back if she got knocked over by a tram. How do you know when a sheep's clever, anyway?'

'Same way you know a human is.' His smile was becoming annoying.

Fred, who had been asleep on the job, came loping up, and he was friendly enough, but Monica refused to have anything to do with him, or to use his name. 'Well,' she said to Billy, 'I do think your dog ought to do a better job of keeping them in once place.'

'Will you come here a minute, Monica?' said Billy. He seemed to be changing the subject.

'Why?'

But she'd sort of known, because she gave a quick look about. There were very few people on the Heath, despite the beauty of the day. A wasp came between them as they closed in on each other, but Billy brushed it aside with a smile. He gently took hold of Monica's hand and led her into the middle of the Tumulus trees, where the mixture of sunlight and shadow made magical effects.

He was a good kisser, and it had been what's called a French kiss, which you wouldn't have thought a person like Billy would know about. But then again, there was no such thing as an English kiss (which was probably just as well). There was not much to say afterwards, as they stepped back out of the trees. Already the Heath seemed to be filling up with afternoon strollers, several of them convening at the foot of the Tumulus with their silly knapsacks and wondering stares at a boy and girl not of the same class emerging from the trees. Well, let them stare. She felt like taking a bow; she and Billy might almost have been emerging from a church, having got married in those trees.

Billy and Fred disappeared from the Heath soon after, which was perhaps why he'd done the kiss in the first place – by way of a goodbye, but surely he wouldn't have done it if he didn't like her? It was very hard to imagine Billy and Fred so comfortably accommodated anywhere else. The new shepherd was twice Billy's age and twice as soppy. He actually *dressed* like a shepherd, and he – and his dog – made themselves available at every opportunity to be photographed and painted by tourists and trippers.

★

For a quiet place, Venice was becoming rather noisy. Monica was approaching St Mark's Square, and all the shops were for tourists now. Well, she herself was a tourist, so perhaps she should do what tourists did: that is, buy something. She knew from the guidebook that a common question asked by tourists in Venice was, 'Is it an original?' to which the answer was always, 'Yes,' so there was no point asking the question. You had to be a bit cuter, asking, 'What is the date of this?'

and 'Do you have proof?' and so on. It was generally quite hard to avoid having a row with Venetian shopkeepers and as Monica peered into the shop she was alongside, which sold seashells, she didn't much care for the look of the proprietress: a cross-looking woman – overdressed, with a lot of Venice lace about her bosom. And her eyebrows met in the middle, like Monica's, so trouble was obviously in prospect. Monica walked in, nevertheless.

The woman – or someone – had tried to make the shells look special by displaying them on embroidered napkins, and some had gold chains attached, but most were no more notable as specimens than some shells Monica had collected with Leo on one of their visits to Brighton. She had boiled them up in a cocoa tin before forgetting about them entirely. Monica then remembered that there was a shell amid the tawdry collection of ornaments on the mantelpiece of the Holloway flat. If she bought a shell from this shop, obtaining proof of purchase and mentioning to this woman that she was buying the shell for her guardian, it would look as though she did not believe her guardian could possibly be dead, so this would be evidence in her favour in case Driscoll *should* be dead.

Monica picked up a shell that looked similar to the one on the mantelpiece (which also looked similar to the cake she had just eaten). The woman said something snappish in Italian. She obviously wanted Monica to put the shell down, but Monica did not see why she should do that, given that she was about to make a purchase. She put the shell to her ear, as though trying to hear the sea. She knew that would annoy the woman, and it did. She continued holding on to the shell as she took her purse from the chatelaine bag and took out a two-lire bank-note, but the woman was making a dismissive gesture. Either the shell cost more than two lire, in which case Monica would not be buying it, or the woman was one of those superstitious Venetians Driscoll had so dreaded encountering: the ones who would only take coins.

In order to be as provoking as possible, Monica said: 'Would you kindly explain what you mean?' But as she spoke, three people entered the shop under a cloud of cologne: a grand-looking couple, possibly Russian, and a puffy-faced boy in a sailor suit, who began picking up shells as the woman smiled and spoke pleasantly to the parents. Monica put her shell down and walked towards the door. She was about to step out into the street when she noticed a box of small shells – a sort of lucky dip. Monica looked back at the grouchy woman, grouchy no longer because of the wealthy Russians. It seemed likely that if Monica put her hand into the box and took a shell, she would not notice.

Monica put her hand into the box. She looked back to check on the woman. She was still sucking up to the Russians, so Monica picked up a shell and stepped out of the shop, all of which she'd done quite slowly. Once back in the narrow street, though, she began running, with fast-beating heart and a feeling of great satisfaction, following the direction of *'Per S. Marco'* signs and tapping the ground with her parasol after every four running paces. Then she stopped. *'Per S. Marco'* would be too obvious a direction if the woman gave chase, so Monica diverted right, where she came to a canal overlooked by a crowded café terrace. A man came up to her, walking fast and with a threatening look, but he was only a waiter, requir-ing to know – seemingly as a matter of urgency – if she wished to be seated. She shook her head and moved to the edge of the water, where she opened the chatelaine bag. Seeing Charlotte lying there, she said, 'Little present for you,' and dropped the shell into the bag.

New people were coming up to the café terrace all the time. It must be a fashionable spot. Perhaps Monica should take a seat after all. She glanced down at herself in the water, at her fluctuating form, and she thought she looked rather *chic*, like one of the Impressionist paintings Leo admired. It was the second time she had stolen something, unless you counted things like apples off overhanging trees. A few days after her mother died, she had taken a box of Fry's Chocolate Creams from Challoner's Grocery on Highgate High Street. She was living between her father and Leo at the time, and receiving no pocket money, for it was her mother who'd given her it (a shilling every Friday), and she didn't feel she could raise the matter with her father just then. Also, Mr Challoner was such a prosperous-looking man, made positively shiny by money, and when he broke up the toffee for you, with his little silver hammer, he didn't give you the bits that had skidded off the board and flew over the counter. Monica had once asked him why not, as he primly swept them up with a little brush. He said they were only fit to be thrown away after they'd been on the counter, but she knew he put them back in the jar as makeweights when the customer had left. So she rather hated Mr Challoner. He deserved to be stolen from, and it had only been the small, not the large, box of Chocolate Creams.

She was watching two rather presentable men. They had risen from their places on the café terrace and were removing their boots. It was very intriguing, since they appeared to be about to get completely undressed. They looked racy types and were speaking French, so she had them down as *boulevardiers*, *flâneurs* or similar. She wondered if the French were quite welcome in Venice – after all, it was only about a hundred years ago that Napoleon had conquered the city – but these Frenchers seemed very welcome, and there began to be some cheering now that they had lain aside their suit-coats and were unbuttoning their shirts. The undershirts and trousers came off next, so they had nothing on but their white pantaloons, and they certainly did look fine in them. If Driscoll were here, she would have been walking away by now and commanding Monica to follow her. Monica thought of a genteel expression – 'I didn't know where to look' – which was only ever said by females, but the women on this café terrace knew where to look, all right. It was the men of the café who were embarrassed, because they were not as handsome as this pair who now dived into the water – a rather disappointing upshot, Monica thought, but it brought a round of applause from the terrace.

Monica had just been thinking about Napoleon, and now she saw the man himself, standing by the café terrace. But, of course, it was just a Venetian soldier in what looked like Napoleon's hat, coat, breeches and boots. He looked absurdly antiquated, and yet he obviously saw something amiss with *Monica's* appearance. He was staring at her, anyhow. You'd have thought he would be more interested in the men in the canal, who had resurfaced from their dives looking like a pair of seals because of the way their hair was slicked smooth by the water.

The staring soldier was small, somewhat beetle-browed. His natural expression would have been a frown, but just now he was not so much frowning as scowling, and you don't want to be scowled at by a man carrying a rifle with a dagger stuck in the end of it. Monica recalled that she had just stolen a seashell. It was about the smallest thing you could steal, but theft was theft, and there could hardly be a clearer case. The seashell had been in the cross woman's shop; now it was in Monica's bag.

The two swimmers were climbing out of the canal; the women of the café terrace, and a few sheepish men, were applauding again, but the soldier appeared to notice none of this. Or was he a policeman? Very likely. A soldier wouldn't be wandering about on his own, and there was bound to be something picturesque about the Venice police. He continued to stare at Monica as he began fishing about inside his tunic. What he produced was shocking, but also perfectly logical: a piece of paper. He was glancing down at what was written there, and it was only now that Monica recollected her other possible crime: the murder of Driscoll. A phrase from unsuitable literature came to Monica: her description was being 'circulated'.

The French swimmers, having climbed out of the canal, were being encouraged to join a party of half a dozen well-dressed Italian men and women, whose boldness suggested that none of them were tourists; they *belonged* here. In order to deflect the stare of the policeman (which is what Monica was now sure he was), it was necessary for Monica also to look as though she belonged. She heard French being spoken directly to her left: two young women stood on the margin of the terrace, waiting to be seated. They might look presentable enough, but their conversation was about as special as a bus going down the Holloway Road.

'*Il va faire chaud,*' one was saying.

'*Il va faire beau toute la journée,*' the other replied.

Monica moved towards them.

'*Bonjour!*' she said, loudly.

At first, neither woman responded; Monica had effectually stunned them. Both were pale and dressed entirely in white, but one of them had a bloodshot eye, so it was like when a spot of blood shows through a bandage. Monica was grateful that, despite this affliction, the woman eventually nodded and returned Monica's greeting, albeit warily. Monica glanced towards the policeman; his scowl was subsiding back to a frown, but he was still looking at her. It was necessary to convince him that she was French. '*Oui*,' she said, smiling unnaturally to both women in turn, '*il fait certainement beau temps, mais souvent, en Septembre, il pleut ici.*'

The policeman had returned the paper to the inside of his tunic; he seemed to be looking around for something else to do. Then again, the two perfectly normal eyes of the other French woman were now on Monica.

'*Qui êtes* vous?' she said.

This no longer mattered because the policeman had now *found* something else to do. Amid loud French and Italian shouts, a table had turned over in the middle of the café terrace: a row between the swimmers and the men of the party who'd invited them over. It was all very . . . what was the word? It came to Monica as she was running along another alley: *operatic*.

Instead of washing lines, telegraph wires were suspended over this alley, and Monica wondered whether her description was being circulated by telegram, or perhaps even telephone. She was a fugitive from justice. She might become a heroine of the *Notable Trials* – a warning to other lonely girls, stranded in the Holloways of the world. Some people reading of the case would sympathise with her; others wouldn't, and it might be said that a trial for murder would be quite in keeping with her life so far: a tragedy.

After a while, Monica stopped running and began walking; she turned into another of the endless supply of alleyways, and in this one, a drinking fountain was waiting for her. She looked away immediately, but she had already seen the small, horrible iron spewing face. The water noise echoed in this alley of old stone as she walked fast to the end of it, and turned into another, which held no drinking fountain, but only walls of stone. Monica knew that if there had been a window and she had seen her reflection, her face would have been white again. What else but a description of her could the policeman have been reading? And why had the description been issued? It could only be that she was wanted for murder. But if Driscoll were dead, how would they know about her? Who would have 'furnished' them with the description? There were possibilities: Zita, for instance, whose address in Venice would be somewhere among Driscoll's papers, or Stefano the gondolier. And any number of people might have seen her leaving the house. She was following another arrow for St Mark's Square. She was closing in on it now, walking amid narrow but grand shopping streets. She passed windows full of lace, ribbons, hats, shoes, jewellery. This, according to the guidebook, was *Le Mercerie*, where the alleys were lined with potted palms like the corridors in good hotels, and where the promenading men were dark and sleek, the women white and flouncy.

And now Monica had reached the culmination: the arch that led to St Mark's Square. If Driscoll were not dead, she would be waiting for Monica in the grand café called Florian at half past twelve.

The Piazza

'Of all the open spaces in the city, that before the Church of
St. Mark alone bears the name of piazza, and the rest are called
merely *campi*, or fields.'

From *Venetian Life*, by William Dean Howells, quoted in
Venice, by Augustus J.C. Hare & St Clair Baddeley

The opulent shops had gradually calmed the fast beating of
Monica's heart; St Mark's Square completed the job. It was as
if Monica had been holding her breath in the narrow streets,
but now she exhaled; or it was as if she had been kept wating
outside a theatre, and now she was *in* the theatre, and the performance had begun.

There was a great openness – more than enough room
for everyone, and there were many saunterers in the square,
progressing slowly towards nowhere in particular. Or perhaps
the chequered tiles of the piazza gave their movement significance, as if the people were counters in a game that they did
not themselves understand. What betokened the sauntering?
The slow twirling of parasols among the women, the leisurely
smoking of the men. Elderly wandering Italians carried trays
of postcards, but everybody was in a postcard anyway. There
was a thoughtfulness to people's movements. Monica saw a

man walking while reading a book: he was heading towards the boat landing and therefore the sea. Would the book prove sufficiently enthralling that he would walk into the water? Other people would walk a little way, then strike an attitude: a balletic twirl or a bout of staring at sea or sky. The piazza invited everybody to make fools of themselves, but it didn't mind, being a free and easy host.

The famous basilica was to Monica's left. She imagined that actual religion must be going on inside, along with all the touristic gawping. She had read that, in Venice, the host was being served at any given time of day. All Italians were Catholic, of course, especially the pope, and a good Catholic took communion every day. But they couldn't take it if they hadn't confessed, or so Harriet Beck, who *was* a Catholic, had told her. Monica wondered whether you were allowed to confess even if you weren't a Catholic. Perhaps she should do so. You had to begin, 'Forgive me, father, for I have sinned,' whether you had really sinned or not, but Monica had definitely sinned.

Next to the basilica was the ducal palace, or whatever it was called, that frilly building, peach-coloured and seemingly made of doilies. Driscoll would surely approve. The sky was engaged by flags on tall flagpoles, and there was something of a breeze up there, provided by the nearby sea, which redoubled the freedom of the piazza, and there were the two tall stone columns, which culminated in high, but rather surprisingly small, statues, as if the money had run out at the last minute. One was a man – some sort of sailor, Monica believed; the other was a winged lion, symbol of Venice, and it did look like a great, strange bird that had settled there for a moment. Then, to the right, marking a sort of corner where the small part of the piazza joined the big part, was the famous campanile, which, in spite of its fame, had rather embarrassingly fallen down about ten years before, but was now almost completely rebuilt, with scaffolding around the top, on which a workman stood – only he *wasn't* working, but just gazing around like everybody else.

The sea was on sparkling form and there was a large ship on it, steaming ponderously from left to right, an antidote to all the fussy gondolas. As the ship moved, it revealed to the left an island of churches, like a part of Venice that had broken off and floated away. To the right of the ship was another island, somewhat more ordinary-looking, and rather sulky in the sunshine: it had dock cranes, factories and chimneys that surprisingly smoked.

Bells were ringing in celebration of everything and nothing, and there was music, rather confused, like several music boxes all opened at once. It came from the cafés of the piazza. Florian was on the north side. At half past twelve, Driscoll might be there, or perhaps even now, for she would tend to be annoyingly early for everything. A quick glance at the drinkers and diners on its terrace had not disclosed her, but Monica believed that half past twelve was some way off. Perhaps she ought to flag down a saunterer and ask the time? She would do so in a moment.

Monica had been walking towards the sea, but now she diverted in a leisurely arc towards the left and the benches in the colonnade of the ducal palace. Being in the shade, most of the benches were taken, but the one nearest the sea was available. She sat down. There was a pillar a few inches beyond the end of the bench. Monica rested her head against it and within half a minute, she had commenced to dream.

★

She was approaching a school on a hill – no, it was on a cliff, for there was a dark sea below. 'We call it the Point,' said a

friendly big girl who was walking beside her. 'It's not a high
school, but it has a top form.' They were walking across fields,
in some of which girls were playing tig. 'No tigs back!' someone shouted. 'It's a school rule!'

'We also play badminton at night,' said the friendly girl.

'I like your school skirt and jersey,' said Monica.

'Yes,' said the girl, 'and we have light frocks for the dancing
afternoons. I wasn't born with my clothes on, you know. That's
why a tig must be given on the skin.'

'What is the food like?'

'It's prime. But you can have a small or a very small if you
don't like it.'

'What do you do as a prefect?' Monica asked the friendly
girl.

'Nothing, of course, but we have a prefects' room. We have
heavy wallpaper with a heavy warning on the door, but people
can come in if they knock politely. We are like ants to the little
ones.'

'Ants, did you say?'

'No, *aunts.*'

'And we have a fire alarm in there, of course.' The big girl
was lighting a cigarette. 'I am going to smoke,' she said.

'That's all right,' said Monica.

'I wasn't asking your permission.'

She was such a cool girl – and the smoking suited her. 'We
also have a swimming pool and a prison,' she said. 'And there
are cracks in the wall in the sea room, and we're always making
scrapbooks in the rec. Once, we froze the playground to make
an ice rink.'

An even bigger girl than the big girl walked past, coming
away from the school. Her hair was blowing in the wind.

'She is a former pupil,' said the first big girl. 'She used to sit on the radiators, but only when they were turned off.'

'She has ginger hair,' said Monica.

'Be careful with that,' said the friendly big girl. 'You ought to say auburn.'

Monica turned slowly to the left, and there was the sea the school overlooked.

But, of course, it was the wrong sea, and Monica was back in the piazza. The weather of the dream had been largely bad, so it was shocking to be reacquainted with the sunshine of Venice. There was no mystery about the dream: in the first place, it definitely had *been* a dream; second, it was part of a whole series, in which Monica was in the early stages of attending a school on the South Coast of England.

Earlier that summer, Driscoll had taken Monica to an office in High Holborn – a sort of agency for schools. There she had met a senior girl and a headmaster from a school on the coast near Eastbourne, to which it appeared that Driscoll, in consultation with Mr Farmery and Mr Walker, had applied on Monica's behalf. Monica liked the sound of a school-on-the-sea, and, of course, she would have to board there, so she would escape Holloway. She wanted to have a uniform and walk in a crocodile and convene with friends in rooms, the names of which she would confidently abbreviate, like 'the rec.', 'the san.', 'the dorm.' Driscoll had gone in to see the headmaster, while Monica walked up and down High Holborn – which was extremely hot just then – with the senior girl, who was ginger-haired, as Monica had been unwise enough to mention.

'I love your ginger hair.'

'It's auburn, actually.'

The senior girl, who was a prefect, had spoken to Monica of many things mentioned by the girl in the dream, although more logically, of course. The girl appeared slightly rebellious, despite being a prefect, and Monica's second mistake might have been to play up to that. She mentioned some unsuitable school stories she had read and, in response to the questioning of the girl, she answered that she jolly well would sit on the radiators if it was cold, yes, and, no, she never would 'split' on another girl who had broken a window, even if the whole class was given a detention. But Monica believed the girl must then have been guilty of 'splitting' on *her* to the headmaster, having deliberately 'led her on'.

The headmaster was a pleasant enough man, if pompous. 'By all accounts, you are a diamond in the rough,' he had said. But her performance in the exercises he then set her must have changed his mind, demoting her to some less precious stone. In arithmetic, for example, she would have been surprised if she'd got any marks at all, given that all her answers were guesses.

★

Monica wondered about the time. A loud fat boy, belonging to the family on the next bench, was studying his father's watch, and he seemed to want to get very close to his father, to sit on his knee, even though he was far too old for that – and far too fat. It must have been distressing to the father, who was quite elegant, to have a son who looked like Tweedledum (or, indeed, Tweedledee), right down to dressing like them, in white trousers, pea jacket and jockey cap.

'Do you suppose it's slow?' said the boy, and the father laughed.

'My gold Hunter?' he said. 'Slow? I rather think not.'

Monica, irritated by this verbosity, said, 'Excuse me, but what *is* the time?'

'You're about to find out!' shouted the boy, which was *intensely* irritating, since Monica was only about to find out if he was about to tell her, there being no clocks in St Mark's Square. But she saw she was wrong about that, for the boy was indicating a beautiful blue-and-gold one over the arch by which she had entered. At least, it looked like a clock. It was certainly *round*, but it seemed overcrowded with numerals, and generally very involved – and there were no hands. She wondered if it was a sort of sundial, since it seemed to be exchanging flashing signals with the sun. It occurred to Monica that she and the fat boy's family were not the only ones staring at this clock. Almost everybody in the piazza was doing so, but their attention was on the action taking place on a platform above it, rather than the clock itself. Here, a pale green mechanical man had begun striking the hour, by tentatively hitting a pale green bell with a hammer, as though testing either the bell or the hammer. The man was dressed in green leaves, but otherwise looked so lifelike that Monica hoped he had a head for heights, given the altitude of his stone platform. He had now hit the bell once, and Monica waited for him to hit it again. At this rate, it would take him forever to get to twelve o'clock, but he appeared to have seized up. Perhaps there was a fault with the mechanism. But now the other green man hit the bell with his hammer in the same cautious way. Well, of *course* . . . The second man wouldn't be up there for no reason. The striking of twelve was evidently going to be a joint effort. But now the second man froze as well. What on earth was going on? Had Monica really slept right through to two o'clock?

'But it's not *two* o'clock!' shouted the loud fat boy, and his father laughed again, even though this was not in the least funny.

'The hour is struck twice,' the father said. 'The figures represent youth and age. The first figure tells us one o'clock has arrived; the other says it has already passed – so you'd better get on with things.'

'*She* doesn't believe you!' the loud fat boy loudly declared, pointing at Monica.

Monica realised she had been staring at the pair; her distaste must have been evident. She waved her hand, as if to dismiss them. She stood up, to begin skirting around the campanile and walking towards Florian. So the time had settled down at one o'clock – Monica was only half an hour late, and Driscoll would surely wait half an hour for her. She had certainly done so in the past, on those occasions when Monica had deliberately tested her.

Some dandified men were among the parasol twirlers, she noticed – Italians, of course. One of them was cooling himself with a fan and might be wearing kohl around his eyes. Leo would have been very interested in those men. She was now facing the wide terrace of Florian. The interior of the café itself glowed in the background like a series of golden caves. Were there *saloons* or *salons* in there? Probably both. The musicians of the small orchestra were in the centre of the terrace, beneath a white canopy, to shade them. The delicate music they made seemed rather lost in the open air. Their canopy had been made by extending a pair of white curtains out from the two arches of the portico behind them. In the other arches, the white curtains remained unextended, so the people on the terrace sat in the sun.

Surveying the terrace, Monica felt she was like a person in a theatre watching the stage, and she was looking out for an actress playing a very minor role. *She will naturally be on her own*, thought Monica, *and most likely on the edge, not in the centre*. But Monica had already failed to spot Driscoll on the left-hand side, and she was now commencing her examination of the central area.

At a typical table, there would be a man and a woman; at the next most typical, a family. Few people sat alone. You could tell the couples who were in love because they looked like conspirators, and they were the ones who really belonged in Florian.

Most of the others seemed too conscious of the grand surroundings and were intimidated by the waiters, who moved with an arrogant ease between the tables, their silver trays sending out blinding flashes as they caught the sun. Monica's survey of the terrace had reached the right-hand side, and there, at the outermost table, a lonely woman peered out towards the piazza crowd. Was it Driscoll? It was certainly a Driscoll type, and there weren't many of those. If the woman stood up, she would be tall, and she looked as if she didn't belong in Florian, or anywhere. Yes, it had to be Driscoll.

Monica didn't know who had fallen into whose trap. She closed her eyes and breathed a sort of official and formal sigh of relief. Instead of being tried for murder, she was merely going to be berated by Driscoll for having left the palazzo without her — for not waiting for her to wake up. How should Monica respond? She could hardly say, 'Well, I thought you were dead.' Still less, 'I thought you were dead because I had killed you.' She would probably say, 'I decided to let you have a nice lie-in. You worked so hard, dear, to arrange everything and you were obviously exhausted. And, of course, I knew we had the arrangement to meet at Florian.' Monica did feel a *small* disappointment at the prospect of having to speak to Driscoll again, and it must be admitted that she thought *slightly* less of herself for not having killed her. Monica was obviously a more ordinary person than some previous events might have suggested — those events signified by all the drinking fountains of the world. She opened her eyes and looked back towards the right-hand edge of the terrace.

The lonely woman was no longer there.

New customers – a couple – were being shown to the table at which she had been sitting. Had she crossed in front of Monica while Monica's eyes had been closed? If so, she must have seen Monica – the square wasn't so very crowded as all that. Perhaps she had spotted Monica and decided to ignore her? No again, because the reason Driscoll had come to the square was to *rendezvous* with Monica. Or had she gone away *behind* Monica? She swivelled around. A herd of monks was sweeping across the square from west to east, passing in front of the two smaller cafés on the north side and so, like a dark curtain, obliterating any saunterers who might be on the other side of them. Where the monks had come from, Monica couldn't imagine, but they were surely making for the basilica. Yes, the foremost monks had reached the basilica now and were flowing in through the entrance (the tourists having been moved aside) with the inevitability of bathwater going down a plughole . . . and they were leaving in their wake different scenes on that side of the piazza, with new saunterers, or the same ones doing slightly different things, and no sign at all of Driscoll.

But it seemed increasingly likely that the lonely woman on the Florian terrace had not been her after all. Driscoll would have waited more than half an hour, and the dress had been quite wrong. It had been a very lightweight pale green dress. Bizarre sea creatures that never saw the light of day were that colour, Monica believed, as were certain types of dead and perhaps drowned people. The lace collar had somewhat resembled coral. Of course, Driscoll was keen on lace, but would she have gone in for that sort of ghostly green? It was the opposite of a useful colour. And a dress of such lightness . . . it might almost have been silk. Was it possible Driscoll was aiming at 'sex appeal'? Monica thought of the Valentine's card in the locked drawer. Of course, the 'A' must stand for Driscoll's special friend, Aubrey. Or had she sent it to herself, since it had paper roses and a good deal of lace stuck on it? And the letter 'A' squared with her lack of imagination, being first in the alphabet, therefore the first one her logical mind would come to.

The lonely woman's hat had also not been one Monica associated with Driscoll, and it certainly was not the wide, rolling one Monica had seen on the train. It had been a small, white hat – rather like those worn by modern sailors. So might it be that Driscoll had, in a moment of insanity, gone all in for the maritime theme? But Driscoll never had moments of insanity; that was the whole trouble with her.

Monica was now running along the north side of the piazza, looking for any lonely woman, but they were a rare commodity in sociable Venice. There was no Driscoll in the two cafés on this side, or in any of the trinket shops selling postcards and lace. She was not in the gloomy 'Change' office; the equally dim interior of the post office – where electric fans turned laboriously – disclosed no sign of Driscoll either. Monica stopped outside the post office and removed Driscoll's letter to Sarah Kelly from the guidebook. Ought she go in and post the letter? It might do the job the seashell was supposed to have done – provide proof that Monica thought Driscoll was alive. Because you wouldn't post a letter on behalf of a person you thought dead . . . would you? But there were long queues for the counters, and she would have to join one of them to buy a stamp for England.

It was so humiliating to have to pursue Driscoll in this way, and meanwhile everything was changing: time was putting on a spurt; pigeons arrived and departed, as did café customers; tables were cleared and set; new bells rang as the sun boiled. It was probably quarter after one already.

Monica walked back towards Florian. She was thirsty; she would have a glass of water and a *chocolat* – and perhaps Driscoll would return. Monica had to correct herself: Driscoll *did* have moments of insanity. What else could account for last night's drama on the gondola? Was it possible the whole notion of Venice had gone to her head and quite unhinged her? It amounted to this: the chances of the lonely woman having been Driscoll were about equal to the chances of the supposed dream of killing her being real. As she stepped onto the Florian terrace, Monica said, 'Fifty-fifty.' It was an American expression, she believed, which had been called to mind by some American voices around her. Monica walked towards a table alongside the couple who had taken the lonely woman's place. She sat down.

The woman of the couple was reading a guidebook while stirring her coffee, which was irritating. Monica wished she would concentrate exclusively on either the book or the coffee. 'This is the only piazza,' the woman said to the man. 'The other squares are *"campi"*.' She stopped stirring and raised her face to the sun. 'It's so festive here – almost like a carnival.' The man muttered something along the lines of, 'The real carnival is happening in Paris.' . . . Some mention of Paris, anyhow. He must be a well-travelled person, or perhaps he was speaking metaphorically. The woman was now looking behind her, towards the café interior. 'Apparently,' she said, 'the Italians go into the room of red velvet, while the Austrians favour the room of green velvet.'

'It's the other way around,' said the man.

The woman tipped her face to the sun again. She still hadn't drunk the coffee she'd spent such a long time stirring. 'The temperature must be very high,' she said.

'It's ninety degrees at least,' said the man, who reminded

Monica of her father, in that he seemed to know everything. It wouldn't necessarily stop him dying of a cancer, though.

A waiter came up to her – a small, efficient-looking man. Rather too efficient, for all he said to Monica was, 'Yes?'

Now this was also rude. The English were the top nation, of course, but it was annoying to be *taken* for an English person when abroad, especially for Monica, who, with her dark eyes and hair, rather fancied herself an Italian type.

She said, '*Chocolat, per favore,*' a combination of French and Italian that, with luck, might have annoyed the waiter. There was no need to ask for water; she saw from the surrounding tables that it came automatically. The waiter gave the slightest of nods to show he had understood the order. Men were supposed to like Monica, and usually they did. You couldn't legislate for the ones who were simply uncivil.

When the waiter had departed, Monica again looked out into the piazza for any sign of Driscoll. She then looked at Driscoll's letter in the guidebook. The flap of the envelope was imperfectly gummed down; it only held at the tip. Even so, Monica would leave a visible tear if she tried to open it. The couple had finished their drinks and were taking their leave. They had been sitting on the right-hand side of Monica; they now crossed behind her, to speak to the man – a rather dishevelled figure – sitting at the table to her left.

'Your post-meridial plans?' he said.

'Nothing very original, I fear,' said the woman from the couple.

'But this is not an afternoon for originality,' said the dishevelled man.

'We felt that a swim at the Lido might be called for,' said the man from the couple.

'I would say it's positively dictated,' said the dishevelled man.

When the couple had departed, Monica studied the man. On closer inspection, he was elegant, on account of a blue-and-white bow tie amiably askew, and a blue handkerchief flowing out of the pocket of his rather grubby but (Monica suspected) expensive white suit-coat. His hair consisted of a few sweaty black curls that had at first – until he spoke to the couple – led Monica to believe he must be Italian. But she was now considering that he might be at least part-Indian. He was looking over towards the basilica, and nodding his head in time to the music, while obviously not really paying attention to it – humouring the music, so to speak. Monica tried to catch his eye, until she realised that he would be immune to her stares. He was blind; his eyes looked down to the right, up to the left – always seeking out things that weren't there. His white walking cane, Monica saw, was propped against his chair. A pretty woman walking past touched him gently on the shoulder, which did not stop the agitation of his eyes, but he smiled the moment he felt the touch. The woman leant down and spoke to him, and he replied with a single happy word. It seemed he was highly popular. When the woman had gone, the man appeared to be trying to see inside his own head. His eyes were of a very faded blue, and Monica wondered whether they would have been that colour if he could see. She also wondered if having blue eyes disqualified him from being Indian, but she didn't believe that was the case.

The waiter returned in fairly short order with the *chocolat* and the iced water. He didn't say anything as he put them down, so Monica didn't see why she should thank him. Instead, she drank the water off straight away, which was not an elegant thing to do, but she was free, this afternoon, to do inelegant things. The waiter had now compounded his rudeness to Monica by giving a cheery greeting to the elegant and scruffy man: '*Buon giorno, avvocato!'* the waiter said, and they began a short conversation as Monica wondered about *'avvocato'*. Bobby Harper, being a barrister, sometimes referred to himself as an 'advocate' . . . so this interesting man to her left was probably the Italian equivalent of a barrister, a profession embodied on the one hand by Mr Harper, bicycling off to do scraps of 'pleadings' in his shiny suit; on the other by the barristers whose photographs appeared in the *Notable Trials*. Their names were liable to go on for ever: 'E.A.G. Mitchell-Innes, Esq. KC', for example, and these KCs – the King's Counsels – had their assistants, called juniors, who were junior only in the sense that they were younger than the King's Counsels. They weren't younger than many other people.

Now this man was shaping up to be a very fascinating person indeed: scruffy, yet refined-looking, and probably rich; very English in a way, but possibly at least half Indian; blind yet learned. Well, his knowledge of the law combined with blindness might have been heaven-sent as far as Monica was concerned. She would be able to quiz him while disguising her identity. As the waiter moved away from him, Monica stretched out her left leg and kicked over his white cane.

'The waiter's just knocked over your cane,' she said.

'The waiter?' the blind man said, somewhat bewildered. He clearly didn't believe the waiter would have done it. The waiters knew him, and they knew to look out for his cane. But Monica must press on. 'I'm just going to pick it up for you,' she said, and she did so. 'I don't think the waiter noticed,' she added. 'Otherwise, he would have picked it up himself.'

But the calculation going on behind the blind man's eyes suggested she ought to drop the subject of the waiter.

'Would you mind if I asked you a question?' she said.

'I don't mind your asking, young lady, as long as your parents have no objection to my answering.' Use of gerunds – that was promising, too. 'They will have advised you,' he continued, looking up at the sky, 'against speaking to strange men, I'm sure.'

'Oh, my parents are not here just at present. They're coming along shortly.'

Monica realised that she was attempting to *sound* pretty, and the effect on this clever man must be quite horrible. She half stood and shifted the chair beneath her in the direction of the man. It made a grating sound that must also have been horrible, and the man's eyes flickered with apprehension.

'What is your question, dear?' he said.

But Monica hadn't decided on it yet. At any rate, she had not decided on her *first* one, and it was as if the man, being so gracious and clever, knew it, because he gave Monica breathing space by offering his hand. 'I'm Humphrey De Silva,' he said. 'I'm very pleased to meet you.'

'Pleased to meet you, too,' said Monica, hoping he would not notice that she had withheld her name. In any event, Humphrey De Silva would be too polite to ask it.

He appeared to be looking towards the top of the campanile. He would 'look', if that were the correct verb, anywhere but at Monica, and the effect was rather gentlemanly, indicating a becoming shyness. On the table before him was a silver cig- arette case, a box of matches, an empty coffee cup and some sort of pink alcohol in a rather scientific-looking glass

Monica said, 'Are you Humphrey De Silva, *KC*?'

'I must admit that I am, dear, for my sins. Now how on earth did you know that? Do you mix in legal circles?'

'Not precisely,' said Monica, still sounding ridiculous, 'although I used to know a barrister – a Mr Bobby Harper. Robert Harper, I should say.'

'I can't say I know him. What's his Inn?'

The barristers worked – and sometimes lived – in the Inns of Court. One of them, Lincoln's Inn, came up a good deal in *Bleak House*. She didn't know which one Bobby Harper belonged to. She decided to make a joke of it.

'I think the inn he most favours is The Flask at Highgate!'

Humphrey De Silva smiled. 'A lot of my colleagues are similarly inclined. But you still haven't told me how you know my identity.'

'The waiter called you "*avvocato*", which means lawyer, I think. You don't look like a solicitor to me. You look like a barrister, and you are obviously very clever, so you must be a successful one – and they're called King's Counsels.'

'Well, that's very clever of *you*, young lady.'

'It was elementary, my dear De Silva,' she said, and this time he laughed properly.

'I feel you are destined for the music-hall stage, my dear.'

Monica did not care to hear that, in view of what she might be really destined for. Humphrey De Silva was signalling for a waiter who was chatting away about three tables to the right. This second waiter, who was rather long-haired, looked more amiable than the first, but less efficient.

'. . . And you are clearly an admirer of the Great Detective,' Humphrey De Silva said to Monica.

'I've read almost all the short stories. I don't mean to boast – it's just a fact. But I've only recently got round to *The Hound of the Baskervilles*.'

'And what do you make of it?'

'A little disappointing. Holmes has gone off on his own and sent Watson to Devon.'

'Yes, which is really Cornwall – old tin mines and all that.'

'Of course, Watson's a nice man, but not very interesting.'

'Not without Holmes around to insult him. Have you come to the part where Holmes says something like, "You are not yourself luminous, Watson, but you are a conductor of light . . . in noting your fallacies I was occasionally guided towards the truth"?'

Monica shook her head, before remembering that shaking one's head wouldn't do in this case. 'No,' she said, 'I don't believe I have. It's *awfully* rude, isn't it? You wonder why Watson puts up with him sometimes.' Monica was also wondering about another matter, namely how Humphrey De Silva could have read *The Hound of the Baskervilles,* or indeed anything at all. But there were special books for blind people – they could read by touch. Or perhaps he had seen stage plays of the Holmes stories. (Well, not *seen,* strictly speaking.)

'But I had better say nothing more about the book,' he said, 'in case I spoil the mystery. You had a question for me, dear?'

'Yes. Yes, I do. You see, I have a friend . . .'

That was a lie, for a start.

Humphrey De Silva was signalling again towards the second waiter, who continued to betray his location by the sound of his chatter. When Humphrey De Silva clicked his fingers twice (and very expertly), the waiter did see him, and he began to approach.

'He's coming over,' said Monica.

But then he *wasn't* coming over.

'Oh, now he's gone inside the café.'

At this, Humphrey De Silva sighed and closed his eyes very decisively, as if switching off an electric light. Given that he was already blind, this seemed a twofold retreat from the world. It was quite alarming, this sudden cessation of his great charm, and Monica had internally counted to five before he reopened them and gave her his full attention once again.

'I have a friend,' she continued, 'who's worried that they might be in trouble with the law.'

'They must have good reason for that anxiety.'

'Well, you never know with this person. They probably do. I'm not entirely sure.' Monica was pleased with that – distancing herself from herself.

'Is this person a child?'

'Yes.'

'What age?'

'Is the age important?'

'Yes. It is presumed that no child under eight can be guilty of any offence.'

'The person is fourteen.' (Which was a bit close to home, but still.)

'Very well. There is also a presumption that a child aged between eight and fourteen is incapable of committing a crime.'

'Is that eight to fourteen inclusive?'

'It is.'

'Oh,' said Monica, because while this was good news, it seemed illogical. Monica herself, for example, was perfectly capable of committing a crime, as she had proved most recently only today.

'But this presumption is rebuttable,' Humphrey De Silva continued. 'It is expressed in the maxim *malitia supplet aetetem*. How's your Latin, my dear?'

'Not very good.'

'An evil disposition makes up for a lack of years.'

'How might this evil disposition be proved?'

'Evidence of precocious malice; of similar acts other than the offence charged.'

That was definitely bad news.

'What would happen if she was arrested?'

'It's a girl, then?'

'Yes, didn't I say that?'

Monica knew perfectly well that she hadn't. The cat was out of the bag now, and in danger of being recognised even by a blind man. Humphrey De Silva took a sip of his drink – finished it, in fact.

'Now that's unusual,' he said. 'Crime is almost exclusively a masculine pursuit. The Lady Macbeths of this world are rare birds indeed. She would be released on bail or sent to a remand home.'

'Released on bail?'

'Upon a recognisance being entered into by a parent or guardian.'

'What if there is none?'

'No parent or guardian?'

'Yes.'

'Then by any person interested in the child.'

'A family lawyer, say?'

'The family lawyer would be the prime candidate, yes.'

Monica tried to picture herself living with Mr Farmery while on bail, but she couldn't.

'. . . Unless, of course, it's homicide or some other grave crime. But I doubt your friend is a murderer.'

A woman in the piazza who had been feeding pigeons had now let herself be covered in them – like the opposite of a scarecrow. Perhaps if they all clutched on to her, she would take off. The sun was so hot, it seemed to be making the air bend.

'The thing is,' said Monica, 'she might be.'

The pigeons were flying away from the woman, who looked for a moment as though she were engulfed in a grey flame.

Humphrey De Silva had seemed to look in that direction. He now put out his cigarette (having only smoked an inch or so of it) and turned towards Monica. 'My dear,' he said, with his eyes looking slightly to the left of her, 'I am about to express a sentiment that might seem rather severe for this beautiful sunny day, but if you suspect your friend of murder, you should arrange for the police to be informed of it at the first opportunity. Have you confided in your parents about this?'

'Not yet. It's probably nothing anyway. My friend is rather an over-imaginative girl.'

'Well, let us hope so.'

Monica felt that her imaginary friend was becoming implausible. 'What are you drinking?' she said, indicating the pink stuff in Humphrey De Silva's glass.

'Something I shouldn't be.'

But Monica felt she had to get back to the case of her supposed friend, no matter what. 'If she *had* done a murder, she couldn't be hanged for it, could she?'

'This is not the eighteenth century, dear. A fourteen-year-old girl cannot be executed.'

'Is that quite definite?'

'Quite definite, because of the Children Act 1908. But even before it, the execution of our hypothetical child would have been very unlikely.'

'So the courts are quite merciful?' It was a possibility she hadn't considered, her ideas of children in court having largely come from reading *Oliver Twist*.

'The *law* is merciful, you could say.'

'But she could still go to prison for many years?'

'She could spend many years in custody, yes.'

'Decades?'

'I'm afraid so.'

And they would be the years that were supposed to be the best ones of her life.

The first waiter – the efficient one – was passing the table. Humphrey De Silva grasped his sleeve, almost with violence, and a rather fast and tense conversation ensued. It was in Italian, of course, but Monica could make out that Humphrey De Silva was complaining about the other waiter, for he kept gesturing towards the direction in which he had been standing. His voice was completely different when he was cross – with a rather mechanical clatter that did not at all suit his friendly, crumpled appearance. The original waiter – presumably more senior than the other – seemed mortified and was apologising. He departed into the café interior, returning a moment later, still apologising and holding a small silver pot, which he placed on the table: an ashtray. Only now, it seemed, could a more amiable discourse begin, and the waiter asked: '*Cosa le porto, signor De Silva?*'

Humphrey De Silva answered in English, and Monica was thrilled to realise that this was probably for her own benefit. 'Another grappa for me, please, Luca,' he said, 'and would you care for another hot chocolate, dear?'

Monica was doubly charmed: first, by the contrast between Humphrey De Silva's ferocity on the subject of the second waiter and his solicitousness towards her, and second, by the cleverness with which he divined that she had been drinking a *chocolat*. 'Yes, I would like another, please,' she said, 'but really – how did you know?' (She hoped he couldn't smell chocolate on her breath. That would be rather disgusting.)

'I knew by the sound of your cup on its saucer, my dear, which disclosed the weight of it. That wasn't quite conclusive. It might equally have been a *caffè latte*, say, but given your age, a *cioccolata calda* was the favourite.'

'But you don't know my age.'

At this, Humphrey De Silva nodded for a while, as though accepting the reasonableness of the remark. Then he said, 'Do you mind if I smoke?'

'Not at all.'

All the best men asked first. As he lit the match, Monica thought, *Now this is going to be interesting*, but he knew exactly where the match flame was in relation to the end of the cigarette. Practice made perfect, she supposed. But then, after shaking out the match, he dropped it on the floor, rather than using the newly acquired ashtray. Perhaps truly sophisticated smokers took the meaning of ashtray literally and disposed of matches separately. Or perhaps he was not using it so as to punish the waiters for its late arrival.

'I would say you were fourteen, my dear.'

Silence for a space. Humphrey De Silva lit another cigarette. Clearly, Monica had said too much, but then again, she had meant to. Was she embarking on her confession? She couldn't quite say. She was certainly being rather reckless.

His words coming out along with the smoke, Humphrey De Silva said, 'Do you live in London, my dear?'

'Yes,' said Monica, but she really had better choke him off a bit, so she added: 'In Wimbledon.' That was the first London suburb that came to mind – because of the tennis. Unfortunately, 'Wimbledon' was rather a long word, and she had almost lost confidence in the lie halfway through, so had said it in two distinct halves.

A length of ash was developing at the end of Humphrey De Silva's cigarette, which he held in his right hand. That hand was now gravitating across the table in the general direction of the ashtray, but what if he should miss? Monica nudged the ashtray, somewhat in the direction of Humphrey De Silva's hand, and a small collision occurred. He closed his eyes again, with the same abruptness as before – the gesture of irritation. Monica was appalled at her clumsiness and her pre-emption in assuming he would not be able to locate the ashtray. Of course he could have, after all these years of smoking! But his eyes opened more quickly this time (after only a count of two) and, even though they were quite useless, they were very beautiful as he smiled a forgiving smile. 'Thank you, dear,' he said, flicking the ash skilfully into the target. 'And you are at school in Wimbledon?' he continued.

'I'm not at school yet. I'm being coached up at home.'

Humphrey De Silva nodded.

Another lot of well-wishers came up to him: an Italian family, all very pretty, but too perfect and small, like a collection of dolls, and he was speaking to them in Italian. The word 'Lido' cropped up here, too. That was the beach of Venice; it seemed everybody was off there, and as Monica contemplated the shimmering piazza, it did seem rather arid, the sea being out of sight around the corner on which the campanile stood. Her *chocolat* came, and Humphrey De Silva's drink, brought by the efficient waiter, with further apologies, and these were received by Monica, Humphrey De Silva seeming not to notice the waiter, but directing all his charm towards the Italian family. While it was gratifying for Monica to be apologised to, the perpetuation of the conversation with the family was becoming rather annoying. They were clearly talking about some frivolous matter, whereas she had important business with Humphrey De Silva. But as she sipped her chocolate, she realised the important business was over, really; she had found out what she needed to know. It was just that she would like to prolong her acquaintance with Humphrey De Silva. She realised she was in love with him, in a way. As the Italian wittering continued to her left, she said his name softly to herself between sips of *chocolat*.

'Humphrey . . . De Silva . . .' Humphrey had a Dickensian ring to it, and even De Silva did, in a way. Of course, there was Master Humphrey, who cropped up in various Dickens tales and didn't appear to have a surname.

To her intense delight, Humphrey De Silva was now reaching out his right arm and resting his hand on Monica's left shoulder. She stopped her greedy glugging of the *chocolat* in order to receive this honour, and she dabbed her lips with the napkin, before smiling to face the Italian family, as Humphrey introduced her to them. She should have known he wouldn't forget her. Of course, he was introducing her in Italian, but he seemed to be enthusiastic about her. She caught the word '*amica*', which probably meant friend in some way. She said, '*Buon giorno*,' to the Italian family and left it at that. She felt proud of being Humphrey's quiet companion. Only a person who knew him well would sit so quietly by his side. She did wonder how he had got around the awkwardness of not knowing her name, and she felt ashamed all over again for not having told it to him.

She recalled that Dickens's Master Humphrey was a lonely old man. Perhaps Humphrey De Silva was lonely, despite these cheerful conversations with half of Venice. In which case, Monica might make herself useful to him, as the cure for his loneliness. She might be curing it even now, just by sitting by his side.

Finally, the Italians left.

'Sorry about that, my dear,' Humphrey said. 'A rather garrulous quartet – perfectly charming with it, of course. Now, where were we? The matter of your age.'

'I think it was my friend's age.'

But he didn't agree about that. He was a person of integrity: he would not go along with lies, which was admirable, while also annoying.

'I don't think my friend could really have done a murder. She's rather over-imaginative, as I say – not a very reliable witness.'

'No?'

'She sometimes mistakes her dreams for reality . . . and reality for dreams.'

The day after she was told of her father's death, Monica had woken up in 47 Sycamore Gardens to find Leo in the kitchen. She said, 'I want to go and see Daddy in the hospital.'

'But, my dear,' Leo said, 'I told you yesterday that—'

'I dreamt you told me he was dead.'

'It wasn't a dream, dear.'

'It *was*.' And they had actually argued about it, even though Leo was dressed in mourning black.

It was generally a bad thing when her dreams turned out to be reality, because the dreams were invariably bad. It was therefore much better if they remained as dreams.

Humphrey De Silva said, 'My dear, I am completely certain that your friend is guilty of nothing more than an overactive imagination. But here is a purely speculative scenario – just for the sake of comprehensibility, since you are such a clever and curious young lady . . .'

'Thank you,' said Monica.

'You mentioned her dreaming . . . It is not unknown for people to commit crimes in their sleep, as it were.'

Monica felt the pounding of her heart, accompanying a dizziness; the piazza seemed to be tipping. She had thought there were only two possibilities: she had killed Driscoll, or she had only dreamt she had killed Driscoll. Now here was a third: she had killed Driscoll in her sleep.

140

But, no – it wasn't very likely. She had no history of sleep-walking and had never woken up anywhere but in her own bed. She was just somebody who occasionally filed her memories in the wrong place (as Leo was always doing with household bills), putting them in the folder marked 'dreams' instead of the one marked 'reality', or vice versa.

Even so, Monica asked Humphrey De Silva, 'Is it correct that, if she had done it while sleepwalking, she might be found not guilty? Or be found not *so* guilty?'

'A defence of diminished responsibility would be available to her. The judge would decide whether the jury had the option of finding her not guilty of murder but guilty of man-slaughter.'

'And if they decided it was the latter?' (Monica had felt rather lawyerly saying that.)

'Well, that would affect the sentence.'

'She might not go to gaol?'

'She might not.'

That would be good: all the glamour of being a tragic young criminal while still being at large in the world. She could write her memoirs; she saw herself in saloons or salons. But then her speculative thoughts collapsed.

She said, 'How do we know we're not in a dream now?'

'That was the very question put by a philosopher called Descartes.'

'I daresay,' said Monica, who was impatient for an answer and didn't care to hear about philosophers she'd never heard of.

'We don't know. But I strongly suspect we're not.'

'Why?'

'Dreams are incoherent. We're being coherent.'

'My dreams are often very coherent, whereas I myself am often not.' She was fishing with that last remark, she knew, but

Humphrey De Silva was too clever to rise to the bait.

'It is also believed that people cannot feel physical pain in dreams,' he said.

Some time ago, Humphrey De Silva had lodged his cigarette in the ashtray. She held her palm close over the red tip until she could feel the heat, and the beginning of pain.

'Don't do that, dear,' said Humphrey De Silva. (But how could he have known what she was doing? By sheer cleverness!) 'Perhaps we are indeed such stuff as dreams are made on,' he continued, 'but then, so what? If we are all dreaming all the time, the notion of a dream loses all meaning.'

Monica still loved Humphrey De Silva, but she felt he deserved a small punishment for bringing her to this dead end: 'By the way,' she said, 'can you see in your dreams?'

'That is a very familiar question,' he rudely replied. 'It depends on what you mean by "see".'

Monica was damned if she would answer him, but she still did wonder about his eyesight and his reading. Perhaps he had some little drudge of a clerk who read everything for him and knew what to pass on and what was not worth mentioning, and it might be quite a perilous situation if the little clerk himself were losing his eyesight, for it would be impossible to coach up another reader so attuned to Humphrey's mind.

'Do you read Milton?' she said. It was a silly question, really. As if a blind man would make a point of reading books by other blind men.

'He's rather hard to avoid, isn't he?'

She tried another question: 'Are you in Venice on holiday?'

'In a manner of speaking.'

'Where are you mainly based?'

'I'm quite often at my flat in London, and sometimes in the country near London.'

'But you come here regularly?' Monica asked, for she didn't want him drifting too far from Venice.

'Yes. In fact, I'm thinking of buying a place here.'

'A palazzo?'

'Well . . . a small one, yes.'

'Are you buying it with your wife?' Monica realised she hadn't kept the anxiety out of her voice. She hoped very much that he wasn't married. She would hate his wife if he were. But then she was mortified, for she could see that she had hit a nerve.

'I'm not married,' he said. 'I—'

Monica must spare him the embarrassment of having to reveal – or not reveal – a painful truth. 'Of course, you don't *have* to be buying it with anyone,' she said.

'With my sister,' he said. 'We have a place in mind.'

What a relief; he mustn't be married if he were buying a place with his sister. Perhaps he had been married once, and his wife was now safely dead.

'Do you do your legal work here?' she asked.

'Not if I can help it.'

'Where are you staying just now?'

'The Danieli.'

The Danieli was a top hotel of Venice, if not the very top one. There was a big advertisement for it at the back of the guidebook. She said, 'That's quite near here, isn't it?'

Humphrey De Silva waved his hand towards the round-the-corner part of the piazza. 'It's over there, opposite the boat landings,' and from the way he spoke, you wouldn't think the Danieli was grand at all, which made Monica say, 'It's *terribly* grand, isn't it? How long are you stopping there?'

'Oh, a few weeks, but you mustn't think I'm rich, dear. I once helped them with a legal matter, and they let me stay there free of charge a certain number of weeks a year.'

'It must have been a very important matter.'

'They thought so.'

'Have you ever done murder trials? Defending murderers, I mean?'

'In my criminal days, yes. I don't mean the days when I was a criminal, of course, but when I practised criminal law.'

'What law do you do now?'

'Not much, I'm half retired.'

'Have you ever wanted to kill anyone?'

She had been careful not to emphasise the 'you', which would have implied that Monica herself had. Humphrey De Silva smiled and took a sip of his drink.

'Well now, let me think. Yes.'

(He hadn't thought for long, Monica noticed: what a divine man he was.)

'Why didn't you?'

'There were certain difficulties.'

'Because you're blind?'

He laughed. 'Exactly.'

'When was that?'

'Long ago. When I was a hot-headed undergraduate.'

Monica had finished her second *chocolat*. She had reluctantly decided that the time had come to leave, and Humphrey De Silva seemed to know that. He said, 'I don't believe you've told me your name, dear.'

'It's Lucy,' she said. 'Lucy Moore.' She was always good at making up names, but now, full of shame at the lie, Monica pushed her chair back with a horrible scrape. She rose to her feet, saying, 'It's been lovely talking to you, Mr De Silva, but I've just spotted my family.'

'Are they coming here?'

'They're sort of hanging about in the middle of the piazza. I'd better go to them.'

Humphrey De Silva kept silence. He did not believe in her family. If he had believed in them, he would have said something along the lines of, 'Give them my regards.' Monica had her chatelaine bag open. In its silky interior, Charlotte seemed to have turned away from the seashell, and quite rightly. Monica had made her a receiver of stolen property. Humphrey De Silva's goodness made her very aware of her own badness. She took out her purse and lay down a two-lire note to cover the cost of the *chocolats*. To be quite sure, she put another note on top, but Humphrey De Silva picked up the notes and handed them back to her.

'Thank you, my dear, but you have been my guest.'

'But I insist.'

She put the money down again; he handed it back again.

He said, 'Would you want to compromise the reputation I have acquired, however unjustly, for chivalry and hospitality?'

'But nobody will know where the money came from.'

'Oh, I think we are probably being watched by a dozen pairs of eyes at least.' As Monica surveyed the terrace, people turned away from her one by one.

'I suspect we have been exerting a sort of Beauty-and-the-Beast fascination,' he said.

Monica replaced the money in her purse. She said, 'Mr De Silva, you do not know whether I am beautiful.'

'Oh, yes, I do.'

'Mr De Silva, I must warn you of something. I am about to kiss you. It is coming in now from the right-hand side.'

When she had done it, he extended his right hand. She squeezed it and he squeezed back. 'I am worried about you, dear. But you know where to find me.'

Monica was running across the piazza, scattering pigeons, and with tears in her eyes. As she glanced back at the café terrace, Humphrey seemed to be trying to see her. At the campanile, she turned right, and there was the wide, soaring sea. She went right up to the steamboat landing. Taking the seashell from her chatelaine bag, she threw it back to where it belonged, so that Charlotte could rest in peace. While standing and facing the sea, which looked to have been charged with electricity. She took the guidebook from the bag. Hare and Baddeley had quoted Dickens about the basilica: 'A grand and dreamy structure, of immense proportions; golden with old mosaics; redolent with perfumes; dim with the smoke of incense . . .' She could take it as read. Dickens had seen it and dreamt it for her. As for the Doge's Palace, she remembered that there was a dungeon in it, so she didn't care to visit that either. She would do something else instead.

She turned left out of the piazza, to begin walking along the dock.

The Vaporetto

The boat landing was on one side of her; on the other, a line of big, pastel-coloured hotels. Everybody was on the move, walking in and out of the hotels, stepping on and off the motor launches – vaporetti was the plural – that kept booming up sideways in a friendly and inviting sort of way, and there was something enjoyable about how the men on the dockside chalked the destinations quickly on blackboards, as though with excitement – as though they'd just *thought* of the destination and realised people might like to go there: Murano, Burano, Torcello . . . these were all islands off Venice, no doubt crammed with churches, and there was also the Lido – a kind of beach in the middle of the sea.

As Monica looked along the boat dock, a swirl of the crowd revealed a troublesome sight. She was looking at two Napoleons – that is, in all likelihood, two policemen. They had not noticed Monica, but they *were* staring at a girl of about her age, which was almost as bad. The girl had dark hair and a sailor hat somewhat like Monica's. As she walked, she was eating an ice with a tiny spoon. 'Do they think she's me?' said Monica to herself. But the men's suspicion was falling away rapidly: something about the slow, self-satisfied way the girl was eating the ice . . . and now it was clear that she was in the company of a very upright-looking old lady, perhaps her grandmother. *They can't possibly think* she's *a murderess*, thought Monica; then she said out loud, 'Perhaps they just think she's pretty,' which she was – slightly. But what of Monica? Was she an attractive person? Once, in Oxford with Leo, she had walked past two undergraduates, and one had said (when he thought she was out of earshot), 'Well, *I* thought she was pretty.' So it seemed to be debatable.

The Napoleons had been joined by another man, who looked slightly comical in a different way – more like an English policeman: his uniform seemed to have been made by some very Italian person trying to copy an English police uniform but with only a faint memory of it. He wore a tunic of heavy blue serge (in which he must have been fairly roasting), with a white sash, a dome-like hat and white gloves. He was somewhat overweight and carried no gun. The three obviously knew each other of old. They were talking in a desultory sort of way, while looking about. Any minute now, they were going to spot Monica.

She glanced towards the beginning of a narrow street; it ran at right angles to the boat dock, and a sign pointing along it read '*Gabinetti*', which meant lavatories. Monica did need to 'go', and, of course, the policemen would not be able to follow her into the part of that building reserved for ladies. She hurried over to the beginning of the street, and as she turned into it, she looked over her shoulder at the policemen, whereon one of the two Napoleons met her eye. 'Damn,' she said, and she nearly broke into a run, but checked herself: that would look suspicious if the man was still watching. The street seemed very civilised, being full of old-fashioned bookshops. It smelt fustily of books in the sun, much as Leo's sitting room in Pond Square had done when the weather was right. A man came out of one of the shops with a woman trailing behind him. The man had a port wine stain on his face; he was the rower of the early morning. The woman, still in her flowery hat, was only slightly less ugly than Monica had suspected. 'Well, that was highly embarrassing, Henry,' she was saying. 'Fancy asking the man if he had any books on cricket. They don't *play* cricket in Italy.'

'Well, they jolly well should do,' said the man, who was looking at Monica. 'Hello, young lady! Didn't I see you this morning?'

Monica couldn't think of anything to say; she was trapped.

'You were standing at a window,' said the man. 'I looked out for you when we went back the same way an hour later.'

'You went back the same way?' Monica blurted.

'Yes, indeed.'

'Was anything going on?'

'How do you mean?'

Well, of course, if there'd been a body floating in the water, he would have mentioned it.

'Come along, dear,' said the woman. 'I'm sure the young lady would like to run along back to her family.'

'It was all quiet at the house?' Monica said.

'Absolutely,' said the man. He raised his hat and wandered off with the woman.

Monica looked back; the three policemen had entered the street, conferring as they walked. They did not seem in any particular hurry, were still a good way off, and there was quite a crowd between Monica and them. She had reached the culmination of the street, where it opened into a small square, and here, enshrined like some important monument, was the gabinetti: a fancy white building with a drinking fountain attached – a horrible thing with dirty pigeons scuffling in the grate beneath, and an iron cup on a chain, which was a bit too prison-like. A lot of worrying things were all happening at once. The port wine man had reported a peaceful scene at the house, but he had provided no assurance, really. He might have been rowing his boat over the dead and drowned body of Driscoll. Monica felt very overheated, but on no account would she take a drink from the fountain. She looked back once again; the police weren't here yet. She walked into the women's half of the gabinetti, where the combination of heat and some chemical smell brought on a fainting feeling. She saw that you had to pay a woman to use the facilities, and perhaps that was why Driscoll had about-turned in those at the railway station. She didn't have the right money, and nor did Monica have it now. She offered a one-lira note, and the woman waved it away with a smile, which cheered Monica up somewhat, but she insisted on paying anyway. She felt much better for having 'gone', and when she emerged from the closet, she went directly to the looking glass over the sinks, where she had a wash and prodded at her hair a bit.

The attendant said, '*Bellissima*,' which was very obliging of her, because that (at a guess) meant beautiful. Monica hoped she wasn't doing it just because of the banknote. Was she *really* '*bellissima*'? Humphrey De Silva had said so, but he was blind.

She stepped back into the blazing day, which was full of milling tourists, but empty, it seemed, of police. 'Good,' said Monica. She crossed the square, entering a shadowy food shop that had bottles of water in a barrel of ice. She bought one, together with a bread roll that contained a slice of something mysterious. In the square, she began drinking the water from the bottleneck, having turned her back on the drinking fountain, which, of course, was a deliberate snub. When she'd finished the water, she burped quite loudly – a sort of celebration of not having Driscoll on hand. All *her* burps were silent, although the same could not be said of her farts, about which she was quite unashamed, oddly enough. As she 'let one go' (to use Leo's term), Monica would frown at her in a questioning sort of way, and Driscoll would say something like, 'It's a perfectly natural part of digestion, dear.'

Monica felt much better for the water, although, of course, it would have been prudent to have drunk it *before* visiting the gabinetti. She put up her parasol as she walked again along the book street towards the sea. It was so hot that she had to supplement the parasol by walking on the shady side. Presumably this man heading towards her now considered her *bellissima*, because he was smiling and raising his hat. Such beautiful eyes, the Italian men had – a class of people with jewels in their heads – and Monica began thinking of the general question of 'it', which in turn called to mind Harriet Beck.

Harriet Beck was very interested in 'it' and made no secret of the fact.

Monica thought back to early summer – June, it would have been – of the previous year. She was still in Pond Square; Leo was still alive. Driscoll was looming large but was still only her governess. Monica had been walking on the Heath with Leo, and they'd ended up between the Men's Bathing Pond and the Model Boat Pond. But then Leo had gone off on another 'tramp', probably to the Spaniards Inn on Hampstead Lane. Then she spotted Harriet Beck, hanging about near the Men's Pond, perhaps watching them dive in. It occurred to Monica that Harriet was on her own, which was most unusual.

'Would you like to see something, dear?' Harriet said. 'Something very *interesting*. You have to swear not to split, though.'

Harriet led Monica into a clump of trees on the other side of the Men's Pond. They had arrived at a wooden wall – in fact, the back wall of the changing room, and Harriet was peering through a crack in it. 'Your turn,' she said, after half a minute, during which she'd gone quite red. There were about a dozen men in the changing room – which wasn't a room at all, really, being open to the sky – and most of them were *not* changing but sitting around talking or reading newspapers; two were doing 'exercises', and none of them had any clothes on.

'What did you think of that?' said Harriet, as they emerged from the trees.

'What do you mean by "that"?' said Monica, who had decided not to be shocked, which she wasn't particularly. She had seen men's 'privates' several times before. Leo didn't often have a bath, but when he did, he took it in the scullery, and he wasn't too particular about closing the door. Also, a man sitting opposite her on the Tube had appeared perfectly normal one minute, the next he'd had his 'thing' out. She'd been with Driscoll, who didn't appear to have noticed the man (she was reading *The Times*), but, in fact, she *had* done because she whispered, 'Ignore him, dear, and we'll get off at the next stop.'

'I meant the really *enormous* one,' said Harriet. 'How could you not have seen it? It was perfectly horrid!'

Monica had emerged from the book street and was once again on the dockside. She could not see any police. People paid for their rides on the vaporetti on disembarking, she noticed: a matter of dropping coins into a box (it didn't seem to matter how many) as the gangplank (that couldn't be the right term) was lowered. She sat down on a sort of giant iron toadstool on the water's edge, took the waxed paper off the bread roll and bit into it, with highly satisfactory results. The mysterious something inside was a kind of spicy ham, which beautifully complemented the sliver of cheese that was also secreted in there. But now Monica saw the police again. They were making straight towards her and one of the Napoleons held the cursed bit of paper that must contain her description. There must be carbons of it in all the police stations or police barracks of Venice, but what about the islands? If she boarded a boat, she might escape arrest. It would only be temporary, but everything in her life was now temporary – always had been, come to think of it. She stood and pitched the remainder of her delicious sandwich into the Adriatic Sea. How she hated these three pantomime police who'd made her do that. They were advancing – starting to run now – from the direction of the boat landings, so boarding a vaporetto was out. They were about a hundred yards off, with many dazed tourists between her and them. Monica ran left, away from the sea; she was in an alleyway that ran parallel to the book street. It culminated in a small, kinked bridge, and she was on and over this in a flash. There was now a choice of two alleys: a big and a small. She took the small one and began charging towards an obstacle in the shape of a man who was ringing a doorbell by pulling on a chain. But he was not a policeman, so he stood aside for her before resuming his ringing. The echoing clatter of the bell spurred Monica on to faster running. Everything in this alley spurred her on: a barred window, which looked prison-like, a dog barking out of sight, a torn poster that might have been a police poster advertising a 'wanted' person. Monica had once seen a paper called the *Police Gazette* in the Holloway Library. She believed it had been left behind by an actual po-liceman. It was horribly fascinating, full of what were called 'Apprehensions Sought' – drawings of brutal-looking men, and their descriptions: 'bald on top', 'stooped', 'missing most teeth', 'weak chin'. None of the men were handsome, but, of course, the police wouldn't have said so even if that were the case . . . although Monica had to admit they'd been fairly civil about the only woman whose apprehension was sought. She was a *young* woman who had escaped from a reformatory. She wore a brown uniform dress; her complexion was 'bright', hair 'abundant'; she 'stammered slightly', and Monica had felt very sorry for her.

She could not keep up this speed of running; she felt sick. When a person had died – as Driscoll obviously had done – you were meant to mourn, not start charging pell-mell through a strange city. She stopped and looked back – couldn't see the police. When Monica came to a shopping street (or alley), she slowed. It might be an idea to copy the female saunterers in this street, most of whom had their parasols up. Monica did likewise, keeping the thing low, to screen her face. How its lacy edges seemed to be mocking her. The street, she realised, looked familiar, as did the arch that now approached. A moment later, Monica was back in St Mark's Square. She commenced running again, scattering pigeons and people, and wondering whether she was the only woman in Venice ever to have run with an opened parasol in hand.

She was back at the boat dock, and it was perhaps rather clever of her to have come full circle, because would the three policemen really think she would return to where she'd started from?

A boat was departing. She must go with it. The boat was a clear two feet from the dock when she leapt; for a moment, she could see the oily water churning beneath her wedding shoes. As she landed on the deck, she received what she believed was a look of admiration from the deckhand – the person who ought to have pulled across the iron gate that would have prevented her from boarding. But he had for some reason not got around to doing so, probably because he was too busy smoking a cigarette. As Monica had leapt, the vaporetto had let out a trumpeting blare from its horn, as though indignant at Monica's late intrusion. Monica had further spoilt the 'swaif' effect by stumbling as she landed, which caused Charlotte to fly out of the chatelaine bag and go into a skid across the deck boards, until she came to rest amid the standing part of the boat crowd. A woman picked Charlotte up and handed her to Monica as she regained her feet. 'No damage done!' Monica said, even though the woman was almost certainly Italian, so would not understand. She looked very kindly as she asked – in Italian – the question Monica hoped she had just answered.

The deckhand came up, still smoking. He watched with fascination as Monica bundled Charlotte back into the chatelaine bag. It was as though he couldn't believe that anyone who could make such a violent leap would own such a girlish thing as a doll. Then he was pointing at something else on the deck. The wooden heel – the left one – of Monica's wedding shoes had broken off. She limped over and picked it up. The deckhand had moved away; two passengers were questioning him about the destination of the boat.

Monica heard a shout from the dock – one hoarse syllable. It had come from one of the two Napoleons. If anybody else on the boat had heard it, then it had not signified with them. The officer who looked like an English policeman was waving at the boat as if saying goodbye; in fact, he was beckoning it to return, but fruitlessly. She could also now see the second Napoleon. He was diminishing rapidly in size, but she could make out that he was approaching a kind of box-on-a-stick on the dockside, and it appeared he had done so with a key in hand, for he now unlocked the box and opened its door, so it was effectually a cupboard on one leg. The man removed from the box something that remained attached to it by a cord: a telephone instrument. Anybody wearing such old-fashioned clothing had no business using anything as down-to-date as a telephone. No telegraph wires were attached to the box (Monica believed that telephones used the same wires as the telegraphs); they must run underground in this case, and the question was whether they would continue all the way under the Adriatic Sea to where Monica was going . . . And where, incidentally, *was* she going?

Monica stood at the rail, watching the receding city. The policemen were no longer distinguishable, and nor was the dock. It had become part of a low line of sunlit buildings. Not quite *all* were low, however; every so often a tower protruded, and now Monica saw one that was leaning quite dramatically. It was frightening that something so large could be so wrong. 'It reminds me of Driscoll,' she said, 'tall and awkward,' and suddenly Monica was crying. Poor Driscoll. She took her handkerchief out of her bag to dry her eyes. It was comforting to see Charlotte lying in there. Whatever her destination, Charlotte would be with her. She put the shoe heel in the bag, taking care to avert the dirty side from Charlotte. It was quite symbolic, possibly, that a wedding shoe should have broken. She could always take it back to Ed's Original for mending, but she doubted she would be seeing Holloway again.

She could buy some new shoes wherever they were going; she had enough money for a cheap pair. It occurred to her that she might change her appearance more generally. Ought she to discard her sailor hat? She couldn't bear to. She loved it even more than her wedding shoes. Strictly speaking, it was a leghorn straw hat, and, like the shoes, it had been an odd thing to see for sale on the Holloway Road. She took it off and looked at it, adjusting the taffeta ribbon that trailed prettily from the brim – that was Driscoll's doing . . . Monica was nearly crying again. Instead, she put the hat back on and stood up. She must find out where she was going.

She approached a languid man with one well-polished boot resting on the lower rung of the rail. He was smoking a small cigar, which seemed to go with his small moustache. He was handsome, albeit probably a cad, because of the cigar. She was about to ask her question in French, but he was smiling so cynically that she thought that would come over as pretentious, so she said it in English, and she decided she would dish out a bit of slang into the bargain.

'Where are we off to?'

The man frowned, and he was not the frowning type, being such a cool customer, so Monica was forced to conclude that she'd asked a bizarre question, possibly an incriminating one. Some amendment was required. 'I boarded rather hastily,' she said. 'I'm not quite certain . . . we're for the Lido, I assume?' So she had swung from slang to pomposity. As for 'the Lido', she had simply invoked the place she *hoped* they were heading for. The man had understood her all right, but he was making her endure a veritable eternity of his cynical smiling before he conceded as much.

'The bus,' he said (using a word that proved he was an old Venice hand, not impressed by the term 'vaporetto'), 'is for the Lido, yes.' He was nearly English, but a little 'off' . . . perhaps American, therefore? Monica did not believe he was Italian, for he did not have beautiful eyes. His eyes – light brown – were merely efficient; he relied on the neatness of his face and the moustache for his effects.

'I'm obliged to you,' said Monica. (She'd started out pompous, might as well carry on with it.)

'Its destination might come as a surprise to some of these folks,' he said, indicating the other passengers.

'Why is that?'

'It left from the berth normally used by the Murano boats.'

'Why?'

'Your guess is as good as mine,' he said, but he clearly didn't believe that. 'They're forever changing the arrangements at the Riva.'

'The what?'

'The Riva degli Schiavoni: where we left from.'

'Oh.'

'They like to do it at the busiest times, you know.' And so saying, he threw his cigar into the sea.

Monica repeated her thanks and walked towards a seat at the rear of the boat.

The man called after her, 'Young lady . . .'

She ignored him; she was confident he would be too lackadaisical to pursue her.

'The Lido,' she said, sitting down. 'Good.' But it seemed not everybody welcomed the prospect of going there, as word of their destination spread among the passengers. She pictured the Lido as a sliver of sand with waves in front and behind, which couldn't be the reality, of course. She looked back over the rolling blue waters: nothing there but the wake of the steamer. No police boat followed, but, of course, they wouldn't give up now, and more police might be waiting for her at the landing stage . . . and only now did she appreciate the significance of the intelligence she had just received. The pantomime policemen might have subscribed to the common mistake about the boat's destination; assuming they could get into touch by telephone

158

with their comrades, they would be waiting for her at Murano, and not at the Lido. And here came another good thought that should have occurred to her before: what if the police were after her not as a murderess, but as a missing person? For, if Driscoll were alive, she would naturally have reported Monica's disappearance to the police. The trouble with this theory was that Driscoll – if alive – would surely have turned up for luncheon at Florian. The theory could not be discounted, however, as the detectives tended to say, and Monica ought to keep in mind that she might be not only 'missing' rather than 'wanted', but also innocent rather than guilty. But a succeeding thought – and a memory accumulating in her mind – quickly scotched that happy notion.

Everything was now preordained. You could tell by the way the boat was following a set path, guided by wooden poles in the water that were at crazy angles but regularly occurring. Monica was going where she had been going all along; anybody who knew about her past would be able to guess her future.

The Drinking Fountain

'Every Venetian boy is called Giovanni, as every girl is Maria – names which are supposed to protect them from the power of witches.'

From *Venice*, by Augustus J.C. Hare & St Clair Baddeley

Since her removal to Holloway, Monica had occasionally revisited the Heath, sometimes in the evening and without Ethel, her supposed chaperone.

After some hard campaigning by Monica, she and Ethel had come to an arrangement. Monica pointed out that chaperoning had not been strictly enforced by Leo and had gone almost completely by the board towards the end of his time in charge. Driscoll was much keener to enforce it, which meant more work for Ethel.

'And yet I think you are on the same wage as under Leo?' Monica had suggested to Ethel.

'I don't see what it's got to do with you,' said Ethel.

'I don't want to be chaperoned, and I don't think you want to chaperone me.'

Ethel had said nothing to that, but a few days later, she announced: 'What you were saying about the chaperoning . . . I talked to my John about it.'

'And what did he say? I'll bet it was something good.'

'He said, "Do what you like."'

What Ethel did *not* like, she now told Monica, was having to be a chaperone on top of her other duties, '. . . especially as you are so often very rude'.

The arrangement they made was this: Monica could walk unaccompanied; she would then rendezvous with Ethel on Highgate Hill, and they would take the tram back down to Holloway together. The suggestion would be that they had been together all along, and Monica was happy to lie in re-inforcement of this fiction. But Ethel never quite lied, and she would take a little turn on the Heath herself while waiting for Monica, so that when Driscoll asked Ethel, 'Did you have a nice walk?' or 'Where did you go on the Heath?' she would have a truthful answer.

Monica began taking her walks at night because the Heath by day – especially a sunny day – reminded her too painfully of her life in Hampstead and Highgate. But one hot day at the start of the present summer, when the Holloway Road was fuming away, she had spotted a flyer (it actually *was* flying, blown along in the wake of a tram) that spoke of something to do with the Highgate Model Yacht Club. She couldn't imagine how this flyer had drifted down to Holloway, or who, on that workaday road, should be interested in such a whimsical thing, but Monica had stooped and collected it up.

'It's litter, dear,' Driscoll had said.

'Not any longer,' said Monica, and she had pocketed it in her pinafore.

'What *is* it, dear?'

'Not telling.' (It hadn't been one of Monica's wittier days.)

'Highgate Model Yacht Club,' she read, when she got back to the privacy of her bedroom. 'Nineteenth Pick-Up Summer

Regatta . . . Saturday, 15 July, 1911 . . . Entries by 9 June to Commodore Wakefield, West Winds, Millfield Lane, Highgate . . .' and so pompously but endearingly on. It was so redolent of Highgate, the Heath and lost romance. Monica did not believe she had ever actually attended the regatta, although she had sometimes observed the preparations, as, for example, last year, when she had watched Jack Linton towing the little boats he made across the water. Jack Linton was well known in Highgate. He was a carpenter in a small way of business, with premises in a yard behind the high street, and he was associated with the Model Yacht Club, as a sort of lieutenant to Commodore Wakefield, who lived in a big house on Millfield Lane, right next to the Heath.

Monica knew she ought not to go to the regatta because she was exiled from all that world now.

She did go, however, and she took the tram up Highgate Hill with Ethel. Monica had brought a book to read on the tram, while Ethel looked out of the window. They had told Driscoll they would be back by eight, but they separated, as per their new arrangement, when they reached the Model Boat Pond. Perhaps a couple of hundred people were already there. The atmosphere was highly festive and jolly; the sun was raying down quite mercilessly, and it was as though celebratory oompah music were playing, although it wasn't actually. On the south side of the Model Boat Pond, between it and the Men's Bathing Pond, a trestle table with a white cloth had been set up. Various trophies were displayed, and programmes were available for a penny. A couple of trophies were big, jug-eared silver cups, another was a bowl of the kind used for displaying flowers (a little placard informed Monica that it was 'The Hogan-Portland Rose Bowl'), but others looked rather pathetic: a teaspoon (that was the prize for the race called the

Commodore's Invitation) and a couple of coins or medallions with engravings of sailing ships on them. Bunting hung from a kind of clothesline behind the table.

Of those around the pond, most were spectators, but some were competitors, and these were the ones studying, and discussing, the pond, even though nothing was yet happening on it. There was much anxiety about the little breeze ruffling the waters. It was evidently a bit flighty, rather enigmatic as to its direction. A father was gesturing at the water and saying to his son, 'Imagine the wind as a colour, Davey . . .' Another man was lamenting, 'They ought never to have chopped down that oak.' He seemed to think that had affected the wind.

Most of the competitors were fathers and sons, with the mothers hanging about looking spare beneath their parasols – although one woman was doing something useful: sitting on a folding stool in order to stitch some sails. The boats were either being clutched by the sons or lying around on the banks like dead swans. Commodore Wakefield was stomping – and sometimes running – around the pond, making announcements through his megaphone and giving a countdown to the start of the races. 'The first race, which is the young children's race, commences in ten minutes . . . The young children's race commences in five – repeat, five – minutes . . .'

People kept scurrying after the commodore, asking him for advice, or to make rulings on things. He was saying to one boy, 'I will certainly *not* tell you the direction of the wind, young man. It's up to you to work it out!' The commodore was a famous Highgate figure, known to be charitable, if overbearing. Monica believed that, in spite of his blue and gold uniform, he had no connection to the full-sized navy but had made his name in some tremendously boring sphere, like stockbroking (whatever that was). He was a loud, bearded man, who seemed to have clicked that he was even louder without his megaphone, which he now held down by his side as he marched around the pond barking out various rules '. . . that shall apply to all – repeat, all – competitors'. The main one, repeated several times, was: 'If your boat becomes entangled in the weeds on the east side of the pond, you may *touch* it off from the bank, and you may use a pole or cane as necessary. But you must not – I repeat, must *not* – *push* it off.'

Monica knew by sight or name some of the faces around the pond, although not as many as the ordinary sort of Highgate girl would have known. After all, Monica didn't go to school in Highgate (or anywhere), and Leo, while an occasional swimmer in the Bathing Pond, had never had anything to do with the model boating lot: 'hearties', he would have called them, which was what he also called people who played golf. Some of those familiar faces did acknowledge Monica, in that slightly pitying way to which she had become accustomed even before Leo had died. She had already heard the words, whispered in her wake, '. . . lived with that one who went under the tram'.

The young children were lining up on the south bank – where the races began – for the first event. They were *very* young, and Monica knew immediately which one she would be 'supporting': the only girl competitor. She was probably about eight, and wore a tam-o'-shanter that was too big for her and nearly fell into the water as she lowered her boat in. The race was begun by a young 'starter' who did it by firing a gun into the sky with an embarrassed look on his face. One of the boys, having been warned of this, stood behind his boat with his fingers in his ears and a silly grin on his face. The boats began moving, at varying speeds, wavering somewhat. It all depended how the sails had been set. Halfway across the pond, one of the yachts simply came to a stop, as though defying the wind to move it, having suddenly realised the futility of the whole proceeding. Monica hoped desperately that it wasn't the little girl's, but she believed it was, by the way the girl was staring fixedly at that boat with an unfathomable expression.

A few minutes later, the race had finished, and the boy who'd blocked his ears was leaping about with joy, while the girl slowly removed the tam-o'-shanter from her head and held it in front of her, like a much older person at a funeral. Her boat was still in the middle of the pond, and Jack Linton, wearing waders, was walking into the water to collect it. A man (the girl's father, presumably) put his hand on the girl's shoulder to commiserate. She barely responded but just watched in a kind of daze as her boat was being collected. 'She'll remember this forever,' Monica said to herself. 'I won't have it; I simply won't have it.' She must affect the memory, if possible, so Monica walked quickly – half ran – around the pond towards the girl. 'I just wanted to say that I absolutely *adore* your tam. Won't you put it back on? You look so pretty in it.' The girl silently put her hat back on, and she smiled at Monica when she'd done it. Monica then dashed off happily, not knowing where she was going, but thinking she might buy an ice from the barrow on Millfield Lane.

Then she saw Harriet Beck talking to a boy, and all her happiness fled.

This had been coming for a while, of course: Harriet and boys. Even when she was ten years old, she had seemed to like doing cartwheels and handstands when boys were around, to show off her knickers, and Monica knew for a fact that she had kissed several boys in the garden of a dance – only one dance and yet several boys.

Harriet and the boy were on the grass bank that rose up from the south side of the pond. He was obviously older than

Harriet, perhaps sixteen, and big for his age. He was quite handsome, Monica supposed, but rather fleshy; in fact, he looked like a big, brutal baby. He was holding his yacht, as if it were a trophy he'd already won. He looked slightly familiar, so he might be at Highgate School. She would see those boys walking in their crocodiles, playing football, or – in the case of the older ones – just hanging about after school, because, of course, boys did not require chaperones. There was another girl near the boy but hanging back slightly, which must have been irritating to Harriet, who was saying to the boy, 'So it's a gaff-rigged topsail cutter?'

'You got it right at last, Harriet!' he said.

'And you really think you've got a chance?'

'I know my boat, and I know the wind,' he said.

. . . *Probably because he's full of it*, Monica thought. She walked straight up to them and said, 'Hello, Harriet, dear.'

'Oh, hello, dear,' said Harriet, obviously disappointed to see Monica at this important moment in her love life. 'I haven't seen you for a while. I was so sorry to hear about Leo. Are you still living in Highgate?'

'No,' said Monica. 'I'm living in Holloway Road. With Driscoll.' Those words, Holloway Road and Driscoll, were so horrible they were like weapons that you could hit people with.

'Well, that's not so far away, is it?'

The Brutal Baby was eyeing Monica in such a way that Harriet had no choice but to introduce him.

'Monica,' she said, 'this is my friend Gareth. Gareth, this is Monica.'

So his name's Gareth, thought Monica; *does that mean he's Welsh or something?* It wasn't a very intelligent name, anyhow.

'How do you do?' he said, rather nastily but perhaps

flirtatiously, and his next remark did suggest flirtation: 'You're obviously not very interested in model sailing.'

'How do you make that out?' Monica said, being nasty in her turn.

'The book,' he said, indicating it with a nod of his head.

'Monica's a great reader,' Harriet said, trying to get back into the conversation. 'She's quite an intellect on the sly.'

'And what is it?' said Gareth, nodding again at the book.

Definitely flirtation, thought Monica, *but don't let it go to your head. He probably flirts with any girl.* And she was beginning to feel a bit sorry for Harriet, who was obviously in love with him.

'*The Mill on the Floss*,' she said, 'by George Eliot.'

'That's a woman, isn't it?'

'It is.'

It was quite impressive he should know that, since most boys knew nothing of novels or novelists.

'Have you ever read it?' she said.

'Nope.'

He got points there, too, Monica had to admit, by, on the one hand, not declaring that it must be trash or, on the other, by pretending he *had* read it.

She nodded at his boat. 'What race are you in for?'

'Several,' he said. 'With *this* one,' he said, indicating the boat, 'the Commodore's Invitation.'

'That's the one where you win a spoon, isn't it?'

'It's a *silver* spoon,' he said.

Monica decided not to make the obvious tart remark, which was that he'd got one of those already – jammed firmly in his mouth since birth. The boat was called *Atlanta*.

'Atlanta,' she said. 'Isn't that the city under the sea?'

'No,' he said. 'It isn't.'

It was quite rare that people, other than Monica herself, were so rude. *I've met my match here*, she thought. He also didn't mind leaving long silences, and Harriet tried to fill this one. 'Oh, well,' she said, 'Gareth and I are just off to . . .' But Gareth continued to look, with amusement, or perhaps bemusement, at Monica.

He's weighing me up, she thought, *trying to decide if I'm pretty*. It went also to his credit that he hadn't immediately discounted her upon learning that she lived on the Holloway Road with a person who sounded like a rainy day.

'I'm awfully sorry, Monica,' said Harriet, 'but Gareth and I have to go off now to see some of our friends.' She was indicating the crowd around the pond – could have meant anyone.

Monica let them go off. Good luck to them. Out of sight, out of mind – that was the way. It was quite an effort not to look, though.

The spare girl – the one who'd been hanging back – came up to Monica. She looked nice: a broad, rather moon-ish face that was pretty in its own unique way. She was perhaps two years older than Monica.

'Oh dear,' said the girl.

'How do you mean?'

'Are you *very* close friends with Harriet?'

Monica couldn't decide how to reply. Would a confidence from this stranger be more likely if she said yes or no?

'*Quite* good friends,' she said. 'We used to live near each other.'

'I've tried to warn her off Gareth, but it doesn't seem to be working.'

Monica couldn't remember the last time anyone had said something so interesting. She mustn't deflect any further intelligence by one of her wrong remarks. She settled on, 'How do you know him?'

'He's my brother. He has his points, Gareth, but someone like Harriet brings out the worst in him. And, of course, he's too old for her . . . Are you off to the tea?'

'What tea?'

'After the last race – for competitors and their friends. If you want to come along, just say I invited you. It's in the commodore's garden.' She indicated the large, peaceful houses of Millfield Lane.

'What's your name?' Monica said.

'Oh, sorry. Katherine. But most people call me Kitty – Kitty Hall.'

Monica thanked her and drifted back into the crowd of spectators. She wandered about, half watching the races. The pistol was fired to start so many in such quick succession that you'd have thought a gunfight had broken out. She recognised Harriet Beck's parents. So she was under their control, but on the long leash. She wondered what they made of Gareth Hall. Perhaps he had not yet emerged with any definition from the ranks of Harriet's friends, accumulated at the many parties they either attended or gave as a successful Hampstead family. She kept seeing him in the crowd, with Harriet always tagging along. Gareth Hall seemed quite a celebrity in the model yachting world. But Monica believed that, unlike the commodore, he would not linger in that world when he was a fully grown man. He would have bigger fish to fry.

Monica saw Ethel on the far side of the pond. She was with her young man, John. They were looking about, occasionally whispering to each other. She walked over to them.

'Hello, John,' Monica said. (There was no need to say hello to Ethel.) 'How are you keeping?'

'Hello, Monica,' he said. 'I'm keeping very well. How are you?'

'I'm very well too, thanks.'

They always said exactly the same, and their conversation had never gone any further, and it wouldn't go any further this time either, because – after touching his cap again at Monica – John drifted over towards the trophy table. He was quite a pleasant-looking man, but always seemed slightly dusted with plaster – a potential ghost. At the very least, his dark hair would go grey prematurely, Monica believed. On the other hand, a plasterer was unlikely to be lost at sea, and Monica supposed this was part of his appeal to Ethel: he was 'steady'. But Gareth Hall was not steady. He was dangerous. She could see him just then, holding forth about his boat – or it might have been a different boat that he carried now. Monica pointed him out to Ethel.

'See that fellow over there, Eth? The one in the white top-coat and black trousers holding the boat?'

Ethel nodded slowly.

'Have you seen him about in Highgate?'

Ethel nodded slowly again.

'Well, where *exactly* have you seen him, for God's sake, and what was he doing at the time?'

'He's one of those that hang around at the stink pipe.'

Stink pipes were quite common in North London and, as far as Monica knew, throughout the world. They were vertical gas pipes that somehow ventilated the horizontal ones buried under the pavements. The stink had to be taken on trust, because the tops of the pipes were high in the sky – at least twice as high as the usual street lamp. But Highgate had a notable example, in that it was only a little taller – although much wider – than an ordinary street lamp, and the excess gas was put to use, burning in a big glass that would glow so brightly white you could hardly look at it. The stink pipe was on the corner of two tree-lined avenues Monica couldn't remember the names of, but one of them – and possibly both – began with 'B'. She pictured the scene the stink pipe illuminated: the big red-brick villas belonging to Highgate School, where the boarders lived.

Gareth Hall was now setting the boat he'd been holding down in the water for the start of another race.

'What's he like?' Monica asked Ethel.

'You can *see* what he's like,' she said.

Gareth Hall was now waving away an older man who was presuming to advise him on some nautical matter like sail-setting.

'My John and me are off for a bus ride,' said Ethel. 'It would be more convenient if you and me could meet on the Road.' She meant the Holloway Road, of course.

'Where?'

'Under the railway bridge.'

'All right.' Because it didn't matter where they met as long as they returned to the flat together, and since the railway bridge was so much closer to the flat than their usual meeting place – Highgate Chapel – they could afford to meet later.

'How about eight o'clock?' said Monica.

'That's when we're supposed to be *back*.'

'I know. We can be a few minutes late.'

'She gets very worried, you know,' said Ethel.

'Well, it's hard lines, isn't it? Driscoll has practically kidnapped me, and you're in danger of turning into her accomplice.'

'You're off your head, you are,' said Ethel, and she went off to find her John.

The gun was fired. The race was run (if that was the term), and it seemed Gareth Hall had won it from the way he was being congratulated by his fellow males, with a good deal of, 'Well done, old man!' and, 'Now for the big one!'

'The big one' was the Commodore's Invitation, which took place an hour later, during which time Monica had eaten an ice and read a chapter of *The Mill on the Floss*. A man in knicker-bockers had come up to her as she sat on the grass, with her hat on the ground beside her. 'What are you reading, young lady?'

She'd thought of saying, 'A book,' or, 'I don't believe we've been introduced,' for the sun had given her a headache, and reading George Eliot was not helping. Her characters were well drawn, but in fact too realistic, and therefore exhausting.

'It's called *The Mill on the Floss*,' she said, 'and it's by George Eliot . . . who's a woman.' She'd felt the need to add this because she wouldn't be able to bear the stupidity of this man saying, 'I don't believe I've heard of him,' and so failing the test Gareth Hall had passed. She'd looked the man up and down. Of course, he'd already failed *all* the tests Gareth Hall had passed, and he'd seemed to know it. At any rate, he'd touched his boater and walked off.

The Commodore's Invitation was announced with extra-loud shouting by the commodore himself, and everybody was paying attention as the competitors approached the water's edge on the south side. It must be that the smallness of the prize reflected inversely the importance of the competition – just as, in cricket, England and Australia competed for a sort of egg cup full of ashes. The competitors in this race were certainly a cut above, and their boats – all clippers, she supposed – were the most graceful and swan-like. Gareth Hall turned out to be rather shabbily dressed in comparison with the others; he was the only one not in a lounge suit, and he looked much the youngest. Monica would generally support the underdog, and Gareth Hall seemed to fit the bill – except that he still smiled nastily.

The best lounge suit – best pressed and best cut (as far as

Monica could judge) – was worn by a tall, thin, somehow foreign-looking man, who had walked down to the water in company with a more plainly dressed companion, who carried a splendid-looking yacht. This second man placed it in the water and crouched down to set the sails, apparently at the behest of his elegant governor.

At the firing of the gun, all the cutters positively shot away from the bank, their sails finding every last breath of the invisible wind. At first, Gareth Hall's boat was in the lead, but then it began to veer to the right, crossing in front of the others as though it had a different destination in mind. Gareth Hall's boat was undoubtedly heading into the notorious weeds of the east bank, and he was running around the pond anticlockwise towards it, carrying a cane in his hand. Monica also set off around the pond, going the opposite way to Gareth Hall (it might actually have been that she was going anticlockwise and he clockwise – the terms always confused her), but they were both heading towards those weeds. The commodore was there, too, and it seemed to Monica that only the three of them saw what happened next, the rest of the great crowd being distracted by an apparently greater drama of two other clippers colliding in the middle of the water.

Gareth Hall leant into the weeds and pointed his stick at his yacht. The commodore was watching him with a friendly smile, which was most unlike him. The commodore said, 'No mudlarking now,' which perhaps meant, 'You mustn't step into the weeds.' But Gareth did not need to step in; he simply gave his boat, *Atlanta*, a mighty shove with his cane, causing it to instantly speed away from danger. He did this as the commodore turned and trotted away. Had he seen what had happened? That Gareth Hall had 'pushed' rather than 'touched' the boat off? Gareth Hall, too, moved rapidly away from that incriminating corner of the pond, but not before he had given a guilty glance Monica's way. He knew she'd seen what he'd done.

He won the race and received the spoon in a little ceremony at the awards table. Most of the crowd cheered, but not the elegant, foreign-looking man, of course. Monica looked up at the pale blue, blameless sky as she called to mind the correct word for his expression: inscrutable.

She spent much of the remainder of the afternoon entangled with George Eliot's people, who gradually became realer than the boating crowd. Finally, the regatta ended with a volley of gunshots, and the attendees either drifted home or to the tea party at the commodore's place, depending on their importance.

Monica had been telling herself that she wouldn't try to attend the tea party, but now she was reconsidering that resolution. She actually walked in a little circle on the Heath as she tried to decide what to do. But she realised she was only pretending to be doubtful, and when she uncoiled herself from the circle, she walked directly to Millfield Lane and West Winds.

In the event, she didn't have to explain to anyone that she knew Kitty Hall, but just opened the gate and joined the throng. The tea party was pretty opulent, of course, but not as good as it should have been. It was held mainly on the lawn, which had evidently been dying for weeks in the heat. A churchy-looking woman played droning music on a harmonium. The cakes weren't as various as they first appeared and cream did not feature, presumably on account of the heat. The sandwiches had little flags in them, which was some sort of nautical joke, but they'd been too long in the sun, like all the guests, whose boats had been placed in the ornamental pond, alongside which was a small sign reading 'Marina', which was another semi-joke. A frog was crawling over them, trying to get into the water. People were saying tired, complacent things like, 'A noble tradition, a noble tradition . . . the commodore looking fighting fit as usual . . . competition keen as ever.' The 'life force' that people in books spoke of was represented at this place and time by only one person. Monica watched Gareth Hall helping himself to a glass of punch; you were supposed to wait to be served. Then she watched him doing various other arrogant things, like staring down at his left boot, which he twiddled while some man tried to interest him conversationally.

Harriet Beck was usually standing close by, of course, and not eating or drinking, probably for fear of looking indelicate. It struck Monica that, instead of her habitual two pigtails, she wore only one, a bit more flowing than usual, and trailing down to the side, which was a clever idea, since it stopped her head looking so very rectangular. 'Handsome' was the word for Harriet Beck, rather than 'pretty', and, of course, Gareth Hall would always require pretty girls and, quite soon, pretty women. He would be in the sixth form, Monica supposed, therefore on the brink of Oxford or Cambridge.

Whereas she was looking at him a good deal, he never looked at her. It was as though she had ceased to exist, but then she had hardly existed for him to begin with. He was no more likely to remember her than she was to remember a butterfly she'd seen on the Heath that afternoon. Or could it be that he did remember, and he was ignoring her deliberately because she had seen him cheat in the race? Monica removed the flag from a sandwich. You had to do that before you could eat them, obviously, and Monica began removing a good many flags, making herself feel less and less like the butterfly that had just crossed her mind. A couple of people came up to her to commiserate about the various disasters of her life, while obviously, by their furtive glances, trying to figure out who had accompanied her to the tea.

Every so often, Gareth Hall and Harriet Beck would converge as they moved around the garden. They spoke to each other perhaps more than they spoke to any third person, but Monica was pleased to see that it was always Gareth who broke off the conversations. Monica told herself that she didn't want Harriet Beck involved with Gareth because he would hurt her (possibly physically), but she knew very well there was a bit more to it than that.

It must have been about six o'clock when Monica saw Harriet's parents in the garden. Obviously, this would be 'curtains' for poor Harriet, whose father was continually looking at his watch despite being told not to do that by his wife. And now here came Harriet, dragging Gareth towards her parents for what was probably going to be both hello and goodbye at the same time. After Mr Beck and Gareth shook hands, Mr Beck began some dutiful enquiries about the prizewinning boat, and Gareth, clearly irritated, said, 'Not exactly. She's classified as a cutter – a gaff-rigged topsail cutter.'

Shortly after that, Harriet was trailing sadly behind her parents towards the gate. Monica did not attempt to say her own goodbye. That would come over as triumphant, for Harriet was being removed while Monica remained in the same hallowed location as Gareth . . . although he seemed, for the moment, to have disappeared. Monica did another lonely round of the garden and the conservatory, then she sat down on a chair more or less in the middle of the garden and read a bit more of *The Mill on the Floss*. She knew this was the height of rudeness, but then again, it was everybody else's fault for not coming to talk to her. After ten pages of George Eliot, she decided she had better be getting off to the Highgate tram stop for the glum descent to Holloway. She was about to rise from the chair when she felt a gentle touch on her shoulder. Her heart leapt. She turned around expecting to see Gareth, but it had indeed been a *gentle* touch, so, of course, it was not him but his sister, Kitty.

'I do wish *I* had the nerve to read a book at these dos,' she said, smiling.

'Where's Gareth?' said Monica, and Kitty frowned, probably wondering whether this was another helpless schoolgirl falling into his clutches.

But she answered casually enough. 'Not sure. Probably gone off to see his pals at the stink pipe.'

Ten minutes later, Monica was walking towards the junction where the stink pipe was located. 'I won't try to talk to him, of course,' she said to herself, 'because it'll be all boys there. But it'd be interesting to see from a safe distance what he's up to.' What she really wanted to do, she realised, was to make sure he was just as horrible, and just as attractive, as she had been thinking all afternoon.

Her route from Millfield Lane to Bishopswood Road (she had remembered one of the two names) could have taken her past the Highgate School chapel and its pretty powder-blue clock, which, *being* a clock, told the time. But she wanted to avoid the time, so she cut across the Heath to get there. The sky was just beginning to darken, and the lamps had just been lit; the evening air smelt of faded flowers.

On Bishopswood Road, the villas containing the school dorms, often guarded by massive cedar trees, were silent. It was the summer vacation, after all. There wouldn't be many boys available to convene at the stink pipe, but some of them, she knew, stayed all summer. When Bishopswood Road kinked, and the stink pipe came into view, Monica saw that there were only two boys. One of them was sitting on top of the pillar box adjacent to the pipe, king-of-the-castle like, and talking down to his companion. Both were smoking, and the one on the pillar box, of course, was Gareth. Both were as brightly illuminated by the pipe's lamp as if they'd been on stage. Its bright blue-ness put to shame the other street lamps, but it was extraordinarily ugly, and might have been created to show off the elegance of the ordinary lamps. It was like a prototype lamp; primitive, elephantine, and with a stooped look, because of the way a branch of the pipe was bent, as though weighed down by the great lantern that hung from it, like a flower too heavy for its stem. Monica was perhaps 150 yards away from this horrible object, and she and the two boys seemed to be the only people on Bishopswood Road. As she looked on, two exciting things happened. First, Gareth, from his high elevation, spotted her; second, the boy on the ground stamped out his cigarette and, looking up at Gareth, seemed to say, 'Toodle-oo, Jim' – which was perhaps Gareth Hall's nickname – and walked away. Monica noticed that Gareth, who had begun smiling a twisted smile when he spotted Monica, made no attempt to detain his friend. *Is it possible*, she wondered, *that he would rather speak to me?* He gestured that she should approach his high throne.

'What brings you here?' he asked, rudely.

Her heart was beating twice as fast as before she saw him.

'Just passing. I'm on my way home.'

Gareth blew out smoke.

'Funny way of getting from the Heath to Holloway,' he said.

The lamp seemed to seethe and shake.

'Is it wise to smoke so near that?' she said. 'There might be an explosion that would kill us both.' (*It would be an absolutely classic case*, she thought, *of 'death by misadventure'*.)

'You can always walk away, can't you?'

'That is what I'm just about to do,' she said.

He jumped down, stumbling slightly, and he touched her shoulder as he steadied himself.

'Sorry,' he said. 'Clumsy of me.'

'No harm done,' she said, a response she was very pleased with.

Gareth Hall had coloured up slightly. He threw down his cigarette and rubbed it out with his boot – this to 'cover his confusion', as the novelists tended to say.

'That other boy . . .' she said, indicating the direction in which that person had walked off.

'*Young man*, you mean,' said Gareth Hall.

'That other young man . . . called you Jim.'

'He did.'

'Why?'

'It's my name. I have quite a few. My family call me Gareth, which is actually my second name. My first is James.'

Here was an opportunity for Monica to say she liked either James or Gareth, but she couldn't decide which would be the most diplomatic.

'I have several names myself,' she said. 'I'm Monica Alice Phyllis.'

'Mmm . . . you've got the right one at the front.'

'You think Monica's a nice name?'

'I just said that, didn't I?'

'Not exactly.'

He was lighting another cigarette.

'Don't mind, do you?' he said, as he flicked away the match. Of course, he should have asked her in *advance*, but still.

She shook her head.

He said, 'You think I cheated, don't you?'

'Well . . .'

'Come on, Monica, out with it.'

'Well, you didn't *touch* your boat off. You *pushed* it off.'

He gave a snarly smile. 'I might touch you off in a minute.'

'I'd like to see you try.'

'I believe you would.'

'Did the commodore see what you were about?'

Gareth Hall shrugged. 'He wanted me to win, anyhow.'

'Why?'

'It's not because he likes me, I'll tell you that. It's because he *doesn't* like the fellow I was up against.'

'The tall, well-dressed one.'

'He's certainly tall,' Gareth said. 'He dresses like a cad if you ask me. He's called Thomas Durand. Name mean anything to you?'

'No.'

'Of the Durand banking family. He's bloody French. Do you suppose he built his yacht himself?'

'I suppose not,' said Monica.

'Do you know who built mine?'

'Jack Linton.'

'He helped a bit, but I designed it, and I rigged it. Total cost about a pound. Guess how much Durand's cost?'

'Three pounds,' she said.

'*Ten.* You could very nearly buy a full-sized yacht for that. He's the champion model yacht racer in London, although he does nothing but turn up at the races. He has an entire team to help him – a sort of crew. His old man drives him to all the regattas in the family car. It's a Mercedes – yellow. Did you not see it on Millfield Lane?'

'If I did, I didn't notice it.'

'You're a clever girl. If you'd seen it, you would have noticed it. I'll tell you this for nothing: the commodore noticed it, and he's sick of the sight of that car.'

A silence fell – and there were not many people who could silence Monica.

'You live on the Holloway Road,' said Gareth Hall, 'but I think you once lived in a big house in Hampstead, near Harriet.'

'Your data is correct.'

'Here's another fact. Your uncle's the one who went under the Highgate tram. Do you know why?'

'What do you mean, "why"? It was an accident.'

He looked at her, smoking thoughtfully, apparently revolving a number of possible remarks.

'Have it your way,' he said, eventually, and she was grateful to him for only skirting reality, not quite broaching it. 'You're quite nicely dressed,' he continued, 'but you've come down in the world and, naturally, you're resentful. You probably think I'm rich. It's true, I'm at an expensive school, but I'm on a scholarship. It annoys me when people make that mistake about me.'

'Maybe they wouldn't if you were less arrogant.'

'A reasonable point. Now – enough talking,' and he pitched away his cigarette. 'Would you care for a kiss?'

Monica did, very much, but surely she ought to refuse?

Monica looked up at the stink pipe. It seemed big-headed, like Gareth Hall.

'I take it the answer's "no"?' said Gareth Hall.

From somewhere in the greenish gloom, beyond the lamp's halo, came the sound of a horse's clip-clop accompanied by trundling wheels. That sound stopped. There came next the clump of a carriage door, then a relentlessly swishing skirt.

'Here comes fun,' said Gareth Hall.

As Monica turned to see Driscoll, the words formed in her head: *This is the worst moment of my life.*

'You are to come home this instant!' Driscoll yelled.

She was as heavily loaded with flowers as any porter at Covent Garden Market, and they were all on her head. Monica had hoped never to see this vile hat again. Driscoll had recently acquired a new, slightly less absurd, summer hat with a rolled brim, which therefore had room for only a small quantity of waxen roses, whereas there must have been twenty around the brim of this present one. They were worn in honour of her name, which was Rose: Rose Driscoll. People were meant to say, 'A rose by name and a rose by nature' or, 'A rose by any other name . . .' Things like that.

'You are to come home this instant!' she said again, in more of a shriek this time. 'Do you hear me?'

Gareth Hall seemed to be staring at Driscoll with something between horror and fascination. Perhaps he was counting the roses. 'Off you go,' he said to Monica, smiling his dangerous smile. Monica decided it would be best to say nothing. It would be unbecoming to begin a row with Driscoll, or a physical fight, within earshot of Gareth Hall.

As she rolled back to Holloway in the cab with Driscoll, however, Monica said three things.

When they had regained Hampstead Lane and were approaching the school chapel (which showed the time to be half past eight), she said, 'How can I go home when I don't *have* a home?' As they began descending Highgate Hill (just as they were passing Mr Farmery's office), she said, 'Your hat is absolutely ridiculous!' and when the cab broached Holloway Road, she screamed, 'I *hate* you!' The peculiar thing was that Driscoll may not even have heard that last one, what with the rattling of the cab, and her anxiety about paying cabmen having resurfaced, causing her to begin counting and recounting a quantity of increasingly sweaty coins.

But she probably *had* heard it.

Nothing further was said between them that evening, or indeed the next day, the Sunday, almost the entirety of which Monica spent in her bedroom. The inquest did not come until the Tuesday, when Ethel returned after her two days off. It appeared that seven, not eight, had been the time specified by Driscoll for their return, and Driscoll did not agree that there was any room for doubt. Eight o'clock *had* been mentioned when she was making the arrangement with Monica, but only as the time at which she was definitely not to stay out *until*.

'Even if you assumed it was eight o'clock, though,' Driscoll said, 'you were making no attempt to return at that time. When I saw you with that boy, it was already gone eight.'

'I lost track of the time,' said Monica. 'Perhaps I will save up my pocket money for a watch. I should have enough after about five years.'

'If you had a watch, I don't believe you'd look at it, except to admire its prettiness.'

'I doubt it would *be* very pretty, on what I could afford. I would have got away from that boy sooner, but he was being rude about Leo, and I wanted to stick up for him.'

'What did he say about your uncle?' said Driscoll, but then she immediately negated herself. 'Never mind.'

Ethel, who had waited until quarter past eight under the railway bridge, was not in so much trouble as Monica, about which Monica was glad. Ethel had not been party to the making of the arrangement – the curfew hour had merely been relayed to her by Monica – but she was on the hook to the extent that she ought to have been accompanying Monica at all times. Monica, realising that Ethel would not be able to invent an excuse even if she were morally inclined to do so (which she was not), said, 'We became separated at the end of the regatta. There was such a crowd,' and Ethel did at least have the wit to keep silence on that point. There had then been the grudging apology from Monica, which Driscoll accepted by offering her cheek for a kiss.

She said, 'We will put that behind us, and progress to other things – in particular, Venice. I'm going to make you some light dresses. I think four. I'll need to send off to Butterick's for the patterns this week. Shall we look at the catalogue together?'

'I suppose so,' said Monica. 'I mean, yes.'

But Monica believed there could never be any true reconciliation between them, and she believed that Driscoll thought so, too.

★

Three weeks after the regatta, Driscoll went to the gymnasium on a Monday evening. That being one of Ethel's nights off, Monica was left alone in the flat – quite a rare event at that point. It had apparently not occurred to Driscoll that Monica would go out – to the extent that she didn't tell her not to do it. But Monica had to escape the flat. The sun had been boiling all day. At noon, Driscoll had walked over to the window in despair at Monica's failure to comprehend basic arithmetic.

'Writing "QED" after a guessed answer doesn't make it any more plausible, you know,' she said, as she pulled back the lace curtain to see a workman and a more smartly dressed official examining the Road, while a policeman diverted the traffic. 'I think the macadam is melting,' she said, sadly.

Driscoll had gone to the gymnasium at six. At half past, Monica took the tram up to Highgate. It was the wrong thing to do, she knew, and for about a hundred reasons. On the way up, a row broke out on the tram between the inspector from the tram company and the driver, who the inspector accused of running late. Monica was on the side of the driver. She didn't see why the tram company *needed* an inspector. He was only there to split on his comrades, and Monica hated splitters. Finally, a calm, pipe-smoking passenger had to intervene: 'It's the end of a long day, and we're all very hot and bothered, I'm sure.'

It was a bad omen.

From Highgate, Monica walked onto the Heath, albeit avoiding the ponds. As she was walking through some trees near Kenwood, a man was lighting lamps she'd never previously noticed. Monica felt very blue, which was her new word for 'sad'. The rejection from the Eastbourne school had come through. It was not a very brainy sort of school; if she couldn't get in there, where could she get in? Of course, there had been a 'splitter' in that case, too, but Monica had certainly failed the tests. Obviously, heaps of stupid girls did go to school; it was just a question of paying a lot of money. But Driscoll had had two meetings with Mr Farmery recently, so perhaps something was amiss on the financial side of things.

Monica walked past a mother and child. The mother was saying, 'It's getting dark now, so stick close together.' Monica was tempted to stay on the Heath until midnight. That would bring matters with Driscoll to what was known as the 'crisis point', so that she might end up being handed over to Mr Farmery. Monica had begun writing a letter to Mr Farmery, asking for that to happen, but she probably would never post it.

Coming to Hampstead Lane, where the Heath ended, she turned right, the direction for Highgate, and this time she did look at the chapel clock. It was only eight. Driscoll was never back from the 'gym' until ten.

Monica decided to turn left, rather than proceeding straight on to Highgate Hill and the tram stop. She came to Archway Road, east of Highgate. It was nothing like as quaint as

Highgate, consisting of rows of tall, thin, red-brick buildings with shops on the ground floor and flats above, and these were called parades – a depressing word. The shops were all closed but still illuminated in the warm blue gloom. Further down, towards Holloway, Archway Road began to run in a dark groove between high stone banks, and the great iron bridge traversed it, carrying Hornsey Lane over. At present, nobody was jumping off it. The only thing occurring was the rumble and roar of the traffic.

She walked further east again, on to Muswell Hill Road, which boasted woods on either side: Queen's Wood and Highgate Wood. You'd have expected Highgate Wood to be the more select, Highgate being a top-drawer sort of place, but Queen's Wood was the one preferred by naturalists. Monica had paused on Muswell Hill Road to think of that last word, and as she did so, she heard the ringing of the keeper's bell in Queen's Wood, and the cry of, 'All out! All out!' So she wandered into Highgate Wood, which remained open. Highgate Wood was too thinly planted, the local naturalists would complain, and there weren't enough wildflowers, berried trees or birds. It did have a well-known drinking fountain, though. When he had first arrived in Highgate, about twenty years ago, Leo had been involved with the do-gooders who had raised the money for the drinking fountain, and they had settled on an inscription:

Drink, Pilgrim, here; Here rest! and if thy heart
Be innocent, here too shalt thou refresh

The words were from a poem by Coleridge, who had lived in Highgate. Leo had been recruited onto the committee by his friend Arthur Housman.

Highgate Wood being a little on the sparse side, you were aware of the people still left in it towards closing time, and there weren't many – probably a number in single figures and decreasing by the minute. Monica was heading away from the gates and into the middle of the trees when she saw Gareth Hall. Her heart pounded as their eyes met. She had often thought of Gareth Hall – usually at night, for he belonged in the night. She had known they would meet again, and, of course, there would be trouble, but they would keep meeting and each time the trouble would be less, and they would gravitate towards each other, like Jane Eyre and Mr Rochester.

But it was immediately clear that there would be no gravitation in reality, only trouble, for Gareth Hall was with a pretty woman.

She was certainly a woman rather than a girl. Her skirt was pleated with expensive complications, and the hem was high, revealing rather muddy button boots; they were of good quality, though. Monica wanted to tell her to pull her clothes down, just as Driscoll told Monica when her own skirts rode up. She and Gareth Hall were sitting on a fallen tree trunk, and they looked so evil to Monica that she might have believed the woman if she told Monica they had just pushed the tree over. Gareth Hall, naturally, was sitting on the higher part of the fallen tree, and the woman was plucking the berries off a purple flower, probably a privet. She seemed to have yanked a whole branch off some poor hedge, and now she was destroying it further. She was staring insolently at Monica, while Gareth Hall smiled his bitter smile.

Monica said, 'Hello, Gareth.'

'Do you know this person?' said the woman, and Monica was thrilled to see that she hated the idea.

The agitation of anger was overcoming Monica. She wanted to move about, and she realised she was kicking mud with her boot heel.

'It's the Holloway girl,' he said.

'My name is Monica,' said Monica, 'as you know perfectly well.'

'Shouldn't you be at home in bed, Monica?' said the woman, before turning to her beau. '*How* are you acquainted, Gareth?'

'Oh, I witnessed a rather rowdy scene between her and her guardian. A good deal of shouting in the street. Pretty embarrassing for all concerned.'

Monica said, 'Have you touched off any more cutters recently, Gareth?'

'What *is* she on about?' said the woman, whose voice just then combined slang with refined pronunciation – the worst of both worlds, therefore.

Monica said, 'Gareth and I share a secret, don't we, Gareth?' She would keep saying his name, to shame him for not saying hers.

'Nothing of the sort,' said Gareth, and, of course, he had to use distraction tactics now, to prevent the woman from getting 'the wrong idea'. 'You might recognise her,' he said, indicating Monica to his companion. 'She used to live in Highgate. Her father was the one who went under the tram.'

'He was *not* my father; he was my uncle.'

'Yes. Sorry. He went under the tram, at any rate.'

But the distraction hadn't worked. The woman was frowning at Gareth – a menacing, questioning look – and he jumped down from his high position (just as he had jumped down from the top of the pillar box), not being confident enough, in the present adverse circumstances, to maintain it.

'And do you know why he went under the tram?' he said.

Because, of course, he must 'up the ante' in search of the distraction.

Monica, kicking the mud more fiercely, said, 'It was an *accident*.'

Gareth Hall shook his head. 'It was suicide. And if you don't know why, I'm not going to tell you.'

Monica had been looking down as she kicked the ground, but now she faced Gareth Hall. 'You obviously *are* going to tell me, or else you wouldn't have said you weren't. Anyhow, I would be interested to know what you think.'

'I think you would be upset.'

'I'm not easily upset.'

'I believe you are, so I'm not going to tell you what your uncle was. Personally, I don't mind. Live and let live, I say, but it's illegal, and he was in bother with the law . . .'

Monica had never felt so exposed to words as weapons. It was perfectly clear that Gareth Hall was going to tell her everything about the world that she didn't want to know. She must escape him before he did so.

She turned on her heel and walked away fast towards the exit from the woods, but she was not quick enough to avoid hearing the continuation of Hall's speech: 'Her uncle's the . . . who was being had up by the coppers. So he went and threw himself under the tram.' Monica wasn't certain of the word she'd missed hearing, but she knew its meaning, and she would never forgive Gareth Hall for uttering it.

As Monica approached the exit, there was late movement in the wood. The bell was ringing at the gate, and the shout of 'All out!' was going up from the keeper or his deputy. Monica swerved away from the exit; she must keep walking, fast and quietly, through the trees. Emerging from a thicket some minutes later, she saw that Gareth Hall had ignored the shouts, for he was a little deeper into the woods than before – and about to take a drink from the fountain. He was probably on the point of leaving, and his companion seemed to have already done so, for she was nowhere in sight, but, being thirsty, Gareth would help himself, as he always did. The inscription on the fountain said, 'if thy heart be innocent', and he wasn't, so he was not entitled. It – the water fountain – looked somewhat like a tombstone, and perhaps that's what gave Monica the idea of making something really bad happen to him there, whether for Leo's sake or her own. Also, the relative stillness of Gareth Hall, as he stooped, lapping from the spout, seemed to demand some correction, so she charged towards him from the rear. Under the force of her shove, he clashed his head against the brass tap and the granite. He went down, onto the hard mud, seeming to twist and look at the sky with a lost expression as he fell, and you could see that he was just a schoolboy, really, which was why he went in for model boating. Monica's energy was not quite spent, and she was pacing – almost prancing, really – around the prostrate form of Hall, watching him, waiting for him to stir, at which moment she would run for the exit. But he was not stirring.

Down in Holloway, Driscoll had a glum little pamphlet: *What to Do in Emergencies*. Monica would flick through it when bored; words from its pages now came to her. Gareth Hall was surely 'unconscious' . . . 'insensible' . . . and sometimes in those types of emergencies there was nothing to be done, for an injury to the brain might have been sustained. On the other hand, he might simply be 'stunned'. Monica had retreated into the trees; she now advanced a little way back towards Gareth Hall, deliberately making a noise by stepping on dry, dead leaves. He did not stir.

She cleared her throat, a ridiculously genteel way of announcing oneself in the present circumstances. No response from Gareth Hall, who lay on his side, so that she could see half his face, and not only was it very white (as Monica knew her own must be just then), there was also a sheen of sweat on it. 'Clammy' – that was a word from *What to Do in Emergencies*, and it was, Monica seemed to recollect, one of the warning signs of brain injury. She caught up a twig, pitched it experimentally towards Gareth Hall, but it fell short with barely a sound, and so, naturally, it had made no difference. She picked up another and threw it harder. The moment it left her hand, she knew it was going to be on target, and so this would be the moment of truth. It landed squarely on Gareth Hall's shoulder, where it remained, rising and falling slightly – so he was breathing, albeit shallowly. She ought to go over and loosen his necktie, perhaps?

There came an impatient clatter of the keeper's bell. Five woodland tracks intersected at the fountain. *Choose the wrong one*, Monica thought, *and you'll end up face to face with the keeper.* She chose a track; it gave her a clear run to the main gate.

On the tram back to Holloway, Monica dropped asleep, as she often did when 'under stress'. She arrived back at the flat before Driscoll and went immediately to bed. In the morning, she found a cup of cold cocoa by her bed, presumably a confused peace offering from Driscoll, who had noticed that Monica had not eaten any supper.

All that day, Monica stayed in bed. She said she had a headache, which was true enough, and it arose from the great tangle of her thoughts. Had she killed him? Would the police come knocking on the door at any minute? She didn't want to have killed Gareth Hall, partly for his sake, and partly for hers – a confusion that added to the headache. If she *had* killed him, it was his fault, because of what he had said, as she would be explaining to the police, but then again, *she* was at fault – not so much for what she'd done as for having no control over herself. That was the truly shocking thing. And the noise from beyond the window of the infernal Road made everything worse.

In the late afternoon, there came a great hammering on the front door. It was as if the Road itself had come knocking, and Monica said, 'Of course, it's the police and it's for the best. At least I will be taken away from here.' But it was the milkman wanting, perfectly cheerfully, to be paid. He always came in the afternoon, liberated from his cart, to collect his money.

At what must have been about midnight, Monica was woken by another knock. She heard Driscoll walk downstairs to answer, and Monica could make out the voice of the caller. He sounded different, but it was obviously Gareth Hall. He said he was sorry to bother Driscoll; he then explained at length how he'd discovered the address. Monica could tell what he was saying, even though she couldn't quite hear the words. It was perhaps not necessary for him to explain at such length about his finding the address, but the longer his explanation of such an ordinary thing continued, the less of a worry he became. Finally, he said what Monica had been longing to hear, and these words came floating clearly up the stairs in a much more musical version of his previously rather bitter and snide voice: 'Tell Monica I am very sorry for what I said.' Monica turned over in her bed and went contentedly back to sleep.

In the morning, she was somewhat confused about the events of the night, but she was certain that Gareth Hall had paid a late visit. She walked into the kitchen, where Driscoll was buttering bread while reading *The Times*, and Ethel was washing up.

'There was a boy in the flat last night,' said Monica.

Ethel froze at the sink.

'There certainly was *not*,' said Driscoll. 'You have been dreaming, Monica,' and she turned a page of the paper.

Ethel resumed her washing up.

On the evening of the day after *that*, Monica found herself looking warily – from halfway across the living room – at a copy of the *Hampstead & Highgate Express*, which graciously spread the news from those glamorous locations to humbler spots such as Archway, Holloway and Islington. Driscoll bought this paper every week, from Baxter, the newsagent up at Nag's Head, where she also bought *The Times*, quite early every weekday morning. Her morning routine was to pass on the day-old *Times* to an old lady who lived three doors down, who consequently lived in the past, before heading off in the opposite direction to buy the new one from Baxter. So *The Times* never persisted in the flat, unlike the *Hampstead & Highgate Express*. When Driscoll had finished with this, she put it on the hearth, in the fire basket with the kindling, and that's where it lay now. If the outrage suffered by Gareth Hall were to be written up in any newspaper, this would be the one – and Monica knew the very page where it would be: the one towards the middle where bits of something-or-nothing, but usually *grim*, news (sometimes labelled 'Stop Press') jostled for space with advertisements, some of which made regular appearances, such as the one for Marcella Cigars: 'The Cigar That Stands Alone', and there was always a picture of one of those smokables standing upright like a rocket. Why the Marcella people wanted their cigars mentioned on a page mainly devoted to news of factory fires, windows broken in railway carriages and motor smashes on the Holloway Road, Monica could not imagine.

Dare she look at that page for news of Gareth Hall? It was not yet the fire-lighting season, but all day the rain had been falling heavily on the dark Road, increasing the fury of the traffic. Driscoll and Ethel had been out in it, and now Driscoll wanted some of their clothes dried, and others aired. Monica had been set the task of lighting the fire – one of the few household chores she enjoyed. She began dismembering the paper, reserving the important page. Once the fire was lit, its cheerful glow (which almost redeemed the horrible flat) emboldened Monica to read the page. Her heart was already racing as she scanned the columns; it was fairly pounding as she came to:

UNPROVOKED ASSAULT

A police investigation has commenced into an incident occurring on Monday in Highgate Woods. James Gareth Hall, a pupil at Highgate School, was refreshing himself from the drinking fountain at about closing time when he was violently pushed from behind, clashing his face against the stone of the fountain. Hall, aged seventeen, was found unconscious by Mr Saul Hudson, deputy keeper of the Woods. An ambulance was summoned, and Hall is presently in the Royal Northern Hospital. He is not expected to . . .

To continue reading, it was necessary to go to the top of the next column. The upright cigar pointed the way, but Monica couldn't bear to discover what was not expected in the case of Gareth Hall. She crumpled the page and threw it onto the blaze.

The Lido

'Steamers leave the Schiavoni constantly for the Lido, returning every hour, and it is a very pleasant excursion on late summer evenings, and worth taking even for the beauty of the return to Venice, when all her lights are reflected in the still waters.'
From *Venice*, by Augustus J.C. Hare & St Clair Baddeley

There were two lessons to be learnt from that reflection, thought Monica, as the Lido dock came bouncing into view. The first was that she was capable of terrible actions, which suggested she had indeed killed Driscoll. The second was that she could take a dream for reality (she had been really convinced that Gareth Hall had visited the flat to apologise), which suggested she had *not* killed Driscoll.

Two more editions of the *Hampstead & Highgate Express* had been placed in the fire basket since she had read of her 'Unprovoked Assault', and there they would remain until the fire-lighting season. Monica had not dared consult them. It was curious (and not much to her credit) that while she'd had the courage to make the initial assault – for a certainty in the case of Hall and possibly in that of Driscoll – she did not have the nerve to discover the consequences. Well, it was the difference between rage and courage; she was at the mercy of her temper. It — together with her tendency to fluctuate between dream and reality — had led her into a perpetual uncertainty as to what she had brought about. It was high time she embraced reality.

The vaporetto roared up to the dockside, giving it a sideways kiss, in a flamboyant sort of way — quite the opposite of an apology to all the people aboard who thought they were off to Murano.

She dropped some coins in the box and stepped off the boat. There were no police to be seen. Probably, a veritable squadron of them awaited her at Murano, wherever that was. It was no easy matter confronting hard reality when you had such a faltering force as the Venice police after you. But then, it seemed that the London police were no better. They must have presumed it was a man who had attacked Gareth Hall, either some enemy of his — and surely there must be quite a number of those — or some passing ruffian. In North London, there was no shortage of those either, and it was not recommended that lone walkers enter Highgate Woods in the evening. Of course, Hall had been accompanied by that female, but she had quit the woods before Hall made for the fountain. What might be Hall's view of the matter, assuming he was capable of forming a view? That is to say, not dead or suffering the effects of some brain injury. She didn't believe he had seen her make her approach, and surely he would have assumed she had quit the woods, since she was going in that direction when he *had* last seen her. If he did suspect Monica, he might well not say so, out of shame at being the victim of a young girl.

Monica stood on the Lido dock, still lost in her reflections. Since reading the initial report, she had been capable of going for days without thinking about Gareth Hall. Of course, the sight of a drinking fountain would trigger recollections, and sometimes – depending on her mood – her conscience. She was sure that, if he really had died, the news would have been on the front page of the *Hampstead & Highgate Express*, and other papers besides. Word would somehow have got back to her that a star of Highgate School and the great regatta had come a cropper.

There was a map on a dockside noticeboard, and it confirmed that the Lido was a skimpy thing – a long, thin island. She limped as she started walking away from the dock, on account of her broken shoe. It was strange to see plodding horses and motor cars again, and normal, large shops selling large things like furniture. She walked up to a woman who was sitting on a café terrace. An English newspaper – the *Continental Daily Mail* – was folded on the table in front of her.

'Excuse me, which way is the sea?' Monica asked, because she had not been able to work out the direction from the map. 'The *other* sea, I mean.'

'Do you want the beach, dear?' the woman said.

'That's it,' said Monica, although she suddenly didn't know what she wanted, she was feeling so tired.

'It's that way, dear,' said the woman, indicating a side street. 'You'll start to smell the ozone after a minute or so, then just follow your nose!'

Monica thanked the woman. When, having walked away for half a minute, Monica glanced back, she saw that the woman was looking at her. There was a post office on the corner of the side street the woman had indicated. Monica thought of Driscoll's letter to Sarah Kelly. Should she go in and post it? No, she wouldn't be doing that – not before she'd read it.

She walked on. The air smelt of horse dung and heat; no ozone yet, whatever exactly that might be. (It was a fancy word for 'sea air', possibly.) She was on a road of large houses – villas, really – with large gardens full of colours you didn't get in England: mauves, flame-like reds, oranges. She sometimes saw families in the gardens, all dressed in white. These people must be on holiday all the time. The favourite activity here seemed to be to sit in a swinging garden seat with a white sun canopy overhead as you stared rather rudely at people walking by. Monica stared back as she limped along. She had given up trying to screen her face with her parasol, which, in its folded state – in tandem with her limp – must have looked like a walking stick to the garden people, who were no doubt all congratulating themselves on not being her.

Up ahead stood a row of giant buildings, all with their backs to the villas, for these giants were facing the sea. Two minutes later, she had reached the dusty junction of the villa road and the one on which the large buildings stood. They were hotels, of course: a whole parade of them running left and right of where Monica stood, but mainly to the left. They were proudly ship-like, as though about to breast the waves, with flags on their roofs. On the other side of the road was the beach and the sea, or rather, a series of barriers that half concealed the beach and the sea. Monica turned left, walking along the front and skirting these barriers, which had gates in them, guarded by rough-looking men in grubby sailor-suits and straw hats. The different parts of the beach obviously belonged to the different hotels. Monica paused to think of the word that described these hotels – not so much a word as a French phrase: *hôtels des bains*, that was it, bathing hotels, and they really were of disproportionate size: great castles, endeavouring to anchor the sliver of sand.

If you did penetrate the barrier, you were on a sandy boardwalk, then came the beach. Monica stopped at one of the gates for a proper look. The Lido beach, like the commodore's tea party, was not quite as good as it should have been. The sand was greyish, as indeed was the sea, which had what you might call wrinkles or ruffles on its surface rather than waves. The day was still hot, but the heat came through a white haze and had passed its peak. There were not as many people on the beach as she had expected.

A young man in a bathing suit was doing a headstand before a small audience of older people in beach chairs. A rather beautiful-looking woman – from a distance, anyway – was walking in the shallows, kicking up the water. She looked very dissatisfied. Monica admired her loose, red bathing dress. It would be worth learning to swim – properly, that is – for the sake of wearing one of those. Most people on the beach wore swimming things with white beach robes on top, and some did rather look as though they had wandered out of a sanatorium. A seller of what might have been pieces of cake wandered between them. Things were a little livelier on the sea. There were half a dozen little wooden boats, all blue and green, of a similar shape to the boats you make out of folded paper. Each was big enough for one person, but most had two or three, so they kept capsizing in the shallows to shouts of laughter. There was also a stray gondola on the sea, but if it was offering rides, there were no takers.

A ball rolled across the beach towards the boardwalk. A boy in a bathing costume with a sweater worn over the top came chasing after it. He seemed to be looking towards Monica as he said, with an American accent, 'You're not quite dressed for the beach.'

Monica was thinking of a reply (she had decided to be polite) when another girl, standing behind her on the road, seemed to answer for her. 'My things are in the cabana,' she said. *This girl looks quite like me*, Monica thought, for she was petite in a white dress and a boater. Of course, her shoes were intact – that was one difference.

The boy said to the girl, 'Where are your folks?' and the girl waved towards the hotel.

'Mother's relaxing on the terrace,' she said, 'in theory, anyway.'

So she was quite a clever girl.

'She thinks she has a touch of sunstroke,' she added.

'Good grief,' said the boy. 'What are the symptoms?'

'A bad temper seems to be the main one.'

'Come on,' he said.

And the girl ran onto the beach after the boy. It was as if Monica had not existed.

Now a new person came walking along the beach road: a man in a swimming costume with (unfortunately, since he was not very elegant) no bathrobe or sweater on top. He was holding a lighted cigarette and singing a song – something about 'I get lonesome'. Well, you could see why. He seemed cheerful enough, though, and he smiled when he saw Monica, which was quite encouraging, being proof that she did exist after all. Since 'lonesome' was an American word, it seemed possible this man was another 'Yank', but all she could say for certain was that he looked like a fish, in that he had a narrow, pale face with colourless hair, not much chin and bulging eyes, which were blue but not blue *enough*. She spoke to him partly to find out whether he was indeed American, and partly because she believed he found her attractive.

'Am I allowed on the beach here?' she said.

He looked at Monica, then peered along the road behind her, as if to discover who she was with.

'Oh, I should think so,' he said – and the 'Oh' had nearly been 'Och', so he was neither English nor American, but

Scottish. (There did seem to be a drastic shortage of *Italians* in Italy, Monica was thinking.)

'Anyone can just wander on?' Monica said.

The man took a draw on his cigarette. 'Aye, more or less.'

'Thanks.'

'That's quite all right. Can I offer any other assistance, my girl?'

Monica shook her head, and the man stepped onto the boardwalk, then the beach, which – now that she paid attention to it – seemed rather muddy at this point, with an ugly wooden fence or barrier trailing off into the water. There was a word for those things, but Monica couldn't think of it. She stepped onto the boardwalk and the word came to her: 'Groynes,' she said. The Scotsman, who'd been heading for the sea, stopped and turned around.

'Beg pardon?'

She decided to change the subject: 'If just anyone can walk on to it,' she said, 'this must be the worst bit of beach.'

'What a cynical young girl you are,' he said, and he obviously loved saying the word 'girl', which he pronounced 'girr-ul'.

She had not only arrested his walk to the sea; he was now coming back towards her. She regretted having engaged his interest, since he was too nearly naked. He ought at least to have a towel over his shoulder, and his legs were so bloodless and fishy as to have a hint of blue in them: varicose veins. Leo had had the same complaint, as he had admitted to Monica, in a rueful sort of way, on Brighton beach. He had traced the line of one of the offending veins, but they were somewhat disguised in his case, since even though Leo couldn't grow a beard, he had rather nice, hairy legs. The Scottish swimmer said, 'This bit of beach belongs to the Excelsior, but the beach manager is away home at four – so it's anybody's after that.'

The Excelsior must have been one of the hotels, presumably the great red, sunburnt-looking castle that overlooked them just now. 'The cabanas belong to the hotel, too,' said the man, indicating the row of huts on the landward side of the boardwalk. Some of them used the boardwalk as a kind of veranda, with beach chairs set out on the wood. The man exhaled smoke, watching Monica. But if she had been somewhat 'leading him on', she would be stopping now, since he really was quite repellent. She looked away from him until he resumed his walk towards the sea. When he was a few yards short of it, he threw his cigarette into the sand and ran towards the water in a silly way.

Monica wandered along the boardwalk. Some of the doors of the cabanas (each had double doors) were closed. Where the doors were open, families sat inside, usually reading around a table or – in one case – all staring silently out to sea. Every cabana held a kettle and tea-making things on a trestle table, and it seemed this kit came as standard. She arrived at one cabin where the doors were open but there was nobody inside. Its small kettle sat on a spirit stove, with a box of matches lying invitingly alongside. You could open letters with steam. People did it all the time in unsuitable stories. Monica entered the cabin and walked up to the copper kettle – a friendly-looking little thing. She picked it up; there was a weight of water in it, and it seemed to be winking at Monica and saying, 'Here's your opportunity!' She lit the spirit and set down the kettle. If anybody turned up, she would say she had mistaken this cabin for one belonging to a friend of hers. She would add, for good measure, that she was staying at the Excelsior.

The cabin smelt of wood oil and trapped sun. There was really very little in it, aside from the now-simmering kettle, and the tea things nearby. There was an empty bottle of champagne:

'Dry Élite,' said the label. A canvas bag on the floor held beach towels, possibly. She laid down her parasol, removed Driscoll's letter from the chatelaine bag and applied it to the steam. Yes, the flap was coming unstuck. She would say this had happened naturally, if anybody ever required to know. She glanced at the floor to see a shadow stretching from the doorway.

'What are you doing in here, my girl?'

It was the Scotsman again, and he was perfectly dry – seemingly hadn't been in the sea at all.

'Is it your cabin?' she said, withdrawing the letter from the steam.

'Whether it's mine or not is quite immaterial. It's certainly not your own cabin, and yet you are in here.'

'I suppose you think I might be a thief,' she said, returning the envelope to her bag.

'Och, I couldn't possibly say. But it's not beyond the realms of possibility.'

It was said the Scots spoke English better than the English. But this one so liked the sound of his own voice that he made a meal of every sentence.

'Yes, it is,' Monica said.

'Well now, it just happens there's a detective in the hotel. Perhaps we should go in and speak to him.'

'Why?' said Monica.

'So we can settle the question of what you're about, my girl.'

'I mean, why is there a detective in the hotel?'

She didn't believe in this detective.

'Because he is a *hotel* detective, my girl, and the security of all the guests and their belongings is his responsibility. I'm sure he will be interested indeed to hear why you have come in here.'

Interested indeed – what a windbag he was.

'I came in here to turn off this kettle,' she said.

'Now I believe you *did* come in here to do *something* with the gypsy – like make away with it, perhaps.'

On the face of it, this was a puzzling remark, but Monica took his meaning. About two years ago, a man who had a caravan like Mr Toad's had parked it on the edge of the Heath on the Highgate side, which was illegal. He had been sitting on the steps of the caravan while his tethered horse grazed on the Heath grass (also illegal) as Monica walked past. He had asked her if she fancied a cup of tea, and she had said, 'Yes,' because she did. He asked if she wanted to see inside the caravan, and she had said, 'I'll just have the tea, thanks.' She had been able to see inside the caravan from where she stood anyway. It was interesting but ugly – a lot of crude wooden furniture, painted relentlessly green. 'I'll just put the kettle to boil on the gypsy,' the man had said, so this was obviously a term for a sort of travelling stove. The man had made the tea, which they drank near the horse on the Heath. The tea was perfectly nice, and the man was charming, although when he spoke of his valet – 'My valet usually makes the tea for me' – she didn't believe him. When Monica returned to Pond Square, she told Leo about the man and his caravan – which was called *Wayfarer* (the name had been painted on the side) – and Leo said, 'Oh, yes, I saw him. He looks an oddball. I meant to warn you not to speak to him.' It was typical of Leo to warn her of danger after the danger had passed.

Monica was now associating the half-naked Scotsman with the caravan man: a dangerous person she ought to have been warned about.

'Why would I steal a kettle?' she said.

'Because you have-nea got one of your own.'

Obviously, it was her broken shoe that had made him say that.

The man was blocking the doorway, and Monica could no longer help noticing that a wrong bit of his body had rudely declared itself, like an uninvited guest.

'Now if you will kindly mind out of the way,' she said. 'My family will be getting worried about me.'

'And where are they?'

'In the Excelsior Hotel.'

He brought the two doors of the cabin to. He was shaking his head and smiling as he turned towards her. The twin doors behind him were not locked, but he was definitely barring her way. A distant clock commenced striking the hour, the chimes floating on the sea sound. It would be five o'clock or so; Monica didn't wait to hear the chimes to the end, but said, 'My family will be here very soon. They're coming for tea, you see. We always have it about this time.'

'Aye . . . well, it's teatime right enough.'

'Precisely. And there are quite a lot of *people* in my family, including some very large brothers.'

'I believe y'are a lettle bet crazy, lassie.'

His accent was becoming stronger, and he was shaking his head again, flatly denying the truth of her statements, but smiling at the same time. He began pushing aside the material of his costume, where it covered his right shoulder. 'Wee bet son born,' he seemed to say. It occurred to Monica that he was complaining of a sunburn, but there was no sign of any redness, just more of his very unsavoury whiteness. His costume was now a skimpier thing, reminiscent of the kind of asymmetrical leotard worn by a circus strongman, and the alteration going on down below was continuing. The next revelation would be the other shoulder, and then . . .

Monica contemplated screaming – there were plenty of people milling about outside to hear. Or she could make a dash for the doors, but she didn't see why she should be reduced to that indignity. Her fear was becoming anger – the kind that prompted her to act.

The man took another step towards her. He said, 'Let's have a lettle bet talk, you and I.'

He turned his i's sideways; they were recumbent. 'I *think*,' said Monica, taking care to pronounce the 'i' sound correctly, 'that you should be on your way,' and this was by way of a final warning, but the man gave no sign of moving, so she caught up the kettle and flung it at him.

But she had only flung it *towards* him, for he had sidestepped the water with no trouble.

'Messed!' he said, with satisfaction, as though this were the start of a game.

There came a blessed bang on the double doors, a rattle of the handle. 'Open up there!' A stranger speaking – an American one. 'This is our cabin. Who's inside?' Perhaps the speaker had first thought the doors were locked, hence the knock, but now he had pushed them open, revealing himself to be a handsome American father with his perfect-looking family arrayed behind him, all in soft, relaxed-looking holiday clothes.

The fish-like man was perhaps shamed by the beauty of the family; he certainly ought to have been. He quickly reversed his coquetry, restoring the costume to his shoulder. As he quit the cabin, which required him to push past the family in a most undignified manner, his voice was reduced to a mutter – something about having seen this young lassie trespassing in the cabins. He had perhaps taken this family for Monica's, even though they were quite obviously American. There were a lot of brothers in it, after all. Well, two, as against one girl, and they had all been staring at the Scotsman – and now that he had gone, it was Monica's turn to be stared at. She said, 'He's lying, obviously.'

That was perhaps not quite enough, so she added, 'I made a simple mistake.'

Clearly, the mother was the most intelligent one in the family, for she had fixed her gaze on Monica's broken shoe, and she continued to look at it as Monica limped off.

Monica turned away from the beach and walked back to the sandy road. The evening air was warm and changing colour, although electric lights in the hotel gardens were complicating the question of *what* colour. A pretty little tram approached. It was pinkish and light green, with a frilly effect around the roof (although it must not be forgotten that a similarly fanciful vehicle had been enough to kill Leo in Highgate). Monica was stationary by the tram lines; in a moment, she would have to move out of the way in order to board the tram, which would carry her back to the boat landing, since there was really no-where else for it to go. She would then take the boat back to St Mark's Square, where she would be arrested.

Her loathing of the fishy man and what he had done was not subsiding. What was a person like that doing in Venice? He had negated its magic spell. She held him personally responsible for the present greyness of the sea and sky. She was pondering, from a long list of possibilities, the single most hateful thing about the man. Was it that he had not believed she had a family? That was so unreasonable of him, given that the vast majority of young girls *did* have families, but that wasn't quite his worst offence.

Whereas Gareth Hall had sought to wound Monica by telling her things about the world that she already knew but didn't want to know, the revolting Scotsman had *embodied* those things. Men like him were interested in girls of Monica's age, and probably almost any girl of Monica's age would do. There-fore – unlike in the case of Gareth Hall – there was no question of any backhanded compliment being paid. She thought again of his fish-like pallor. There had almost been – the word slowly came to her – a *luminosity* about it. She also thought again of the development that had been occurring inside his swimming costume. She doubted the scene would ever pass from her mind; it would have a lasting effect on her. There ought to be some lasting effect on him. She had (she imagined) done permanent damage to Gareth Hall, and she had almost *liked* Gareth Hall, even if part of the liking was disliking.

The tram came on, tinkling a musical bell, perhaps the only means available to it of encouraging her to get out of the way, for she realised she had been repeatedly kicking the toe of her good shoe into the groove of the tramline. She stepped aside. The tram came to a halt, inviting her to board, but her con-tinuing agitation would not allow her to do anything so meek.

She spurned the tram and, as it moved on, she quickly re-crossed the road and surveyed the beach again, while pacing back and forth. The bathers had thinned out. There were small parties of people, widely spaced, and it was the talking phase of the evening, the swimming and boating phase being over. She saw the Scotsman almost immediately, and he betrayed no sign of shame or remorse at his recent actions. He was speaking to a woman who wore a long loose robe: a comfortable-looking person – unexpectedly jolly-looking, and laughing with the man in such a way that made Monica hate her even more than she hated the man. She must be extremely misguided to be so cheerful in that man's company. She must, in point of fact, be a halfwit. And now she was going so far as to touch the man's flesh: only some light touches on his arm, but signifying affection nonetheless – and signifying also goodbye, for they were now parting. Monica did not care where the woman went. With luck, she would take a late swim and drown, the lifeguards having all abandoned their posts, leaving behind the unnaturally tall stepladders on the beach, from which they had surveyed the waves.

Monica watched the man as he returned to the line of cabins and began walking jauntily along it. He entered the very last one, and he did so with a certain air . . . The word came to Monica: proprietorial. It was *his* cabin. Monica realised that she hated to see people who belonged anywhere, and this man belonged at the Lido. Monica belonged nowhere, except perhaps in gaol. Well, she had nothing to lose – might as well be hanged for a goat as a sheep, or whatever was the arrangement of animals in that expression.

She commenced to walk for a second time along the line of cabins. Most of the doors were closed. She pushed at one with doors ajar, and there was a lonely-looking woman drinking tea, her kettle on the table behind her. Monica made a very sweet apology (she thought) and walked on. After a few more tentative proddings, she found an unoccupied cabin. Unlike the one she had entered to steam open the letter, this one was very happily cluttered with holiday goods: fishing nets; a canoe propped upright, like a strange wardrobe; a half-finished painting on an easel – at least, she hoped for the sake of the painter that it was half finished. It showed an extremely horizontal scene: flat beach, flat sea, with rudimentary people dotted about, like notes on a musical stave. Behind the easel stood the usual trestle table, kettle and spirit stove with a box of matches alongside. It was a large box of matches, decorated with a flame that had a smiling human face. There was no water in the kettle, but a bottle of mineral water stood adjacent. Monica filled the kettle and lit the spirit. As the kettle boiled, she removed both her broken shoe and the good one so that she might run. She tied the laces together and put the shoes around her neck. Her stockinged feet on the wooden boards felt very free and ready for fast action.

The kettle came to the boil, as kettles will do.

Picking it up, she walked lightly along the rougher wood of the platform in front of the cabins. Pushing open the double doors of the end cabin, she was confronted with an appalling sight. The man's tendency towards nakedness had been fulfilled. He lay on his stomach on a day bed, smoking a cigarette and reading a newspaper. It was incumbent on her to nullify this terrible vision as soon as possible. Why, it was practically a public duty, given that strangers passing the open door might also be exposed to it. She removed the kettle lid entirely and threw it with a pushing action, in hopes that the water would hit him first, with the hot kettle following through as a kind of grace note. Her hopes were more or less fulfilled, and she was already walking away fast as he screamed; then she began to run, giving a little skip of joy and dropping the kettle lid (for which she had no further use) as the second scream came. 'It's lucky for him,' she said, running, 'that he was lying on his front.' She was quite convinced that shame would prevent the man from complaining to the police.

Monica slowed when she regained the road; another amiable-looking tram was approaching. 'And he was such a baby,' she said, as the tram – obviously not minding that she had spurned its predecessor – obligingly stopped for her. 'At least half the water missed him entirely.'

The tram further demonstrated its good nature, in that no conductor troubled Monica for a fare. She felt truly blessed; it was as though she'd had the opportunity to go back in time to rectify her earlier mistake. When she reached the boat landing, she put her shoes back on. She had left her parasol, she realised, in the first beach cabin, but that was probably just as well, and she would have to take further steps to differentiate herself from the person described in the circulating police paper. Removing her hat, she placed it on a vacant bench. 'Goodbye, sailor hat,' she said, and she walked on swiftly to the vaporetto dock, for it wouldn't do to stay on the Lido.

She would go wherever this boat waiting at the dock took her. She did not trouble to discover its destination, but just marched straight towards it, and the milling crowd on the dock parted to let her do so. Of course, they all stared – and from a safe distance, in case whatever ailed Monica might be catching. Her lower stockings were quite filthy, and now she was hatless into the bargain. She had retained the chatelaine bag, however, and Charlotte within it. When she sat down on the boat, she placed Charlotte on her lap. With a slightly shaking voice, she said, 'It's been a long day, my dear, but it'll soon be over, and whatever happens, you'll be with me.' For a long time, though, the boat didn't go anywhere, but simply growled away, belching smoke, while tethered to the dock, along which – she now saw – ran telephone wires. The boat was obviously being 'held'. Trains would also be held, and eventually, if they were held for long enough, the passengers would be told why. A man would come stomping along the corridor, shouting about signals or a broken rail up ahead. But since this boat was surely being held to await the arrival of the police, the reason would not be declared, in case Monica ran away.

In light of all these depressing thoughts, Monica was quite surprised to see the deckhand untie the ropes. Soon, the boat was bounding over the sea, which now really began to *smell* like the sea, and it had regained the line of poles, which meant she was heading once again (it was inevitable, really) for Venice proper and St Mark's Square. There were lanterns on some of the poles, not yet illuminated, but they would be soon. There must be some seagoing version of a lamplighter who would come along and do it. Others had become perches for great grey seabirds that looked anywhere but at the smoking, speeding boat.

The Letter

'This First-Class Establishment enjoys the reputation of being one of the Best-Kept Houses on the Continent. It has been entirely refitted and is now replete with all modern comforts.'
Advertisement for the Hotel Danieli, in *Venice*, by Augustus J.C. Hare & St Clair Baddeley

As Monica disembarked at Venice, there were no police. The colours of the day had been decaying further on the lagoon, with pink and violet creeping into the picture. In the vicinity of St Mark's, the change was being noted by a mass ringing of bells. Crowds flowed along the dockside, better dressed than earlier in the day – fewer parasols among the ladies, more canes and stiffer hats among the men. Everyone was heading to drinks, dances, saloons and salons. What was required at this time of day was that you had somewhere to go, and when Monica saw the fantastical pink building with windows in the shape of bishops' hats and thin white letters running across the façade reading 'DANIELI', she knew she, too, had a place to go.

She entered what she supposed was called the lobby, which glowed orange and pink, and had gracious violin music playing. An old-fashioned staircase ran up the walls; there were also galleries, so it was all quite theatrical. The lobby was hot and smelt strongly of flowers. Monica always had to be very careful of that combination, but this was a heavenly place that Humphrey De Silva had found for himself. He couldn't *see* it, of course, but he could perhaps imagine it based on the music from the small orchestra. People moved up and down the staircase, as though to demonstrate its properties. The light was the colour of candlelight, but it was all by electricity. Fans twirled in a relaxed manner. Monica knew very well that the doorman who'd stepped aside to admit her was staring at her, probably contemplating her removal. At the reception, by contrast, she was being deliberately ignored. But, eventually, she was able to put to them the question: 'Is Mr De Silva in?'

A second clerk leant over and whispered to the first a few words that included 'De Silva'. 'My friend,' said the first man, 'informs me that Mr De Silva has gone out for the evening.'

The clerk was looking over Monica's right shoulder, clearly confident that something was about to happen, and Monica turned to see the advancing doorman. It was getting to the point where her presence wouldn't be tolerated anywhere in this city. She quit the hotel without waiting to be told. She turned right and right again into St Mark's Square, where the lamps glowed very prettily but sadly.

She stared over the water, where a haze of small birds moved back and forth above the mysterious factories of the island called Giudecca. She saw no fewer than eight gondoliers, rowing a giant gondola somewhat resembling a galleon in a children's storybook, and they were heading into the path of a steamboat. They'd better get a move on. It might be a sort of training exercise, or a gondoliers' social club, for what else would a gondolier like to do at the end of the working day than some more gondoliering, only this time with his colleagues? Perhaps they were all singing in unison; if so, the bells of the city were drowning them out.

Monica was beginning to be slightly cold. If Driscoll were here, a flouncy shawl would be produced. She looked up at the Campanile, with its crown of scaffolding, sticking out in all directions, rather like Jesus's crown of thorns. It was probably not yet contributing to the mass ringing of bells. What a terrific ceremony the Venetians would lay on when the bells were brought to the tower. They would come by boat, no doubt, from some island specially dedicated to the making of bells, a crazy sort of place where new-made bells were ringing incessantly, to test them out, and the citizens all wore ear defenders made of sea stones.

The sophisticated evening phase had begun at Florian. Everybody had wine on the tables before them, not coffee. The women tended to be touching their hair, having removed their hats, while leaning towards their men. They all seemed to be conspiring about different things, but, of course, they were all conspiring about the *same* thing. In most cases, the waiter attending any given table was handsomer than the man sitting at the table. She assumed most of the women had noticed that, but had determined to ignore the fact and make the most of a bad job. Either way, this was where children began. Monica thought of Hampstead in the evening: the lights at the high nursery windows all blazing like so many lighthouses – guaranteeing the continuation of civilisation. She thought of Driscoll, and Driscoll's monthlies. A little machine working away to no purpose; a machine that could – for a few years, until the clockwork wound down – make a child if a man came along, but no man ever had done, and probably never would, even if Driscoll were still alive. Monica took in the whole of the Florian terrace, looking from left to right, as she had done at one o'clock. But no woman sat alone.

She crossed the piazza in a crowd of pigeons. Couldn't doves have been arranged? She returned to the stone bench, the exact place in which she had dreamt of the Eastbourne school. She sat down heavily, removed the envelope from the chatelaine bag, took Driscoll's letter from the envelope.

She began to read . . .

My dear Sarah,

Thank you so much for your latest. I wanted to reply immediately, which is why I am writing this on the train between Paris and Venice – which, in turn, is why my handwriting might appear even more lamentably spider-ish than usual! I must set one little matter straight as soon as possible. Please disregard <u>immediately</u> my morbid fantasies about the Archway Bridge because that is all they are – fantasies. As long as I have your dear sister for weekly guidance sessions (at which badminton also happens to be played), I will not be resorting to panic measures. There is a much more sensible way out of the predicament in which I find myself. I could simply resign my guardianship of the girl. It is a job, after all (or at least, that is what it has become), and not the kind of job that anyone can hold you to, least of all that perfectly reasonable, if, in my view, somewhat weak-minded, lawyer, Mr George Farmery.

This would be a drastic course, certainly, and I would probably not be able to afford to keep on the flat, but I am inclined to give it up in any case. The girl obviously hates it (she is like a house agent in reverse, pointing out all its defects on a regular basis) and her jaundiced opinion has begun to 'rub off' on me. It <u>is</u> too noisy; it has become a prison for both of us, anyhow.

It is not, of course, the financial consideration that has prevented me from resigning so far, but my feeling of obligation towards the girl. But you will have spotted the weasel word in that sentence, dear. It is the word 'obligation'. There ought to be something more than that between the child and me; there ought to be some measure of affection, and I fear there is precious little of that.

Earlier today, she made a hateful remark about me to a French railway attendant. She appears to think I am over-reliant on the occasional glass of wine. Well, she has divined correctly; she is a highly intelligent person, after all, but I wonder whether she has the wisdom to make a further divination: that my disposition towards the occasional glass, which (do not be alarmed, dear!) amounts to no more than about a bottle and a half a week, is entirely on her account; and does she make the further intellectual leap of connecting my small weakness here with the rather larger one of her previous guardian and looking for the common denominator?

She also appears to find my attempt to draw up a programme for our Venice stay highly amusing. If she knew the nerve-strain this trip has imposed upon me, she might think twice (although I doubt it). 'See Venice and die,' somebody said. I am beginning to understand the conjunction, and I haven't even got there yet! I am to her a perpetual object of satire, and what is so dispiriting is not that her satirical view of me is incorrect. It is that it is all too correct: my attempts to keep her in check have made a martinet of me. Perhaps I would have been one anyway, with any child, even one of my own. I am indeed overcautious, given to pedantry and generally lacking in girlish vivacity . . . and I think I will now terminate this list. (The shade of our dear Miss Jones looms: 'This is the day that the Lord has made; let us rejoice and be glad in it.')

But she is <u>such</u> a capricious girl, alternating between depression and vivacity, and for all the trouble she gives, she can be really kind; there are flashes of affection, like the sun coming out from

219

behind a cloud. (*Not the most original simile, granted. How Miss Parker would have lamented!*) She can be very charming, especially of course where men are concerned, and trouble awaits in that direction, I am sure; but I am equally sure that if she is determined on sexual delinquency, there will be nothing I can do about it. Having lost all respect for this apparently dipsomaniac old maid, she is quite out of control.

It was in your letter before last, dear, that you asked some questions about the girl, and I don't believe I answered properly, but merely subjected you to my litany of grievances. I will attempt to answer them now.

My predecessor as guardian, as you know, was her uncle Leonard – Leo to his friends, of whom he had many, not all of them quite respectable. Leo treated the girl kindly, as far as I could see, but somewhat negligently. In particular, he neglected her education, to the extent that when I was taken on as governess, she was barely up to Standard One in mathematics, and had no science whatsoever. As for languages, she did have tolerably good French, but it was a case (as the saying goes) of 'little Latin and less Greek'. Leo, of course, had a house full of books, not all of them (to say the least) suitable for a young girl, but he gave her the run of that library and seemed almost to be tutoring her in Bohemianism. She continues to read a great deal, but for no other purpose than to fuel her wild imagination, and hers really is wild, perhaps even dangerous.

Towards the end of his life, Leo seems to have been under severe duress and it is beginning to transpire – the evidence emerging from various unsavoury quarters and relayed to me in regretful and bowdlerised terms by the chivalrous Mr Farmery – that his death was not accidental. The fact that this most disorganised of men should have made a will only a month beforehand does rather point in that direction. Incredible as it seems, the possibility of blackmail by his former tenant, Robert Harper, has come up, and perhaps this explains (or even excuses?) Leo's failure to apportion from his income the 'reasonable' sum stipulated by his late brother for the girl's education, and he does not appear to have investigated any schools on the girl's behalf.

Unfortunately, the 'reasonable' sum does not go as far as the girl's poor father envisaged. The plan I had agreed with Mr Farmery and Mr Walker (my fellow trustees) is that she should be coached up for a scholarship, which I thought might be attainable largely on the strength of her written work (which does reflect her total immersion in literature), if only she could be brought up to a tolerable standard on the maths and science side — by which I mean the rather <u>low</u> standard found acceptable in most girls' schools.

But hope for that plan is fading fast. Despite professing a keenness to go to school — a boarding school especially ('to get away from you', as she was kind enough to put it) — she simply will not apply herself to her studies. Consequently, the establishment at Eastbourne that I mentioned last time — which is not a very advanced school — turned her down point-blank. The headmaster, a Latinist, described her to me as 'both supra- and sub-normal'. He reported in his letter that he might have 'taken a chance' on her, on the strength of her exceptional articulacy, both vocally and on paper, but that he had received disturbing reports from one of the senior girls as to her conduct and remarks when they had fraternised briefly before she took her test.

A few days after the failure of that application, I did end up conveying to Mr Farmery (I had not meant to do it) the degree to which the girl and I have become antagonised. It was the prospect of our forthcoming excursion that had brought it on, and, I think, the fact that I had been deprived of the wise counsel of your sister that week (the badminton having been cancelled!).

I was in such a pother! It was the apparent perversity of Leonard's stipulation of a holiday in Venice, of all places, for the girl that so vexed me, and for no better reason, really, than that she had read and enjoyed some silly novel about it. (I gather that he had then rashly promised her that she would see Venice, so perhaps the stipulation was honourable, after all.) But a city on water . . . when neither I nor the girl can swim! At least, I don't <u>think</u> she can; she has resorted to bluster on the two occasions I have mentioned it. I admit that I have not pressed the point as I should have, being afflicted with a prejudice amounting almost to phobia of any public swimming bath. (It stems from some childhood incidents that would be painful for me to relate, and tiresome for you to read.) Well, after an interval of silently and sadly nodding his head at my maunderings, Farmery very surprisingly suggested that he and his wife would be willing to consider 'taking the girl on', providing she were at a boarding school somewhere for most of the time.

Now that did set me thinking . . .

This letter, you may have noticed, is rather haunted by memories of our own alma mater. In light of Mr Farmery's offer, I began mentally drafting a letter to the eternal Miss Jones, asking whether she thought I would be well advised to go into a school. I suppose a course at teacher training college would have to be on the cards (although perhaps that is not necessary for we 'intellectuals' equipped not merely with certificates but actual university degrees?). This fantasy, in which I gradually ascended to the rank of headmistress of some leading London school, persisted for a few days, but it would amount to failure, pure and simple.

The fact is, I have come to see in the girl an opportunity to do good, to rectify the series of terrible misfortunes that have befallen her. She apparently sees herself as akin to a 'parcel', constantly passed on − or likely to be so − from hand to hand, as in the parlour game, although the metaphor does not quite apply, for it is her conviction that nobody involved wants to find themselves unwrapping the parcel and taking ownership of the contents. It is heartbreaking that she should view herself in this way, as an unwanted chattel, and I can't help but think it excuses, or at least explains, any amount of unruly behaviour.

My dear Sarah, I am determined not to perpetuate the 'game'. I know the girl suspects my motives, but perhaps she will one day realise that I made the offer of guardianship to Messrs Farmery and Walker ex gratia, and with no thought of the modest income associated with my role. One speaks of one's 'Christian duty' with reluctance, but . . .

Enough! How pompous I am becoming in my old age!

Please tell me what you know about this ladies' cricket team your dear sister is proposing to 'get up'?! Have you been recruited? She is being rather mysterious about it. I told her I think it would make an excellent project for next summer. I might just about do as a bowler, but I would never make a 'batsman' with my eyesight. Perhaps I could make the tea? Or I could be seamstress of the team. What do lady cricketers wear? White bloomers? I dread to think!

Sorry to go on so dreadfully about myself, dear. It is really your own fault, you know, for being such a very sympathetic and kind sweetheart. Is it any wonder that I remain your deeply grateful and ever-loving,

Rose

P.S. I see that I have referred throughout to 'the girl', which is quite wrong. Please do make the mental substitution of 'Monica' each time – but I know you will anyway, being a so much kindlier soul than your correspondent!

P.P.S. Aubrey, as I think you know from Mary, has been so kind to me in my recent travails (if such they can be called). The dear man has invited us (Mary and I) to another concert in October, and this time he has arranged the programme, which is to be 'Mostly Mozart'. He is a very remarkable person. How many 'high-ups' in Islington Council, I would like to know, have the talent and breadth of interest to write music reviews of great liveliness and insight for the magazines − reviews beginning, for example, 'In this recital, devoted to the Modern French Masters (Debussy and Ravel), something seems to have got lost in translation . . .' and continuing in the same witty vein? When I told Aubrey about how it was such a trial finding a school for Monica, he replied, 'It sounds to me as though a good reformatory school would fit the bill,' and it was such a tonic to hear levity brought to bear on this fraught question.

Well, dear, I must be like that eminent author (whose name temporarily escapes me) who observed, 'Anything awful makes me laugh.'

P.P.P.S. I have it! Charles Lamb!

Monica looked up from the letter. Fast-flying birds were skimming low over the piazza − swifts, perhaps, making a high, zinging sound in celebration of returning home at the end of a long day.

Mr Farmery was willing to take her on!

. . . As long, at any rate, as she was at a boarding school most of the time, but that was all right. Mr Farmery was a very nice man with, presumably, a nice house somewhere near his office in Highgate: a quiet, neutral place where one could bide one's time amid gently ticking clocks and garden views. But he was a solicitor, not a barrister, and therefore more or less officially a dull person, so it would suit them *both* for Monica to be away much of the time.

And then Monica felt ashamed of not having first thought about the revelations concerning Leo. As far as she knew, he had been drinking in one or more of the Highgate pubs when he and the tram coincided, and it was mainly the drink, rather than his intention, that had caused the collision. But perhaps drinking that much amounted to slow suicide in itself? That he was being somehow menaced by Bobby Harper did not surprise her; no terrible revelation ever would, she believed. The thing about Bobby Harper was that he did not *do* enough; he had spare energy for *some* purpose or other.

She glanced down at the letter again.

'Supra- and sub-normal!' Monica said out loud. Well, she didn't mind that, really. Obviously, she had made an impression. She had stretched the little man from Eastbourne to the very limit of his stale Latinate vocabulary, but a bad thought lurked. If you combined supra and sub, you ended up with whatever was the Latin for average or mediocre. 'I didn't want to go to that damned school anyway,' she said.

The letter seemed to become jollier as it went on, and Monica tried to recollect, from the train journey, whether Driscoll had been drinking wine at the same time as writing it. Monica had to admit that Driscoll came out of the letter quite well. The exclamation marks were bad style, of course, but she wrote rather fluently and with some humour, albeit rather stilted . . . and it seemed there really might be, to coin a phrase, 'a man in the case', namely Aubrey, sender of the Valentine. Monica could have done with a bit more about him and a bit less about Mary Kelly, but then she was the sister of the person to whom the letter was sent, so Driscoll probably thought it polite to bring her in regularly.

Monica thought about Mary Kelly.

Even though she would absent herself when Mary Kelly called at the flat, she wouldn't go far, and would try to hear, through whatever door had just closed behind her, what they were about. Mary seemed keener on socialising than Driscoll, and the purpose of her calls was often to take her out, whether to the gymnasium, a concert or a talk. Monica believed that Aubrey was present at the latter kinds of events, if not actually giving the talk himself. She was encouraged in this by Driscoll's habit of not taking her glasses when she went out with Mary and wearing her better (or, at any rate, more expensive) hats. It was possible Mary Kelly was advising Driscoll to marry Aubrey. Once, she had distinctly heard Mary say, 'I know Aubrey would love to see you, dear.'

Mary Kelly had better not be fixing on marrying him herself. It was a close-run thing, but she was slightly prettier than Driscoll. She didn't need specs, for a start, and while she was just as tall as Driscoll, she didn't seem quite so protracted, owing to having a neater face, its symmetry emphasised by the circular hat, while her grey eyes were complemented by the long, silky blue coat she wore, which was always slightly shiny, as though she'd come in from the rain, which, in point of fact, she often had. Also, she could – and did – play the organ, mainly at St John's Church, Upper Holloway, which must impress the musical Aubrey, provided she played well, which Monica could hardly believe she did. It also seemed likely that she wasn't as clever as Driscoll; few people were, after all.

The letter was, in truth, a little . . . disingenuous. It didn't give the whole story. There was no mention of all the times when Driscoll had crumpled up one of Monica's maths exercises and pitched it into the waste-paper basket, saying, 'I've heard of *improper* fractions, but yours are *ridiculous*,' or simply, 'Dateless girl!'

Monica glanced again at the beginning of the letter. Driscoll had written about Leo as though he were a hopeless case, but it appeared she herself had held suicidal thoughts.

'And I am the cause,' said Monica.

The swifts were still zinging about, but now with an air of panic, as if trying to close down, or at least escape, the social night of the humans unfolding below.

'You are something of a trial,' Monica said. 'You are not very efficient in maths or Latin. You give trouble. You must be kept in check.' She paused before adding, 'And you're off your head.'

The lights were burning more seriously in the far cafés, emphasising Monica's separation from civilised life. She thought of the wound she had inflicted on the white rear of the Scotsman. Was that the result of madness? Either way, she did not regret it, but if – as seemed increasingly likely – she had murdered Driscoll . . .

Monica was folding the letter and putting it back in the torn envelope. 'You were horrible to her, and then you killed her,' she said. She felt that she was coming apart from herself; she seemed to see the events of last night from a different angle – not from the point of view of someone pushing Driscoll through the open window, but from the point of view ('perspective' was the correct word) of somebody watching Monica doing that from the sidelines, so to speak.

Monica put the letter back in the chatelaine bag, and she realised she was crying as she did so. She walked out into the piazza. The clock was beginning to strike. That is, the high, green iron man was striking the bell. He did it eight times. His colleague began doing the same, but Monica was looking at the first man. When he had completed his strikes, he had seemed to make an extra mechanical movement, as though glancing down at Monica and saying, 'It is time.' She wondered what he could mean, but not for long. A tall man stood before her, overshadowing her. He had beautiful blue eyes and a grave expression on his face.

The Blue-eyed Policeman

'The scene is most animated toward evening, when Venice is
"in piazza".'

From *Venice*, by Augustus J.C. Hare & St Clair Baddeley

He was a policeman. At first, Monica couldn't have said precisely how she knew, which went to the man's credit. Yes, he
had one of those very sideways hats, but there was nothing
pantomimic about his elegant, grey tunic. Then she saw an
assortment of other police, of the more ridiculous sort, arrayed
behind him.

'Monica?' he said, making her name sound lovely.

She nodded.

He was holding before her a small leather wallet that contained nothing but a silver star – proof, she supposed, of his
identity as a policeman. Yes, for he now said, *'Polizia.'* It was
a dreadful word to hear, of course, but if anybody had to say
it to her, she would rather it be this man than any other. He
asked her a question in Italian, which she didn't understand; or
he might have been saying 'Good evening' in a courtly sort of
way.

She said, *'Parlez-vous français?'*

He slowly shook his head.

'English?'

At this, he shrugged – a curious response.

He took her gently by the arm and began leading her across the piazza, just as though they were a married couple, or a couple actually *getting* married, with the other policemen following behind as a guard of honour. They quit the square on the south side. They were briefly on a shopping street, where all the shoppers stared at their progress in a rather gratifying manner. Of course, Monica wanted to ask many questions about what she might or might not have done (principally, 'Is Driscoll dead?'), but, true to her traditional failing, she would not dare ask many.

They entered a small, plain-looking building, evidently a police office. It smelt of carbolic, was too brightly lit by electricity, and a throbbing of engines came from beyond the windows on one side. There was a touch of Holloway bleakness about it. A policeman of the English type stood at a wooden counter, and the blue-eyed man started talking to him in fast Italian. Neither smiled, betokening a serious matter. One of the Napoleons now took Monica's arm, more roughly than the blue-eyed man. He led her into a pale green corridor, along past a glass cabinet, containing an assortment of casually piled guns. Monica began to cry again, at which the Napoleon turned and shook his head, which might mean anything. He must be taking her to a prison cell, except that this place did not seem big enough to accommodate such a thing, and, in fact, now they were out through the other side of it, standing on a small, hot dock where two motor launches awaited. A moment ago, there would have been three, but one boat had just roared off into the darkness of the side canal on which the berths were located. A policeman of the English type had started the engine of one of the boats. He stood at the wheel, which was to the rear of an outsized chimney. There was a small cabin behind him, with a low, barred door. At the front were primitive seats – just planks, really. The Napoleon pointed to one of these; Monica climbed down onto the boat and meekly sat.

The man at the wheel called out to the Napoleon and Monica discovered from this that the Napoleon's name was Adriano. Monica saw, with horror, that the man at the wheel was holding aloft a pair of handcuffs; Adriano shook his head. And now, to Monica's relief, the blue-eyed policeman came out of the back door of the police station, and he was immediately giving orders to the boat driver. All their conversation was now conducted in the sing-song not-quite Italian: the Venetian dialect. The blue-eyed man climbed onto the boat and sat down next to Monica as naturally and companionably as if they'd had two theatre tickets booked. He looked directly at her; he could see she had been crying. He gently touched her arm and said something that was drowned out by the uncouth roar of the boat's engine starting.

Monica's mind was racing in circles; if she hadn't been sitting down, she would probably have fainted. But a small part of her also began to enjoy the beauty of the unfolding scene. In the lighted rooms they passed, a lot of cooking was going on, and hisses of smoke would come out through opened windows. There was a food smell, and she could hear the clatter of kitchen activity, echoing up the high, peeling walls. They passed a shrine set into one of the walls – just a hollow in the stonework, with two candles illuminating a painting of the Virgin Mary. It was very pretty, the Catholics being so much more artistic than Protestants. She thought of Highgate Hill, where the Catholic church known as Holy Joe's stood on one side of the street, as big as a railway station, with many jolly people, often Irish, continuously coming and going. On the other side of the road was the thin, pale Presbyterian church whose name she couldn't remember, and which was patronised by thin, anxious-looking people – Driscoll types, and indeed Driscoll herself, on occasion. If it was a stand-off, then Holy Joe's came out the winner.

Maybe she ought to say a prayer, Venice being such a religious place, with God perhaps close at hand? Yes, he was a local here. She closed her eyes and said very quietly, 'Please let Driscoll not be dead, and let her marry Aubrey, if that's what she wants.' The blue-eyed policeman was consulting his watch. From around some distant corner came the shout of an unseen gondolier: 'Oyeee popay!'

They were approaching a watery junction. Crossing in front of them was an extra-long gondola, hung with lamps and filled with people, and one gondolier serenading all of them. Adriano had something cynical to say – or to mutter under his breath – about that; the man at the wheel muttered something back. The rapidly darkening sky held tones of purple and green. And now Adriano was speaking at a louder volume, calling up to a hatless man in shirtsleeves, who stood on a high balcony, something in the lilting Venetian tongue. The man waved dismissively in response.

Here was a question that might be safely asked. Turning to the blue-eyed policeman, Monica said, 'What did he say to the man on the balcony?'

Her companion turned the full blueness of his eyes on her. 'He said, "All your family ees dead dogs." Eet ees a joke-a.' And he was smiling the loveliest smile; Adriano was smiling, too, and Monica turned around to verify that the wheel man was smiling also. A full house! Perhaps they were not taking her to prison, after all.

But an atmosphere of death was accumulating. They were

passing a broken gondola. A large crab was right beside them on a ledge. A darting movement ahead in the water suggested a rat. Monica heard a splash, not over-loud, but somehow resonant. Then came a succession of black, barred windows. The boat turned a corner, and there before them in the water was the back of Driscoll's head.

'Ay-eee!' cried Adriano.

Driscoll twisted, and there was her white face. Then she was going under, and since she had disappeared in a downward direction, Monica instinctively looked up – to see the tall window of the palazzo and the stone balcony that had come into its own as a kind of diving board, albeit belatedly. As Monica's gaze had ascended, so had her spirits. She had not killed Driscoll! And not only was she not a murderer, but she must now prove Driscoll's saviour. For surely, she was still alive? She stood, ready to dive. The blue-eyed man and Adriano were already in the water.

The man at the wheel was shouting – perhaps trying to stop Monica doing what she was about to do, for she was making the diving shape she had seen at the Hampstead Swimming Pond. But whereas she wasn't *certain* whether she could swim, she knew for a *fact* she couldn't dive, and so, in the end, she bathetically jumped, like so many of the Hampstead men.

She was going down in the dark water, but she wasn't scared; she knew she was in with a chance of resurfacing and aiding the rescue of Driscoll; it would be a fair fight with the water, which had a rather pleasant velvety warmth. It occurred to her that today had been Saturday, so now it was Saturday *night* – bath night in Holloway, only this time Driscoll had gone in first. When Monica surfaced, she told herself, 'Keep your chin up,' and she realised she *was* keeping it up, so the first part of her plan was working out, but there was no sign of Driscoll.

The blue-eyed policeman came up for air alongside her. It was very noble of him to have gone in because, hatless, it was evident that he was almost bald. He and Monica went under again, but she already knew she would achieve nothing in the water. Then again, she had learnt that she could indeed swim. When Monica surfaced again, she saw that Adriano and the blue-eyed policeman were jointly propelling Driscoll towards the palazzo, but she seemed lifeless, at which revelation, the palazzo seemed to tower higher above Monica, and a fainting feeling threatened to come on.

The servant, Zita, had now appeared at the water door – evidently newly arrived via the *back* door. She held outstretched the boathook that had been stowed in the basement.

Driscoll grabbed it with great, greedy suddenness, and Monica knew then she was going to be all right. She averted her eyes from the process of Driscoll's extraction – it was bound to be a bit undignified, since it was much easier to go in than to come out (she had just had a brief glimpse of Adriano pushing at Driscoll's rear end, in an attempt to get all of her onto the narrow landing stage). Monica began swimming towards Charlotte, who had floated out of the chatelaine bag (which Monica had stupidly been holding when she jumped in) and was now drifting peacefully on her back. Monica was glad to have this excuse for further swimming, although she did realise, as she collected up Charlotte ('Got you!' she said), that she was being shouted at from the landing stage. Monica turned in the water to see Driscoll looking practically naked in her sodden pale green dress, and with newly enormous eyes. Almost everything beneath the dress was clearly revealed, and Monica saw that Driscoll wore a brassiere instead of her usual corset, so she really had 'modernised', and the water had destroyed her sugarloaf hairstyle, which was also to the good. Her thin, careworn, hollow-eyed face looked really beautiful, Monica thought.

Adriano and the blue-eyed policeman were swimming towards Monica, which was perfectly absurd: she did not require rescuing by *one* man, leave alone two. She found that she could even swim while holding her bag out of the water, although that itself was a futile act since the bag and everything in it, including the guidebook and Driscoll's letter to Sarah Kelly, was thoroughly sodden. She met Adriano and the blue-eyed policeman in the middle of the water and was attempting to explain that she did not require any assistance even as they began dragging her towards the palazzo. At the small dock, she heaved herself up.

★

Half an hour later, Monica and Driscoll were in dry clothes; the blue-eyed policeman and Adriano remained stoically in their wet ones. They had more important things to do than dry themselves. The blue-eyed man had twice tried to speak to Driscoll – had succeeded, after a fashion, but she had answered as though he were not there, and very briefly. The word she said was something like '*incidente*', which presumably meant something close to 'accident'. Well, she had tried to leave the world, and here it was starting up again, like a magic lantern show forced upon her. In the big room, the lamps were lit; a fire burnt in the pretty grate, its flickering seeming to animate the children depicted on the surrounding tiles. Kindly Zita had done all this, of course, and she'd got the water on the boil in the copper. Her mother, the cook, would not be coming for some reason, but Monica didn't mind, because Zita was laying out the fresh bread she had brought, along with cold meats, cheeses, olives, fruit and an apple tart and cream – and there was red wine for Driscoll, of course; also for Adriano, who drank several glasses very quickly while talking loudly (and apparently humorously) in fast Venetian-Italian, most of his remarks being addressed to Zita, who seemed embarrassed by the attention. Adriano was what's known as a 'character'. The English-style policeman, easily the dullest of the three, remained mostly on his boat (it was perhaps necessary that he guard it).

Every time Monica looked over at Driscoll, Zita made a gesture indicating that she should look elsewhere, and Monica quite understood that you wouldn't want to be the centre of interest if you had lately tried to kill yourself. It would be embarrassing, not least because you had just tried to escape from all the people scrutinising you so intently. Monica's second choice for someone to look at was the blue-eyed policeman. Monica was not sure she had ever seen a handsomer man, and certainly not a handsomer bald one, but she wanted to go up to him and reprimand him for not having explained the situation: that he had wanted to return her to her guardian, rather than take her to prison for murder. But perhaps he had thought she would try to run away, in that case. Or perhaps his English was not up to it.

Presently, it became clear that he was leaving and taking the other two policemen with him, and this was a sad moment. As he approached the door, he summoned Monica with the tiniest movement of his head. She went up to him rapidly, expecting him to say something – goodbye, at the very least – but he kept silence, practically forcing Monica to speak.

'Don't worry,' she said, indicating Driscoll. 'I will look after her.'

'Yes,' he said, rather sceptically. 'And she will look after you' (only with extra syllables thrown in).

Monica wasn't sure what to make of that. Surely the events of the evening proved it was Driscoll who needed looking after?

But she'd better not protest. No doubt, as far as this man was concerned, Monica's 'running away' had been the cause of all the trouble. Furthermore, he was a policeman, and Monica had that very day committed an assault (albeit with good reason), and it remained possible, depending on the health or otherwise of Gareth Hall, that she had done worse in England. Yes, policeman of whatever nationality were to be given a wide berth.

It was a rather disappointing leave-taking, nonetheless.

★

When they had gone, Zita was carrying a pitcher of hot water out of the room; she would be taking it upstairs to fill the bath. Driscoll sat by the fire with several blankets over her shoulders, looking both old and young, and still very white and large-eyed. Monica sat down on the chair opposite, at which Driscoll gave a half-smile. Finally, she spoke to Monica, as Monica knew she eventually would. After all, wine unlocked so many things.

With a tip of her head, Driscoll indicated the stairs and by implication the bathroom to which they led.

'You must have the "hot", dear,' she said, which proved she was not yet fully in her senses, for if anyone merited the first bath it was Driscoll at the present time – as Monica pointed out, using far too many words, and beginning with, 'It was you who nearly drowned . . .'

'But you nearly drowned, too, dear,' said Driscoll, when Monica had finished, 'and all on account of me.'

'No, it was all on account of *me*.'

Driscoll was looking all around the room. Presently, she said, 'Where is your hat, dear?'

'I left it at the Lido.'

'We must both go back for it.'

Monica, thinking of the naked Scotsman, shook her head.

Zita bustled back in, collected more 'hot', departed again.

'Shall we both go up?' said Monica, for she wanted to escape Driscoll's weird stare.

They both stood, and as a direct consequence of doing so, they embraced.

'You poor thing,' said Monica, 'to have had an accident like that.'

She was rather pleased with that: a lie, obviously, but a necessary one.

'I was in such a pother!' said Driscoll, some normality returning to her voice.

'You obviously weren't thinking straight,' said Monica. 'It's so easy to trip over those little walls they have around the balconies. It might happen to anyone.'

Monica was less pleased with that. It was over-egging.

They walked slowly upstairs, to find Zita waiting in the candlelit bathroom with the red enamel jug in her hand. Was that dear lady starting to get the idea that the two mistresses had had a row, and that Driscoll had tried to make away with herself? But Zita merely reached out towards Driscoll, thereby confirming that Driscoll would indeed have the 'hot'.

Monica moved towards the door, but Driscoll checked her.

'Did you like my dress, dear? Oh, I know it was soaking wet, but what did you think? I so wanted to look nice for you.'

Monica nodded. She knew she would cry if she spoke, and her tears would be for Driscoll, but they would also be tears of happiness, because she was not a murderer.

After their baths, they ate the delicious supper, at which Monica called Driscoll 'Rose' for the first time. They *both* drank wine, and Monica had two glasses, because when Driscoll poured out her third, she poured another for Monica without being asked. Zita stayed for the first part of the supper and left only after assurances from Driscoll that she – Driscoll – would be absolutely fine. She then gave Zita quite a lot of money, and a phrase came into Monica's mind. It would come up in unsuitable stories of one kind or another, and Monica believed it was hyphenated: 'hush-money'. Driscoll was paying Zita not to go around saying this crazy Englishwoman had tried to kill herself.

With Driscoll's dress drying in front of the fire (but not too near, because of the silk), they talked about clothes for a while. Driscoll was very insistent that they should return to the Lido in hopes of retrieving the sailor hat. 'The taffeta ribbon was really lovely – and so expensive, dear!'

Monica said she had noticed the ribbon and lace shops near St Mark's Square, and perhaps they should visit those.

Driscoll said, 'Yes, I was meaning to buy some Venetian lace.'

But then they both remembered it would be Sunday tomorrow, so the shops would be closed.

A silence fell. They both looked over to the drying dress.

At length, Driscoll said, 'I made it when you were in bed in the last days before we left London. It's a muslin-silk weave. I wore it to Florian at half past twelve, hoping you might stick to the arrangement.'

A further silence. Monica took up the poker and stirred the fire, quite pointlessly. Driscoll sipped her wine, looking suddenly very sophisticated.

'But I knew that, since you'd run away,' she said, 'you must be so upset that it was unlikely you'd come. I waited half an hour, dear, cursing myself for having slept in – it was just that I was overdone by the heat and so worn out by all the preparations and the trouble with the gondolier last night – and then I became so agitated that I began charging all over the city like an absolute madwoman looking for you.'

'Just out of curiosity,' said Monica, 'when did you tell the police?'

'I did that straight away. As soon as I got up and realised you were gone. I stopped the first one that I saw: a carabinieri, you know? I described you to him.'

'You furnished a description.'

'What, dear?'

'That's what people do with descriptions. Furnish them. They are then circulated.'

'I daresay.'

'The carabinieri . . .' said Monica. 'I call them Napoleons. They're partly soldiers, I think. It was one of those that found me and brought me back.'

Another silence.

'But you were glad to be found and brought back, I hope . . . dear?'

'Oh, yes,' said Monica.

She was wondering about the timing of it all. Had Driscoll alerted the police soon enough for the first of the day's Napoleons to be holding a piece of paper bearing Monica's description? Perhaps the paper in that man's hand had concerned some other matter entirely?

Monica couldn't decide whether to be honest about her day. Ought she to say that she thought she had killed Driscoll? That she had seen her at Florian but hadn't been able to believe it because of the dress? It might be best to remain enigmatic about the details, and certainly she should *not* mention the dream. Let Driscoll think it was her mistreatment of Monica that had resulted in her running away. But did Driscoll *really* think that? The letter suggested she had regarded herself as 'more sinned against than sinning', but perhaps she had now changed? Could you be the same person again after you had tried to kill yourself?

But perhaps the attempt had *not* been genuine? Had she only made the leap when she heard the approaching motor launch? Or perhaps when she heard Zita coming in through the back door? Had she known she would likely be rescued? Monica didn't think so, and there wasn't much difference between the two things anyway. Whether Driscoll had intended to die or not, she had taken 'panic measures', to use the phrase from her letter.

Monica asked Driscoll, 'What did the blue-eyed policeman say to you?'

'He was very kind; he told me the address of the British consulate here, but I already knew that. He asked if I would like the police to visit again in the morning; I said that wouldn't be necessary . . . His eyes *were* rather wonderful, weren't they?'

'It's just such a shame he had no hair,' said Monica, who had now definitely gone off the man, because of what he'd said as he left. 'Shall I tell you who else has very nice eyes? Your friend Aubrey.'

No response from Driscoll, so Monica decided to raise the ante.

'And *he* has a great deal of hair.'

All Driscoll said to that was, 'Yes, dear.'

They looked again at the dress.

Monica said, 'It *is* lovely – and rather daring, dear!'

'I was worried about that.'

'You shouldn't be. You have the figure to carry it off.'

Driscoll said, 'Where else did you go, dear?'

'The Lido, as you know. Apart from that, I just wandered about. I'm so sorry to have been such a trial for you,' Monica added, and she realised it was a phrase from the letter, but Driscoll didn't seem to notice.

'And I to you,' said Driscoll.

About an hour later, when Monica was lying in bed, she said quietly to herself, 'The only thing for it is to *change* things. That is the lesson of today. Because, otherwise, we will both go back to square one.'

But how much could Monica change? Surely, she was stuck with her own nature. She began thinking of a grammatical nicety. She *may* not have killed Driscoll, but she *might* have. She had in the past felt motivated to do so. And she may have killed Gareth Hall at the drinking fountain in the woods. That remained to be seen. (It occurred to Monica that, despite being 'off the hook' as far as Driscoll was concerned, she was still on it as far as Hall was concerned.) In any event, she had certainly hurt Hall, just as she had hurt the Scotsman at the Lido, and she did not regret those actions. She did not want to have *killed* Hall, but was that not for purely selfish reasons? Because she did not want to be detained at His Majesty's Pleasure. Meanwhile, she was, in effect, detained at Driscoll's pleasure.

She began to hear a sound from Driscoll's room – the sound of crying. She got up and tapped on the door. No answer, so she walked in. Driscoll was at the window, looking down.

'Now don't go jumping again!' said Monica, hurrying towards her – so the cat was finally out of the bag, and Driscoll made no denial, but just said, 'The window is closed, dear,' which was true enough. 'I was so silly,' she said, '. . . so silly.' With a kind of blind, groping gesture, she put out her two arms. An embrace was on the cards, so Monica moved towards her, and the embrace began, with Monica's face pushed right up against Driscoll's chest – her breasts indeed, which, in spite of their smallness, seemed to be working together to suffocate Monica. After about twenty seconds (Monica had counted), the embrace ended, and Driscoll gave a great sniff. 'I was so silly,' she said again. 'You see, I thought you had left me . . .'

That did seem to be the end of the sentence, but Monica supplied a different ending, one less momentous.

'. . . Left you a note? To say where I was going? Of course, I should have, but I hardly knew what *I* was doing.'

The two walked over to the bed, where they sat down. Monica put her arm around Driscoll, and Driscoll put hers around Monica, so they sat there like two drunken men, although neither was in the least drunk.

'*Shall* we go to the Lido tomorrow?' said Driscoll.

'Well, what about the activities for First Day? Shall we jump straight to Second?'

She'd said the word again. What an idiot she was.

'You are to forget *all about* First and Second Day,' said Driscoll, smiling.

'Just as well, dear, since I lost the guidebook in the water, I'm afraid, and there was a letter of yours in there. I'd taken it to post. I'm awfully sorry but that's gone, too.'

Neither statement was true, of course; both objects were in Monica's bedroom, but it seemed the simplest way out with the letter.

'I think perhaps we should go home tomorrow,' said Driscoll. 'Do you mind, dear?'

'Not a bit,' said Monica, rising to her feet, and she really didn't, because somehow she knew she would be back: the paradoxical lesson of all the late turmoil was that she belonged here.

'When we get home,' Driscoll said, 'we will make a new start. I already have in mind a change that I'm sure you'll like.'

'Oh, I'm sure I will,' said Monica, thinking nothing of the sort, because only a return to Venice would do. 'Are you all right now, Rose?' she said.

'I will be 'ere long,' said Driscoll, and Monica didn't care for that phrase, which reminded her of the wearisome Holloway Road, and then Driscoll went and repeated it: 'We'll *both* be all right 'ere long.' And she compounded her sin by saying, 'We'll win through in the end, dear!'

Holloway

'If Cupid have not spent all his quiver in Venice.'
From *Much Ado About Nothing* (1.1), by William Shakespeare,
quoted in *Venice*, by Augustus J.C. Hare & St Clair Baddeley

Monica woke. Monday on the Holloway Road. She'd had a
few short dreams in the night – scraps of Venice floating back,
as they had done regularly since her and Driscoll's return two
weeks before. Last night, a room that was somehow a larger
version of her bedroom also turned out to be St Mark's Square.
A gondola had been displayed in a window that turned out to be
a ship in a bottle. There'd been other indoor-outdoor perplex-
ities, but these were amiable dreams, and Humphrey De Silva
was on hand to explain and reassure. He was always present
in the dreams, even if in spirit only. Of course, it was simply
intolerable to dream you were floating pleasantly through the
Hotel Danieli only to wake and find yourself on the Holloway
Road again without taking steps to rectify the matter. She
was determined to return to Venice, under the guardianship
of Humphrey, and she kept the guidebook (somewhat warped
after being in the canal) close about her as a token of this ambi-
tion. Not the least benefit of living in Venice with Mr De Silva
was that you would get to know the city really well, so you

wouldn't need to bother with Hare and Baddeley, although, naturally, you would always have a few copies to hand, to dish out to your English guests when their constant questions about churches and frescos and whatnot became tedious.

Her commitment to returning to Venice had not diminished, although it had to be admitted that relations between herself and Driscoll were somewhat improved since the night of the canal plunge. There were lapses, of course, usually brought on by Monica's academic failings, and she had no doubt that the *status quo ante* (more or less permanent warfare) would eventually be restored.

At the outset of the journey back from Venice, Driscoll had ushered Monica towards the café in the railway station, where she had bought her a hot chocolate – perfectly produced by a large steel machine, which, fittingly for a station, emitted steam. In that same place, Driscoll had bought for Monica a tin of biscuits, or *biscotti*, with a design of little gondoliers rowing around the circular lid. Then Monica had been invited to choose a volume from the English-language books in the bookstall. She'd picked out another Wilkie Collins, *The Moonstone*, handing it to Driscoll as a kind of test, sure she'd be asked to choose again. But there was no expression of disapproval, only a small smile and, 'Well, if you really must read this kind of novel . . .'

'Yes, I really must, dear.'

That small smile had persisted throughout the journey back, and indeed since. It seemed to have replaced what would formerly have been a sigh.

Driscoll had planned the outward journey at length and with anxiety. The journey back she improvised, almost with happiness, smiling at the railway guides and rippling their pages to give herself a cooling breeze in the hot stations and carriages she was taking in her stride – and all this because she was returning to, rather than heading away from, a world she knew, which naturally suited her better, being a person without imagination.

The return arrangements required them to put up in a hotel near the Gare du Nord in Paris. They had walked along a short street full of hotels that lay between the Gare du Nord and another station, which was called, with delightful aptness, the Rue des Deux Gares. Driscoll had been aiming towards a rather plain hotel, but Monica preferred the looks of one over the road that had ivy growing over it, as though it were not in Paris at all.

'And it has a cat,' said Monica, because there was a dear little white one sleeping on the doorstep.

'That's hardly a clinching argument, dear,' Driscoll had said, but the small smile came, and she relented again. They had shared a room, of course, but with twin beds on opposite sides, thank goodness. Monica had slept soundly, lulled by train noises that seemed to regulate the night, keeping true darkness at bay. She had dreamt, of course, but it was an encouraging dream, opening on a warm day on Upper Street, Islington, which started just beyond Lower Holloway. In the dream, there were more trees than in reality, fewer motors and more prettily trotting horses. Monica – wearing her navy coat-frock (no top-coat being required) with the green check – was waiting outside the Town Hall and reading the stone plaques affixed thereto (the words 'affixed thereto' being distinctly pronounced by a helpful voice in the dream). The plaques commemorated the distinguished and presumably deceased officers of the Council, and Monica was reading the name 'Aubrey', even though he was not deceased, of course. On the contrary, he was standing next to her and smiling – and giving no indication that he thought Monica ought to have been in a reformatory school. He looked very smart and, at the sight (as it were) of his mane of hair, another word was pronounced by the kind voice: 'Leonine.' Monica started in straight away with an amazingly detailed description of a musical concert that was coming up. She named the players of the violin, viola, piano, and the vocalist, and described the programme, which would be performed at the 'Large Hall' (with which both Monica and Aubrey seemed perfectly familiar). Monica named works by various composers, or at least by people whose foreign names sounded like those of composers. 'Rose,' Monica added, 'very much hopes you will accompany her. She also sends you her love, by the way.'

'Oh, but I know,' Aubrey said, rather complacently. 'We are about to be married. We will be removing to the countryside. Of course, we won't be able to keep you on, but I believe you have developed a lovely plan for yourself.'

When Monica woke up, the room was full of light, and Driscoll, sitting up in her bed, was smiling at Monica, as though she had shared, and endorsed, the dream.

★

At the end of the first week back, Driscoll had knocked on Monica's door, asking whether she would care for a walk.

Monica had been sitting on her bed finishing an exercise set by the grammar book Driscoll had given her. It was the kind she liked: 'Make up a story using the interjections *hush, alas, oh.*' Her story concerned a lively young girl (modelled on herself) who was seeking to evade going on holiday to Skegness (a famous, but presumably horrible, resort in the North) with a tedious aunt (modelled on Driscoll). The girl and the aunt were walking through a wood in Hampshire (for some reason) and the moderate wind in the trees made sounds like 'hush', 'alas' and 'oh', and by incorporating these words, the girl's speech became gentler and more diplomatic than it otherwise would have been, and the aunt accepted her case that she ought to stay in Hampshire in order to attend to the anxieties of her sickly mother (who had not been invited to Skegness).

'A walk where to?' said Monica, without bothering to get up from the bed.

'Oh, not far.'

'No, thanks. I'm working.'

'Might I come in, dear?'

This in itself was part of the new, gentler regime. Before Venice, Driscoll would have entered without asking.

'All right,' said Monica, at length.

'What are you working on?'

'Read it if you like,' said Monica, noisily ripping the page from her notebook.

'Don't do that, dear,' said Driscoll, 'and please take your pen off the pillow. You know how it leaks.'

But she was already reading the story, and when she'd finished it, she looked raptly at Monica for a while, as though seeing her for the first time. 'That's lovely, dear. I couldn't have written that in a million years.'

This was pleasing to hear, but also somewhat disturbing. It was too fulsome, rather like the Venice embrace.

As Driscoll laid the story reverently back on the bed, Monica said, 'Of course you could have written it, dear. And your semicolons would have been where semicolons should be, unlike mine, which I put in when I get bored of commas. But where do you want to go on this walk?'

'You'll see, dear.'

'Is it a surprise?'

'Yes.'

'Rather than a nasty shock?'

'Yes, dear.'

Soon after, they were walking beneath a neutral blue-and-white sky towards Lower Holloway.

Monica said, 'We're off to Islington, aren't we?'

'We're *going* there, yes, dear.'

This was promising, in view of her Paris dream.

Monica thought about Islington. It hadn't been a village since about 1700, and its only bit of remaining greenery was Highbury Fields, but its main road, Upper Street, was more elegant than the Holloway Road, which it adjoined at a right angle. There were trees at regular intervals, fewer big, fuming railway stations, and prettier – because older – shops, usually with a touch of gilding.

They were now veering left, crossing Highbury Fields and approaching one of the grand houses overlooking it. At the doorway, a small man with a large moustache awaited them.

'Who's that?' said Monica.

'A house agent, dear. We're going to view a flat that's for rent.'

'Is it the new start you promised?'

'We'll have to see.'

The house agent did not remove his hat as they approached; instead, he rudely took out his watch.

'Are we all here, then?' he said.

He probably thought Monica and Driscoll were mother and daughter and that the man of the family was on the way. They climbed a wide, bright staircase, which led Monica to expect similarly attractive rooms, but the one they entered – evidently the main one of the flat – was hardly bigger than their existing living room. It was slightly more appealing, of course, but there were too many flowers on the bumpy wallpaper, and while the window did overlook a corner of Highbury Fields (which was, in truth, only *one* field), it seemed more interested in the back view of Highbury & Islington Station. The Holloway Road itself was detectable only as a faint rumble – at least, that was the situation with the windows closed.

'Might we have the window opened?' Monica said, addressing the house agent, who had embarked on some boring talk of the rates. It was Driscoll who answered.

'Why, dear?'

'I want to find out if we can hear the Road.'

'What road?' came the words from behind the agent's moustache.

'The enormous one about two hundred yards to the left,' said Monica.

'That's the Holloway Road.'

'I know that.'

'Why do you want to hear it?'

'I *don't* want to hear it.'

The agent turned, frowning to Driscoll, who said, 'I don't think it will be necessary to open the window.'

The agent, turning back to Monica, said, 'It's sealed shut just at present,' and then, as though out of pure spite, 'I ought to tell you two: we've just had an offer at the asking price.'

'So much for the new start,' said Monica. Refusing Driscoll's offer of looking at the other rooms, she said, 'I'll wait outside.'

'It's probably just as well,' Driscoll said, after she'd emerged with the agent, who'd positively sprinted away to more important business.

'No, it isn't,' Monica said, but that was her own thought exactly. The flat had been a red herring. Her new start would come in Venice, and Driscoll's would come when she was married to Aubrey with Monica off her hands.

They hardly exchanged a word that evening.

The next morning was devoted to trigonometry, and they had their first row since the return from Venice. Some sighing from Driscoll at Monica's wrong answers – and the muttered remark, 'Heaven help us when we come to algebra' – had brought it on. Monica threw her maths exercise book vertically towards the kitchen ceiling, where it just missed the gas mantle.

'Killed by Sine, Cosine and Tangent,' she said. 'That's what they'll write on my gravestone.'

'Yes,' said Driscoll, 'and mine will read "Killed by Trying to Teach Someone Trigonometry", and we will lie side by side.'

After supper, Mary Kelly turned up, as she had been doing regularly since Venice. She had presumably got wind of what had happened there and was concerned that Driscoll might go charging off to the Archway Bridge for another go at suicide. She would prise Driscoll out of the flat – usually to go to the gymnasium, the visits thereto signified by the big, white canvas boot bags in which they carried their kit.

Monica read the situation as follows: Mary Kelly did not like Monica; she probably blamed her for Driscoll's distressed condition in Venice, and if Driscoll married Aubrey, she would have to relinquish Monica, because Aubrey also didn't like her. (Much of this, of course, Monica had got from reading Driscoll's letter to Mary Kelly's sister.) So the irony was that, even though Mary Kelly couldn't stand Monica, she was, in a roundabout way, on her side. These speculations led on to the question of where Monica might end up, should the parcel be passed again, and here a complication had arisen. She probably would not, after all, be received by the kindly lawyer, Mr Farmery, owing to the death of Mrs Farmery, which had occurred while

Monica and Driscoll had been in Venice. (Driscoll, heavily beribboned in black, like a frayed crow, had attended the funeral two days after their return.) It was a cancer, of course, that killed her, and what amazed Monica was that it had been Mrs, and not Mr, Farmery who'd died, since whereas almost everyone Monica got acquainted with did die, she had never met Mrs Farmery.

As usual, Monica retreated to her bedroom when Mary Kelly arrived, while trying to overhear their conversation through the door, should they wander into the hall.

Driscoll was knocking on that door. Monica opened it.

'I'm going out, dear,' said Driscoll.

Mary Kelly stood behind her in the hall. No sign of the canvas boot bags, so perhaps an assignation with Aubrey was on the cards.

'Where are you off to?' said Monica.

'Mary's giving an organ recital at St John's.'

'Oh,' said Monica, quite pleased, because Aubrey had surely been roped in to attending that.

When they'd gone, Monica went into the living room and looked at the cold fireplace and the fire basket, where the *Hampstead & Highgate Expresses* continued to accumulate. Two more had appeared since they'd returned, and Driscoll was forbidding fires until October. Monica still hadn't looked at the page where Gareth Hall's fate was likely to be reported. Of course, she could simply have removed the papers from the basket, and any number of excuses could be employed to explain their absence. It was Driscoll herself who recommended the use of crumpled-up newspaper for (as she unpleasantly phrased it) 'leaching the moisture' out of shoes.

But she dared not face the potentially incriminating newsprint just then.

★

Early on Tuesday afternoon on the third week back, Monica embarked on one of her lopsided conversations with Ethel. Like most of these, it took place in the kitchen while Driscoll was out. Ethel was chopping carrots; meat was bleeding on the sink drainer.

'What are you making, Eth?'

'Stew.'

'What's the meat?'

'Shoulder.'

'Shoulder of what? Oh, forget it. I'm sure it'll be lovely. Do you want a cup of tea?'

'No, thanks.'

'Have you heard of her ladyship's friend Aubrey?'

'Yes.'

'Yes? Well done, Eth. What do you think of him?'

'He's quite well-off.'

'Really?'

'And quite tall.'

'So you've *seen* him?'

Ethel had walked over to the meat. Monica said, 'Please go on, Eth. I almost thought you were on the verge of some interesting statements. How do you know he's well-off?'

'My John knows a builder who does some work for Islington Council, and it's him who gives him the work.'

'Aubrey?'

'Yes. He's the fellow we're talking about, isn't he?'

'Don't get batey, Eth. The subject of your sentence wasn't clear. I suppose that means he – Aubrey – is quite important.'

'I daresay.'

'But *really*? I mean . . . anyone might give work to a builder.'

'It's a building *firm*.'

'Eth . . .'

'What?'

'We've established that he's quite tall, but do you think he's good-looking?'

'. . . Yes.'

Monica didn't know why she'd bothered asking the question. Ethel would never say anything rude about anyone, no matter how many chances you gave her.

'*When* did you see him, Eth?'

'Last Wednesday.'

Monica couldn't recollect last Wednesday.

'Where?' she asked.

'Walking down the Road.'

'The *Holloway* Road?'

'Course.'

Monica could hardly bear to ask the next question, for fear of the wrong answer: 'Who were they with?'

'Each other.'

This was surely too good to be true.

'Just the two of them?'

Ethel was dusting flour over the cut meat. 'And Mary, of course,' she said.

The meat knife lay on the drainer. It would be very easy to stick it into Ethel.

'Why didn't you tell me that at the start, you idiot? You really are such a blockhead, Ethel. Does John know how stupid you are?'

That last, rhetorical question had been asked from the hallway, Monica having quit the kitchen and slammed the door behind her, it having been absolutely necessary to perform some violent act at that moment – and the noise had perhaps obscured those final words. From her self-exile, Monica immediately hoped so. She walked back into the kitchen where, sure enough, Ethel was in tears, like a beautiful actress in a melodrama.

'Everything I've just said is completely wrong,' said Monica, standing before her. 'You are not a blockhead, Eth. Your head is beautiful, just like all the rest of you, and you are very far from being stupid. You have just as good a reason for being mad as everyone in this madhouse, but you are clever enough not to be, and I'm very, very sorry, Eth. Can you forgive me?'

Ethel looked sidelong through her tears.

'Eth?'

'What?'

'*Won't* you have a cup of tea?'

A nod, possibly, so Monica lit the gas. Ethel was slowly grinding pepper over the meat.

Monica said, 'It's just that I so want Rose to be with Aubrey.'

'Why?'

'So they can be happy.'

'You mean so *you* can be.'

'Yes, because then they'd have to get rid of me.'

'But where would you go?'

'Venice. Hold on a minute.'

The word 'Venice' had reminded Monica of the *biscotti*, which she had been saving unopened as something between a souvenir and a token of her eventual return to Venice. She brought the tin from her room, and made the little gondoliers circulate by unscrewing the lid. She presented the tin to Ethel. 'Have one,' she said and, handing over the lid, she added, 'Have them all.'

Ethel cautiously put a biscuit (they were surprisingly small) into her mouth.

'But,' Monica continued, 'she never sees Aubrey without

Mary-bloody-Kelly hanging about, does she? Sorry for swearing, Eth, but it's just the absolute bloody limit.'

'He's her brother,' said Ethel, swallowing the last of her biscuit.

'What? *Whose* brother is he, for God's sake?'

'Mary Kelly's.'

Ethel was now fishing about in the kitchen cupboard for the frying pan, and there was a musicality about the sound, like so many pennies dropping.

The letter Driscoll had written on the way to Venice, and that Monica had read *in* Venice, had taken no pains about describing or introducing Aubrey, and that, as Monica now realised, was for a very good reason. Being Mary Kelly's brother, he was also the brother of the letter's intended recipient, Sarah Kelly. Monica had never seen Sarah Kelly, but presumably she was tall, with greyish eyes, just like Mary Kelly and Aubrey Kelly, a man whose surname Monica had never known until now, but who had seemed perfectly summarised by his pretentious forename alone.

'If Mary's out of the picture,' said Monica, 'he's gettable. So why doesn't she get him?'

'Maybe she doesn't like him in that way?' said Ethel, who now had the pan warming on the gas next to the kettle.

Just in time, Monica stopped herself from invoking the Valentine's card.

It was a hopeless mystery. And why must she be forever trying to understand the actions of other people? She must perform actions of her own. As she filled the teapot, she formed a resolution that made her much happier, and she found she had a little happiness left over for Ethel, too.

She said, 'You love your John, don't you?'

'Course.'

'What do you do when you go walking out with him?'

(Ethel had Sundays and Mondays off, residing back at the Sailors' Orphan Girls' Home on those days. She would always see John on the Sundays.)

'We like going on buses.'

'What's the best bus route, Eth?'

'It depends where you want to go.'

'Are you going to marry your John?'

'Yes.'

'When?'

'After Christmas.'

'*Soon* after Christmas?'

'Yes.'

'Eth?'

'*What*? You *are* in a funny mood.'

'Congratulations, dear,' Monica said, kissing Ethel.

★

A few minutes later, Monica commenced the drafting of a letter while sitting on her bed, the paper resting on Driscoll's writing tablet. After much redrafting over the course of the entire afternoon – and some reading of drafts aloud to Small Charlotte – the letter ran as follows:

2, Holloway Road Crescent
Holloway Road
London
England
My dear Mr De Silva,
I hope you are keeping well, and that you don't mind my taking the liberty of writing to you.
You may remember a somewhat strange conversation you had with a young girl on the terrace of café Florian, Venice, some three

weeks ago. The girl called herself Lucy Moore, which, as I suspect you realised, was not her true identity. In fact, her name is the one signed at the bottom of this letter, and I must own up to being the mendacious creature in question.

I do not seek to excuse myself for perpetrating a falsehood, but I hereby apologise, and I will also seek to give an explanation.

I was somewhat troubled at the time, since I was labouring under the misapprehension that I had caused harm to my guardian, a Miss Driscoll, and that I might accordingly be 'in trouble with the law'. It transpired, however, that I was quite innocent of any transgression, Miss Driscoll having suffered a 'crise' entirely of her own making. I will not go into details, but let us say that the results of her actions might easily have proved fatal to herself.

So much for the part of my letter concerning the past; I now come to the part concerning the future. You will have gathered from my use of the word 'guardian' to describe Miss Driscoll that I am an orphan. I have only been under the care of Miss Driscoll for a short time, and while she is a kindly and dutiful person, I fear that the arrangement does not quite suit either of us, and that her recent 'crise' might not prove an isolated incident. Her guardianship of me is regulated by the terms of my late father's will, and there are trustees in the matter, one of whom is a lawyer – not an eminent barrister like yourself, Mr De Silva, but a Highgate solicitor called Mr Farmery. I am well aware that, being only fourteen years old, I am not at the age of legal majority, but I am sure Mr Farmery – an honourable and decent man, I believe – would take my reservations about Miss Driscoll seriously if I were to put them to him, and I do mean to do that in due course, with the aim of seeing whether a new guardian might not be found, allowing Miss Driscoll to retire, so to speak, from the role.

I am forming in my mind a short list of possible replacements for Miss Driscoll and now I come to the main thrust of my communication to you, my dear Mr De Silva. I am sure you have anticipated the question I am going to ask, and I can only hope it will not be too troubling for you.

Might you be a candidate to 'take over' from Miss Driscoll?

Rest assured, in the first place, that you would not be 'out of pocket', the costs of my upkeep and education, etc., being provided for in the will, and it occurs to me that I ought to say something straight away on the matter of my education. Miss Driscoll, I believe, aspires for me to attend a London day school, whereas my preference is for boarding, ideally in the country, and so you see that I would be 'off your hands' for much of the time, only returning to you in Venice in between terms. Or perhaps I might sometimes be at your London residence, as I do believe you have a pied-à-terre (to say the least) in this city. It further occurs to me that it might be even more convenient for me to attend a school on the Continent within 'striking distance' of Venice. For example, there are several estimable girls' schools in Switzerland, I think.

But, of course, these are all what are called mere practicalities; the important question is whether you would be willing to 'take me on', and if the answer to that is in the negative, believe me, Mr De Silva, I will bear you no ill will. On the contrary, I will always treasure the memory of our meeting at Florian: all the charm of La Serenissima seemed to be embodied in that place and time, and in your own person above all.

I know I may rely fully on your discretion and, hoping very much that you will excuse the trouble I am giving, I remain, yours truly,
Monica Burnett

Monica surveyed the letter. She was forced to admit that the overwhelming feeling it provoked in her was sympathy for the person about to receive it – viz. poor Humphrey De Silva. On the other hand, she'd been refining the letter for hours (it was now getting for on for six; the darkening sky and increasing traffic on the Road told her as much) and it was as sane as she could get it. She was pretty certain about the Swiss schools – Harriet Beck had mentioned a friend of hers as having gone off to one of them.

She'd overdone the inverted commas, obviously; that was by way of apologising for the use of colloquialisms, and so was rather craven, and bad style. And she wasn't at all sure about the close – the business about relying on his discretion. She'd copied that from a book she'd consulted in the Holloway Library: *Practical Mercantile Correspondence*. She assumed its meaning was obvious enough: that he should write back to herself and not Driscoll. Of course, Driscoll would demand to know the contents of any letter from Venice, so Monica would just have to be first to the front door when the letters arrived for the next few weeks. That wouldn't be easy, given the early hours kept by Driscoll.

Monica had been revolving the idea of the letter ever since her return from Venice, and she'd been advised at the Holloway Post Office that it might reach Italy in anything between two days and a week. 'You're putting yourself in the hands of the Italian Post Office,' the clerk had said with a sigh. The cost of sending to Italy was surprisingly cheap – a penny ha'penny – and Monica had already removed three ha'penny stamps from Driscoll's bureau. (Quite typically, Driscoll bought all her stamps in ha'pennies, but the advantage to Monica of this was that she could never keep track of them all.) On the envelope, Monica wrote, 'Mr Humphrey De Silva, KC, Esq.' That being done, she copied the address from the guidebook, reading it aloud: 'The Hotel Royal Danieli, Riva degli Schiavoni, Venice, Italy,' and the very word 'Italy' seemed to demand a swirly underlining . . . which she managed to resist. She added the date – Tuesday, 26 September 1911 – which she always did last, because you were committed to sending the letter soon when you did that.

She would post it in the morning, but she sealed the envelope now and slid it into the pages of the guidebook – so it was almost as though it had reached Venice already.

But then Monica froze.

Mr De Silva was blind! He wouldn't be able to read the letter!

But then she unfroze. He must, as she had previously surmised, have arrangements in place: some secretary who read documents out to him . . . or possibly his sister did it; otherwise, how could he be a lawyer? It was a shame that a third party would be reading her letter, but Monica had no doubt that, one way or another, its meaning would be conveyed to Mr De Silva.

She then rolled over on her bed and, after talking to Small Charlotte for a while, commenced to dream of a boat that collected her on the Holloway Road (which was now a river) and took her to some narrow Paris rivers (or streets), with Venice evidently in prospect. But she was woken by a knock on the door.

'Please come in,' she said, the gracious mood of the dream lingering.

Driscoll entered, holding a small, ominous book, which banished the gracious mood.

'Sorry, dear, were you asleep?'

'Yes,' Monica said resentfully, 'and having such a lovely dream.'

'I'm sorry.'

Monica and Driscoll both glanced at the writing tablet – *Driscoll's* tablet, currently placed more haphazardly (half under

Monica's bed) than it ever had been in Driscoll's room.

'I was writing a letter,' Monica said, defiantly.

'Of course, dear,' said Driscoll, and then came the small smile, which had begun to irritate Monica even more than the previous sighs.

'Where've you been?'

'Supper with Mary. She very kindly gave you this book.'

Monica read the title: *A First Book in Algebra*.

'It will also be my last, you know,' she said, causing another small smile.

'Can I sit down next to you, dear?'

But Driscoll already had done. She smelt of smoky rain, and possibly wine. She was holding the book open at its introduction, where Monica read:

Algebra is so much like arithmetic that all that you know about addition, subtraction, multiplication and division, the signs that you have been using and the ways of working out problems, will be very useful to you.

'What do you think of that?'

'It's very badly written,' Monica said, which succeeded in dispelling the smile.

'In algebra,' said Driscoll, 'we assign a numerical value to letters to help us discover unknown numbers.'

'I know,' said Monica.

Driscoll was indicating another page in the book. Monica read:

Illustrative example. If the difference between two numbers is 48, and one number is five times the other, what are the numbers?

'I haven't the foggiest notion,' said Monica, but to her horror, Driscoll had taken out her pocketbook and the associated propelling pencil, which she now sharply twisted to begin writing, stabbing down small, fast numbers and saying, 'Let x equal the lower number, 5x be the greater one, 5x minus x equals 48, *or*—'

It was the 'or' that did it.

'Shut up! Shut up! Shut up!' said Monica. 'I don't know what you're on about, and I never will do.'

Driscoll stared fixedly ahead for a while, then came the small smile, like some purely private spasm. She stood up.

'I'm sorry, dear. You're very tired. It really is much easier than you think.'

Bending to collect up the tablet (thank goodness the letter to Humphrey was not inside it), Driscoll said, 'I was wondering whether we might go over the road for breakfast tomorrow?'

'Over the road' meant the Workingmen's Café, which also condescended to serve working *women*, and in which Driscoll and Monica had dined two or three times.

'Why?'

'A little treat.'

'But your treats never come up to scratch, do they?'

On the other hand, she did like the way they crisped the bacon in the Workingmen's Café.

'And I have some news.'

'Are you getting married to Aubrey?' Monica asked, hopelessly.

'Of course not, dear. May I give you a goodnight kiss?'

'No.'

She did it anyway.

★

When the waiter in the Workingmen's Café asked if they would like a 'slice' with their breakfasts – meaning a slice of fried bread – Driscoll said, 'The young lady would like one,' even though Driscoll disapproved of frying bread ('It takes all the goodness out'). So heavy news was obviously in prospect.

'I'm going to put you in for a scholarship exam, dear.'

Monica merely sighed.

'For a boarding school, I hope.'

'No, dear, for an excellent day school – the Camden School. You know of it, I think?'

Monica did, chiefly from its advertisements in the Tube carriages, which sat oddly alongside ones for cigarettes and hair oil. The adverts showed a black-and-white drawing of a castle-like building that had been somehow crammed into a Camden side street. The date of whatever term was coming up appeared underneath, along with the slogan, 'Electric Cars Pass the Entrance', the word 'trams' obviously being too un-dignified. It was universally known as 'the Camden School', although its official name was longer, and it was operated, Monica believed, in tandem with a grander school for richer, and possibly also cleverer, girls, which she couldn't remember the name of. Sometimes the Camden girls could be seen at large in Holloway – just passing through, of course, on their way to, and from, swankier spots, and recognisable by their black pleated skirts and surprisingly casual and soft grey hats. Monica rather liked those hats, and the Camden School was quite toney; girls from Hampstead might even go there, for instance. But what the news of the scholarship attempt meant chiefly to Monica was that the world of everyday, the un-Venetian world, was closing in fast.

She said, 'I'll never pass a scholarship exam.'

'I have every faith in you, dear.'

'That doesn't mean I will, does it? And what happens when I fail?'

'Don't start going on like that, dear.'

She would work in a shop, perhaps . . . become a type-writer and go clerking, another slave of the Road.

'You've talked to them about me, I suppose?'

Driscoll nodded.

'I dread to think what you said.'

'I said you were a delightful young lady.'

'I'll bet.'

Driscoll was smiling really quite prettily. She liked talking about schools.

Monica said, 'You didn't tell them I give no end of trouble?'

'Certainly not. I said that you were rather inclined to let your imagination go free; that mathematics wasn't much in your line.'

'But it's very much in theirs, I suppose.'

'It's a component of the examination, naturally. But only a modest competency is required – and I did secure you an exemption from German.'

'Just as well, since I can't say a single word in it.'

'They usually require a second modern language after French, you see, but in view of the disrupted circumstances of your early life, dear . . . And, of course, your French is excellent.'

'Assuming I pass – which I won't – will there be nothing at all to pay?'

'As near as makes no difference. I'm putting you in for the spring term. It starts on 15 January next year.'

'And when's the examination?'

'On 5 December. It's a Tuesday,' Driscoll added brightly.

Monica was shaking her head.

'You have an absolute age to prepare,' said Driscoll. 'Practically ten weeks.'

Monica was still shaking her head as the breakfast arrived, so Driscoll took her hand across the table. 'You will do it, won't you, dear?'

'I suppose so.'

In hopes of undermining Driscoll's plan, she made an excuse to get away from her the moment breakfast had ended, and she posted the letter to Humphrey De Silva at the Holloway Road Post Office, from where, she believed, letters were despatched more carefully, and quickly, than those entrusted to an ordinary pillar box.

★

The scholarship preparation began the moment Monica returned from posting the letter: Latin (only a slight amount, thank God), French, English grammar and composition, science, or at any rate biology, a subject which – for the purposes of the exam – boiled down to botany, and further down to something called photosynthesis. And then, of course, maths, including its most sinister manifestation: algebra. A sort of swift steeliness had come over Driscoll's teaching now that they had a target to aim at. But she certainly was not entirely relaxed about her progress, and Monica concluded it would be 'touch-and-go' as far as the scholarship was concerned.

On the third day of scholarship training, Mary came for Driscoll, and they set off for the gymnasium with their shapeless bags. Driscoll had been reluctant to go because Monica, she believed, was developing a head cold. She had actually asked whether Monica minded if she were to go out, and, of course, Monica didn't mind in the least.

She sat in the living room, reading one of her favourite Holmes stories: 'The Five Orange Pips'. She'd had the idea of revisiting the story because Driscoll had squeezed the juice from an orange for her, on account of the supposed head cold. The story, of course, began with Holmes and Watson sitting by the fire, and Watson noting that the 'equinoctial gales' were screaming along Baker Street. Monica loved the words 'equinoctial gales'. A less distinguished wind was currently hurtling along the Holloway Road as well, and making ghostly sounds in the chimney, above the unlit fire. Monica glanced towards the fire basket. A new edition of the *Hampstead & Highgate Express* lay there – the third Driscoll had bought since their return, being so dogged in all her habits. Altogether five had accumulated since Monica had read the brief report of the hospitalisation she had brought about, and they were all in the fire basket.

Monica reflected on what she had read those few weeks ago: 'He is not expected to . . .' Surely the completed sentence could not possibly read, 'He is not expected to *live*,' just in case Hall himself should come upon it and be demoralised . . . or if any of his intimates should. Monica thought of the girl he'd been with in Highgate Woods – his paramour (she had only just recalled this word and rather liked it). What would she have made of events, for she must have heard of the assault? Had she perhaps undertaken a bedside vigil? No . . . hadn't looked the type. She must also be quite stupid not to have pointed the finger at Monica when questioned by the police, as she presumably had been. But maybe she thought Monica had quit the woods before closing, as she herself had done? Either that or she assumed the assault must be the work of a man.

Then again, she might not have 'come forward' as a witness at all. No doubt, she wanted to keep out of the picture altogether. Young women weren't supposed to be in rapidly darkening woods with the likes of Gareth Hall. And what if she were married? She had looked old enough, just about.

It was far more likely, Monica thought, that the sentence she dared not read ran as follows: 'He is not expected to be detained in hospital beyond Tuesday,' or, 'He is not expected to suffer any lasting ill-effects.'

It then occurred to her that she had every right to be as cosy by the fireplace in reality as Holmes and Watson were in the story, and she would be killing two birds with one stone if she used the *Hampstead & Highgate Expresses* to get the fire going, thereby removing the temptation to discover the fate of Gareth Hall. Yes, Driscoll's rule was 'no fires until October', but October was just around the corner, and Monica did have a cold, and she would arrange to be coughing – perhaps while prostrate on the couch – when Driscoll returned. She commenced to make faggots out of the pages of the paper, averting her eyes from the words, in case Hall's fate should be inadvertently disclosed. The fire, when it was going, did its best to make the room cheerful, and the flames quelled the moaning in the chimney. As for Gareth Hall, he could go to hell, if he were not already there.

When Driscoll returned at about ten, Monica knew there'd be trouble, because she hadn't paused to remove her hat in the hall. Monica coughed, but apparently to no effect, for Driscoll said severely, 'I saw the smoke coming out of the chimney.'

'Yes,' said Monica, 'well, that's what smoke tends to do.'

'You know the rule about lighting the fire.'

'But I have the most dreadful cold.'

'I'm so sorry, dear, of course you do. Are you any worse, do you think?' and she lunged for Monica's forehead. 'I don't *think* you're running a temperature, dear.' She sighed, fairly dragging her hat off her head. Evidently, the evening had not been a success.

'Did you have a nice evening?' Monica enquired.

'Thank you for asking, dear,' Driscoll said, sitting on the couch next to Monica. 'Mary has asked me to become the editor of the St John's parish magazine, and I really don't want to do it.'

'Why not? You *are* religious, aren't you?'

'Not especially, dear. And it's so frightfully pious.'

'But you mustn't fall out with Mary,' said Monica, in a tone of panic. Driscoll had already thrown Aubrey over. If she were to do the same with Mary, there'd be no one in Driscoll's life but Monica.

'Of course not, dear. I shall decline diplomatically. Would you like a toddy?'

Monica thought of saying, 'Oh, don't bother on my account,' perpetuating the martyrdom, but she'd had one of Driscoll's toddies before, and it had been a revelation: honey, lemon and whisky – the latter obtained, presumably, from some even more secret sanctum than the top drawer.

'Yes, please,' she said.

★

The cold persisted in mild form; Driscoll or Ethel supplied frequent glasses of hot orange or lemon, but Monica's condition merited no reprieve from the cycle of tuition, which, Monica concluded, spoke volumes about Driscoll's view of her chances of success. Not a minute could be wasted.

A week after she posted the letter to Humphrey De Silva, Monica supposed that she might now begin to expect a reply. So she climbed groggily out of bed at seven in the morning, so as to intercept the post before Driscoll. This was a matter of descending the stairs to the gloomy, green communal hall of the house that contained their flat, where the Road's thunder echoed horribly and a rubber plant on a stand was slowly dying (not much photosynthesis underway there). On the mat lay one lonely letter, addressed to the lonely man in the top-floor flat. Monica did her duty, picking it up and popping it into the wicker criss-cross affixed to a green baize board propped next to the plant – an object for which there was no name, as far as Monica knew.

There came footsteps on the staircase lino.

'What on *earth* are you doing?' said dressing-gowned Driscoll. 'Are you *trying* to catch your death of cold?'

'I was expecting a letter.'

'Who on earth from?'

'We are all on *earth*, dear,' said Monica. 'It's quite a well-known fact. There's no need to keep mentioning it.'

The question was a reasonable one, though. Monica hardly ever got post. She received books occasionally, and letters from the library pointing out that other books were overdue, or, more charitably, informing her that a book she'd requested had become available. Mr Farmery had once sent her a postcard from Swanage. And she had once sent a postcard to herself. She had bought it from an Upper Holloway junk shop; it showed New York, photographed from some high vantage. She had written:

Dearest Monica,

I think you would like New York. The buildings are high, the prices are low; the streets are amazingly long.

Your dear friend,

Elizabeth Collins

Driscoll had propped it on the breakfast table.

'You have a postcard, dear. Who's it from, if I might ask?'

'Surely you know.'

'Do you suppose I've read it?'

'Yes.'

'I did notice that the handwriting is remarkably similar to your own,' Driscoll had said.

As Monica ascended the stairs, Driscoll, awaiting her half-way up, said, 'Please promise me you won't do this again, dear.'

'All right,' said Monica.

Early the next morning, she once again stood beside the expiring plant in the communal hall. This time, the absence of any letters at all seemed to make the sound of the Road even louder. As Monica turned to climb the stairs again, she was shocked by the rattle of the letterbox. But it was a rather con-stipated thing, that letterbox, and again there was just a single letter. It was addressed to 'Miss Rose Driscoll', the postmark reading 'Stock' and 'port' in two half-circles. Nothing too sur-prising in that. Stockport was somewhere north, near Driscoll's native Manchester, possibly even part of the same glum bundle of factory towns. Monica left the letter where it was.

She didn't bother going down the next day. Driscoll wouldn't dare open a sealed letter addressed to her, and in fairly short order, she gave up expecting any reply from Humphrey De Silva.

★

A week after its commencement, the cold worsened somewhat, so Driscoll withdrew bothersome mathematics until Monica should feel up to it again.

'How about some irregular French verbs?' said Driscoll. 'I know you like those.'

'That's putting it a *bit* strongly,' said Monica.

Over the following days, the cold evolved into a cough, and Monica was beginning to think it had been sent by some providential force to spare her the scholarship examination.

There then came one early morning, with light oozing through the closed curtains, when Monica woke to see Driscoll standing beside her bed looking stricken. It was her just-having-fallen-into-a-canal face, and Monica thought she must immediately disappear, this being a dream. But it was reality, and Monica was coughing.

'That's on your chest, dear,' said Driscoll. 'We must have the doctor to you.'

'What doctor?'

The answer turned out to be the ideal kind, a handsome, humorous man with curly black hair decorated with streaks of silver that made you want to stop time on his behalf, because eventually the silver would overwhelm him.

As he took Monica's temperature, Driscoll stood fretfully behind him. She did appear somewhat relieved when the doctor said, 'A little high; no fever,' and to Driscoll, 'Veno's ought to shift the cough.'

Monica, who felt fine apart from being simultaneously too hot and too cold, did a bit of coughing to justify the doctor's having turned out, and in the hope of keeping him in the room a little longer, in which she was successful.

'What are you writing, Monica?' he said, and it was lovely to hear her name. She explained that she had been writing one of her grammar stories. Invited by the exercise book to place some adjectives in a fictional setting, she had come up with the tale of a man who experienced a cold chill every time he heard certain complimentary ones, such as 'kind', 'industrious', 'thoughtful'.

'Can you think why?' she asked the doctor, at which Driscoll attempted to intervene, saying that Doctor Plummer (his slightly disappointing name) was too busy for parlour games. But he rather thrillingly put up his hand to silence her, saying, 'Wait a bit. Let me think.'

When he said, 'No, I give it up,' Monica said, 'They're all words that appear in his obituary after he's died.'

The doctor looked down at Monica, puzzlement obviously giving way to admiration, and then he laughed. 'We have here a very remarkable young lady,' he said to Driscoll, who seemed almost in tears as she said, 'I know, doctor, I know.'

'What *is* going on with that woman?' Monica asked Small Charlotte when her visitors had quit the room. She then looked more closely at Charlotte. She had never been quite the same since her immersion in the canal: she was paler and parts of her eyebrows had been washed away. You were bound to be changed by falling into a Venetian canal. Monica herself had been changed for the better: it had been a sort of baptism, the moment she fell in love with Venice, having realised she had not murdered Driscoll. But Driscoll had tried to murder herself in the canal, so the change must have been even greater for her, and Monica had seen the consequences just then. Was it possible that Driscoll had truly come to love her? Or perhaps she had simply decided that life was too short to hate her? Monica preferred the latter idea.

★

It was the start of a very strange day. Even with the cough, the work must continue, and Monica was assigned the task of finding all the pronouns in some Tennyson poems. Breaking off from this, she discovered Driscoll writing in the kitchen as Ethel cooked. Standing at the kitchen door in her dressing gown (she kept a theatrical distance from the other two, lest she infect them), Monica asked *what* Driscoll was writing, only for Driscoll to withdraw, politely enough, into her bedroom, saying, 'Admin, dear. Just admin.'

'What's up?' Monica asked Ethel.

'I'm cooking rabbit pie.'

(She was actually opening a tin of prunes.)

'I meant with her ladyship . . . But *why* are you cooking rabbit pie?'

'For you.'

'Why would I want a rabbit pie?'

'Because you like it.'

That was true enough. Monica adored rabbit pie.

'And you have a cold,' said Ethel.

'I do.'

'And you *feed* a cold.'

'Of course. Where's the rabbit, Eth?'

'I'm off to Scott's for it in a minute.'

Scott was one of two butchers near the flat. The other was called Bartlett. Both had rabbits hanging in the window.

'Why Scott and not Bartlett?' Monica asked.

'Because Scott's reliable.'

'Meaning what, exactly?'

'He has clean fingernails.'

Monica stepped aside to let Ethel into the hall, where her hat and coat awaited.

Monica's grammatical exercise completed, she intermittently read Wells's latest, *The History of Mr. Polly*, and dreamt. At some point when she was asleep, someone – well, it must have been Driscoll or Ethel – had lit the fire in her room. It had never been lit before; Monica didn't know it *could* be lit. She watched it for a long time, trying and failing to understand its beauty, this little labyrinth of perpetually crumbling red grottoes; very moving, the way it destroyed itself for her benefit, but it would be reborn, for the fire had gained an ally in the form of a small coal scuttle.

At about six, Driscoll brought her rabbit pie on a tray, and in the light of the day so far, this was not so very extraordinary.

When she came back half an hour later, Monica assumed she'd come to remove the tray, but she was holding a glass of red wine, so Monica was obviously in for some other new experience. Driscoll merely removed the tray to the bedside table before sitting on the bed beside Monica. She sat down, in fact, on *The History of Mr. Polly*, which had been partially under the covers.

'What's this?' she said, holding it up.

'Oh, just the novel I'm on.'

Monica didn't want to be quizzed about it, since Mr. Polly had attempted suicide halfway through. Driscoll took a sip of her wine. Monica watched, fascinated, and Driscoll, observing this, said, 'Don't worry, dear. I haven't become a dipsomaniac overnight. I had a lot on today. I've got through most of it, so I thought I'd have a glass to celebrate.'

'The admin.'

Driscoll nodded.

'I've sent away for a new Latin primer. I don't think the Fox is up to the required standard.'

Fox was the author of the primer Monica had been using. It was worrying that she had evidently been proceeding below par. She knew her Latin wasn't very strong, but she'd rather thought it was 'in the bag'.

'I'm worried about the maths,' said Monica.

'You're making great strides, dear. You've fairly sailed through mean, median and mode.'

'Sailed' was not the term Monica would have used, although it was true that the three Ms were a slightly more ingratiating mathematical trio than Messrs Sine, Cosine and Tangent. But algebra still lay in wait. Evidently, Driscoll did not dare revisit that yet.

Monica was a little uneasy about having Driscoll next to her in bed, but she was ill, so these were special circumstances, and she was flattered in a way. Driscoll took another sip of wine, and Monica thought how sophisticated she looked when she did that – this woman who knew mathematics, Latin, science (not just botany) and the verse of Tennyson. She did not seem in the least drunk, but her skirt had ridden up slightly when she sat on the bed.

'You have nice legs, dear,' said Monica.

'Not bad. My mother – now *she* has lovely legs.'

'*Has?*' Monica blurted.

'She still has them, love.'

So the envelope in the locked drawer was not a coffin. It *was* an envelope, though, which was a peculiar place to put a picture of a living person – a kind of banishment.

'Tell me about your mother,' said Monica. 'What's she called?'

'Anne.'

'You don't see her very often.'

'Not at all, I'm afraid.'

'Does she see anyone very much?' (Monica thought it would be polite to imply that Driscoll's mother was a sort of hermit.)

'My sister – all the time. She lives with her, and with my sister's husband, of course.'

'Wait a bit. Your *sister*? What's *she* called?'

'Violet.'

'Violet and Rose. Two flowers!'

'Yes, but only one of them bloomed, as far as Mother was concerned. We always got across one another, Mother and I. I gave a lot of trouble as a child.'

'That's hard to credit,' said Monica. 'I'd have thought you were a model child.' She closed her eyes until the word came: 'A paragon.'

'Not a bit of it. I was rather arrogant. The world didn't come up to my ideas.'

Driscoll was beginning to sound remarkably like Monica.

'And I was a frightful little swot. I insisted on getting an education, whereas Mother wanted me out to work as soon as possible. We were quite poor, you see, ever since Father died.'

'Of what?'

'A cancer.'

Well, of course, thought Monica.

Driscoll took another sophisticated sip of wine, but then she frowned down at the glass as if there were something amiss. Could she be a *connoisseur*?

'It wasn't only a question of money,' she continued. 'Mother thought that any young woman who received a good education would turn into a young man.'

'Really?'

'Not literally, of course . . . Well, a man or an old maid, which is what I am getting to be.'

'Nonsense,' said Monica.

'My sister is of a similar opinion. She used to say she hated the smell of ink.'

'Does ink *have* a smell?'

'It does if you don't like it.'

'How is she . . . situated just now?'

'Violet has three children.'

'What's her husband? I mean, *who* is he?'

Driscoll finished the rest of her wine in one go, so there couldn't have been very much wrong with it.

'Alistair Jenkinson.'

'A rather *indigestible* name,' said Monica, triggering the small smile.

'He's a brilliant mathematician.'

Monica scrutinised that statement for any hint of sarcasm, but she found nothing there other than pure admiration. There were people who could do 'maths', people who could do 'mathematics', and then there were *mathematicians*.

'Like you,' Monica said.

'Oh, Alistair leaves me standing.'

'But how do you know? It's not as if you've both taken the same exam.'

At this, Driscoll alarmingly stood up and left the room, but she returned a moment later with her glass refilled.

'That's just what we have done, Monica,' she said, sitting down on the bed again, 'taken the same examinations. You see, we were at university together.'

'Oh,' said Monica – not a *very* clever remark, but there was such a lot to take in, so many questions to ask. 'What does he do – for a living, I mean?'

'He's the deputy town clerk of Stockport.'

Monica said, 'Do you need maths for that?' although that's not what she was thinking.

'Of course, dear. You need mathematics for everything.'

Monica was thinking of the letter postmarked 'Stockport'.

'Is that where he lives, then? In Stockport, with your sister and your mother?'

'That's it.'

'And you don't keep in touch?'

'I send Christmas cards and so on. I do make the effort, dear, but they never reply.'

Monica said slowly, in the manner of a famous-trials barrister at the momentous point, 'So you *never* hear back from Stockport?'

Driscoll had almost finished her wine again.

'I don't. For all I know, Alistair might be the actual town

clerk by now. They might have had another child, making the score four–nothing to Violet.'

'Well, it's not a competition,' said Monica.

'No, dear,' said Driscoll, 'you're quite right.'

'In any case, you have *me*,' said Monica, it being the obvious thing to say, even though it was the exact opposite of what she wanted Driscoll to be thinking.

'Yes, dear,' said Driscoll, 'I do,' and she began patting Monica's hand with such rapidity that Monica thought some great stifling embrace was in prospect. Instead, and to her relief, Driscoll turned the other way and quickly left the room, either to hide tears, or out of shame at having lied, for she almost certainly had done that.

★

The cough proved a paper tiger and after a couple of days, Veno's Syrup had lived up to its name ('Lightning Cure'). The next evening, Monica declared that she was 'off for a walk'.

Driscoll made no attempt to detain her, merely saying, 'It's *milk* that goes off, dear. And wrap up warm.'

It seemed Driscoll would be going out, too, for she was standing before the hall mirror in a hideous new hat, with a great swollen rosette of purple ribbons on one side.

'That's a nice hat,' said Monica. 'Are you off . . . I mean, are you *going* somewhere special?'

'Oh no. I'll just have a little stroll myself, I think.'

Monica didn't believe her, and why should she? For Driscoll was a proven liar.

Any walk would do after Monica's confinement, even one along the Holloway Road. This early evening, the shop lights were lit, as were the public-house lanterns. The sparks flying up from the various mistakes and misconnections of the trams showed pale blue against the darker blue of the sky. Monica tried to imagine how the Road would seem to somebody who approved of it: someone like Ethel, say, or Driscoll. They might detect a certain harmony in the racket, a great orchestration of people doing their best to 'rub along' with each other.

She made her customary tour. There was Mrs Stern's shop, for instance, at 126A. Number 126 itself was one of the many coal merchants of the Road and therefore a gloomy sort of place, to which Mrs Stern brought 'light relief', for she made incandescent mantles, and her shop window in the evening looked like the universe, with all the little mantles glowing white against a backdrop of black velvet.

So that was quite a pretty place, but most of Monica's haunts she visited out of morbid interest: there was Mrs March, for instance, who made and sold birdcages, of which some had stuffed birds within, but some held real ones, so her shop was also a gaol. Then there was Mr Symonds, the artificial teeth maker, and the big question with him was whether he himself wore – or *sported* (hard to know the right verb) – artificial teeth. Monica had once entered his shop with a query about a kindly old man she had invented who needed some new teeth, but, in replying, Mr Symonds had not opened his mouth wide enough for her to reach any firm conclusion.

Two doors along from Symonds's place was Mr Herbert's photographic shop, where cameras, photographic albums and frames were sold, and you could have your picture taken on the premises. Oddly enough, you could also (if you were a man) get your hair cut, and some of the portraits displayed in the window promoted that side of the business: that is, they showed men who'd recently had their hair cut in the shop, and none of them looked very pleased about it, but then nobody ever smiled in photographic portraits. Increasingly often, it seemed to Monica, people looked away from the camera, as if, far from having paid a lot of money for the privilege, they were being photographed under sufferance. Well, that must be the fashion.

Alongside the portraits, Mr Herbert's window also displayed what he called 'Scenes of Local Interest', and Monica always looked at these, marvelling at what Mr Herbert deemed 'of interest'. A new tram stop on the Road might qualify, for example. Sometimes Mr Herbert roamed further afield with his camera, and on this occasion, several photographs showed Hampstead Heath scenes. One caught Monica's eye and immediately set her heart racing. 'Highgate School Steeplechase, 9 September 1911' read the attached label. It showed, in the foreground, a man clad in an oilskin coat and holding a stopwatch. He was being approached by a line of muddy, agonised-looking schoolboys in long shorts and undershirts. Both the mud and the timekeeper's oilskin suggested a rainy day. The boy coming second (assuming the one in front of him to be the first-placed runner) had a good deal of mud on his face and Monica couldn't be absolutely certain of his identity, but, surely, this was Gareth Hall, pictured only around a month ago, and evidently completely recovered from Monica's assault upon him, his pained expression reflecting no *real* pain, but only the determination – so characteristic of his competitive nature – to overtake the first-placed boy?

Experiencing intense relief that Hall apparently still lived – mingled, when she recollected the arrogant way he had stared at her from the top of the pillar box and other vantage points, with a twinge of regret about the same – Monica turned on her heel and headed back to Holloway Road Crescent. The flat was deserted. One mystery having been resolved, it was time to confront another.

She walked into Driscoll's bedroom, and to the tallboy,

where she shook the key to the locked top drawer out of the rolled-together gloves in the one below. On opening the drawer, she immediately saw a new item in the silky nest: a blue pasteboard file decorated with a diagonal red ribbon, a similar receptacle to the one that held the Valentine's card. Inside, Monica was appalled to see her own story about the young girl guided in her conversation with the elderly aunt by the noises in the trees suggestive of certain exclamations. Monica had wondered what had become of that. There was also a poem Monica had written on the back of a dining-car menu, on one of the trains back from Venice. Entitled, 'From the Window of the Train', it ran:

> From the window of the train, I see
> Flying backwards away from me
> Other trains and other lines
> Sunbeams, buildings, trees and time
>
> And here is the lesson I presume to teach
> The world is a whirl
> A girl is a girl
> And some accommodation must be reached

'Not up to much,' Monica said, but the quality of the poem was not the important matter.

Monica having more or less formally presented it to Driscoll when they were evicted from the carriage for the second sitting, it was perhaps not so outrageous that Driscoll should have held on to it. But the poem and story together threatened to be the start of a collection, and Monica didn't want to be commemorated in this drawer because it was full of dead things, souvenirs of a life only half lived.

Monica stopped her rummaging. Had she just heard a noise from the hallway? Looking towards the half-open door, she decided it had been a noise from the Road. She turned her attention to the item she had come about: the Valentine's card. She read again the frustrating inscription: 'I hope you will . . .' followed by the three illegible words, the first two separated by an 'a', followed by 'to', then 'this particular', with the large 'A' on the line below, and the three kisses underneath. The question was this: since the 'A' seemed unlikely, on the strength of recent intelligence, to stand for 'Aubrey', might it not stand for 'Alistair'? Alistair Jenkinson, mathematical genius, and deputy town clerk of Stockport . . . and husband to Driscoll's sister? It was the word 'mathematical', triggering baleful thoughts of algebra, that allowed Monica to decipher the inscription:

I hope you will assign a value to this particular
A
xxx

Yes, Alistair must be the sender, but when? Surely not *after* he had married Driscoll's sister? Northern people didn't get up to such scandalous deceptions. Monica looked again at the front of the card, and the apparent heart became something else: the pile of confetti was in the shape of a number 99. *Well, of course it* would *be a number*, thought Monica, *Alistair being a mathematician*, but then she had a better thought: it was the number of the year: 1899. Driscoll would have been eighteen or nineteen then, her university age. She would have been – what was the word . . . ? – an undergraduate when she received this, and Alistair an undergraduate when he sent it. So here was young love, and what had become of it? Alistair had been lured away by the prettier, albeit (and this was necessary for the symmetry of the scenario) stupider sister.

Another noise from the hall? No, the Road was again the culprit.

The revelations were coming so easily . . . it seemed that another lay close to hand. Monica picked up the locked cedarwood box, which still didn't rattle. She had to know what was inside. Driscoll was not overly imaginative, to say the least. Where would she have hidden a second key? In the same place as the first, perhaps? Monica picked up the gloves and separated them. She shook both over the top of the tallboy, and a small key tinkled down from the little finger of the left glove.

With heart racing, Monica opened the box. It contained letters: half a dozen, all unopened. The top one was postmarked 'Stockport' and so, of course, were all the others. Did they emanate from Alistair, from the sister, Violet, or the mother (whose name Monica couldn't recall)? But it didn't matter who in the household had sent them, the point was that Driscoll had cut herself off from her family, not the other way around, and about this, she had most definitely lied. As Monica locked the box and replaced it in the drawer, along with the pasteboard folder, she had a hollow feeling. The one possible virtue of Driscoll had seemed to be her moral steadiness, a quality that Monica knew she herself lacked. But it seemed that Driscoll lacked it, too.

And there she was, standing in the doorway.

'I'm sorry,' said Monica, 'you see, I—'

Driscoll was approaching with her right arm raised and tipped backwards – a grotesque, primitive sight, contrasting horribly with the elaborate hat, as if she were about to throw an imaginary spear. Clearly, she meant to strike Monica.

She did not do so, however, because Monica said, 'I thought

I was having my first monthly, so I was looking for the stuff.'

Driscoll lowered her arm.

'But you *know* where the towels are.'

'I forgot.'

'And *are* you having a period?'

'No,' Monica said. 'I thought I was, but I'm not. The key to this drawer fell out of some gloves when I was looking through the next one down.'

'Are you in pain?'

'No.'

Driscoll stared at Monica, who thought, *The best I can hope for is the small smile.*

She hated it when it came, though.

Hampstead

'The piazza is quite unrivalled . . . It was not beauty, nor magnificence alone, nor grotesqueness. It was a sort of sublime quaintness – the work of a mighty child, with all the strange and lively fancies, and yet with none of the weakness or innocence of a child.'

From *Life and Letters of Dean Stanley (A.P. Stanley)*, edited by Rowland E. Prothero, quoted in *Venice*, by Augustus J.C. Hare & St Clair Baddeley

Monica woke.

Another Monday on the Holloway Road: the start of a new week, the third one in the workaday month of October. You'd think there might eventually come a Monday on which the people of the Road would resolve to do things differently, but it wasn't going to be this one. Monica had been woken by the squeal of tram wheels at the Seven Sisters junction, and some altercation was proceeding beyond her window.

'Leave off out of it, won't you?' somebody was shouting – so there were seven words conveying no meaning whatsoever.

Driscoll was in the kitchen, cooking (or undercooking) bacon, since Ethel was off on Mondays. Driscoll didn't like Monica to be in the kitchen when she was making breakfast;

she would knock on her bedroom door when the food was ready. On the table lay the day's *Times* and an opened envelope, evidently lately arrived, from which one of Driscoll's haberdashery catalogues protruded. Monica had given up on Humphrey De Silva. She pictured him lounging about in the Hotel Danieli, wafting her letter towards the wastepaper basket. Now that she came to think of it, he had made an appearance in her dream of the night before: he had been the large man with the empty smile who had tried to prevent Monica from exiting Venice railway station and entering the city.

Monica said, 'Could you crisp the bacon, dear?'

'I will if you go back to your room and look at your Latin, dear.'

She did crisp the bacon, so Monica felt obliged to comply when, at four o'clock on that Monday, Driscoll requested a favour. Would Monica go up the road with a letter for the vicar at St John's?

'What's it about?' Monica asked point-blank, when the letter was handed over.

Driscoll smiled the small smile and said, 'I'm explaining why I can't edit his parish magazine. I want him to get it as soon as possible.'

So it seemed that Mary Kelly had rather landed Driscoll in it.

Monica went by tram. Unlike Ethel, she usually sat on the lower deck of the Holloway trams. Where Ethel liked looking at the Road – a matter of turning left or right on one of many forward-facing seats – Monica was more interested in the people, and you had no choice but to stare at your fellow travellers on the lower decks, for they had just two seats facing each other: very long seats, of course, made of comfortable, albeit dirty, upholstery.

The weather on the Road was the standard offering: wind

and rain flying together from Lower to Upper Holloway, and it was a relief to board the warm tram, although Monica did so amid grey, defeated individuals saying the usual Holloway things, such as, 'You must never trust the weather,' and, 'Now isn't that just typical?' But the tram, for once, contained some undefeated people: three girls, two seemingly a little older than Monica, and one a good deal older – all wearing the dark pleated skirts and endearingly shapeless hats of the Camden School. As Monica took her seat opposite, the girl who was positively the prettiest, and probably the youngest, turned to the one next to her – the middle girl, in Monica's mind – and commenced softly singing into her left ear, as though *confiding* the song to her. Monica could just make out the words over the clatter of the tram:

> *On wings of song, my darling,*
> *I'll bear thee on and on*

She sang beautifully, Monica thought, but the middle girl received this musical tribute with a kind of amused frown. The older girl, meanwhile, was looking directly at Monica and smiling, and her smile came very naturally. The three of them quite transcended the tram. Rain-misted Holloway scenes beyond the windows behind them seemed to belong to a different world, or a cine film. The saggy hats were meant to impose a uniformity, but they only emphasised the girls' differences. The two smaller ones were dark, and the singer's hair was a mass of ringlets, not unlike Monica's; the older one was fair. Their smiles all went in different directions, but there was one curious consistency: they all had sleepy eyes.

The song continued:

The lotus flowers are longing
To see their sisters soon

The stops for the Underground and Nag's Head Junction came and went, and Monica barely noticed. The conductor was approaching. Monica usually enjoyed a little flirtation with the tram conductors, who invariably had a kind of music-hall swagger, all the more fascinating for being tragically wasted. But this time, she paid her thruppence over impatiently, and craned around the man to keep hearing the song, which was now approaching its conclusion, as suggested by the greater intensity of the singer, the way she moved closer to the listener's ear, as if she had reached the most scandalous part of a secret:

Together we'll rest beloved
Praying the gods will send
A dream that knows no waking,
A love that knows no end

Monica only just stopped herself from applauding. The singer was looking at the middle girl, awaiting her verdict. The tram had arrived at Monica's stop, the one outside St John's, but Monica didn't get off; she wanted to hear how the song had gone down.

The middle girl turned to the singer and said, 'Can you not give them an *instrumental* presentation, Doro?' which seemed very cruel of her, and the singer landed a fairly powerful, but still essentially playful, blow on the other's left shoulder. Then, to Monica's astonishment, the middle girl looked directly at her, the directness of her gaze mitigated only somewhat by the sleepiness of her downturned eyes.

'She can play the piano rather nicely, believe it or not,' she said, indicating the singer, which earned her another punch on the arm.

'I can very *well* believe it,' said Monica.

The singer now also looked at Monica. 'Thank you very much,' she said.

The older one, who had commenced reading a book, looked up and smiled in such a way that she seemed to approve of Monica being involved in the conversation. So Monica said: 'Are you all at the Camden School?'

It was the middle girl who answered. 'For our sins, yes.'

'And you have a musical concert coming up?'

'An event,' said the singer. 'We call it an event. I'm giving a recital. She gave hers last year, and *she* gave *hers* the year before,' she added, indicating the other two.

Whereas Monica hoped this might be the start of a conversation, it turned out to be the end, for the girls were collecting up their belongings (the younger two had boot bags, the older one a book bag) and preparing to disembark. The older girl said, 'Bye, dear;' the middle one lifted a hand in salutation; the singer nodded. Monica ought to get off here as well, since she was already beyond her stop. But that would look too much like tagging along behind the three girls, and if they thought she was doing that, she would forfeit their smiles. She did walk to the end of the tram, though, where she stood on the open platform, getting rained on as she tried to see where the girls went – for she really couldn't imagine them in any location on the Road.

They were collected at the tram stop by a pretty woman in a good grey-and-green coat, the grey parts being fur. The older girl immediately began talking to the woman; the other two fell in behind as they all walked off, like ducklings behind a duck. Well, of course, the sleepy eyes had not occurred coincidentally: the three were sisters. As they receded from view, she saw that the three had stopped outside Mr Boulton's excursion shop, and were looking at the notices in the window, of which the least seductive ones, Monica always thought, were those proclaiming 'Holidays in the Homeland'. The girls and their mother wouldn't settle for those; they would be after a continental trip, and Boulton could supply those, even if not as many as Cockspur Street. And now they were entering his shop, seeking another treat in a life that must be a succession of treats.

Monica regained her seat. The places that had been occupied by the three girls had been taken by a scowling, thunderous-looking man, a pale, tremulous woman (a Driscoll type) and an uncouth, yawning boy. Would Monica ever see the three girls again? She doubted it, and the fact that such lovely people should be at the Camden School only seemed to make it more unlikely that Monica would ever be admitted to it. She was surely not fated to pass the scholarship examination, for she was not like those girls: she was not in a family; she was not essentially serene and happy, and she doubted that any of them had ever committed murderous assaults.

The tram gave a jar and sparks flew up beyond the window, like the end of a rather nonplussing conjuring trick.

'Terminus!' bawled the conductor.

★

That night, Monica had a nightmare. She was in a too-small tram, with too many people in it for her to alight when it came alongside the great compressed castle under heavy skies that was evidently the school where she was to take a long examination in algebra. She was shouting to the conductor that this was her stop and she must alight or she would miss her chance in life, but the tram moved on, and not only could Monica not escape, she also could not breathe, until she woke up gasping.

★

On the following Sunday, with the wind and rain again in alliance on the Road, Driscoll returned earlier than usual from church, and then spent most of the morning in the kitchen, sewing a new brush braid onto the bottom of Monica's best coat (as opposed to brushing the mud off the old one) and polishing up her 'Sunday boots'. At midday, she said, 'We're going out this afternoon, dear.'

Monica, who had been reading Tacitus officially, *The History of Mr. Polly* (for a second time) unofficially, said, 'That's what *you* think.'

'Now, dear . . .'

'Have you seen the weather!'

'I want to look at a new pair of everyday boots.'

'Then go and look.'

'Boots for *you*. You will need a good, plain black pair for the school.' (The Sunday boots were brown.)

'I'm probably not going to get into the school.'

'You'll need a good pair even for the exam, and for the interview with the headmistress. And you will need a good pair *full stop.*'

'Anyhow,' said Monica, 'it's Sunday.' (Any boot shop would be closed.)

'But they're in the *window* of a shop, and I want you to look at them.'

'Why?'

'I've just told you that, haven't I?'

At three o'clock, Driscoll walked into the living room holding Monica's best coat and a new hat, which was green (with a red ribbon) and triangular in shape, with a purposeful coming-to-a-point at the front, like the hat of Robin Hood. Monica thought it rather trim and *swaif*.

'I bought this for you, dear. I added the ribbon.'

'Thanks. It's nice.'

'It's called an Arundel. Try it on.'

Monica put the hat on and looked in the glass over the fire.

'It's still nice,' she said. 'And, of course, yours is lovely.'

For Driscoll wore the horrible cockeyed purple one that had already been unveiled. That was relatively new, and beneath her good Norfolk jacket (she also had a less good one), Driscoll wore a showy, ivory-coloured blouse that Monica had not seen before.

'All this to go and look at some boots?' said Monica.

'We might take a walk afterwards. Maybe we'll go to Evensong.'

'Where?'

'The place where we're going. Come along, dear.'

'*No*,' said Monica, and some short smiles came and went from Driscoll, like when the gas sputtered out. 'I don't believe you. Tell me the truth about where we're going and then I might come – or I might not.'

Driscoll took the poker and began spreading the coals in the fire, a routine only performed when it would be left a long time, so she was obviously confident that Monica could be persuaded to leave the flat. She turned and said, 'We're going to see Mr De Silva.'

'Humphrey!' Monica fairly screamed in delight. 'So he's come to London? Oh, what a stupid question!'

Driscoll was already in the hallway, taking a last look in the glass, otherwise she would have been embraced.

'I didn't want to over-excite you,' said Driscoll, as they stepped from Holloway Crescent onto Holloway Road.

'Well, I'm sorry, but I *am* over-excited, and I have so many questions, dear.'

'They will all be answered soon, I'm sure,' said Driscoll.

'Yes,' said Monica, 'how wonderful! Meanwhile, I will shut up!'

. . . Because Driscoll did look somewhat overstrained. Naturally, she would find the company of so sophisticated a man as Humphrey quite intimidating, or perhaps she had already found it so, having met him previously to make today's arrangements. They were heading towards Lower Holloway, in the direction of Islington. Why that way? But Monica must reserve her questions and suppress all speculation for the time being; she would simply go where Driscoll took her – to the *rendezvous*, and what a beautiful phrase that was.

The wind had relented; an old-fashioned, rather agreeable sort of mist had taken over, as if Humphrey had brought some interesting weather with him specially for the occasion. They were entering Highbury & Islington Station. They were not going into the middle of London, therefore; they would have needed the Tube for that. The trains from Highbury went across the top of town, so to speak. This being Sunday, there was no queue at the ticket window, but Driscoll ignored it anyway. She had bought the tickets at some earlier point, and Monica thought of her recent, mysterious absences from the flat. The platform they now headed towards was, according to numerous signs, served by trains heading in the general direction of Willesden Junction.

'Surely we're not going *to* Willesden Junction?' said Monica, thinking of that place where grimy goods wagons were eternally shuffled, like a sad old man playing patience. Humphrey wouldn't be seen dead there!

295

When the train came in, they boarded a third-class compartment and sat facing each other. Driscoll did look quite done in, overwhelmed by the new hat, so that Monica felt sorry for her. She remembered about the much nicer and lighter hat she was wearing, which Driscoll had bought her, after all, so she moved across to sit next to her. 'I love this hat,' she said, and she was leaning forward to look at herself reflected periodically in the carriage windows, as the train ran through its railway canyon made of high walls and, when the walls ran out, house-backs – and which was even more mysterious than usual today, being filled with the wintry mist as well as the engine's steam. Eventually, the houses seemed to take a step away, revealing foggy gardens and trees. Glancing sideways at Driscoll, Monica saw that her eyes were closed and she was breathing deeply, as though trying to gather her strength. Of course, journeys generally did make Driscoll nervous.

When they were approaching Hampstead Heath Station, Monica knew this must be the destination. It was the stop for South End Green, a pretty enough spot for Humphrey, with its attractive little cluster of shops on the margins of the Heath.

'Is this us, dear?'

It was indeed.

The station partook a little of the nearby Heath, with pretty lampstands and flowers in baskets, albeit mostly half dead because of the smoke. Emerging from it, they crossed the road to the boot and shoe place, the place that had formed the basis of Driscoll's attempted lie, but it had only been a white lie. Naturally, it was closed, but gaslight, retained at a low level, showed a selection of girls' black boots in the window. The next-door shop was the haberdashers, and Monica saw in its window a hat identical to the one she was wearing.

'There's my hat,' she said. 'Did you buy it here?'

Driscoll only nodded, as if not trusting herself to speak.

It seemed likely, therefore, that this was Driscoll's second visit in quick succession to this bit of Hampstead. They stepped onto the Heath, which Monica hadn't visited since that unfortunate evening she couldn't bear to think about. Their way lay along an avenue of plane trees. Driscoll had taken hold of Monica's hand; she was holding it tightly. Most of the trees' leaves had fallen, and their trunks looked grey in the misty dark, so they resembled giant bones, and walking between them was like being Jonah in the Whale. But the trees were also beautiful, and they seemed to say to Monica: 'Welcome back.'

She saw an interesting man ahead of her. He was rather large and carried a pale-coloured cane. He was side-on to Monica, who felt a contraction in her stomach as he turned towards her. It was Humphrey De Silva.

'The game's afoot!' cried Monica, and, turning to Driscoll, 'You're such a dark horse, dear.'

For Driscoll had evidently been working behind the scenes to secure an exemption for Monica, not only from German, but from the whole world of everyday! How clever and kind of her to secretly plot this reversal of all the misfortunes of Monica's life. She would trounce the sleepy sisters! Because, whereas they might one day take an excursion to Venice, Monica would be living there!

Humphrey hadn't seen them yet. Well, of course he never would exactly 'see' them. He was still about fifty yards off. Monica badly wanted to run to him, but it would be rude to disengage prematurely from Driscoll's hand.

Her thoughts ran pell-mell. The scholarship examination was obviously a red herring – or had become one, after Humphrey De Silva had resurfaced, presumably in response to Monica's letter. Probably, Driscoll had doubted Monica's chances of success all along, but it was to be expected that she would not immediately break off her teaching: that would tell Monica that something was 'up', and in any case, it would do no harm for Monica to be presented to Humphrey De Silva as a rather better educated and more cultivated person than when she'd first met him. He would have some Venetian or international school in mind for her, and she must be up to the mark for it, but there would surely be no question of having to win a scholarship, for Humphrey De Silva was *rich*.

A small, fine-featured woman with a mass of greying hair stood at Humphrey's side.

'There's a woman there as well,' said Monica, a little concerned that this person might come between her and Humphrey.

'That's Mr De Silva's sister, Lavinia,' Driscoll said. 'She's quite a well-known educationalist.'

'You mean a teacher?'

'Not exactly.'

Possibly she was a headmistress, then – of some attractive and exotic establishment, for that's what Lavinia De Silva herself looked like.

Humphrey seemed to know she was approaching.

'It's me!' Monica said, coming to a stop about four feet in front of him, and then, remembering her grammar, she amended the statement: 'It is I!'

Humphrey, looking (more or less) in her direction, smiled and began to laugh in such a way that she walked up and kissed him. 'My dear girl,' he said, looking just above her head – at her new hat, in fact. Since there was no point hoping she *looked* nice to him, Monica hoped she *smelt* nice. Thank goodness she'd had a bath only last night.

'Exactly on time!' said the sister, revealing herself to be a sensible person. Well, an educationalist would have to be that. Her eyes were large and dark, and might have been melancholic, but this was contradicted by her practical manner.

'Sorry to drag you onto the Heath, Rose,' she said to Driscoll, 'but we must make sure Humphrey has his constitutional.'

'It's lovely here,' said Driscoll, '. . . such a gorgeous spot.' She sounded like a more elevated version of herself; it was her talking-to-Aubrey voice. 'Just perfect for a constitutional.'

'Yes,' Humphrey said, 'well, I've had it now, and I'm sure our friends are cold, so let's go and get our tea.' He had been addressing the space in between Driscoll and Monica, but now he turned to Monica in particular. 'How are you, my dear?'

Monica said, 'I've dreamt about you so often!'

Lavinia De Silva was smiling at Monica, but in such a way that made Monica qualify her previous remark. '. . . Which, of course, is a total non-sequitur, I do realise that.'

Lavinia De Silva smiled again, in much the same way as before.

'Well,' said Humphrey. 'Once encountered, I'm not so easily got rid of – bad penny and all that. This is my sister, by the way: Lavinia.'

'I already know that,' said Monica, as they shook hands, and, again, this was probably not quite the right thing to have said. Another addendum was required. 'Lavinia's such a nice name,' she said, thinking she couldn't really go wrong with such an insipid remark.

'It's lovely to meet you, dear,' said Lavinia De Silva. 'I've heard so much about you.'

'Oh dear!' said Monica, hoping to dislodge Lavinia's enigmatic smile in favour of a laugh, but Monica couldn't make out the result of her joke, for Lavinia was now looking to her right, indicating Downshire Hill.

'Shall we . . .?' Lavinia said, as though she *owned* Downshire Hill. Monica recollected that Humphrey De Silva had owned a flat in London, which he perhaps shared with his sister, as he would be doing with his place in Venice. Maybe the flat was on Downshire Hill, which they now began walking along.

Downshire Hill was what was called a 'preferred address', the houses, behind their long gardens, being extremely quaint. There were a number of small schools on it. Monica had seen the pupils at one of them dancing in the front garden, and that appeared to count as a lesson of some sort or other! Lavinia De Silva and Driscoll were walking ahead. Monica was next to Humphrey, and she didn't know whether anyone in that position automatically became his guide.

She said, 'May I assist you, Humphrey?' having decided she had better get used to calling him by his first name.

He had come to a stop; Monica was terrified for a second that he was about to make some sort of speech reproving her for her familiarity, but he was only lighting a cigarette, in his expert and languid way, and when this was done, he proffered his left elbow (the cigarette being in his right hand).

'Thank you, my dear,' he said, as they set off again.

What an honour to be guiding a King's Counsel! It was only inconvenient to keep her hand on his arm in the sense that she felt like skipping down the street. Glancing to the right, she saw, above the adorable, cottage-like houses and above the mist, a beautiful sunset forming. It was as if an artist had used the same orange pigment for the sunset as that he'd employed to illuminate the house windows, and this effect, of harmony between buildings and nature, was something never seen on the Holloway Road.

'There's the most extraordinary sunset,' she said.

'Tell me about it, dear,' Humphrey said – a charmingly

poetic request, and it seemed they had resumed where they had left off in Venice, conversing easily and enjoyably. The conversation of the two women walking ahead was not quite so animated, but they did not appear to be at odds.

Of course, in asking her to describe the sunset, Humphrey had set her a stiff challenge, but Monica did her best, describing how more and more purple was being mixed into the orange of the clouds – but she checked herself. 'Oh, but these colours . . .' she said, for she was bandying terms that must mean nothing to Humphrey.

'My dear,' he said, 'you convey far more than you could ever know,' and now there were tears of happiness in her eyes, and there would be tears in her voice, too, if she carried on speaking, so she kept silence for a while.

Downshire Hill really was the most beautiful street, and to be walking *up* Downshire Hill – it sounded like the title of a song! Of course, Humphrey would always be in beautiful places: Oxford or possibly Cambridge as a young man; the quarters of the barristers – the Inns of Court – which she had once visited, and were so pleasantly tumbledown in spite of the important business conducted there . . . and then, of course, Venice.

Monica thought of Venice: the buildings endlessly contemplating their own beauty in the looking glass of the waters. '*La Serenissima*', they called it, perhaps because, once a person was there, they wouldn't want to be anywhere else. It was true that Monica hadn't been particularly serene during her stay in the water city, what with all that running away from the police. But it wasn't enough to be a tourist: for true serenity, you had to live there permanently. Could this *really* be the prospect awaiting Monica? Surely such blessings were not very often bestowed in the real world, the world of everyday? But *Humphrey* lived there, for at least some of the time. The real world had been pretty good to *him* (aside from his being blind, of course); it had once been good to Monica, too – before everybody started dying – and was she not owed a few favours by the real world?

Humphrey's sister and Driscoll were some way ahead now. It suddenly occurred to Monica that only she herself had been introduced to Lavinia. Obviously, Driscoll had met her before, and presumably also Humphrey. But when? A couple of days after posting her letter, Monica had embarked on her phase of mild illness. During this time, she had slept a good deal and was not aware of Driscoll's movements in detail.

Humphrey, having received Monica's letter, must have replied to Driscoll rather than herself. Thereafter, telegrams might have taken over. Had Humphrey come to London specially to negotiate, as it were, with Driscoll? Or perhaps (a less flattering scenario) he had been coming to London anyway?

'I dread to think what you made of my letter,' she said. 'It was rather . . . *gauche*, wouldn't you say?'

'First, my dear, I must apologise for replying to Rose – to Miss Driscoll, that is – instead of to yourself, but it seemed the right course, given your young age.'

'My tender years,' she said, rather foolishly.

'Exactly.'

Well then, Humphrey was forgiven.

'It did make me rather worried for you, dear,' he said.

'Oh, it wasn't meant to do that,' Monica said, but, of course, it *was* really.

'. . . And worried also for your guardian – for Rose.' He indicated the two women walking ahead.

Monica recollected that she had spoken of the '*crise*' suffered by Driscoll in Venice. Monica did not want to look ungrateful by harping on this.

'She's much better now,' she said.

'So I gather,' said Humphrey. Therefore, he must have spoken with Driscoll about the matter. But Monica wanted to put their conversation back on a happier footing.

'Have you bought your house in Venice yet?'

'We are in negotiations about a property.'

What an important world Monica was entering.

'Is it on a canal?'

'Well, they're all on canals, really, if you think about it.'

'I'll bet it's very beautiful.'

'What's certain,' he said, 'is that it's very expensive.'

'Where is your place in London?' (It was very sophisticated to say 'place'.)

'Oh, that way,' he said, indicating south – Belsize Park sort of direction – as airily as he had once indicated the Danieli. So they evidently weren't *going* to his flat for their tea, which was a *little* disappointing.

'It's not in Hampstead then?' Monica asked.

'Near. I'm very fond of Hampstead. I spent part of my childhood here.'

'So did I,' said Monica.

Silence for a space.

'You have met Driscoll – Rose – before, haven't you?' said Monica, for she must have this confirmed.

He nodded.

'Was it in Holloway?'

'No, dear.'

'I *knew* it wouldn't be!'

They walked on; he was being rather quiet. He would be more like his old self with a glass of whatever he had drunk at Florian.

At the top of Downshire Hill, Driscoll and Lavinia De Silva

awaited them. They all turned right onto Rosslyn Hill, and here an exchange was made: Lavinia Da Silva fell into step next to Monica, while Humphrey dropped back to walk with Driscoll, and this manoeuvre, Monica suspected, had been planned in advance.

'How are your studies coming on, my dear?' Lavinia De Silva asked.

Now it was important to make a good impression with Lavinia De Silva, who was obviously part of Humphrey's household, so they would be seeing a good deal of each other. She must be honest and sensible, yet not dour. Charming – she must be charming.

'You are doing some science, I think?'

'Biology, yes.'

'Now that's a Greek word. Do you know what it means?'

Monica thought about it. 'The study of life.'

'Indeed. Very good, and you will have touched on photo—'

'—synthesis, yes.'

'And how does that help we humans?'

'The plants need only the hydrogen element from water, so they release the oxygen back into the atmosphere.'

'That's—'

'—which we then breathe.'

'That's exactly right.'

'So they give us their leftovers, so to speak.'

'Indeed. And how's your French, Monica?'

'*Pas mal,*' said Monica, showing off now. '*Mais mon accent est choquant.*'

'On the contrary. And I've already been told that your English is very strong – grammar *and* composition.'

'I adore English composition. I think I would like to be a writer, when one would be doing it all the time.'

304

'And mathematics?'

Lavinia De Silva had obviously been alerted to Monica's deficiency here; she wouldn't get points for trying to gloss the situation.

'Well, I don't like mathematics, and it doesn't like me, but I'm making a little headway. I'm pretty well up on fractions, I think.'

'And how about trigonometry?'

Monica looked back: Driscoll and Humphrey were talking – but hesitantly, and with a good many pauses. They probably had little to say, the arrangements for the transfer of Monica having been already agreed. And perhaps Driscoll did feel a twinge of sadness at letting her go. Any major change had an undertow of melancholy, but she would be a new woman with Monica off her hands. Glancing back again, she saw Humphrey throw down his cigarette stump, and – with great sureness – put his boot down on it in mid-stride. Evidently, he was as good at extinguishing cigarettes as he was at lighting them. He must have detected Driscoll's disapproval of smoking, and that was the other thing about the two of them: they had nothing in common.

'I'm sure you can tell me the area of a circle,' his sister was saying.

'Pi times radius squared . . . or something like that.'

'It's that exactly. You have hit the nail on the head! Now, if I were to say to you four numbers – for example, five, nine, seven and three – could you tell me the mean of those numbers?'

'Six,' said Monica.

'Excellent. I do think you're being too modest, Monica. Miss Driscoll tells me you are coming along satisfactorily in all departments.'

It suddenly occurred to Monica that she didn't *want* to be

coming along satisfactorily. If she were coming along satisfactorily, there would be no need of a removal to different circumstances. The thought came to her with great, almost violent force: Venice was by no means a *fait accompli*. She was going to have to work for it, not as far as Humphrey was concerned – he was 'in the bag' – but his sister would be harder to capture.

Monica felt quite sick. Never had Rosslyn Hill seemed so steep. The tall, grand houses looking down on her seemed to be saying, 'You will never experience peace and comfort such as we afford.' Monica watched a very large rocket-like white motor car coming down the hill. You didn't often see white cars, and it was flared out at the back, so that it reminded Monica of a sort of motorised wedding dress. This was not the kind of observation you could share with Lavinia De Silva, however. But now a man came scorching down the hill on a very lean and fast bike. He was clearly courting an accident, and this did demand comment.

'Looks like he's trying to break a record,' said Monica.

'Some bones, more likely,' said Lavinia De Silva, thereby disclosing a glimmer of humour that Monica thought she might exploit. Perhaps her pitch ought to be: the charming but eccentric young girl, engaging but in need of refinement such as continental society could provide.

'Have you ever read *The Wheels of Chance*, by H.G. Wells?' she said. 'It's a lovely novel about a young man who's a keen bicyclist.'

'No, do tell me about it,' said Lavinia De Silva.

'Well . . .' said Monica, before embarking on a speech just as tedious and rambling as most that begin with that word.

When she'd finished, Lavinia De Silva said: 'And would you say it could be described as picaresque?'

Now 'picaresque' – like 'captious' and 'numinous' – was on Monica's list of words to look up, but she hadn't got around to it. She believed it meant something like 'episodic'. 'Certainly, I can see how it *could* be described as that,' she said, and she had no idea whether she had helped or hindered her cause by so obviously evading the question.

They had arrived at the junction of Hampstead Hill and Willoughby Road, and here another rearrangement occurred. Lavinia dropped back to her brother, while Driscoll advanced to walk alongside Monica, and once again took her hand, holding it tightly, as she had done when they'd approached Humphrey. Monica did not want to be holding hands with Driscoll again, but they were being observed from behind, so it was necessary to continue civilised.

Monica wanted to ask, 'What's going on? Why aren't they talking about Venice?' But what she said was, 'They're awfully nice, aren't they?'

'Very pleasant, yes,' said Driscoll, but with a coolness of tone commensurate with the rather stiff conversations she'd been having with the De Silvas. It occurred to Monica that Driscoll did not care for the De Silvas, or, at least, not for Humphrey. Monica did not want to think about why this might be.

'They're Indians, of course,' Monica said.

'Anglo-Indians, dear.'

There was nothing for it, Monica had to know:

'Did Humphrey show you the letter I sent him?'

'He intimated its contents in his first letter to me.'

So Driscoll knew Monica had described her to Humphrey as essentially mad, while asking to be taken away from her. But had she not been quite correct? Driscoll had tried to kill herself, after all, and that was . . . It was *irresponsible* of her.

Monica's mind was whirling; all she knew for certain was

that things were starting to go wrong this evening, just as they always did. Monica felt that her agitation absolutely must have an outlet. If only she could break into a fast run through a circuit of Hampstead alleyways, in which case she would be running away from the idea growing upon her: that Driscoll was not going to relinquish her, despite, or perhaps because of, what Monica had written about her in the letter. She thought of the 'strange' day – the day of the doctor and the rabbit pie – which had begun when she'd woken to see Driscoll staring at her, with that agonised expression on her face. Was its strangeness accounted for by the arrival, perhaps that very morning, of the letter from Humphrey? By taking extra care of Monica – for which the pretext was her mild illness – Driscoll had also been taking ownership of her. She thought of the stifling embrace in Venice. What had Driscoll said? That she thought Monica had 'left' her? Had she resolved then that Monica would never again leave her? Because she must have something to show for her life – something to put in the scales against the sister's three children, fathered by her former sweetheart? Was it not now certain that Monica was Driscoll's prisoner, as she had long suspected?

But she must resist this terrifying conclusion.

They were passing some of the grander restaurants and seemed to be heading for the older part of Hampstead: the more village-like streets, known paradoxically as 'Town'. Driscoll had come to a dead stop. She was looking at the clock on top of the fire station – which proclaimed the hour of six – and checking her ugly wristwatch by it.

'I hope you're not in any hurry, dear?' said Monica.

'We don't want to be too late back,' said Driscoll. 'The trains become very erratic on Sunday evenings.'

Monica felt her anger rising again as they resumed their slow progress. Driscoll had just confirmed that Monica would not be going off *immediately* with the De Silvas. Of course, that had never been on the cards, in all likelihood, but it was annoying to have the confirmation. More provoking was that Driscoll seemed anxious to cut short the important tea that lay ahead. Monica said, 'I really don't think you should be concerned with train timetables at a moment like this.'

'Somebody has to be concerned with the practicalities in your case, dear, and it seems the role has fallen to me.'

'My *case*,' said Monica. 'You make me sound like a prisoner!'

'Don't be silly, dear.'

'It's right here, I think?' said Lavinia De Silva, who, together with her brother, was following more closely than Monica had appreciated. Obviously, she had heard the exchange, shocking no doubt to such a genteel person, but fairly typical of those between Monica and Driscoll. Very well. There would be no point in maintaining the pretence that all was harmonious between herself and Driscoll. She must go to the opposite extreme and make a pitch to be *rescued* from her.

The party now turned right, into the network of crooked, somewhat Venetian, lanes, illuminated by lonely lamps that showed the mist in their immediate vicinity, and not much else. The place they were making for had a small lane, and a rather large lamp, all to itself.

The interior was dark – with a smoking fire. Driscoll didn't care for it, Monica knew. They were directed to their table by a waitress who might have been Italian, so perhaps that was the theme – acclimatisation to Venice for Monica – but the De Silvas did not speak to the woman in her own language (if, indeed, that *was* Italian), and the menu was entirely and boringly English. Some of the candles in the place also smoked, Monica noticed. Perhaps the De Silvas were not as rich as she had imagined. And now Humphrey was obviously proposing to add to the general pollution, for he'd removed another cigarette from his suit-coat pocket. His sister touched his shoulder, a request that he refrain, but he went ahead and lit the cigarette. This time, an ashtray was already on the table, Monica noticed, but Humphrey hadn't bothered to check in advance. As in Venice, his smoking habit disclosed his wilful streak.

'I'd like a half-bottle of claret,' he said to the waitress. 'Or shall we have a carafe, Rose?'

Of course, Driscoll declined, almost fearfully. Never before strangers – that was her rule.

'Do you like bouillon, dear?' he said, more or less in Monica's direction.

For some reason she couldn't identify, Monica knew about bouillon: a thin, brown soup that came in a silver, trophy-like bowl, from which it was ladled into smaller silver bowls, like the children of the large one.

But Driscoll interjected. 'Oh, nothing hot for Monica and me. Just a sandwich, perhaps.'

'Yes, I think sandwiches, dear,' said Lavinia De Silva.

'But we haven't heard from Monica,' said Humphrey.

She didn't want to get him into trouble with the others, so she said, 'Please don't bother with soup on my account. I'm quite happy with sandwiches.'

And so these were ordered.

And now they must all wait for them to arrive.

Lavinia De Silva said, 'I believe you are a great reader, Monica?'

Monica, feeling suddenly quite exhausted, nodded.

'Could you give me another example of a picaresque story?'

The woman was positively obsessed with that damn word.

'*The Pickwick Papers*?' Monica said, bleakly.

'Yes, indeed. And another?'

Monica sighed a very obvious sigh. 'I'm sorry, I'm rather tired. I'm not *precisely* sure of the meaning of the word. Something like "episodic", I think?'

'Yes. We might add that there is a satirical element, and the central character is usually a person of a roguish disposition, living in humble circumstances.'

'Then I daresay I might qualify.'

Driscoll smiled her small smile, and Lavinia De Silva, it seemed, was equipped with a similar tic.

'. . . In the sense that the character is usually a person of great charm, perhaps,' said Humphrey, who sounded as though he was speaking from a great distance.

When their order arrived, Driscoll said, 'Will you hand the sandwiches, Monica?' and Monica said, 'Of course, dear,' but she hated that expression, as Driscoll must know. When everyone had been supplied, Monica politely waited for someone else to take the first bite, but nobody did. Humphrey was quizzing Driscoll about the railway that had brought her and Driscoll from Holloway. There was, of course, nothing much to be said about the North London Railway, except that it was convenient if you lived in certain parts of North London, as the two of them were now proving.

Monica took a bite of her sandwich. 'I can't quite make out what's in this,' she said.

'Don't eat with your mouth full, dear,' said Driscoll.

A cake stand was brought. Amid some yellowish sponge cakes were a few ripply, dry-biscuity things. 'I say,' said Monica. 'Are they Venetian whirls?'

'*Viennese* whirls,' corrected Lavinia De Silva, and as Monica looked directly across the table at her, seeking some clue about how to proceed, Lavinia De Silva looked away. Monica must at least make her look.

'I do a good deal of reading in the Holloway Library,' she said. 'I'm often left alone there, you see.'

'*Monica*,' said Driscoll, in a warning tone.

'Arthur Mee's *Encyclopaedia*, and so on. I can at least read about the wider world, even if I don't experience it. I was reading about dancing the other day, and thinking about how nice it would be to have a piano in the flat, or at least a gramophone.'

The door of the café tinkled; a large, corpse-like man entered, bringing some of the mist with him.

Still not looking at Monica, Lavinia De Silva said, 'I'm sure there must be places that run subscription dances near where you live.'

'Yes,' said Monica, 'that sounds like just the kind of dances they *would* have on the Holloway Road.'

'She's not old enough for them,' said Driscoll.

'But will be soon, I think,' said Lavinia De Silva, who then began whispering to her brother, who closed his eyes for a full five seconds when she'd finished. She turned to Driscoll: a louder whisper this time. 'Might we have a word, dear?' It went without saying that this was a private word, and they both quit the table.

At the same time, some bowls of fruit salad inexplicably arrived. Everything was spinning out of control; Monica detested fruit salad, as did everyone else, as far as she knew.

'Some fruit salad has arrived,' she told Humphrey. 'God knows why. Might as well eat it, I suppose. I don't get much fruit at Driscoll's place.' She began quickly eating.

'My dear . . .' said Humphrey.

'What?'

It occurred to her that he didn't know what to say, although Monica believed that his sister had given him some instructions. He was a wilful man, but weak in the end, and bossed by his sister, whose questions to Monica had, she now realised, been in the nature of a routine medical examination – one that Monica had unfortunately passed. She had proved herself sufficiently clever and well taught to be left with Driscoll. Whereas, in fact, she had proved herself a total idiot, for she ought to have come over as a neglected waif, twisting in the Holloway wind.

Monica had finished the fruit salad. She dropped her spoon in the bowl; it made a satisfying clatter.

'I've finished,' she said, 'as you no doubt heard. When are you off back to Venice?'

'Tomorrow, my dear,' he said.

So that was that: the horror, fully realised, and it was being embodied by the corpse-like man who, having sat down at the adjacent table, was breathing very heavily and slowly, such that every breath could be his last, and it seemed to Monica that death belonged in this hot little room.

'You're not taking me with you, are you?'

'No, dear.'

'Not now, or ever.'

'My dear, I . . .'

Humphrey was – what? – fifty years old. Monica was fourteen, and yet he was out of his depth with her.

'I'm curious – did you come over to England specially to see me?'

'Not exactly.'

'You were coming anyway?'

'Yes. But we were very *keen* to see you.'

'I believe *you* were. But the question is *why*?'

Through one buckled window of the café, she could see Driscoll and Lavinia. They had convened under a lamp. Neither being imaginative, they probably didn't realise that the mist swirling about them gave the sort of theatrical effect that accompanies an evil revelation, and Monica was learning her fate via the dumb show they enacted: glum nods of agreement, affirmation of the status quo. They had gone out so that Humphrey could break the bad news to Monica.

Monica said, 'Did you not think that by coming to see me you would get my hopes up?'

'I acted selfishly, I suppose. I think a great deal of you, Monica, and I was worried about you. Your letter chimed with an incident I'd heard of in Venice – involving an Englishwoman and a young girl.'

'You mean Driscoll's attempt to kill herself.'

'Yes.'

'And who did you hear it from?'

'The police.'

He would know the police, Monica supposed, being a lawyer.

'I wanted to be reassured that matters had been resolved between you and Rose. So it was necessary to see you both – to make sure . . . well, that you were in safe hands, my dear.'

'But I am obviously in the hands of a lunatic.'

'I don't think so, dear. Rose loves you, and my sister and I are satisfied that she is doing her best for you. Venice is a lovely place at the right time of year, but it really is a backwater, you know, and certainly in the case of a clever young English girl like you.'

'I'll fail the scholarship, of course.'

'You won't,' he said, with surprising sharpness. 'My sister has no doubt whatsoever on that score.'

Monica was glad for him that he had regained some of his

lawyerly quality, but when she said, 'I'll fail the algebra,' he merely looked dismayed, and very blind.

'Tell me,' Monica said, 'were you married before?'

'Before what?'

'Previously.'

'Yes, dear.'

His blind eyes could cry and were about to do so. Monica did not want this to occur but could think of nothing to say that might prevent it, so she took his hand instead. Looking down, she said, 'There's a Sherlock Homes story on my plate.'

Humphrey said, 'Now that's a striking remark, even by your standards, dear.'

'Remember that I have been eating a fruit salad. That's a clue.'

'I have it: "The Five Orange Pips".'

'Correct . . .'

She lifted Humphrey's hand, kissed it and released it, saying, '*You'd* have had me, I know. Your hand smells nice, by the way.'

'Thank you.'

'Tobacco and cologne.'

The women had returned.

'Monica,' said Lavinia De Silva, 'you haven't had any cake.'

Driscoll put a cake on Monica's plate.

'What's that?' Monica asked.

'Lemon cake, dear.'

She took a bite. Speaking with her mouth full, she said to Lavinia De Silva, 'You are an educationalist, apparently. What does that mean exactly?'

'I write about education.'

'So you don't run a school? But you must at least write for an important paper? I assume *The Times*?'

'I edit the *Girls' Day School Gazette*.'

'Never heard of it,' said Monica. She pushed her plate away and stood.

'Sit down,' said Driscoll.

'Well, there's no point hanging about, is there?'

Driscoll repeated her order and Monica complied. 'I mean, I've been told what's what, and we mustn't miss our train back, must we, Rose?'

A metal jug of boiling water came, to replenish the tea. Monica looked at it for a while, as Driscoll and Lavinia tried to resume conversation. Monica placed her right hand against the jug.

'What are you doing?' said Driscoll.

'Experiencing pain, in order to make sure this is not simply the worst dream I've ever had.'

The other three reached out towards the jug but, before it could be removed, Monica had – by way of terminating proceedings – upended it with a simple tilt of her hand. Nobody was really hurt, although Lavinia De Silva leapt to her feet with a small scream.

★

At Hampstead Heath Station, Monica and Driscoll descended towards the platform, where mist and a perfunctory bench awaited. Monica sat down on the bench, as did Driscoll. 'Please don't sit near me,' said Monica, and Driscoll stood, muttering about how Monica really must learn to act her age, making a point of not being angry. She had been making the same show of calmness all the way down Rosslyn Hill, amid the sound of church bells ringing – a rehearsal, no doubt, for some celebratory event that would be occurring in the future, for it certainly was not occurring now. Driscoll had seemed to be almost inhaling the noise, taking deep breaths of her Christian duty.

'I don't mind about what you wrote in that letter, dear,' she had said. 'What I did in Venice was very wrong, but nothing of the kind will happen again . . . I know you're very upset, dear, and I can hardly blame you . . . It really was quite wrong of that silly man to demand to see you. Naturally, he would inflame your imagination. His sister knew that perfectly well.'

Some further words had been drowned out by the bells and the increasing distance between the two of them, but Driscoll raised her voice so that Monica heard the familiar motto: 'We'll win through in the end, dear. You'll see!'

Her calling Humphrey a 'silly man' had almost provoked Monica to speech. The enunciation of her pet phrase 'We'll win through in the end' had come even nearer to bursting the dam, and if it had done, Monica would not have said a great deal, only that Driscoll had denied her a beautiful future purely for her – Driscoll's – own sake.

Banished from the bench but continuing calm, Driscoll had taken up a position in the middle of the platform, a little way in advance of the clock hanging there. She was subjecting the clock to an infuriatingly prolonged scrutiny – far longer than was required to ascertain the time, which was a quarter after seven. The station was in a kind of gaslit trench, the ticket office being above and out of sight. There was somebody in the ticket office, Monica believed, but there was nobody down here except Driscoll and herself. On any other day but Sunday, the station would have been packed out at this time.

To the left was the cutting, with the high houses on either side; to the right lay the tunnel that carried the trains under Hampstead. The train they awaited would come from that direction.

A woman came down the steps leading to the platform opposite. She was all in black, very bulky and dignified despite carrying a somewhat broken umbrella. Monica realised that rain was falling softly on the tracks; you could generally rely on rain having the last word on Sundays. She was protected from it by the canopy of the platform, but she didn't *wish* to be protected; the canopy was just another part of her prison.

A train came rumbling out from the cutting, heading towards the opposite platform. The woman in black awaited it complacently. After it had stopped, there came a great slamming of doors from the opposite side of the carriages to the one Monica could see, but the only consequence was that, when the train pulled away, the woman in black was gone, and some steam had been added to the misty rain.

It was now twenty past seven; Driscoll had walked towards the edge of the tracks. Monica heard a happy shout from the street above the tunnel; it had come from some idiotic person moving rapidly, possibly a bicyclist or, more likely – from the rattle of bootsteps – someone running, and Monica was jealous of this person who was able to expend his energy. She thought again of Gareth Hall, and his face as he tried to beat the first-placed man or boy; no doubt he had succeeded at some point soon after the photograph was taken, causing great annoyance to that other person. 'He will be beating people all his life,' Monica said to herself.

From her position on the platform edge, Driscoll turned towards Monica, thinking, perhaps, that she was attempting to start some sort of conversation: a reconciliation. Monica looked away from her, and Driscoll turned her back on Monica again. The lesson of Gareth Hall's re-emergence into the world, Monica believed, was that nothing and nobody ever changed unless you took steps to force the change. The world was a real world, not a world of fantasy or dreams, hence the existence of people like the Scotsman of the Lido, and you had to take it on

– to affect it, and not in a glancing way but directly; otherwise, your life would never get going.

A train was approaching through the tunnel to the right – apparently a rather shy one, because it was being drawn by a backward-facing engine (trains could be very unceremonious in that way), and it had now stopped in the tunnel, as though afflicted with stage fright. The reality, of course, was that it was being governed by signals, a secret language to Monica and most other people as well. She looked towards the one between her and the tunnel. Had it lately moved? If so, she had not noticed.

But now the signal did move – and with a surprisingly emphatic bang.

The engine came on, steam leaking out of all the wrong parts; it was such a chaotic and lumbering machine. Surely it would take the blame for whatever was about to happen?

Monica had realised that her dream in Venice had not been a dream so much as a message, vouchsafing a plan. Now that a window and canal had given way to a platform edge and an oncoming train, it was time to put the plan into action. Driscoll wanted to die – that was well attested. She had tried to kill herself in Venice and this backward behemoth now approaching gave her a chance to make good that failure. That is how events would be interpreted, and there were no witnesses to say otherwise, especially given the mist, whose purpose had also become apparent to Monica.

The engine, emerging now from the tunnel, was dragging about half a mile of coal trucks. It was like Holloway Road on the move, therefore perfectly suited to the role Monica had allotted to it. She looked over to her guardian. If Driscoll were to take out her spectacles just then and clean them on her cuff before consulting her pocketbook, she would be saved, because even though she had stolen Monica's childhood and killed all her dreams (demolishing the entirety of Venice in the process), Monica would have felt sorry for her. But Driscoll was not moving; she stood almost to attention on the platform edge, defying Monica to act.

'I feel like . . . I don't know what,' Monica whispered to herself.

She closed her eyes; when she opened them again, the train was still oncoming, and Driscoll had not moved. Her stillness was infuriating. Monica computed that she had about two seconds to make her decision; she rose to her feet.

Text Acknowledgements

All chapter opening epigraphs are from *Venice, Seventh Edition* by Augustus J.C. Hare & St Clair Baddeley. London: George Allen & Sons, 1907.

p.2   'Venice' by Arthur Symons. Published in *Knave of Hearts* by Arthur Symons. London: William Heinemann, 1913.

p.102   'Michael' by William Wordsworth. Published in *Lyrical Ballads, Second Edition* by William Wordsworth and Samuel Taylor Coleridge. London: J. and A. Arch, 1800.

p.115   *Venetian Life* by William Dean Howells. London: N. Trübner & Co., 1866. Quoted in *Venice, Seventh Edition* by Augustus J.C. Hare & St Clair Baddeley. London: George Allen & Sons, 1907.

p.147   'The Gondola' by Samuel Rogers. Published in *Italy, a Poem* by Samuel Rogers. London: George Routledge and Sons, Limited, 1890. Quoted in *Venice, Seventh Edition* by Augustus J.C. Hare & St Clair Baddeley. London: George Allen & Sons, 1907.

p.187   'Inscription for a Fountain on a Heath' by Samuel Taylor Coleridge. Published in *Sibylline Leaves* by Samuel Taylor Coleridge. London: Rest Fenner, 1817.

p.245   *Much Ado About Nothing* by William Shakespeare (1.1). Quoted in *Venice, Seventh Edition* by Augustus J.C. Hare & St Clair Baddeley. London: George Allen & Sons, 1907.

p.287 *Life and Letters of Dean Stanley* edited by Rowland E. Prothero. London: Thomas Nelson & Sons, 1909. A.P. Stanley quoted in *Venice, Seventh Edition* by Augustus J.C. Hare & St Clair Baddeley. London: George Allen & Sons, 1907.

p.289– 'Auf Flügeln des Gesanges' by Heinrich Heine. Pub-
290   lished in *Buch der Lieder* by Heinrich Heine. Hamburg: Hoffmann und Campe, 1827. 'On Wings of Song' translated by G.H. Clutsam. Published in *On Wings of Song (The Mayfair Classics)* by Felix Mendelssohn, English words by G.H. Clutsam. London: Murdoch, Murdoch and Co., 1929.

Acknowledgements

I would like to thank Philippa Stockley and Henrietta Irving (for advice about Edwardian clothes); Christopher Elliott and Brendan Martin (about railways to Venice, although I have taken quite a few liberties with strict fact there); Christopher Hamilton (about Venetian language) and Ian Irvine (for putting me in touch with Christopher); Stephen Beamon (for well-informed speculation about the Venetian police). All departures from historical accuracy are entirely my own responsibility.

About the Author

A.J. Martin is an author and journalist living in London. As Andrew Martin, he is the award-winning author of many novels (mainly historical) and non-fiction books.